2003

DON'T CLOSE
YOUR EYES

OTHER BOOKS AND BOOKS ON CASSETTE
BY BETSY BRANNON GREEN:

Hearts in Hiding

Never Look Back

Until Proven Guilty

DON'T CLOSE YOUR EYES

A NOVEL

BETSY BRANNON GREEN

Covenant

Covenant Communications, Inc.

Cover image, by Nick Koudis © PhotoDisc Collection/Getty Images.

Cover design copyrighted 2003 by Covenant Communications, Inc.

Published by Covenant Communications, Inc.
American Fork, Utah

Printed in the United States of America
First Printing: April 2003

09 08 07 06 05 04 03   10 9 8 7 6 5 4 3 2 1

ISBN 1-59156-1881-4

Library of Congress Cataloging-in-Publication Data

Green, Betsy Brannon, 1958-
    Don't Close Your Eyes : a novel / Betsy Brannon Green.
        p.   cm.
    ISBN 1-59156-188-4 (alk. paper)
    1. Women detectives--Fiction. 2. Mormon women--Fiction. I. Title.
PS3607.R43 D6 2003
813'.6--dc21   2002041205

For my daughter Laura,
who has been faithful in all things
and deserves the choicest blessings of heaven.

ACKNOWLEDGMENTS

As always, I owe a huge debt of gratitude to my family. Without their patience and sacrifice, this book would not exist. Thanks also to Mike West, Coroner of Limestone County, Alabama, for technical advice and to Julie B. Brown, BS, RN for sharing her medical knowledge. I am grateful for my continued association with Katie Child and the other wonderful, talented people at Covenant. I believe they publish the best LDS fiction on the market, and I appreciate all their efforts in my behalf. Thanks to extended family members, friends, and readers from across the country who provide much needed encouragement. And finally, my heartfelt gratitude to all the V-girls. I'm honored to be a part of the formation.

PROLOGUE

Matt Clevenger watched the windshield wipers struggle against the warm summer rain as he fought his own battle with exhaustion. His body was accustomed to operating on little sleep, but over the past week he'd pushed himself beyond healthy limits. He was headed home when his cell phone rang. Matt hit the speaker button, and the voice of the department's secretary reverberated through the damp interior of his classic Ford Bronco.

"Sheriff?"

He frowned. The dispatcher on duty should have taken over the phones hours before so that the overworked secretary could go home. "Crystal, what are you still doing at the switchboard?"

"Somebody's got to run this place," she responded. "Chief Ramsey from Eureka City called. Says he thinks he's got a murder and wants you to come take a look."

Matt frowned again. Murders were rare in Coosetta County, and requests for assistance from the city police were even more so. "Inside the city limits?"

"Yes, sir. On Honeysuckle Drive just a few blocks from your grandmother's old house."

Matt glowered at the rain. There was only one reason the Eureka police chief would call the interim sheriff for Coosetta County in on a case—the murder must have been a bad one, and the chief wanted to spread the negative publicity around. "I'll check it out," he told Crystal. "Then I'm headed home."

"Roger that, and not a minute too soon," the secretary replied.

"You might want to take your own advice," Matt said, then disconnected the call and headed into the heart of Eureka.

Matt had only met Ed Ramsey a few times at various meetings and fund-raisers that were a part of his temporary job. The chief was pleasant company, if somewhat condescending. But Matt had been appointed to the office of sheriff on the strength of Sheriff Bridger's recommendation, not based on his own accomplishments. Since he hadn't paid his dues, Matt understood Ed's attitude.

He reduced his speed as he turned onto Honeysuckle Drive. Several police cars were parked in front of a house about halfway down the block. Chief Ramsey was standing on the sidewalk in the pouring rain, waiting for him.

"Ed," Matt said in greeting as he climbed out of his car. "What have you got here?"

"Woman named Robyn Howell. Thirty-six years old, divorced, lived alone, died in her sleep."

"Drug overdose?" Matt asked.

"The on-site chemical test didn't find narcotics in her system. Maybe it was some kind of poison."

"Sounds more like suicide than murder," Matt concluded quickly.

"I would have thought so too, a week ago," the police chief murmured, his eyes straying back to the house.

Matt pulled the collar of his uniform up to impede the flow of rain down his neck. "Was the victim killed outside the city limits and moved here afterward?"

Chief Ramsey shook his head. "She died right here, tucked comfortably in her bed. There were no signs of forced entry or struggle."

Despite his efforts with his collar, Matt felt moisture trickling down his spine. "Then what does this have to do with me?"

The police chief looked up, and Matt was surprised to see fear in his eyes. "It's not the first one."

Matt stared at his city counterpart, oblivious to the rain now pooling in his shoes. "What do you mean, Ed?"

The police chief took a step toward the house. "Let's examine the murder scene. Then we'll talk."

CHAPTER 1

Helen Tyler leaned onto the steering wheel, her attention focused on the rain-slick roads. She squinted to read a sign informing her that at long last she had entered the Eureka city limits. With a sigh of relief, she reduced her speed and checked the map on the seat beside her.

It was almost midnight when Helen parked in front of the little house at 126 Ivy Lane. The other houses that lined the street were dark and quiet, indicating that her future neighbors were asleep. *Like sensible people,* Helen thought as she opened the car door and got out into the rain.

The keys to the house were in the mailbox, as had been arranged. Helen inserted the key into the lock and it turned easily, but the old wooden door was swollen with moisture and resisted momentarily. When it finally swung open, Helen stepped inside and studied the gloomy interior of her new home. The faded wallpaper, threadbare carpets, and aged furniture were very different from what she was used to, and Helen smiled. No one would think to look for her here.

Helen walked back to her newly acquired, pre-owned Escort and unloaded her suitcases. Once everything was inside, she looked longingly at the sagging couch. She wanted to make some hot chocolate and then sit and watch the news on the amazingly modern television set. But she did not want to face her suitcases first thing in the morning, so she forced herself to start unpacking.

* * *

As Matt followed the police chief into the small house, he couldn't help but compare it to his own rental a few blocks away. The floor plans were basically the same, but this house had been extensively remodeled. An officer walked up to Chief Ramsey.

"Photographer's gone and the fingerprint team is finished," he said. "Coroner's on his way to get the body."

The chief nodded and led the way into a bedroom. Matt's experienced eyes surveyed the room quickly, then settled on the woman on the four-poster bed. Matt estimated the victim's height was around five feet. She had short, dark hair, and her hands were folded on top of the lace-edged sheets. Her eyes were closed in eternal sleep, and on the bed was a small, white Bible.

"Who found the body?" Matt asked.

"Officer Gage and Mrs. McBride, the next-door neighbor. She couldn't get Ms. Howell to answer the phone or the door and finally called the police. The officer had to break down the back door and found her just like this."

Matt glanced at a box of Kleenexes and a bottle of NyQuil on the table by the bed. "Looks like Ms. Howell had a cold."

The chief nodded. "The neighbor said she had been fighting one for a couple of weeks, but you can ask Mrs. McBride about it yourself. She's waiting for us in the kitchen."

Matt nodded. "Let's get it over with."

They walked into the small kitchen and found the neighbor sitting at the table. Mrs. McBride's hair was wound around sponge rollers, and she looked like she was on the verge of tears. The men sat down beside her, and Chief Ramsey leaned forward.

"Mrs. McBride, this is Sheriff Clevenger. We'd like to ask you a few questions." Mrs. McBride nodded in acquiescence. "You called the police when Ms. Howell didn't answer the phone. Is that correct?" The neighbor's head bobbed again. "Why were you trying to reach her?"

"Robyn wasn't sleeping well because of nasal congestion. I offered to loan her my humidifier, and she said she'd give it a try. I took it over about eight o'clock, but couldn't get her to come to the door. I tried to call her several times, but I didn't get an answer." Mrs. McBride's eyes moved around the room.

The chief consulted his notes. "You called the station at ten o'clock."

"Yes," Mrs. McBride whispered. "I thought maybe Robyn had slipped in the shower, but I couldn't believe it when the officer said she was *dead!*" The woman pressed a trembling hand to her mouth.

Matt entered the conversation for the first time. "I know you're upset, ma'am, but we need some basic information. Where did Ms. Howell work?" he asked.

"She taught at Eureka High School and the technical college," Mrs. McBride answered, then looked between the two men in confusion. "Robyn had a bad cold, but no one dies from that!"

Matt spoke again. "Did Ms. Howell have a boyfriend?"

Mrs. McBride shrugged her shoulders. "I'm not sure. I don't think so."

"Did she seem upset about anything lately? Depressed?"

Mrs. McBride sat up straight in her chair. "Are you asking me if Robyn killed herself?"

"We have to consider all possibilities," Matt admitted.

Mrs. McBride shook her head. "Robyn was a very optimistic person. She would never take her own life! Besides, she was a major organizer for the Run for Life Marathon sponsored by the American Cancer Society this weekend. If she was going to kill herself, she would have waited until after that."

Matt stood, and Chief Ramsey thanked Mrs. McBride for her cooperation. "We may have more questions later."

"She didn't have any family. Who will plan the funeral?" Mrs. McBride asked.

"I've called her ex-husband in Atlanta, and he's coming down to make arrangements," Chief Ramsey said as he led the way to the damaged back door.

Mrs. McBride didn't look pleased, but she nodded. The men watched her descend the porch steps, then they walked into the living room.

"I think we can rule out suicide," the chief commented.

"Check the NyQuil, just to be sure," Matt said. "And now I think it's time for you to explain what you meant when you said this wasn't the first one."

Ed Ramsey looked around to be sure no one was listening, then spoke. "A lady three blocks over died this same way on Sunday night."

Matt's stomach muscles tightened. "Mary Jean Freeburg?"

Chief Ramsey nodded. "You knew?"

"I heard my mother talking about her funeral. She lived on Westbrook, which is outside the city limits and in my jurisdiction. If it was a murder, why did the city police handle it?"

"You know how people always get confused about whether to call the police or the sheriff's department. The home health care nurse found Mrs. Freeburg dead and called us. I checked it out personally, and if there had been any sign of foul play, I would have notified you. But the woman was elderly, and there was no reason to even consider murder. I might not have ever connected these two if it wasn't for the Bible."

"There was a Bible on the other woman's bed too?"

The chief nodded. "Just like the one here."

"But since you didn't think it was murder, there was no investigation? No autopsy? No pictures? No check for fingerprints?"

"Nothing," the chief admitted miserably.

"Chief!" a patrolman called out as he approached them. "The coroner is here."

They nodded to Phil Norris, the county coroner. "You can go ahead and take the body," the chief said.

"I presume you're sending Ms. Howell to the medical examiner in Atlanta for an autopsy?" Matt verified.

"We've called ahead, and they'll be waiting for her," the coroner confirmed.

Matt waited until Phil disappeared into the back bedroom, then turned to Chief Ramsey. "I suggest you call the ME's office in Atlanta and tell them to report results to you so we won't be at Phil's mercy for information."

The chief acknowledged this with a grunt. "Since the first murder took place outside the city limits, the sheriff's department will have jurisdiction. I guess you'll have to reopen Mrs. Freeburg's case?" the chief asked, and Matt nodded. "The police department will provide as much support as we can."

"Thanks, Ed." Matt gestured toward the bedroom. "What we need right now is to know what killed these women and if there's any connection between the two of them."

Ed Ramsey nodded. "I'll dig up what I can on Robyn Howell and send you our file on Mrs. Freeburg so you can do the same for her. Then we'll compare notes."

Another patrolman stepped up beside the chief. "Sorry to interrupt, sir, but we've gotten several calls from Miss Glida Mae Magnanney. She's reporting an intruder in the empty house next door. Do you want me to send somebody over?"

The chief turned to Matt. "Miss Glida Mae calls about once a day to report one thing or another."

Matt nodded. "I'm very familiar with Miss Glida Mae and her vivid imagination. The empty house she's referring to is mine, and the intruder is probably my new tenant. I'll stop by on my way home and check it out."

Before the chief could reply, the coroner emerged from the hallway and together Matt and Ed watched Robyn Howell leave her home for the last time. Then Matt Clevenger stepped back into the rain.

* * *

It was almost one o'clock when Helen finished unpacking. She was trying to decide whether to watch television for a few minutes or go to bed when there was a loud knock on the door. Helen stared at the door for a few seconds, then crossed the room and removed a small pistol from her purse. There was another knock, and she approached the door with caution.

Helen looked through the peephole, fully expecting to see Harrison Campbell's hateful, handsome face. Instead, she saw a soaking wet stranger. Helen left the chain in place, but cracked the door open. "Who are you?" she asked.

"Coosetta County sheriff," the man replied.

In the dim porch light, Helen could see that the man was wearing an official khaki uniform, and her heart sank. She knew that in spite of her efforts to elude him, Harrison might find her in Eureka and notify the local authorities. But she *had* hoped to have at least a few days of peace before this happened.

"I'll need to see some identification," she said with resignation.

The man on her porch searched through his pockets until he came up with a badge and photo ID. "I'm also your landlord," he added as she examined his credentials. "Matt Clevenger."

Helen sighed with relief, then scowled at him. "Why didn't you say so in the first place?" She closed the door, removed the chain, then pulled it back open.

"Sorry," the sheriff replied. "Force of habit." He stepped inside, then looked down at the rain seeping from his shoes onto the carpet. "Sorry again," he said, as if a little water could worsen the carpet's condition. Then he saw the gun in her hand.

"It's registered," she assured him as she returned the gun to her purse.

He nodded, but his eyes were wary. "I wasn't expecting you until the end of the week."

"I had a change of plans. I hope that's not a problem."

Matt looked around the room. "Not as far as I'm concerned, but it's going to make things a little uncomfortable for you. I didn't have a chance to get the place cleaned up or to warn Miss Glida Mae next door. When she saw lights over here, she called the police to report an intruder."

Helen studied her new landlord. He was about six feet tall, thin, and had dark circles underneath his brown eyes. "The neighbor called the police about me?" she clarified.

Matt Clevenger ran his fingers through the damp hair curling around his head. "Miss Glida Mae has a slim grasp on reality. But once I tell her you're my new tenant and not a wanted fugitive, she'll be fine."

Helen lowered her eyes so she wouldn't have to meet his gaze. "I'll make a point to introduce myself tomorrow."

"I'd appreciate that." The sheriff stepped into the kitchen, and Helen followed a few paces behind. "I'm not even sure everything works." He flipped the switch, and the bulb blew.

Helen walked past him and stared at the mildewed sink. "Maybe faulty wiring is a blessing in this case."

"It could just be a bad bulb." He peered under the sink and removed a corrugated package. Helen watched him replace the lightbulb and hit the switch. The new bulb exploded with a loud pop, and Matt shook his head. "I guess it *is* bad wiring, whether or not it's a blessing." He leaned over the sink to wash his hands, and water gushed from below, splashing his already-wet shoes. He sighed heavily. "I'll arrange for a local handyman to come by tomorrow, and I'll hire a maid service to clean up. In the meantime, you probably shouldn't turn on the water or the lights in the kitchen."

"I'll stay out of here completely," Helen murmured as they returned to the living room.

"I'm sorry the house is in such bad repair," Matt told her when they reached the front door. "But I honestly didn't expect anyone to rent the place."

Helen stared back in surprise. "You advertised it in the paper."

"I let my mother run the ad so she'd stop bugging me about it. But this neighborhood isn't exactly prime property, and I didn't think anyone would answer it!" He stopped as color stained his cheeks. "Sorry."

"It's okay. I needed something cheap," she explained vaguely, then opened the door. "Thanks for stopping by."

"I'll send Elvis first thing to fix the kitchen," he promised.

"You actually know someone named Elvis?" she asked in amazement.

A ghost of a smile played on Matt Clevenger's lips as he stepped out onto the porch. "I do indeed."

* * *

Matt was back in his office before daybreak on Saturday morning. He wanted to be sure that no other possible victims had been misclassified, so he printed out a list of all the unexplained deaths or suicides that had occurred in Coosetta County during the past year. He filled out a request for the files to be pulled, but he didn't want to call Crystal in to work on a Saturday, so he decided to wait until Monday for them.

Next he read the obituary on Mary Jean Freeburg. Mrs. Freeburg was seventy-eight years old at the time of her death and was a lifelong member of the Eureka Baptist Church. She was survived by one son, Martin, and funeral services were held the previous Wednesday. Matt frowned at the small summation of Mrs. Freeburg's life, then dialed the number for the preacher's office at the Eureka Baptist Church. The church secretary, Mrs. Maybeth Hadder, answered the phone.

Mrs. Hadder said that the preacher was in a meeting and offered to help Matt herself. He weighed the pros and cons, then finally decided to risk it. By the end of the conversation, he knew that although homebound, Mrs. Freeburg still paid a generous monthly tithe, received regular visits from the preacher, and was on the church mailing list. Mrs. Freeburg was an accomplished seamstress and a career homemaker, and she had been a widow for almost thirty years. She had a long list of ailments, including diabetes and rheumatoid arthritis, which required daily visits from home health care nurses. Mrs. Freeburg's son, Martin, was the executor of her small estate, and the funeral service had been poorly attended. Matt thanked Mrs. Hadder, then hung up and continued his search.

At midmorning, an officer arrived with the police file on Mrs. Freeburg and the chief's report on Robyn Howell. Matt added the information to what he had and spread out both reports side by side on his desk. Robyn Howell was from Atlanta originally, but she had taken a job at Eureka High School after her divorce. Matt made a mental note to check on the ex-husband. Ms. Howell had a second job teaching computer courses at the local technical college. She wasn't a member of any church, but she was active in several civic organizations and ran competitively. The chief had a tentative list of all Ms. Howell's students and fellow teachers, as well as the other participants in her various civic and running groups. Based on what they had come up with so far, the two women had no mutual interest—no connection. The only trait they shared was that they were both female.

Matt stared at the summaries until noon, when the phone rang. "Matt?" Ed Ramsey's voice came through the line. "I took your advice and asked the ME's office to fax me Robyn Howell's toxicology report. I'm sending you a copy, but if Phil Norris calls to give you the results, don't tell him you've already seen it."

"Phil won't call me." Matt was certain. Notifying Matt would show a respect that none of the local authorities felt for the interim sheriff. Ed Ramsey had only been forced into a friendly relationship with Matt out of desperation. "What did the ME's office find?"

"Nothing," Ed told him. "There were no chemicals in Robyn Howell's body that shouldn't have been there."

"What did they list as the cause of death?" Matt asked.

"Unknown."

"Were they at least able to estimate the time of death?" Matt demanded in exasperation.

"Around 8:30 P.M., and stomach contents indicate that her last meal was chicken soup."

"You think the killer fed Ms. Howell poisoned soup?"

"Assuming it *was* murder," the chief replied cautiously. "We might be jumping to conclusions here."

"You're the one who jumped, Ed, and there's no other explanation for the Bibles."

"Lots of people read the Bible before they go to bed . . ."

"Not Robyn Howell. According to the information you sent me, she was almost an atheist. Any prints on the Bible?"

"Only one, and it belongs to the victim. The Bible is brand new—a 1998 edition of the New World Bible. The First Baptist Church of Eureka sold them for a fund-raiser a few years ago. I got a printout of their sales, and almost everyone in town is on this list, including my wife and your mother."

Matt frowned. "Which means we'll never be able to determine who purchased this particular copy."

"It would be next to impossible," Ed Ramsey agreed.

"Did you talk to Robyn Howell's ex-husband?"

"Yeah, nice guy. He's an accountant in Atlanta, and he gave me most of her biographical information."

"Any way to tell what brand of soup Ms. Howell ate?"

"The lab in Atlanta is working on that now."

"We need to check Mrs. Freeburg's stomach contents too," Matt said slowly.

"And after days underground in this heat, her stomach contents may not be identifiable."

"Or all remnants of her last meal may have been removed at the time she was embalmed," Matt agreed. "But we've got to check. We can get a court order to exhume her if necessary, but I'd like to avoid publicity if possible. Permission from the family would accomplish that."

"And since her murder took place *outside* the city limits . . ."

Matt sighed. "You want me to call Mrs. Freeburg's son."

"Sorry, Matt," Ed Ramsey said.

"I'll forgive you if you can come up with a motive."

"It can't be robbery. Mrs. Freeburg's son would have noticed if things were missing from her house."

"We need to get someone to check Robyn Howell's place."

"The ex-husband is coming from Atlanta to make funeral arrangements," the chief said. "He can do it."

"I'd like to talk to him."

"I'll call you when he gets here," the chief promised.

There was a brief pause, then Matt asked, "Who performed the autopsy on Robyn Howell?"

Matt heard papers rustling, then the chief responded, "Nancy Wilder."

"Never heard of her. Must be a newbie."

"Autopsies from the sticks don't get top billing," the chief agreed. "We were lucky that they handled it so fast."

Matt chewed his bottom lip, then came to a decision. "An old friend of mine is an assistant medical examiner. He's like a forensic genius."

"Does he owe you a big favor?" Ed asked.

"He doesn't owe me anything, but I think he'll help me," Matt said softly. "I'll tell Martin Freeburg we need to exhume his mother, then I'll ask my friend to autopsy both."

"You'll offend our local coroner if you overturn his decision not to autopsy Mrs. Freeburg without talking to him first," the chief warned.

"I don't care about Phil's feelings, and I don't have time to negotiate with him."

"You won't make any friends at the ME's office if they find out you're asking for a second autopsy on Robyn Howell," Ed added.

"That's a risk I'll have to take. We've got to find whoever is doing this before they have a chance to kill again."

The chief was silent for a few seconds. "So we have a serial killer on our hands."

"It's too early to say for sure," Matt said.

"The Bible makes me think our killer might be a religious fanatic."

"Mrs. Freeburg was a perfect Christian. Why would a religious fanatic want to kill her?"

"Murderers are *crazy*, Matt. Keep that in mind." Chief Ramsey sighed.

Matt rubbed his tired eyes. "So if it *is* a serial killer, how long before the next one?"

"Not long," the chief predicted grimly.

CHAPTER 2

Helen woke up on Saturday morning to the sound of someone knocking on her door. She looked through the peephole to see a tall, lanky man of indeterminate age standing on the porch. He wore a tattered baseball cap that shadowed most of his face, and he stood with his shoulders hunched, staring at the ground. The name *Elvis* was stitched above the pocket of his workshirt, and he was clutching a grimy toolbox, so she pulled the door open.

"You must be Elvis," she said, extending her hand.

He didn't answer and made no move to take her hand, so she let her arm drop to her side. She opened the door wide enough to admit him, and Elvis shuffled past her into the kitchen without saying a word. He opened up his toolbox on the counter and began dismantling the light fixture. Unnerved by his odd behavior, Helen clutched her purse that contained the gun while the handyman worked.

An hour later, the kitchen light was operational and the sink no longer leaked, but before she could thank him, Elvis let himself out the back door. Helen locked the door behind him, grateful to be rid of the strange repairman.

She stared at the light fixture. The process of fixing it had been fairly simple, and Helen was sure that after consulting a few good books on home repair, she could avoid another visit from Elvis. She walked into the living room and picked up the outdated phone book from the table beside the couch, looking through the faded pages until she found a phone number for the Eureka city libraries. Then she pulled out her cell phone and called for directions to the nearest branch.

Helen followed her map into downtown Eureka and parked on the street in front of the library. Once inside, she stopped at the front desk and asked where she should go to apply for a library card. A teenager looked up from the date-due cards she was stamping and pointed across the room. "The circulation desk is to your left."

"Thanks," Helen said, and the girl inclined her head vaguely. With a shrug, Helen weaved her way through a group of individual workstations to a desk along the wall.

"May I help you?" a woman asked from behind a computer terminal.

Helen glanced at the woman's name tag. It said *Judith Pope.* "Hello, Ms. Pope. My name is Helen Tyler. I'm new to the area, and I'd like to apply for a library card."

The woman nodded. "I can take care of that for you." Judith appeared to be in her early thirties. She was a few inches taller than Helen and had a modern, spiky haircut. "I'll need you to fill out this application. You can have a seat at one of these desks." Judith pointed to the workstations.

Helen took the clipboard and began filling out the paperwork. When she reached the address line, she paused. "I know my street address but not the zip code."

"What's your address?" Judith asked. Helen recited the information, and Judith smiled. "You're renting Mrs. Pritchett's old house just a few blocks from mine. The zip code is 31805."

Helen printed the numbers in the appropriate space.

"In fact, I've been to your house many times," the librarian continued, and Helen looked up in surprise. "Mrs. Pritchett and my grandmother played bridge together, so I spent a lot of time there as a child. Her grandson inherited the house when she died. I heard he had decided to rent it out since he's afraid to live there by himself."

Helen frowned. "The sheriff of a whole county is afraid to stay in a house by himself?"

This seemed to amuse Judith. "He's not the *real* sheriff. He just assumed the position when Sheriff Bridger had to retire because of health problems. Matt Clevenger is completely unqualified, and when they hold the election in November, Murray Monk from the mayor's office will surely defeat him!"

Helen raised an eyebrow. "It sounds like you don't like Mr. Clevenger much."

Judith blushed, but her lips were tense when she replied, "He was an unpleasant child and even worse as a teenager. Now he's an alcoholic and should not hold a position of authority in this community."

Helen's eyes widened as she returned the clipboard. It disturbed her to know that she was renting from a man with a drinking problem.

"This will just take a minute." Judith typed the information into the computer

"Maybe the sheriff's afraid of his grandmother's house because it's falling apart," Helen suggested. "That's why I'm here—to check out books on basic home repair."

Judith handed Helen a small piece of paper. "Your permanent card will come in the mail in about a week," she explained. "And Matt Clevenger isn't afraid of a leaky faucet or a broken pipe. He's afraid of ghosts."

Helen tried to hide her surprise as she tucked the temporary library card into her purse. "Ghosts?"

Judith's cheeks turned pink as a coworker walked up. "It's time for your break," the woman said to Judith. "I'll cover the circulation desk for you."

Judith nodded, then looked back at Helen. "I hope you'll be able to find the books you're looking for."

"I'm not sure what I'm looking for, so I just plan to check out a bunch of books and hope for the best." Helen turned and started to walk away.

Judith followed her a couple of steps. "Ummm," she began uncertainly, "until you receive your permanent card, you're only allowed to check out two books at a time."

Helen was a little disappointed, but gave Judith a bright smile. "Then I guess I'll just have to come back often!"

Helen found the home repair and improvement section and chose the two books that looked the most comprehensive. While the library clerk was processing her new card, Helen asked the woman if she could recommend a grocery store nearby.

"There's a Piggly Wiggly about six blocks down Main Street on the right, and they give double coupons. Or there's the Wal-Mart Super Center out on Highway 156."

Helen thanked the woman, then collected her books and returned to her Escort. Since she didn't have any coupons and needed more than just groceries, Helen decided to go to the Wal-Mart. Because she wasn't comfortable using a dead woman's sheets, she bought a cheap set, along with towels and a couple of pillows. She didn't dare assume that the stove was operational, so she chose food items that didn't require much preparation.

When she returned to the little house on Ivy Lane, there was a Maids Incorporated van parked in the driveway. Helen carried her purchases inside and spoke to the crew leader, who promised to be through in an hour. Helen put away her perishables, then walked back outside and sat on the porch steps. A few minutes later, she watched as a plump woman with butterscotch-colored sausage curls and a long, flowing gown emerged from the pink house next door.

"Morning!" the elderly lady called out. Her bright curls bounced, and rows of costume jewelry glittered in the morning sunshine. The neighbor's front yard was dotted with birdbaths, statuettes, and ceramic animals, so the golden-haired lady had to follow a circuitous route in order to reach Helen. Elvis, the peculiar handyman, was right behind the woman carrying a stepladder. He stopped under the first window and climbed the ladder without comment.

"Good morning." Helen stood and stepped out into the sun. "I'm your new neighbor, Helen Tyler."

"I'm Glida Mae Magnanney." Wrinkles creased her face, contrasting with the youthful, vibrant hair color. "You probably recognize me from my movies," she added with a demure sweep of her eyelashes. "And that's Elvis Hatcher." She waved at the handyman. "He's going to take the sheet plastic off my windows so I can open them now that it's summertime."

"Elvis and I have met," Helen said with a brief glance in the man's direction. "But it's a pleasure to make your acquaintance, Ms. Magnanney."

"Oh, call me Glida Mae."

Helen frowned. "Your name is so . . . ," she searched for the right word, "distinctive. I love old movies, and if I'd seen your name listed in the credits, I'm sure I would have remembered it."

Glida Mae giggled. "They used my stage name in the credits, and I can't tell you *that!*"

Helen looked at Elvis to see if he was surprised by this strange conversation, but he was patiently pulling tacks from the thick plastic. "Why not?"

"Because the town would be deluged with fans!" Glida Mae Magnanney claimed. "Not so much because of my popularity—although I was quite sought after in Hollywood during the forties—but because of my brief marriage to Humphrey Bogart."

Helen couldn't hide her astonishment. "You were married to Humphrey Bogart?"

The golden curls bobbed again. "And ever since, I've had to hide from his fans. If anyone found out who I *really* am, the town would be simply overrun by people wanting to know about my life with Bogie!"

Unsure of how to respond, Helen took a step back toward her house. "Well, I think I'll go wait on the porch where I'll have some shade."

Glida Mae nodded, then bent to look under some overgrown bushes along the side of her house. "Shadow!" she called. "Darn that cat! I haven't been able to find him all morning." Glida Mae looked up at Helen. "Have you seen him? He's black with white feet."

Helen shook her head and took another step away from the eccentric old woman. "No."

Glida Mae looked up at the handyman. "Elvis! Elvis Hatcher!" she hollered. "Have you seen my cat, Shadow?"

"Don't know nothin' 'bout no cat," Elvis mumbled without turning around.

"I'll let you know if I see him," Helen promised as she hurried toward the front porch of her new residence.

Glida Mae Magnanney followed right behind her. "Are you going to live there?" she asked, pointing at the rental house.

"For a while," Helen confirmed.

"Well, be careful," Glida Mae cautioned. "I saw an intruder there just last night."

Before Helen could explain, the cleaning crew stepped out onto the porch. "We're all finished, ma'am," the leader said.

Helen thanked them and then watched with Glida Mae as they loaded their van and drove away. "It was awfully nice of the sheriff to hire a cleaning service," Glida Mae commented. "They charge a fortune, you know."

Helen thought that hiring a professional to clean up was the very least Mr. Clevenger could do, but she didn't want to argue with Glida Mae. "The sheriff seems like a nice man."

"Oh, he is!" Glida Mae agreed. "And he's sweet on me," she confided in whispered tones. "Always finding excuses to stop by and visit. But my years in Hollywood taught me how to deal with infatuated men. I'm polite, yet careful not to give him false hope."

Helen was still searching for a response when someone called to them from the sidewalk. Helen looked up to see two elderly women. One was tall and wearing a polyester pantsuit with orthopedic shoes. The other had on a dress and sneakers, and both were watching Helen closely.

"Heard the sheriff finally had a tenant," the smaller of the two said. "My name is Nelda Lovell, and I live in the gray house next to Glida Mae."

"Helen Tyler," Helen provided.

"This is Thelma Warren," Nelda introduced. "She lives across the street from me."

"Pleasure," the tall woman said with a nod.

Nelda turned to Glida Mae. "Come on now, it's time for our walk."

Glida Mae frowned. "I don't feel like walking today. The sun is out, and I might get freckles."

Nelda walked up the sidewalk, and Thelma followed a few steps behind. "Glida Mae, you know the doctor said you have to walk *every* day," Nelda insisted.

Thelma joined the little group and wiped sweat from her forehead with the back of her hand. "Whew! Hot already." She turned to Glida Mae. "Heard you called the police again last night."

"There was an intruder next door!" Glida Mae remembered with a horrified expression.

"I'm afraid I'm responsible for your scare last night," Helen said quickly. "I arrived a few days before the sheriff was expecting me."

Glida Mae was vigorously shaking her head. "I saw a man go into the sheriff's basement!"

"It was probably the sheriff," Nelda proposed.

"Oh no! This man was older and shorter than the sheriff," Glida Mae insisted.

Nelda gave Thelma a meaningful look. "Thelma, why don't you and Glida Mae wait for me on the sidewalk?"

Glida Mae didn't seem happy, but she allowed Thelma to lead her away. Then Nelda turned to Helen. "Glida Mae has senile dementia, and sometimes she creates incidents to make her life more interesting. Don't let her rantings scare you."

Helen glanced at Glida Mae. "I'm not scared, but aren't you worried about her?"

"Not really. She's been this way for years. The sheriff keeps her grass cut, Thelma takes her to the doctor, and I see to her meals. She's been having a little trouble with her heart, and the doctor says she must walk daily." Nelda shrugged. "Thelma and I figure it won't hurt us either."

"You all take care of her," Helen said with realization.

"We've been together a long time." Nelda took a step toward the sidewalk. "You're welcome to join us."

Helen opened her mouth to decline as a silver sedan screeched to a stop by the curb, and all the women turned to stare.

"Morning, girls!" the driver called through her open window. "Who's your friend?" She waved at Helen.

"Helen Tyler. She's the sheriff's new tenant," Nelda provided as she moved toward the car. "Helen, this is Maybeth Hadder."

"Hey!" the woman hollered.

Helen stepped onto the sidewalk so the conversation could be carried on at a lower volume. "Nice to meet you."

"Maybeth's the secretary for the Eureka First Baptist Church," Nelda explained.

"Humph," Thelma said with a frown.

"It's the biggest church in Coosetta County," Glida Mae added.

"We'd be glad to have you worship with us tomorrow," Mrs. Hadder invited Helen.

Helen decided not to make an issue of religion. "Thank you," she responded simply.

Then Maybeth Hadder made a startling announcement. "The newspaper said that a young woman on Honeysuckle Drive *died* last night!"

Miss Glida Mae clutched her chest. "The intruder from the sheriff's basement probably killed her, and I could be next!"

Nelda put a calming hand on Glida Mae's arm. "The newspaper made no mention of murder. The article said Ms. Howell died in her sleep and that an autopsy will be performed to determine the reason."

Maybeth Hadder spoke again. "Well, Edith McBride lives next door to the dead woman, and I called her this morning to plan refreshments for the Sunday School party next week. She said her neighbor's house was crawling with policemen taking pictures and dusting for fingerprints. They questioned Edith exhaustively and even called in the sheriff!" Mrs. Hadder claimed. "Doesn't that sound like a lot of fuss for someone who *wasn't* murdered?"

Thelma rolled her eyes, but Nelda frowned. "They asked Matt to help investigate a death that occurred inside the city limits?"

Maybeth Hadder seemed pleased by Nelda's interest. "And while I was making copies of the church bulletin for tomorrow's services, Matt Clevenger himself called to ask *me* some questions! He was very interested in Mary Jean Freeburg, who died this past Sunday."

"Why was he asking questions about Mary Jean instead of the woman who died last night?" Nelda Lovell wondered aloud.

Maybeth Hadder leaned farther out her car window. "He made up some excuse about closing the file, but I think it's because Mary Jean Freeburg died in her sleep just like the woman on Honeysuckle Drive."

"It was the intruder!" Glida Mae cried. "I know it was."

"What intruder?" Mrs. Hadder wanted to know.

"The one who went into the sheriff's basement!" Glida Mae wailed. "He probably goes from house to house smothering defenseless women in their sleep!"

"That's ridiculous, Glida Mae," Nelda dismissed the notion.

"Yes it is," Mrs. Hadder agreed. "He can't be going house to house because the two women lived several blocks apart."

Nelda sighed. "Maybeth, for heaven's sake."

Mrs. Hadder raised an eyebrow. "Well, you've got to admit, it's strange that two women from the same neighborhood died of unknown causes within a week of each other."

Nelda glanced over at Thelma. "All this silly talk is probably making Helen regret her decision to move to Eureka." She turned to Mrs. Hadder. "You'll have to excuse us, Maybeth. We need to take our walk before it gets too hot."

Maybeth Hadder waved good-bye as the women began their slow progress down the sidewalk. "Come walk with us," Nelda said to Helen over her shoulder.

"It's very important to get your heart rate up regularly," Glida Mae contributed.

"And maybe Thelma will tell you why she didn't say a word to Maybeth Hadder," Nelda added with a smile.

Unable to resist, Helen fell into step with the old women. Their pace was so slow she wondered if a walk with them might *reduce* her heart rate. "Don't you like Mrs. Hadder?" Helen asked Thelma.

"Maybeth has always been silly and vain, but right now she is my enemy," Thelma declared.

Nelda stepped into the conversation. "Actually, Maybeth and Thelma are just on different sides of a controversy at church."

"A group of responsible members wants to repave the parking lots," Thelma explained primly. "But Maybeth and her friends want to buy a tacky electronic sign!"

Nelda winked at Helen. "The sign would give information to the community . . ."

"It will give the time—as if people don't have watches—and say silly things like 'Jesus loves you'—as if people don't already *know* that," Thelma said with disdain.

"This is Thelma's house," Nelda interrupted, effectively changing the subject. "Aren't her gardens beautiful?"

Helen agreed that they were as a man walked around the corner of the house. He was wearing a bright orange T-shirt, baggy blue shorts, black socks, and dress shoes.

"Hey, Hugh!" Glida Mae called, and the little man waved.

"Don't forget to water my roses!" Thelma took a few steps across the lawn toward her husband. "And give them some plant food!"

"Just as soon as I get a new coat of paint on the garbage cans!" Mr. Warren waved toward the metal cans sitting by the road. "I swear the trash collectors must be University of Alabama football fans. They put a new dent or scrape on my cans every week."

"Hugh's an Auburn man," Nelda whispered to Helen. "Very devoted."

Thelma rejoined them on the sidewalk. "Thank goodness we still have Hugh to protect us. Otherwise we'd be just a bunch of defenseless women against this mysterious murderer."

Glida Mae frowned. "There's Mr. Nguyen."

"Mr. Nguyen?" Helen asked, struggling with the strange pronunciation.

"The Vietnamese family next door to me." Nelda pointed at a house across the street. "They own Nail Works on Valley Road."

"I don't think we can really count Mr. Nguyen as protection since he works eighty hours a week and can't speak English," Thelma remarked.

"A couple from the North lived here for years," Nelda said when they stopped in front of a dilapidated house. "They both died within a few months of each other, and I don't think anyone ever even tried to sell the house."

"Not as I remember," Thelma agreed.

"Then they tore down the whole next block and built that metal fabricating plant." Nelda gestured toward the building. "I wouldn't mind it so much, except for the dust."

"Helen doesn't have to worry about dust," Glida Mae told them. "The sheriff hired a maid service to clean her house."

Nelda looked impressed. "Well, wasn't that nice of him," she remarked as they crossed the street and headed back up the other side. "The Nguyens' house used to belong to Mayme and Woodrow Camp. He died on Easter Sunday, and Mayme moved to Montgomery to live with her daughter."

"The neighborhood hasn't been the same since," Thelma remarked.

"No," Nelda sighed. "But Mayme was lost without her husband. She's much better off with her daughter."

Thelma shrugged. "She acted like she couldn't stand Woodrow

while he was alive, but once he was gone, she couldn't remember what day it was."

"It happens that way sometimes. This is my house," Nelda said as they inched past a gray clapboard dwelling with green shutters. "Come see me anytime, and I'll give you a jar of Mayhaw jelly."

Helen frowned. "Mayhaw? Is that like grape?"

Nelda shook her head. "The Mayhaw is a berry. It's quite rare, except in Georgia, where it grows wild."

"Especially in that jungle behind the Howarts' old, falling-down house," Thelma commented.

"Mayhaws are a little tart, perfect for jelly. Once you taste it, you'll never eat grape jelly again," Nelda promised. "Well, here we are."

They came to a stop in front of Glida Mae's house, and the alleged actress walked straight inside, locking the door behind her. Glida Mae's apprehension reminded Helen of their original subject. "Why was it unusual for the sheriff to be called in when the woman near here died?"

"The police take care of things inside the city limits, and Matt has responsibility for unincorporated parts of the county," Nelda explained.

"And they are very possessive of their areas," Thelma added. "Chief Ramsey wouldn't call Matt in unless the case was bad," Thelma said.

"Or at least unusual," Nelda amended.

"Well, thanks for inviting me to walk with you," Helen said.

"Join us anytime," Nelda called. "We walk every day except Sunday."

Helen nodded, but was already thinking up excuses as she unlocked the door to her rental house.

CHAPTER 3

Matt turned off his computer terminal at five o'clock and scowled at the computer printouts and other papers stacked on his desk. He was too tired and too overwhelmed to make any sense of it. He hoped after a few hours of sleep he'd be able to think again. Before he could get up from his chair, the phone rang.

"Robyn Howell's ex-husband is at her house," Ed Ramsey's voice came through the receiver. "I told him you'd be by to talk to him."

Matt held the phone in the crook of his neck while he jammed papers into his briefcase. "Any progress on the case?"

"According to the lab in Atlanta, there was no poison in the NyQuil, and the FBI doesn't have a serial killer who leaves a white Bible as a signature. I hope that's good news," Ed replied. "Did you talk to Mrs. Freeburg's son?"

"Yeah. I arranged to meet him at his mother's house on Monday. We'll look around to make sure nothing's missing, and I'll get the Bible. Then I thought I'd ask him how he feels about us digging up his mother."

The police chief missed the sarcasm. "She'll have to come up whether he likes it or not. And make sure nobody touches that Bible."

"There are no fingerprints on the one we have," Matt pointed out.

"Never can tell. We might get lucky with this one. And watch what you say to the Freeburg guy. We don't want the press to get wind of multiple murders in Eureka."

"I'll be the picture of discretion," Matt said with a sigh.

"There's something that's really been bothering me about these cases," the chief said, frustration in his voice. "Why would either one

of those women let someone inside their homes after they were
dressed for bed?"

"The murderer must have been someone they knew."

"But the women didn't have a single common friend," the chief
reminded the sheriff. "There's no connection."

"There has to be," Matt insisted. "We just haven't found it yet."

"We'd better find it quick."

"I'll talk to the ex-husband and let you know if I come up with
anything."

Matt hung up the phone, then turned off the lights in his office
and walked down the hall to the stairs on the side of the building. He
waved to the dispatcher on duty, then descended to the ground floor.
When he stepped out into the warm July evening, he lifted his arms
over his head to stretch his tired muscles. Then he crossed the street
to the lot where he parked his Bronco and smiled when he saw it. The
classic vehicle was his one vice. Parts cost a fortune, it drank gas, and
he knew the sensible thing to do would be to trade it in for a new car.
But year after year he kept it.

As he swung into the Bronco and started the engine, he checked
the clock on the dashboard. His mother would have dinner ready by
now, but the thought of sitting through a cozy family meal made him
shudder, and he was glad to have an excuse to work.

There was a late-model, mud-splattered Jeep parked in Robyn
Howell's driveway, right beside the Lexus that had belonged to the
dead woman. Matt left his Bronco at the curb and walked up to the
porch. The door opened before he had a chance to knock.

"You must be the sheriff," the man said, and Matt nodded. "Scott
Howell." The ex-husband extended his hand, and Matt took it
cautiously. "Wish we could have met under better circumstances."

Matt assured him that he felt the same. They walked into the
living room, and Matt was impressed again with how beautiful the
house was. "Your ex-wife had good taste," he commented.

"Yes, she did."

"Did you ever visit her here after she moved to Eureka?" Matt
asked.

"A few times, but usually she came to see me." Scott Howell
waved toward the couch. "Have a seat."

Matt sat down. "When was the last time you saw her?"

"About a month ago. She came to Atlanta, and we spent the weekend together."

Matt tried to control his surprise, but must have failed because Scott Howell chuckled good-naturedly.

"I know that sounds strange, but Robyn and I really loved each other. We just couldn't *live* together. She was the most," he paused, searching for the right word, "*driven* person I've ever known. She would have worked around the clock if it had been physically possible. She was always looking for a way to make a dollar, then looking for a way to invest it. She was neat to a fault . . ." His voice trailed off.

"And," Matt prompted.

"I was none of the above. I was happy with my position at work and didn't want to move up the corporate ladder. She had enough ambition for both of us, and that drove her crazy. Robyn wanted me to work late, then do tax returns from home on the weekends instead of hunting and fishing. I couldn't seem to remember to put my dirty clothes in the hamper or my dishes in the dishwasher." He spread his hands. "Total opposites. So we finally agreed to end the marriage, and after that we got along fine."

Matt glanced around the living room. "Does the place look about the same as it did the last time you were here?"

Scott Howell made a quick visual survey. "Looks exactly the same to me. Robyn couldn't stand for anything to be out of place."

"Nothing's missing?"

Scott Howell's head jerked up sharply. "Why would anything be missing? Didn't Robyn die of natural causes?"

Matt forced a smile. "We're just trying to check out every angle," he said. "Did you and your ex-wife have a fight recently?" Matt asked, and Scott Howell shook his head. "Did you purchase any extra insurance on her within the last few months?"

Scott Howell stopped smiling. "No."

"Who gets this nice house and all those investments you mentioned earlier now that your ex-wife is dead?"

Scott Howell's expression became downright hostile. "Since Robyn had no family, I wouldn't be surprised if it's me, but I don't know for sure. I don't have a copy of her will and never asked her questions like that."

Matt stood. "Well, I've taken up enough of your time. I've got your number in Atlanta, and I'll call if I think of anything else I need to ask you."

Scott Howell didn't respond or accompany Matt to the door. Matt let himself out and checked his watch. It was only six o'clock—still early by his standards. That home-cooked meal was still waiting, and he had almost resigned himself to that fate when he passed his rental house on Ivy Lane. With a grim smile, he pulled to a stop. As a landlord, it was his responsibility to make sure the repairs had been made.

Helen Tyler answered his knock almost immediately. "Mr. Clevenger?" She tucked a lock of blonde hair behind her ear and regarded him inquisitively.

"Sorry to just drop in on you," Matt apologized. "But I wanted to be sure the kitchen light was fixed and that the maid service came."

She swung the door open for him. "See for yourself."

Matt took one hesitant step inside. "I don't want to disturb you."

"You're not disturbing me," Helen replied, closing the door behind him. "I was just trying to find something on television." She waved at his grandmother's TV. "Which shouldn't be hard with all these channels. Thanks for having the cable hooked up."

"You'll have to thank my mother."

"Maybe you could thank her for me," Helen suggested as she took a seat on the couch. There was a Domino's pizza box on the coffee table, and she lifted the lid. "I ordered pizza for dinner, and there's plenty left if you want a piece."

"Thanks, but my mother will have dinner waiting for me when I get home."

Helen looked up. "You *live* with your mother?"

"I live with both of my parents, actually."

Helen was reminded of Judith Pope's accusations about ghosts. "Why didn't you just move in here instead of renting the place out?" She looked around the room. "With a little paint and some new furniture, it would be okay."

"That was my parents' plan when I inherited the place," Matt admitted. "They pointed out that it's convenient to the sheriff's office."

Helen smiled. "Sort of nudging you out of the nest?"

He shrugged. "Something like that."

"But . . . ," she prompted.

"I just couldn't do it." He waited for her to pursue the painful topic, but she changed the subject abruptly instead.

"That Elvis is a strange person. He didn't speak the entire time he was here."

"He got the kitchen light working though?"

Helen nodded and picked up a piece of pizza. "For the moment anyway."

"You can't blame Elvis for being shy," Matt said in the handyman's defense. "His parents kept him chained in the attic when he was a teenager."

Helen swallowed her mouthful of pizza in one big gulp, and she looked at him with wide eyes. They were large and a strange color, almost turquoise. "Really?" she breathed.

Matt smiled. "No, not really. He's just quiet."

"He's weird." Helen maintained her original position on the subject.

"Well, he does a good job for a reasonable price. And speaking of good," he watched her chew, "that looks delicious, and I'm starving."

Helen pushed the pizza box toward him. "Go ahead and eat some. I'll end up throwing most of it away."

Matt knew it was ridiculous for him to sit there eating this woman's pizza when his mother had a meal waiting for him at home, but he reached over and picked up the smallest piece, telling himself it was just a little snack.

"I also met Glida Mae, but I couldn't convince her that there was no intruder here last night," Helen continued. "She seems dangerously delusional to me, but Nelda Lovell says there's nothing to worry about."

Matt swallowed before he replied. "You met Miss Nelda and Miss Glida Mae and Elvis—all in one day?"

"And Judith Pope, who didn't seem to like you very much."

Matt didn't attempt to defend himself. "I spent a lot of time over here with my grandmother when I was a kid. Miss Nelda's granddaughter Sydney was the best baseball player in Eureka, and she practically lived with Miss Nelda. Whenever we were both here at the same time, we would get up a game. Judith lived nearby and—"

"Let me guess," Helen interrupted. "Judith wasn't athletic."

Matt finished off his first piece of pizza and reached for a second. "Judith was the most uncoordinated child I've ever seen. Always tripping or falling or something. If she was on your team, defeat was certain."

"So you never picked her?" Helen speculated.

"Only if my grandmother made me."

Helen looked disappointed. "What about Sydney?"

"She was more tolerant of Judith for some reason. Maybe it was because she was a good enough ballplayer to compensate for Judith's deficiencies. But anyway, I don't blame Judith for not liking me," Matt said as he picked up the last piece of pizza.

Helen leaned back against the couch. "I also met Thelma Warren, her husband, Hugh, and the secretary from the biggest church in Coosetta County. Maybeth something."

"Hadder," Matt provided.

"Yes, that's it. They were talking about a woman who was killed a few blocks away from here last night," Helen told him, and he had to control a groan.

"Why would they think someone was killed?" he asked through gritted teeth.

"Because a neighbor told Mrs. Hadder that a lot of policemen came to take pictures and dust for fingerprints. And they seemed to think it very odd that you were called in since the woman died inside the city limits. Then Mrs. Hadder said you asked her questions about a member of her church who died in a similar way a few days ago."

Matt sighed. Talking to Maybeth Hadder had been an error in judgment. "I work closely with the city police quite often," he claimed, hoping his voice held conviction. "Two women have died recently in this area. Neither cause of death is known, and the incidents are probably unrelated. But we want the people of Eureka to feel safe, so we try to be thorough."

"It sounds like you might have a big case on your hands," Helen murmured. "I thought the old women were just exaggerating."

Matt winced. "So I should have just bluffed my way through instead of admitting that there's an investigation?"

Helen laughed. "Don't worry. I can keep a secret."

"I'd appreciate that. If there is a killer, we don't want to alert him."

"Maybe Glida Mae really did see something over here last night," Helen whispered, suddenly ill at ease.

"That's very unlikely. Miss Glida Mae is always seeing things, like cats that don't exist."

Helen smiled. "She was looking for one today."

"I'll never forget the summer she had me and Sydney searching for a cat that had been dead for a year. That was one time Judith didn't ask to tag along." Memories besieged him, and Matt grew quiet. "Well, I'd better get home," he said as he stood. "I'll have the phone connected on Monday. How do you want the listing to read?"

"Oh, I don't want any listing!" Helen said emphatically. "I have my cell phone."

Matt was surprised by her refusal to have the phone connected, but he decided not to make an issue of it. "Then I guess you'll need to give me your cell number."

Helen's gaze dropped to the floor. "I don't give my cell phone number out to strangers."

Matt frowned. "I'm not a stranger—I'm your landlord, and I might need to get in touch with you about the house."

Helen considered this for longer than seemed polite. "Why don't you give me your cell number, and if I need something I'll call you."

Matt's cell phone had caller ID, and he knew that the first time she called him, he'd have her number. "Okay." He pulled a business card from his pocket and extended it.

Helen took the card from his hand, then followed him to the door. "Your mother's going to be disappointed when you arrive home without an appetite."

"She's used to it," he muttered.

"To no appetite or disappointment?"

"Both," he answered without a smile.

* * *

Helen leaned up against the door after Matt Clevenger left. He was even more handsome than she had originally thought. He was also charming and intriguing and the last thing she needed in her already-complicated life. With a sigh, she pushed away from the door, only to hear another knock. Helen peered through the peephole and saw Nelda Lovell standing on the small front porch.

"I'm sorry to stop by so late, dear, but choir practice ran long," Nelda said when Helen opened the door. "I wanted to bring you a jar of Mayhaw jelly like I promised and invite you to church tomorrow."

"Thank you so much for the jelly," Helen began. "But I need to attend my own church."

Nelda looked surprised. "You've picked one already?"

Helen took a deep breath. "I'm a Mormon." When she saw the startled look on Nelda's face, she began her Mormons-are-Christians explanation, but the neighbor interrupted.

"Oh, yes, I'm quite familiar with the Mormon Church. My daughter became a Mormon after she married, and she raised all her children in that faith. You'll probably meet my granddaughter at church tomorrow."

"Sydney, the baseball player?"

"Yes, how did you know?"

"Matt Clevenger was here a few minutes before you arrived, and he told me that he used to play baseball with Sydney, but not with Judith Pope."

"Poor Judith. The neighborhood children never really gave her a chance." Nelda looked over Helen's shoulder at the empty pizza box on the coffee table. "You said the sheriff was here tonight?"

Helen nodded. "He was checking to make sure the maid service kept their appointment and that Elvis person had fixed the kitchen light and sink. Then he finished off my leftover pizza."

"Oh, I see," Nelda Lovell said. "Will you at least eat dinner with me after church? Glida Mae always comes, and I'll invite Thelma and Hugh."

"I really appreciate the offer—" Helen started to decline, but Nelda interrupted again.

"It will be a good opportunity for you to get to know everyone," she pressed.

Helen smiled. "Okay. What time?"

Nelda seemed pleased. "Let's say one o'clock."

"I'll be there," Helen promised, then walked Nelda to the door. After waving good-bye to her neighbor, she locked the door behind Nelda and put the pizza box into the garbage can. She had just settled on the couch to watch television when there was another knock on her door. Thinking that one of her previous visitors had returned, Helen opened the door without looking through the peephole. When she saw a stranger standing in the shadows, Helen screamed.

"Oh, I'm so sorry I scared you!" The figure stepped into the light, and Helen recognized Judith Pope from the library. "I would have called first, but you didn't list a phone number on your library card application." She held up a stack of books. "I didn't want you to have to wait a week to get the books you wanted, so I checked these out for you."

Helen put a hand to her racing heart. "That was very nice of you." She took the books from Judith's arms.

Judith stepped back into the shadows. "Good night."

Helen waved good-bye and closed the door. Then she turned off her front porch light and promised herself that she would not answer the door again until morning.

* * *

On Sunday Matt ate breakfast with his parents. It was always a little awkward when he spent time with them. They were trying not to mention anything that would upset him, and he was trying not to remember better times.

"So did Helen Tyler get settled in Granny's house?" his mother asked as she put hot biscuits on the table.

"She looked settled to me," Matt confirmed.

"She sounded like such a nice person on the phone," Rita Clevenger continued. "And Maybeth Hadder says she looks just like Michelle Pfeiffer."

Matt poured homemade gravy onto a steaming biscuit. "I don't remember what Michelle Pfeiffer looks like, Mama. Ms. Tyler is very pretty, and she does seem nice, but don't get any ideas."

"Of course, I'm not trying to match-make," Rita said primly. "After all, she's a complete stranger. She might be married for all we know."

Matt took a sip of orange juice. "She didn't mention a husband, and the lease is just in her name."

"Well," Rita said briskly as she took her seat at the table, "let's eat."

After breakfast Matt mowed the lawn, then loaded the mower into the back of his Bronco. His mother followed him outside, dressed for church.

"Can't you ever take a day off?" she asked.

"I've got so much to do, Mama. I need to cut the grass at Miss Glida Mae's and the rental house." He wiped sweat from his face with the sleeve of his T-shirt. "Then I need to do a few things at the office."

"Even on Sunday?" His mother was apparently not pleased.

"I'm working on a big case."

Rita sighed. "They need to hire you some help."

"The county can't afford more employees."

Rita raised her eyes to his. "I wish you'd go with us to church. I don't think it would be as bad as you imagine."

Matt shook his head. "I think it would be every bit as bad as I imagine. I'd see Julie walking down the aisle in her wedding dress, Chase singing in the children's choir, Chad wearing that awful, four-foot-long gown Julie bought him to be christened in . . ." His voice trailed off, and his mother put a hand on his cheek.

"I'm so sorry, dear."

"I know. Enjoy the meeting, and I'll see you this afternoon."

When Matt got to his rental house, he noticed that Helen Tyler's car was not in the driveway. Mildly disappointed—and irritated with himself for feeling that way—he cut the front and back yards with a vengeance. Then he moved over to Miss Glida Mae's. The elderly woman cracked open her door just as he finished.

"Morning, Miss Glida Mae."

"Morning, Matt," she replied. "Did you catch that murderer yet?"

"Don't have a murderer to catch as far as I know."

Miss Glida Mae pointed a finger at him. "I saw him with my own two eyes on Friday night, and he'll kill me if you don't catch him soon."

Matt realized there was nothing to be gained by arguing. "Yes, ma'am."

"Helen's a Mormon, just like Sydney," Miss Glida Mae continued on a different tangent.

This was news. Matt stood up straight. "Really?"

"That's what Nelda said. She says they're Christians and don't believe in witchcraft, but I'm still not sure after all those strange happenings with Sydney's husband a couple of years back . . ."

Matt smiled. "I guess you'll have to ask Ms. Tyler what she knows about witches."

The golden curls bobbed. "I certainly will."

As soon as he could escape from Miss Glida Mae, Matt went by his parents' house and changed clothes. Then he drove to the sheriff's office. The minute he sat down at his desk, Matt called the Eureka police department. The officer who answered the phone said the chief was at church. Matt left a message, then sifted through paperwork for an hour until Ed returned his call.

"What's up?" the chief wanted to know.

"Remember your question about why these women would let someone into their house after dark when they were already dressed for bed?"

"Yeah," Ed answered.

"Well, since we haven't found any friends that the women had in common, I think we need to look at other types of people who would be trusted."

"Like cops, you mean?"

Matt thought of Helen Tyler's cautious behavior when he knocked on her door that first night. "Mrs. Freeburg maybe, but I don't think a smart woman like Robyn Howell would let a man into her house at night just because he was wearing a uniform."

"So who would Ms. Howell trust?" the chief asked.

"A minister maybe."

"Robyn Howell didn't believe in God, let alone ministers."

"A doctor or a nurse?" Matt suggested.

"Robyn Howell was never seen by a physician in Eureka."

"She'd had a bad cold for a couple of weeks," Matt reminded the chief. "Maybe she called someone to come over."

"Like a house call?" the chief asked. "I didn't know doctors did that anymore."

"Dr. Baker still comes to see Miss Glida Mae."

"I guess I can have somebody check it out," the chief offered.

"Even delivery people like the mailman and the UPS guy need to be checked out."

Ed Ramsey sighed. "We'll start a new list. What did you think of the ex-husband?"

"Seemed nice enough, but got real unfriendly when I asked if he inherited his ex-wife's estate."

The chief chuckled. "If that's what you call being the 'picture of discretion,' I'm glad I won't be there when you tell the Freeburg guy you want his mother exhumed."

"Did Howell tell you that they spent the weekends together frequently? Almost like they were still married?"

"Yeah, that's what he said."

"You sound like you don't believe it," Matt commented.

"After thirty-five years in law enforcement, I don't believe nobody."

Matt smiled to himself. "Well, let me know what you find out about doctors making house calls, and we'll compare it with all the people who provided medical services to Mrs. Freeburg. Maybe we'll find a connection."

"I guess it's worth a try," was the chief's encouraging parting comment.

CHAPTER 4

Helen misjudged the traffic on Sunday morning and ended up being late for church. The sacrament prayer was in progress when she arrived, so she took a seat in the foyer. As soon as the Aaronic Priesthood was dismissed, Helen tried to decide whether she should disturb the meeting by going into the chapel or just sit and listen from the foyer. Then a pregnant woman came through the chapel doors and sat in the chair across from Helen. "It must be 120 degrees in there," she claimed, and Helen nodded to be polite. Then the woman's eyes narrowed. "I don't think we've met."

"My name is Helen Tyler. I just moved into town on Friday."

The woman leaned forward. "Are you Matt Clevenger's new tenant?"

"Yes," Helen admitted. "Are you Sydney the baseball player?"

This earned her a laugh. "In another lifetime. Now I'm an incubator." She rubbed her abdomen.

"When is your baby due?"

"In three weeks—if I live that long."

"The time will pass quickly," Helen predicted.

"For you maybe," Sydney said, then smiled to soften her words. "Don't mind me. I'm crabby anyway, but pregnancy has turned me into a monster. I'm just way too old for all this."

"A lot of women are waiting to have children until later in life," Helen told her. "I read an article that said with drug therapy, some women are conceiving in their fifties."

Sydney frowned. "Do I look *that* old to you?"

Helen studied Sydney and decided she could take a joke. "You don't look a day over forty-five to me."

Sydney laughed and massaged her lower back. "I'll make a deal with you. I'll forget that remark about my age if you promise not to tell my husband women can have babies when they're fifty. I'm trying to convince him that thirty-four is the healthy birth-giving age limit."

Helen nodded. "It's a deal."

Sydney hefted herself up. "Well, I guess I'd better go back into that inferno before my husband comes looking for me. Now that he's in the bishopric, he says I have to set an example."

"I'll follow you in." Helen joined her by the chapel doors.

"Grandma said she invited you for Sunday dinner," Sydney whispered.

"She's trying to help me settle into the neighborhood."

Sydney nodded. "Grandma looks out for everyone."

Helen followed Sydney into the chapel and sat in the first available seat. When sacrament meeting ended, Sydney reappeared. "I'll introduce you to the bishop when he walks by," she said, pointing toward the front of the room where several people were congregated.

Helen studied the men on the stand. "Which one is your husband?"

Sydney raised an eyebrow. "The cute one, of course."

After the introductions, Sydney led Helen to Sunday School, then into Relief Society. The full-time missionaries taught the lesson and challenged each sister to give away a Book of Mormon during the week. When the meeting was over, the elders stood at each door and reminded the sisters about the challenge. "We really appreciate your support," one told Helen as she passed into the hallway.

She looked into his hopeful eyes and couldn't say no, so she tucked the Book of Mormon in her purse and proceeded on to the car. She felt a little depressed as she drove back to Ivy Lane. Sydney had everything—a husband in the bishopric, a baby on the way, and Nelda Lovell for a grandmother. Which all proved that life just wasn't fair.

Helen stopped at a newspaper stand and fed in a dollar and thirty-five cents for a Sunday edition. When she pulled into the driveway of her rental house, she could smell freshly cut grass. Both her yard and Glida Mae's had benefited from a recent trimming, and she wondered if lawn care was part of Matt Clevenger's duties as landlord.

She changed clothes, then planned to read the paper before it was time to go to Nelda's, but as soon as she sat on the sagging couch, there was a knock on the door. Through the peephole Helen could see Glida Mae Magnanney standing on the porch. The old woman's sausage curls were in disarray, and she was still wearing a bathrobe.

"Have you come to walk with me to Nelda's for lunch?" Helen asked pleasantly as she opened the door.

Glida Mae shook her head, looking frightened and confused. "I took such a chance coming over here," she whispered, and Helen let her into the small living room. "But I would never forgive myself if I didn't warn you and something happened."

"What's the matter, Glida Mae?" Helen asked.

The neighbor lowered her voice even more. "I saw him again!"

"Who?"

"Why, the murderer, of course."

Helen relaxed. For a minute she'd actually been afraid. "Why don't you have a seat and let me get you some cool water. It's awfully hot outside today."

"I don't want any water!" Glida Mae exclaimed. "And I don't want to stay inside this house for a minute longer than necessary."

Helen frowned. "Why not?"

"Because this is where I saw him!" Glida Mae cried. "He went into the basement through the door downstairs!"

"You saw a man come into this house?" Helen clarified.

"It's really not safe for you to stay here. You'll have to find another house."

"Thank you so much for warning me," Helen said gently as she led Glida Mae toward the door. "Now let's go down to Nelda's for lunch."

"You don't believe me, do you?" the old woman asked. "No one believes anything I say anymore. Do you think it's because I'm an actress?"

"I believe that you're scared."

"I promise it's true! You are in great danger!" Glida Mae claimed as they crossed her statue-dotted lawn. Then she stopped suddenly. "I can't go to Nelda's today! My Hollywood agent called and said he'd be by sometime this afternoon. They are planning a remake of *Gone with the Wind,* and they want me to play Mellie Hamilton."

"Please come to Nelda's," Helen pleaded. "We can put a note on your door so your agent can find you if he comes during lunch."

"I can't expect an important Hollywood agent to *look* for me!" Glida Mae replied as she patted her pockets. "Now where did I put my keys?"

Helen was watching helplessly as Glida Mae searched for her keys when Nelda Lovell walked up. "Well, Glida Mae, I was coming to get you for lunch, but I see you were already on your way."

Glida Mae gave her friend a confused stare, so Helen responded for her. "Glida Mae thought she saw someone go into the basement of my house, and she was trying to warn me. Now she says wants to go back inside her own house to wait for her Hollywood agent, but she can't find her keys."

Nelda nodded, then spoke to Glida Mae. "It's time for your noon medication, but you're not supposed to take it on an empty stomach. Won't you come eat a little lunch with us?"

Glida Mae shook her head firmly. "I have to wait for Mr. Gregory. Besides," she lowered her voice, "it's very dangerous outside of my house. So dangerous."

Nelda turned to Helen. "She's always worse right before her next dose of medication. Maybe it would be best if we just let her stay home." Nelda led Glida Mae up to the door and helped her find her keys. "You go in and take your medicine. I'll be back in a little while with a dinner plate."

Glida Mae nodded vaguely, then slipped inside her house and closed the door.

"I'm really worried about her," Helen said as she followed Nelda across Glida Mae's lawn.

"It's so sweet of you to worry about Glida Mae, dear. But the only other option is a nursing home, and I think that would kill her for sure."

"It's a lot of responsibility for you," Helen said as they walked through Nelda's back door.

"Glida Mae and I have been friends for a long time," Nelda replied. "She'd do the same for me."

Thelma and Hugh Warren were sitting at Nelda's kitchen table when they arrived. "War Eagle!" the little man greeted.

"Oh hush, Hugh," Thelma commanded, then turned to Helen. "He loves his Auburn University football. Just about everything he owns is orange and blue."

Helen nodded. "I saw the garbage cans."

"Who's your team?" Mr. Warren asked.

Helen thought of the beautiful campus where she used to teach. "The Brownley Buffaloes."

Mr. Warren scratched his head. "Never heard of them."

"They don't win often," Helen admitted.

"Where are you from originally?" Nelda wanted to know.

"West Virginia," Helen replied wistfully.

The little man paused for a second, then asked, "What brings you to Eureka?"

"Now, Hugh, we're not here to interrogate Helen or discuss college football," Thelma told him firmly. "It's Sunday, and we're going to enjoy a pleasant meal."

Helen took a seat, grateful for Thelma's intervention.

"Where's Glida Mae?" Hugh asked after grace was said.

Nelda glanced at Helen before she replied. "She said she saw the murderer again and that she's got an appointment this afternoon with a Hollywood agent."

Hugh looked up sharply. "An agent I can understand, but a murderer?"

"I told you about those two women who died in their sleep," Thelma said with a wave of her fork.

"But you didn't say Glida Mae had seen him!"

"Hugh," Thelma replied patiently, "this is *Glida Mae* we're talking about."

Mr. Warren cleared his throat. "Oh yes, of course. Glida Mae."

"Any developments on the parking lot controversy?" Helen asked in the uncomfortable silence that followed.

Thelma sighed. "The preacher said he's going to leave it up to the finance committee, and since Maybeth's husband is the chairman, I guess the case is closed."

Nelda put a big roast and a bowl of creamed potatoes on the table. "Maybe the parking lot will get repaved next year."

"In the meantime, I might just start meeting with the Methodists," Thelma threatened.

"Well, you'll be able to keep up with Baptist events by checking the new electronic sign," Hugh said with a smile. Thelma gave him a sour look, but Hugh was not deterred. "And speaking of Methodists, did you hear about the missionary couple that got sent back from Indonesia?"

"Why'd they get sent home?" Thelma asked as she got a generous helping of potatoes. "Parasites?"

Hugh shook his head. "No. Adultery."

All eating and conversation stopped. "Where did you hear that?" Thelma demanded.

"Bill Oscar Lee at the filling station told me. Said the husband got a little too friendly with one of the local girls. Might not have gotten caught, but the girl had a baby with blue eyes."

"Hugh Warren, that is scandalous!" Thelma declared, then leaned forward. "What else did Bill Oscar say?"

"That the missionary man confessed it all to the church, and his wife said she wouldn't divorce him. They even brought the baby back to the states with them," Hugh told his audience.

"His wife must be the picture of Christian charity," Nelda said.

"Or crazy," Thelma muttered.

"Bill Oscar said she wanted her husband to have a reminder of his sins for the rest of his life," Hugh contributed.

Nelda shook her head. "So often people choose revenge over forgiveness and end up paying the price themselves."

"At least the baby will be raised here in the States," Helen ventured.

"As a Christian," Thelma agreed.

Nelda stood and got a pie off the stove. "Well, enough of that. If we'd have known our other options, Hugh, we'd have let you talk murder and football throughout the meal."

When dinner was over, Helen thanked Nelda for the invitation and offered to take Glida Mae a plate. "Thank you, dear, but Glida Mae might not open the door for anyone but me," Nelda replied.

Helen walked slowly back to her rental house. She was relatively certain that Glida Mae's murderer sightings fell into the same category as the visits from Hollywood agents, but nonetheless she felt it would be foolish to continue living in the house without checking out the basement. So she retrieved her gun from her purse, then walked around into the backyard. There was a wooden door centered in the middle of the concrete foundation of the house.

Helen used her house key to open the door, then wrapped her fingers around the small gun before pushing inside. She found a light switch by the door and flipped it on. The room looked like a typical basement, cluttered with junk. There were stacks of old books, boxes, broken pieces of furniture, and a metal shelf that held a variety of old paint cans and rusty tools.

Once Helen had assured herself that no one was in the basement, she went out into the hot afternoon sun and locked the door behind her. Then she rounded the corner and ran straight into a tall figure. Thinking that she had met Glida Mae's intruder, Helen pointed the gun and screamed.

"Whoa!" Matt Clevenger said as he caught her wrist and redirected the gun toward the sky. "You're going to end up killing somebody with that thing! Probably me!"

"Sorry." Helen pulled her hand from his grasp and put the gun into her pocket. "The safety was on."

"What are you doing back here?"

"Glida Mae said she saw the murderer in your basement, and I decided to take a look."

"What murderer?"

"The one who killed those two women in their sleep, I guess," Helen said wearily. The uncomfortable look on the sheriff's face did not reassure her. "Did someone really murder them?"

"I told you we don't know how they died."

"But someone might have killed them," Helen whispered.

"You didn't find anyone in there?" Matt asked, and Helen shook her head.

"No, it was empty but kind of creepy."

"All basements are creepy. That's why they play such prominent roles in horror films."

Helen exhaled. "Now you sound like Glida Mae."

"When I start claiming to be Humphrey Bogart's wife, have me committed."

Helen glanced over her shoulder at the basement door. "It might be a good idea to change the locks, just as a precaution."

Matt nodded. "I'll send Elvis over tomorrow."

"And that's supposed to make me feel safer?" Helen asked. "Elvis probably *is* the murderer."

Matt considered this for a few seconds, then shook his head. "No, I don't think Elvis is our man."

"He's weird. You've admitted that."

"But he's too obvious. It's always someone you'd never suspect. Like the butler."

Helen raised her eyebrows. "Is this an observation you're making based on years of police work?"

"No, from years of watching murder mysteries."

She gave him half a smile. "What are you doing here?"

"I left my gas can when I cut the grass." He pointed to the can on her back porch steps.

"I guess I should thank you for mowing the lawn."

"I do Miss Glida Mae's every week. Might as well do yours at the same time."

Another charity case, Helen thought to herself. "Well, I'd better get out of this heat."

Matt picked up the gas can. "And I'll go speak to Miss Glida Mae. She seemed more distracted than usual when I was here earlier."

"She might not let you in unless you tell her you're a Hollywood agent," Helen warned.

Matt gave her a strange look. "Elvis will be over here first thing in the morning to change the locks. As a special favor to you, I'll ask him to leave his hockey mask and meat cleaver at home."

"I can't tell you how much I appreciate that," Helen muttered as she made her way around to the front of the house.

She went inside and stood in front of the window air conditioner until she had cooled off. Then she sat on the couch and opened the newspaper. The bulk of her savings had been used to buy the old Escort and pay the security deposit and first month's rent on this house. Her nice home in West Virginia was untouchable until the lawsuit with Harrison was settled. And since she absolutely refused to ask her parents for money, she needed a source of income fast.

She hoped to do substitute teaching once school started, but until then she would have to find employment of some kind. There were several jobs that looked promising, so she circled them with the intention of calling on Monday.

Helen found an old movie on television and had stretched out on the couch when she heard a noise from her backyard. After pushing her gun into her pants pocket, she walked through the kitchen door and looked outside.

Two children, a boy and a girl, were standing by the fence that separated her yard from Glida Mae Magnanney's. Helen pulled the door open, and they froze in terror when she appeared on the back steps. Both had solemn brown eyes, silky black hair, and were breathtakingly beautiful. Realizing that she must be meeting part of the Nguyen family, Helen smiled. The children remained motionless.

"Hi," she greeted. "I'm Miss Tyler. What are your names?" The boy gathered enough courage to glance at the gate, probably calculating how quickly they could traverse the distance. Helen searched for a way to keep them from fleeing. Then she remembered a bag of Oreos she had bought at the grocery store. "I have some cookies I'd like to share with you. Wait here."

She didn't really expect them to obey, but when she returned, the children were right where she had left them. She approached them slowly, extending the open bag of cookies. Finally she stopped about three feet away. "Here, try one."

They made no move toward the cookies, but Helen waited patiently. After almost a minute, the little girl reached out and grabbed an Oreo, then stepped back to the safety of the fence.

"No, Lin!" the boy cried as he watched her stuff the whole cookie into her small mouth. The little girl chewed furiously, as if she were afraid the cookie would be snatched away.

"So," Helen addressed the little girl, "your name is Lin and you like cookies." Then she turned to Lin's brother. "And it looks like I'm going to have to guess your name." She thought for a moment. "I think your name is Tarzan." He shook his dark head. "Bugs Bunny?" He shook his head again. "Scooby-Doo?" This elicited a small giggle from Lin.

"My name is Tan, and we don't speak to strangers," he said in perfect English.

"Well, I told you my name, so I'm not a stranger. How old are you, Tan?"

Instead of answering, the boy took his sister's hand and pulled her toward the gate. Helen cut them off and handed the package of cookies to Lin. The little girl accepted them, then followed her brother out the gate. She gave Helen one last look over her shoulder as they disappeared around the overgrown hedges.

So much for making friends and eating Oreos, Helen thought to herself as she went back inside. She sat on the couch and had just enough time to get interested in the movie again before she heard a faint knock on her back door. She opened it to find that Lin and Tan had returned. This time they were accompanied by a petite woman whom Helen presumed was their mother. Her lovely face was marred at the moment by an angry expression.

Helen smiled at the trio. "Hello, Lin, Tan," she greeted the children in turn, then looked at their mother. "You must be Mrs. Nguyen. I'm Helen Tyler."

The woman frowned at Tan and issued a series of discordant commands. Tan then turned and spoke to Helen. "My mother says she is ashamed of her rude children who came into your yard and ate your food." Tan's cheeks turned pink, and Helen knew he resented having to accept responsibility for Lin's transgression as well as his own. The little woman stepped forward at this point and thrust a basket into Helen's hands. "She gives you this *thit bo kho* as payment with her sincere apology."

Helen lifted the cloth that covered the basket's contents and found a casserole dish filled with a meat and noodle mixture. Then she looked back at Tan. There was no way his mother could have prepared a casserole so quickly, which meant that the food Helen held in her hands was probably the family's supper. "This is so much food," she began carefully. "Won't you come in and share it with me?"

Tan translated, and his mother shook her head again, but her expression softened. Tan turned to Helen, his disappointment obvious. "She says it is only for you. It is a special family recipe," he told Helen as his eyes strayed longingly to the basket in her hands.

Helen didn't need the food, but she knew their honor was more important. "I am very grateful."

Tan translated for his mother, then waited for her response. "She says to say you are welcome and her name is Yenphi."

"Thank you, Yenphi," Helen said, and the tiny woman relaxed a little more.

Yenphi called to Lin, who was clutching the bag of Oreos to her small chest. The little girl shook her head, and Yenphi stamped a foot. Finally Helen realized that Yenphi was trying to make Lin return the cookies. "Oh, no!" she said, and all three of her guests looked up in surprise. "You have given me this wonderful food." She raised the basket to emphasize her point. "My gift is small in comparison, but you must keep it or I will be . . . sad."

Tan translated furiously, and Yenphi's head dropped in resignation. She murmured a few words, and Tan turned to Helen. "My mother says okay, but she is still ashamed."

"Tell her I'm grateful that her children came to visit, and I'll gladly exchange a few cookies for a delicious meal any day."

The Vietnamese translation of these words seemed to please Yenphi. She smiled at Helen, then motioned her children toward the gate.

"Tell you mother that I'd be glad for you to visit again," Helen called after them. "And I'll get more cookies!"

* * *

Matt frowned as he walked into his office Monday morning. When he'd gone by to check on Miss Glida Mae after retrieving his gas can, she wouldn't open the door more than a crack and was ranting about murderers in his basement. He'd actually considered pretending to be a Hollywood agent to get inside, but he knew Miss Nelda would call him if there were reason for concern.

Once he saw the mountain of paperwork on his desk, he was too discouraged to worry about Miss Glida Mae anymore. He stacked files from several cases that were far from resolved on a corner of his desk and compared the information he had compiled on the two victims. He had copies of their phone records for the past three months. These numbers needed to be cross-referenced with his regional phone book on compact disc. There was a note from Crystal saying that Ms. Howell's cell phone records would be coming soon.

He put the phone book CD into his computer, but before he began the painstaking process of typing each number in, he picked up the phone and dialed a number from memory. After two rings, an answering machine came on. "West Investigations. Leave a message."

Matt waited for the beep, then spoke to the machine. "Brian, this is Matt. I need you to check out a couple of things for me."

Matt put down the phone and waited for it to ring. Thirty seconds later, it did.

"Matt! Put me to work," the private investigator commanded. "Baby needs a new pair of shoes."

Matt smiled. Brian was a confirmed bachelor, and the last things he'd be buying with his exorbitant fees were baby shoes. "I want you to find out everything you can about Robyn and Scott Howell. They're divorced, and she recently died of unknown causes."

"Uh-oh. Let me get a pencil."

"Also check out Mary Jean Freeburg, although I don't think you'll find much of interest. I'll fax you the files as soon as we hang up."

"That it?" Brian asked.

Matt hesitated, then spoke reluctantly. "We're compiling a list of people who are new to the area. I'll send it to you once it's complete, but you can go ahead and run a check on Helen Tyler now. She's from West Virginia." Matt gave the PI the previous address Helen had listed on her lease.

"You got a social security number?"

"No."

"What kind of information am I looking for?"

"Verify that she really did live at this address and see if she has a handgun registered there. Marital status, why she left West Virginia, that kind of thing."

"Sounds like an interesting lady," Brian commented.

"Call me back when you have the results."

"Will do," Brian said as he disconnected the call.

While Matt faxed the files to Brian, he tried to shake his feelings of guilt. Helen was new to town, she lived close to the most recent victim, and she was renting his house. It was reasonable for him to check her out and was certainly not illegal. So why did he feel like a Peeping Tom?

Once the files of the victims were faxed to Brian, Matt looked through his Rolodex and found the home number for Alex Jordan, one of the assistant medical examiners in Atlanta. Matt was mentally formulating the message he would leave when his old friend answered. "Jordan!"

"Alex? This is Matt Clevenger."

"*The* Matt Clevenger has actually picked up a phone and called *me?*"

"Yes, and I need a favor."

"Imagine that! You haven't called me for what—three years now? Then suddenly, out of the clear blue sky, you call your old college buddy and it's not just to shoot the breeze!"

Matt controlled a groan. He had known this wouldn't be easy. "I'm sorry, Alex, but the last few years have been tough."

"You think I don't know that?" Alex demanded. "It's during the tough times that you need your friends."

"Well, it might be a little late, but you're finally going to get your chance to help me."

"Oh man. Why does that scare me to death?"

"I need you to do a couple of autopsies for me," Matt said carefully.

"You folks in Eureka turning out bodies that fast?" Alex asked.

"A Nancy Wilder in your office already did an autopsy on one of them and couldn't find a cause of death for a thirty-four-year-old, perfectly healthy woman. The second wasn't autopsied at the time of death and has been in the ground for almost week."

"You got a repeater?"

"I'm afraid we do. But to confirm that, I'll need you to find chicken soup in the stomach contents of one body and a cause of death for both."

Alex whistled. "When you finally ask a favor, you really come up with a big one," he said respectfully. "You know that during the embalming process, they vacuum out all the major organs and fill them with embalming fluid?"

"I know that if anyone can find something useful, it's you."

"High praise from a long-lost friend. I feel all warm and fuzzy," Alex said with a sigh. "Probably the best way to keep from ruffling any feathers is for me to do your little favor on my own time, what you might call recreational autopsies. This place clears out pretty fast at quitting time." Alex paused for a second. "If you get here about five-thirty tomorrow, most everybody should be gone. I've got an assistant who can be trusted, and I'll get him to stay."

Matt hung up, feeling guiltier than before. He was investigating his renter and using an old friend. How much lower would he stoop? Afraid to answer that question, Matt called the Eureka police department and asked to speak to Ed Ramsey. The officer who answered said that the chief was at home, so Matt called him there. "I've got the autopsies set up for five-thirty tomorrow in Atlanta. My friend's going to do them discreetly after hours to keep us out of trouble with the ME."

"Keep himself out of trouble too, I'll bet."

"Can you call Phil Norris and tell him to have Robyn Howell's body ready at two-thirty?"

"Sure. You just going to put them in your backseat?" the chief asked.

"Thought I'd get you to talk the coroner into loaning me one of his funeral home vans instead."

"You're not easy to work with, Clevenger."

"I'm the one who's got to face the Freeburg man tomorrow," Matt reminded the chief. "And ride to Atlanta with two bodies, then watch double autopsies."

"Yeah, you have all the fun while I do all the begging."

"Thanks, Ed."

Matt hung up the phone and stood to leave, but before he made it out the door, the phone rang again.

"That last name you gave me was a piece of cake," Brian said cheerfully. "Confirmed that Helen Tyler does own a small house in a classy little neighborhood near Brownley College. It's mortgaged, but she has about twenty thousand dollars in equity. Brownley College is, by the way, a private school that you or I could never afford. Miss Tyler has a Ph.D. and taught English Literature at the college. But during her tenure year, she got involved with a student named Harrison Campbell."

"A minor?" Matt asked with dread.

"Naw, guy's twenty-three and in their master's program. Anyway, a nasty scandal resulted, and when classes ended in April, the college didn't renew her contract."

"So she was fired," Matt clarified.

"Basically. She does have a gun registered in West Virginia, and she filed an application for one in Georgia a couple of weeks ago. No mention of a husband, now or in the past. Her parents are antique brokers. You want more?"

"That's plenty," Matt declined.

"Okay then, I'm on to the others."

"Thanks, Brian."

Matt intended to head toward home, but he ended up in front of Miss Glida Mae's pink house on Ivy Lane. As he crossed the statue-filled lawn, his eyes drifted toward the rental house, where lights were on in the living room and kitchen. Miss Glida Mae did open the door, but she kept the chain on as they talked briefly. She didn't invite him in, but she also didn't mention Hollywood agents or murderers, so he felt encouraged by the time they said good night.

He started for the Bronco, then almost unconsciously found himself stepping up onto the porch of his rental house. Helen answered after the second knock. Her shoulder-length, blonde hair was hanging loose, and her eyes registered concern when she saw him.

"Is something wrong, Sheriff?"

He couldn't very well say that he was lonely and the light coming through the windows of his grandmother's house had beckoned him, so he shook his head. "I stopped to check on Miss Glida Mae, and after all that talk this afternoon about murderers, I decided I'd better make sure you were still alive too. And I couldn't call since you won't give me your cell phone number."

Helen nodded and stepped aside. "Come on in."

"I didn't mean to interrupt you," he said as he walked into the living room.

"You didn't." Helen pointed to the old couch. "Have a seat." She took a step toward the kitchen. "If you're just leaving work, I'm guessing that you haven't eaten. I'll heat up some dinner for you. Feel free to change the channel."

Matt perched himself on the edge of the couch, trying to decide whether to stay or go. The local news was on, and they were doing a boring community segment on historical markers in the area. He glanced around the room, and his eyes settled on the newspaper spread out on his grandmother's old coffee table. He shuffled through, looking for the sports section, and underneath found a small blue book. The words *The Book of Mormon, Another Testament of Jesus Christ* were printed in gold letters. Glancing into the kitchen, he saw Helen standing at the stove, so he opened the first page.

At first he read stealthily, like a teenager who had stumbled onto a dirty magazine, but by the time Helen returned, he was so absorbed that he didn't notice her until she placed a plate of steaming food in front of him. Embarrassed, he let go of the book, and the cover closed.

"Sorry," he said. "I just meant to read your paper, but then I saw this and curiosity got the best of me."

"So what did you think?" Helen asked. When he gave her a blank look, she pointed at the book. "I was born a member of the Church, and I always wondered what it would be like to see the Book of Mormon for the first time."

"I didn't get far."

"Take it home and read it at your leisure," Helen offered.

"That's okay," Matt declined, imagining his mother's reaction to a Mormon Bible in her house.

"I promised to give it away this week, and if you take it, my mission is accomplished. So I'm afraid I'm going to have to insist. Now hurry and eat your food before it gets cold."

Matt studied the *thit bo khu,* then looked up in surprise. "You made this?"

Helen smiled. "No. Yenphi gave it to me."

"Yenphi?" Matt asked as he took a tentative bite.

"The mother of the Vietnamese family who lives next to Nelda Lovell. She doesn't speak English, but her son, Tan, said this is a special family recipe."

"It's good," Matt said as he put a forkful into his mouth. "But from what Miss Nelda says, the Nguyen family isn't very friendly. I'm surprised that you've already got them sharing food with you.

Helen laughed. "I *am* irresistible." Matt watched a dimple form in her right cheek and felt his mouth go dry. He swallowed quickly and tried not to stare as she continued. "Actually I found the children playing in your backyard. I gave them some cookies, and apparently the mother considered that an obligation. So she brought me the family's dinner to pay her debt."

Matt shrugged. "Looks like a good trade to me."

Helen stared at the food heaped on his plate. "I can't help wondering what Tan and Lin ate tonight." She waited for him to finish eating, then took his dishes into the kitchen.

While she was gone Matt restacked the newspaper on the coffee table and, in the process, found the want ads that Helen had circled. He glanced over them quickly, then stood when Helen walked back in. "Well, I'd better get home. Thanks for sharing the Nguyens' dinner with me."

Helen gave him a wry look. "You're welcome." Then she reached for the Book of Mormon on the coffee table. "Don't forget this."

"I don't really have much time to read," he tried again to refuse.

"You don't have to read it—just take it. I only promised to give it away, not force someone to scour it from cover to cover."

He accepted the book reluctantly, then moved to the door. "I won't make a habit of stopping by for dinner *every* night," he promised. "I guess I just feel comfortable here."

"Because it was your grandmother's house," Helen said with an understanding smile.

He looked briefly into her wide, blue-green eyes. "Yeah, I guess that's it. I'd appreciate it if you'd call and let me know when Elvis gets the locks changed tomorrow."

She nodded, and he hurried outside before she could see his smile. In a matter of hours, he'd have her cell number.

CHAPTER 5

Elvis arrived at eight o'clock on Monday, and Helen waited impatiently while he changed the locks on all the doors. Once the creepy handyman was gone, Helen called Matt Clevenger.

"The locks are changed," she reported.

"And Elvis didn't try to strangle you?" his voice teased through the phone lines.

Helen smirked to herself. "I guess I'm not his type."

Matt laughed softly, and Helen clutched the phone to her ear. "Well, I'll be by to check on Miss Glida Mae this evening. Maybe I'll see you then."

"Probably," she responded, then said good-bye.

After disconnecting, Helen found the want ads and started calling potential employers. She arranged to pick up two applications and set up an interview on Tuesday morning. During the entire process, her conversation with Matt Clevenger kept replaying itself in her mind. He was such a solemn man—it was a pleasure to picture him laughing. Finally, disgusted with herself, Helen went to collect job applications.

On the way home, she stopped by the Wal-Mart Super Center and bought two bags of Oreos for the Nguyen children, a gallon of milk, and some cereal. Then, hating herself for doing it, she bought fixings for sandwiches in case the sheriff came by for dinner again that night.

When she pulled up to her house, she saw Nelda Lovell standing on Glida Mae's porch. The older woman waved to Helen as she took her groceries inside. Helen put the food away, then walked back outside.

"Is something wrong?" Helen asked as she approached.

Nelda knocked on the door again. "It's time for Glida Mae to take her walk, but she won't come out."

"I'm not going for a walk today," Glida Mae replied through the wood.

Helen looked at the sky. "It's overcast today, so you won't need to worry about getting freckles."

"I'm not worried about freckles!" Glida Mae declared in muffled tones. "I'm worried about murderers!"

Helen exchanged a glance with Nelda, then spoke through the door again. "It's broad daylight, Glida Mae. It seems like a sensible murderer would wait until after dark to go to work."

"This killer is very bold," Glida Mae responded. "He's not afraid of *anything*."

Helen frowned. "How about if I go along then? There's supposed to be safety in numbers."

After a short pause, Glida Mae cracked open the door. She was wearing a nightgown, and her hair was a tangled mess. There were dark circles under her eyes, and her lips were trembling.

"Oh, Glida Mae," Nelda said in dismay. "You haven't been sleeping."

"I can't, Nelda. I'm afraid to close my eyes."

Nelda pushed her way into the house. "I'll help you take a bath. Then I'll brush your hair, and you can tell me how to put on your makeup just like Joan Fontaine did." Nelda turned around and spoke quietly to Helen. "Give me about an hour, and we'll be ready to walk," she whispered.

Helen returned to her rental house and rearranged the kitchen cupboards until the hour was up. Then she went back to the pink house and knocked on the door. Nelda answered promptly. "Doesn't Glida Mae look wonderful?" she asked.

The sausage curls were back in place and makeup was liberally distributed, but the haunted expression was still in Glida Mae's eyes. "Just like Joan Fontaine," Helen agreed.

"Well, Thelma's waiting for us to take our walk." Nelda nudged Glida Mae outside.

"Safety in numbers," Glida Mae murmured, squinting as the light hit her eyes.

"See, it's such a lovely day! Lots of clouds and a gentle breeze! Some fresh air will do us all good," Nelda encouraged.

Glida Mae was nervous, looking over her shoulder continually. But as they walked and Nelda spoke in a soothing tone, she appeared to relax. Thelma joined them when they passed her house. She didn't ask any questions, so Helen assumed that Nelda had called her. The old friends discussed the specials at the Piggly Wiggly that week and a neighbor who'd had foot surgery. Then, as if afraid they were ignoring Helen, Nelda turned to include her in the conversation.

"What brought you to Eureka?" Nelda asked.

"We used to spend our vacations here when I was young. My dad loved to fish on the lake, and we'd camp and eat what he caught." Helen felt unexpected emotion building in her throat and had to pause. "I had so many happy memories, and when I was trying to think of where I could go to start over, Eureka just kept coming to my mind."

"Why did you need to start over?" Thelma asked.

"Thelma!" Nelda apparently objected to the personal question.

"It's okay," Helen intervened. "I lost my job in West Virginia. I could have moved in with my parents, but I've been living on my own for a lot of years now and . . ."

"You wanted to keep your independence," Nelda supplied for her. "That's something you don't have to explain to old folks!"

Helen smiled. "Yes, being independent is very important to me. My move here isn't permanent, but this seemed like a good, safe place to start."

"I don't see how you can be happy here as long as we've got a murderer on the loose," Glida Mae muttered.

Nelda patted Glida Mae's hand and smiled at Helen. "My husband loved to take his boat to the lake and spend hours trying to catch poor, defenseless bass. Does your father still fish?"

Helen shook her head. "My parents are too busy for vacations now."

Before anyone could think of a response, Helen saw Tan and Lin hiding in the bushes by the edge of their porch. She waved, and the children stared back. "Hi!" she called to them. "I hope you'll come see me again soon! I've got more cookies."

The children remained frozen, like deer caught in headlights.

"The Nguyen children have been to see you?" Nelda asked in surprise.

Helen nodded. "Yesterday."

"I've been wooing them for over two months and they still won't come near me," Nelda divulged.

"I made them tea cakes, but they wouldn't take them," Thelma added. "And most children adore Hugh, but he hasn't had any luck with them either."

"Try Oreos," Helen suggested. "But I'll warn you that if they accept cookies from you, their mother will feel obligated to give you their dinner."

The old ladies laughed as Helen described the awkward situation from the day before. "How did the Vietnamese meal taste?" Thelma wanted to know.

"It was very good, but now I'm faced with another problem," Helen said, and the women stopped walking to listen. "I have to return the dish, and sending it back empty seems so . . ."

"Ungrateful?" Nelda suggested.

"Tacky," Thelma amended.

"But if I bake them a cake or something, Yenphi might feel that she has another obligation to me."

"And you can't keep eating their dinner," Thelma said with a frown.

"It's a very delicate problem," Nelda agreed.

After a few seconds of consideration, Thelma spoke. "My advice is to give Mrs. Nguyen a nice thank-you note along with the empty pan. You could even ask for the recipe to show how much you enjoyed the food."

"A thank-you note. Brilliant!" Helen replied.

Thelma smiled. "I can't really take credit for the idea. Thank-you notes have been a standard in the South for *years*."

"Decades. Maybe even centuries!" Nelda corrected, and Helen laughed.

"I'd be glad to help you with the wording for your note if you like," Thelma offered.

"Helen doesn't need help writing a thank-you note. She's a Southerner, just like us." Nelda gave her friend a disapproving look.

Thelma stepped closer to Nelda and lowered her voice. "She's from *West Virginia*."

"Oh, yes," Nelda said softly, then peeked at Helen with embarrassment. "I'm so sorry, Helen. We didn't mean to offend you."

Helen was amused but not offended. "What's wrong with West Virginia?"

"Oh, there's nothing *wrong* with it," Nelda was quick to say. "It's just that West Virginia was never a part of the Confederacy. A lot of people don't consider it exactly a *Southern* state."

Helen nodded. "In that case, I'll take you up on your offer to help me write a proper, Southern thank-you note," she told Thelma.

"Glad to help," Thelma said.

Helen looked at her companions. "And tomorrow I'm going to go by the library to see if they have a book on Vietnamese culture. I'm sure Judith Pope will help me."

"Judith can find anything," Nelda agreed.

"Poor Judith," Thelma contributed. "She was always such a solitary child, and Lavenia was so rigid. I'd try to give her tea cakes too, but Lavenia wouldn't let her take them."

"Lavenia believed in rules," Nelda conceded.

"Why did Judith live with her grandmother?" Helen asked.

Thelma and Nelda exchanged another quick look before Nelda replied. "There was an unfortunate family situation, and the parents couldn't care for Judith. Lavenia assumed responsibility for her when she was an infant."

"And then when Judith was a teenager, Lavenia's health started to fail and Judith had to care for her," Thelma added as they turned up the sidewalk in front of the pink house.

"That must have been very hard for someone so young," Helen replied.

"Yes," Nelda agreed, her tone grim. "She's had a difficult life."

"Like the sheriff," Glida Mae murmured, and all the women turned to her. "So much tragedy."

"What happened to the sheriff?" Helen asked.

Nelda spoke to Glida Mae instead of Helen. "We wouldn't want Helen to think that we're gossips now, would we?"

"Oh, I don't think that," Helen assured her. "But Judith told me he had a drinking problem, and he always looks so tired and sad." Helen paused for a breath. "I just want to be sure that I don't say anything that will upset him."

Nelda considered this as they reached Glida Mae's porch. "Let's have a seat here on the steps." Once they were settled, Nelda continued. "Tornadoes are common here, especially during the spring and summer. Almost four years ago, we had a bad storm that blew up so suddenly that we didn't have much warning."

"We were in Gulf Shores," Thelma explained. "Hugh won a free three-night stay at the Holiday Inn right on the waterfront."

"It was a terrible storm," Glida Mae said as if Thelma hadn't spoken. "It blew shingles off my roof."

Nelda nodded. "Most of our homes sustained some minor damage, but Matt's house was right in the path of the tornado. He was working that night—"

"He wasn't the sheriff yet," Glida Mae clarified. "Just a deputy."

Helen ignored Glida Mae and waited for Nelda to continue.

"His house was destroyed in the storm, and his wife and two children were killed."

Helen felt tears sting her eyes. "Oh, that's awful."

"It was," Nelda agreed. "Poor Matt—left all alone."

"They were such a wonderful family," Thelma contributed, dabbing at her eyes. "His wife, Julie, was a delightful girl, and their boys were so precious. It was a tragedy for the whole community."

"Julie was a cheerleader in high school, and Matt never even dated anyone else," Glida Mae said in her spacey tone.

"Matt got a football scholarship to the University of Georgia," Thelma explained further. "Hugh wanted him to go to Auburn, but Matt was determined to be a Bulldog. It didn't really matter, though, because he hurt his knee the first year. He married Julie right after college at the Eureka Baptist Church—"

Glida Mae interrupted again. "It was a huge wedding! They had the reception outside on the lawn. There were lots of ice sculptures, and everybody was afraid they'd melt since it was June and very hot. But everything was perfect. Very beautiful. Just like in the movies."

Glida Mae's eyes clouded as she turned to Nelda. "Do you remember your wedding, Nelda?"

"Barely," Nelda said with a smile.

"I don't remember it either," Glida Mae murmured with a frown. "Maybe I was in Hollywood at the time."

Nelda patted Glida Mae's hand. "Maybe so." Nelda was quiet for a minute, then took a deep breath and continued. "Well, anyway, after Julie and the boys died, Matt had a bad time. Then the old sheriff was diagnosed with cancer, and Matt accepted his position temporarily. I think it's helped him some."

"Judith told me he was afraid of ghosts, and I thought she was kidding," Helen said.

"Some memories can be crippling," Nelda replied, and Glida Mae started to sniffle. "Well, that's enough talk about sad things." Nelda stood and smoothed her dress. "Let's get you inside, Glida Mae. Thanks for walking with us, Helen."

Helen got up and stepped onto the sidewalk. "I enjoyed it," she said, then watched them disappear inside the pink house.

* * *

On Monday morning Matt got to the office early and started entering phone numbers into the computer. When Crystal arrived, she offered to help him.

"As long as accuracy isn't very important," she warned. "I'm not a great typist anyway, and between phone calls and other interruptions, I can't guarantee perfection."

Matt sighed. Accuracy was essential. "Thanks anyway," he told the secretary and kept typing. He had half of Robyn Howell's calls from the past three months entered into his computer by the time he left to meet Martin Freeburg.

The man was standing in front of his mother's home at ten o'clock, as had been arranged. Martin was in his late fifties, according to the file on Mary Jean Freeburg, but he looked older. *Probably the grief,* Matt thought to himself as he parked by the curb.

"Everything is pretty much the way she left it," Mr. Freeburg said as they walked inside. "I haven't had the heart to sort through it yet."

"The main thing I'm interested in is the Bible that was on the foot of her bed," Matt told the man.

Mr. Freeburg looked confused. "Why?"

"We're just trying to clear up some final details."

They found the Bible on a table in Mrs. Freeburg's room. Matt used gloves to pick it up and put it in a large plastic bag. "We'll return it as soon as possible," he promised. The other man shrugged, and they returned to the living room.

"Well, I'm glad that didn't take long," Martin Freeburg said.

Matt cleared his throat. "There is something else I need to discuss with you."

Mr. Freeburg frowned. "I can't give you much time. I have appointments scheduled today."

"It will only take a few minutes." Matt shifted his weight from one foot to the other, then continued. "There were some irregularities in the investigation," Matt tried, then stopped. "That is, some things should have been done . . . ," he floundered again.

"What are you saying, Sheriff?" Martin Freeburg asked, a line of worry forming between his eyes.

Matt sighed. "We need to have your mother's body exhumed."

Mr. Freeburg's face registered total shock. "Why?" he gasped.

Matt considered his options. "I'm going to be honest with you. I don't think your mother died of natural causes. But in order to prove it, I'm going to need to have an autopsy performed."

Mr. Freeburg put a hand on the couch to steady himself. "Are you saying that someone *killed* my mother?"

"I have no proof," Matt admitted. "But that's what I think. I'm going to have to ask you to promise not to repeat anything I'm about to tell you." Mr. Freeburg nodded warily. "Another woman died in her sleep on Friday night, and there was a white Bible just like this one at the foot of her bed."

Mr. Freeburg looked at the plastic bag in Matt's hand. "That's a strange coincidence, but I can't believe anyone would want to harm my mother." The man's voice cracked, and Matt looked away to give him some privacy.

"I'm sorry to cause you more pain, but I'm afraid there is no other way," Matt forced himself to say.

Martin Freeburg regained control, then asked, "When will it be done?"

"I have a digging crew on standby. You give me a time."

Mr. Freeburg checked his watch. "I can be at the cemetery by noon."

"I'll meet you there," Matt promised.

* * *

At noon Matt stood beside Martin Freeburg as the casket was raised from the ground. Martin wept softly, and Matt was wracked with guilt. They watched as the casket was loaded into a van owned by the cemetery. Then Matt promised Mr. Freeburg that his mother's remains would be returned to her final resting place as soon as possible. Matt waited until Mr. Freeburg left, then he got into his Bronco and followed the van to the Norris Funeral Home.

"So, you think you don't have to go through regular channels like everyone else, is that it?" Phil Norris, the part-time county coroner and owner of the establishment, asked unpleasantly when Matt walked in.

"Afternoon, Phil," Matt replied.

"All it would have taken was a phone call, and I would have ordered the autopsy myself." Phil wouldn't let it go.

"So if we're in agreement that Mrs. Freeburg needs to be autopsied, why are you trying to pick a fight?" Matt asked.

The coroner's eyes narrowed, and he took a step closer. "Because you think you're above following procedure, but come November . . ."

Matt refused to be baited and turned away from Phil Norris's menacing look. "Is Ms. Howell's body ready to be loaded into the van?"

"If you think you're taking a body I'm responsible for up to Atlanta without supervision, then you're crazier than I thought," Phil told him derisively.

Matt raised an eyebrow. "So are you going with me, Phil?"

The coroner gave him an evil smile. "No, Lester will drive you."

This was Phil's revenge, and Matt controlled his expression to keep from giving the coroner any satisfaction. Lester Pody was a chain smoker, had poor hygiene, and never stopped talking. The ride to Atlanta was going to be pure torture. "Do you have someplace to keep Mrs. Freeburg's casket?" he asked, and Phil nodded.

"We'll put her in a body bag and store the casket in the equipment room until you get back—which had better be pretty soon," the coroner added as Matt turned toward the door.

"We'll return them by late tonight," Matt promised, then went out to supervise the movement of the bodies.

Lester smoked, smelled, and talked more than usual on the drive to Atlanta, and Matt wondered if Phil had specifically told him to be obnoxious. They arrived in Atlanta at five-fifteen and waited in the van until exactly five-thirty. Matt knocked on the employee entrance, and Alex Jordan opened the door, then waved the van forward. Lester backed up to the loading dock, and the men transferred the bodies onto gurneys. Then Matt told Lester to wait in the van and followed Alex inside.

Alex introduced his assistant, a college kid who needed his job too badly to report them. The morgue was eerily quiet as they pushed the bodies through the hallway, and Matt's stomach started feeling queasy. "I hope this won't get you into any trouble," Matt said to Alex's back as they walked.

"Me?" Alex said over his shoulder. "If they haven't fired me yet, they ain't going to." He pushed the gurney into a large set of double doors, which flew open, exposing an autopsy room. The tile floor had a big drain in the middle, and the equipment arranged on a table looked like objects of torture. When the smell of chemicals hit Matt's nostrils, he got light-headed. "Where do we want to start?" Alex asked, pointing at the bodies.

Matt looked down at his shoes. "It doesn't matter to me. You pick."

Alex closed his eyes and waved his finger in the air. "I choose—" when he opened his eyes he was looking at Mary Jean Freeburg, "the one who's been underground for almost a week."

Matt felt the room start to spin.

Alex spoke again from what sounded like a great distance. "As I recall, you don't handle these proceedings very well. Why don't you have a seat in the hall?"

Matt shook his head, trying to clear his ears. "I'm responsible for them," he said weakly. "I should stay."

"They won't know the difference, Matt, and we don't want to have to pick you up off the floor. Go into the hall, and I'll come and tell you as soon as I know something."

Rather than pass out in the autopsy room, Matt nodded and walked into the hallway. He sat down on a folding chair and lowered his head into his hands. Later, when Alex touched his shoulder, he woke up with a start. His head felt fine, but both arms were asleep.

"Did you find a cause of death?" Matt asked as he flexed his tingling fingers.

"No, but I took samples of every body tissue. I'll order a comprehensive toxicology report and should have it back in a couple of days."

Matt tried to hide his disappointment. "Well, maybe you'll find something in the other body."

Alex smiled. "Hey, I just said I haven't determined the cause of death. I didn't say I couldn't find *anything*." He held up a small glass vial filled with clear fluid. A tiny white fleck floated inside.

"What is that?" Matt asked, squinting at the vial.

"My guess is a tiny piece of noodle," Alex replied.

Matt leaned closer. "Like from chicken noodle soup?"

Alex nodded. "I think we've connected your bodies, old buddy. Of course, if that means you've got a serial killer on your hands, I'm not sure it can really be considered *good* news."

"In this case, *any* news is good news," Matt assured him as he stared at the noodle fragment. "Will you get in trouble if you send that to your lab and request a comparison with the sample they got from Ms. Howell?"

Alex shook his head. "So many samples go through here in a day, nobody's keeping track. I'll pack it up and send it to the lab first thing in the morning. Now you just sit tight while I redo the other one."

Matt walked down the hall and found a vending machine. He bought a Coke, then looked out the back door to check on Lester. The funeral home employee was asleep in the van. Matt drank his soft drink, then paced the hallway until Alex reappeared. His friend was scratching his head, which Matt took as a bad sign. "You didn't find anything?" he asked.

Alex frowned. "Nothing obvious. The old woman I could under-stand, but a healthy thirty-five-year-old doesn't just die in her sleep."

"Ms. Howell had a bad cold. Maybe that contributed to her death?"

Alex shook his head. "I don't think so. Anyway, I've ordered every test known to man on both of them. It'll cost your department a fortune, but the reports will tell us something."

"Thanks, Alex. I don't deserve your help, but I appreciate it."

"You're welcome," his old friend responded graciously. "And let's try to work in a game of golf soon."

Matt didn't even know where his golf clubs were. Probably in storage with the other things that had been salvaged from his home—Julie's piano, Chase's toys, Chad's high chair. He gave Alex a tight smile. "Sounds good," he lied.

"Well, go tell Igor to come in here, and we'll load these bodies back up," Alex suggested.

Matt smiled, then opened the back door. Lester was leaning on the van, cigarette butts encircling him. "We're ready to go," Matt said.

On the way home, Matt listened to Lester sing along with a country radio station until he thought he'd lose his mind. Finally he got out his cell phone and called Brian West. He left a message, then answered the return call that came in less than a minute. "Have you got anything?" Matt asked.

"I already faxed the reports to your office," Brian responded. "What is that awful noise in the background?"

Matt glanced at Lester, who was still howling at the top of his lungs. "You wouldn't believe me if I told you," Matt promised. "I'm away from the office at the moment, so can you give me a quick rundown on what you found out about the dead women?"

"There were a few little surprises, like the fact that Mary Jean was married briefly to a Horace Kilton, who died in World War II, before her marriage to Norton Freeburg."

Matt considered this for a second. "I don't see how a marriage so long ago could have a bearing on this case." Brian laughed. "Me either, but I'm very thorough. I was also surprised to learn that Robyn Howell's ex-husband gets everything she owned, which was a considerable amount for a teacher."

"He said she loved to earn money and invest it," Matt remarked.

"Apparently."

"Maybe she'd been meaning to change her will and just never got around to it?"

"She added an addendum to her will about some artwork she bought less than a month ago. Seems to me if she was making one change, she could have made others, but she didn't."

"She's an orphan, so she might not have had anyone else to give it to."

"She could have donated it to any number of worthy charities," Brian replied. "Most women would set their money on fire before they left it to their ex."

"So you're saying she *wanted* him to have her stuff?"

"That's the way I see it."

Matt leaned his head against the cool window and pressed the phone more firmly against his ear. "Scott Howell said they were still friendly."

"That also matches what I got. She came to his apartment in Atlanta at least once a month and usually spent the night. So I think it's safe to assume they were at least *friendly*. Besides that, she gave him a large check every month."

Matt frowned at the dirty windshield. "Like alimony?"

"There was nothing official in their divorce settlement. It looks like she just wanted to help him out. They had a nice apartment in Atlanta, and his income is fairly modest. According to her bank records, she paid the rent on his apartment and a few additional expenses like his hunt club dues and repairs on his SUV."

"That all sounds fishy to me," Matt muttered. "Scott Howell said the reason they broke up was because of his lack of ambition and ambivalence toward making money. If that was true, then why was she still supporting his playboy lifestyle after the divorce? I'm telling you, Brian, there was something weird about that guy."

"Like what?"

"He drove down from Atlanta the day after she died to make funeral arrangements. I met him at her house, and he was polite, almost cheerful. He sat there talking about how well they got along, but never shed a tear. Miss Glida Mae shows more sorrow when she thinks she's lost a cat," Matt added, more to himself than to Brian.

"Who?" the PI asked in confusion.

"Nobody. It's just that the only time he showed any emotion was when he felt insulted by questions about life insurance policies and beneficiaries."

"Maybe he was in shock?" Brian suggested.

Matt looked over to make sure Lester wasn't listening, then continued. "I've been there, Brian. For the first day or two after the tornado, I couldn't string together a coherent sentence. Even now, three years later, I can't imagine sitting down with a stranger and talking casually about my . . . ," Matt forced himself to go on, "wife."

"I'll dig a little deeper on Scott Howell," Brian said quietly.

"Thanks."

"And I know you said you had enough on Helen Tyler, but a fax came in this morning that I thought might interest you. There's an outstanding warrant for her arrest in West Virginia."

Matt felt his stomach muscles tighten. "What did she do?"

"Failed to appear in court. Her old boyfriend is suing her for breach of promise."

"You're kidding."

"No joke. The guy said she agreed to marry him, and they bought property together. He says he even made improvements on her house, and then she broke it off. So now he wants her to pay him almost $100,000."

"And she just skipped town?"

"Evidently."

Matt was disturbed by this new information, but since Helen wasn't wanted for murder or even assault, he decided it wasn't important. "Let's just keep that to ourselves for now," Matt suggested.

"Fine by me. I'll be back in touch."

After his conversation with Brian, Matt stared out the window and thought about Helen. She seemed like a nice, sensible kind of person. However, the fact that she had chosen to flee the state of West Virginia rather than appear in court presented a completely different picture. He wanted to trust her, but . . . Discouraged, he pulled his cell phone back out and called Ed Ramsey at home.

"You must be on vacation," Matt said when the chief answered the phone. "You're never at the police station."

"People are *supposed* to be home at night and on Sundays, Matt. That's a lesson you should learn. And just where are you anyway?"

"Headed back from Atlanta in a van with Lester at the wheel and two dead bodies in the back."

Matt heard the chief snicker. "It doesn't get much better than that."

"My friend Alex did the autopsy on Mary Jean Freeburg."

"And?"

"He found a tiny piece of what he thinks is a noodle."

The chief cursed softly. "We've got us a stinking serial killer."

Matt glanced at Lester again. "What we've got are two victims who were apparently killed in the same way. It could be food poisoning, or maybe someone just hated both of them."

"The lab in Atlanta checked for food poisoning and ruled that out. And the two women had no connection—let alone a common enemy. The only reasonable explanation is that the killer picks his victims at random."

"It's too soon to draw that conclusion," Matt urged caution. "Hopefully the ME's office will be able to match the noodle samples. I've ordered the files for thirty-eight unexplained deaths or suicides in Coosetta County. I'll see if any of them look suspicious. Then I'll sift through the PI reports and the phone records, and eventually things will come together."

"When are we going to let the FBI know about this, Matt?" the chief asked.

"When we have an actual theory and some evidence to back it up," Matt responded. "I'll call you tomorrow."

Lester pulled the van up to the Norris Funeral Home at nine-thirty, and they unloaded the bodies. Phil was nowhere in sight, so Matt assumed that Ed Ramsey had already told him about Alex's find.

Mary Jean Freeburg was transferred to her coffin, and Matt confirmed that she would be returned to her grave first thing the next morning. Robyn Howell's body would be released to her ex-husband for cremation.

Depressed by the events of the day, Matt got into his old Bronco and drove through town. He turned on Ivy Lane and parked in front of Miss Glida Mae's house. Every light was on, so he didn't think he'd wake her even though it was almost ten-thirty.

He climbed the stairs and knocked, but got no answer. "Miss Glida Mae?" he called. "It's me, Matt. I've just stopped by to make sure you're okay."

No response. He knocked again, several times, without success. Finally he walked down the steps, then stood surrounded by statues in the small yard and stared at the street, trying to decide whether he should alarm Miss Nelda, who certainly was asleep at this hour. Before he reached a decision, he heard Helen Tyler's voice from behind him.

"Sheriff? Is something wrong?"

He took a few steps toward her. "I don't know. I couldn't get Miss Glida Mae to answer the door."

"Nelda had the same problem earlier." Helen walked out onto her porch. "She finally convinced Glida Mae to let her in, then we walked around the block. But she was very nervous."

"About murderers or Hollywood agents?"

"Murderers mostly. Every once in a while she would make a lucid comment, but the rest of the time she was either silent or ranting." Helen looked over at the house next door. "Do you want me to try and get her to the door?"

Matt shook his head. "No, she might be asleep. I'll come back tomorrow." He walked over and stood at the bottom of the porch steps. "Do you feel safer now that you have new locks?"

"Yes, much safer." Helen's eyebrows pulled together, forming a little wrinkle between her eyes. "I wonder if new locks would help Glida Mae feel more secure?"

Matt considered this. "I don't know, but it's a thought." Helen yawned, reminding him of the late hour. "Well, I'd better head home."

"Would you like me to make you a sandwich to eat on the way?"

"No, thanks. I've eaten too much of your food already." There was an awkward silence, and he knew he should go, but he changed the topic instead. "I've been reading the Book of Mormon. I'm halfway through Joseph Smith's testimony."

She smiled. "I'll have a good report for the missionaries on Sunday then."

"It's interesting," he added.

"Be careful. If you keep reading, it'll change your life," she warned.

Matt raised an eyebrow. "You think so?"

Helen nodded. "I know so." Then she took a step toward the door. "Well, if you're sure about the sandwich, I'll say good night."

"Good night," Matt said. He watched until she disappeared into his grandmother's house, then he got into his Bronco and drove home.

CHAPTER 6

On Tuesday morning when Matt arrived at his office, he stopped in the doorway and surveyed the room. His desk was covered with files, memos, computer printouts, and unopened mail. While he tried to muster the courage to go inside, Crystal walked up. "In addition to that disaster area," she pointed at the desk, "you also have thirty phone messages."

Matt closed his eyes briefly. "I don't even know where to start."

"It doesn't really matter where you start," Crystal replied. "Because it's going to be humanly impossible for one person to sort through all that in less than six months. And by then this entire room will be full of letters and bulletins and . . ."

Matt held up a hand to stop her. "Since you have so much to say about the problem, do you also have a solution?"

"Hire an assistant."

Matt immediately started shaking his head, but Crystal persisted.

"You need someone who can go through those files of dead people and look for similarities with your new cases. You need someone who can type in phone numbers and merge computer files and compare printouts." She pointed to the stacks of information on Mary Jean Freeburg and Robyn Howell. Matt was still shaking his head, so Crystal sighed. "Well, if you won't hire yourself an assistant, hire someone to answer the phone and I'll help you."

"No one else can handle that phone alone, and you're the only person in Eureka who will sit at that desk for eighty hours a week without getting paid overtime."

Crystal didn't smile. "You're in over your head, Matt, and a murderer is on the loose."

Matt chewed his lower lip. The city police had a large operating budget, but since Coosetta County was small geographically and most of its population was concentrated in Eureka, every year the sheriff's department got a smaller piece of the tax-dollar pie. "You know we don't have enough money to hire another employee."

Crystal considered this. "If I called the mayor and told him that we have a possible serial killer . . ."

"We don't have proof of that yet."

"The possibility alone will be enough to strike terror in the mayor's heart during an election year. I'll tell him that in order to solve the case we need a research assistant, but we have no money. He'll pay without an argument, then take full credit when the killer is behind bars."

Matt had to admit it was a pretty good idea. "Assuming we could swing that, how will we find a research assistant who won't run straight to the newspapers with the story?"

Crystal smiled. "We'll cross that bridge when we get to it. So, can I call the mayor and say I'm speaking for you?"

Matt mulled over his nonexistent options for a few seconds, then nodded. Crystal hurried off to set her plan in motion, and Matt turned on his computer. He had almost typed in an entire word when the phone rang. "Hold my calls, Crystal!" he yelled.

She appeared in the doorway and covered the mouthpiece of her headset. "I'm waiting for the mayor to be located." She pointed at her phone contraption. "And I *am* holding your calls. That's Chief Ramsey, and I thought you'd want to talk to him."

Matt sighed. "You're right, I do."

Crystal raised a finger to silence him. "Oh hello, Mayor Brisbane. This is Crystal Vines from the sheriff's department. Yes sir, I'm just fine. How is your wife?" Crystal smiled at Matt and mouthed, "Like putty in my hands," then walked back toward her desk. Matt was shaking his head as he answered the phone. "I thought *you* had gone on vacation!" Ed Ramsey hollered into his ear. "The phone must have rung a hundred times."

"Sorry, Ed. It's crazy around here."

"Well, listen up 'cause I've got some news for you. Good or not depends on how you feel about murder."

"What news?" Matt demanded.

"The ME's office in Atlanta just called, and the noodles removed from both our victims match. It's a brand called Aunt Clara's Wide Noodle Chicken Soup."

"That sounds kind of familiar," Matt said as he wrote the name on an unopened envelope marked *Urgent! Read Immediately!*

"That's because it's the most popular brand in Georgia. Not only is it the best-seller in grocery stores, it's also served in restaurants, hospitals, and school lunchrooms across the state."

"Great." Matt frowned at his notes. "Now if we can just figure out what was in the soup that killed our victims."

"I've got all my fingers and toes crossed," Ed Ramsey claimed.

"Well, uncross them and get busy. We've got a murderer to catch." Matt hung up and resumed the never-ending task of inputting phone numbers until Crystal reappeared in his doorway. From the satisfied look on her face, he assumed she had been successful.

"The mayor's office will pay for your research assistant," she told him proudly. "But he says you'd better wrap this up quickly and quietly."

"You're a miracle worker."

Crystal accepted his praise with a gracious nod. "The *real* miracle will be finding someone who will work for cheap and keep their mouth shut."

Matt shuffled through the disorder on his desk. "What's this?" He held up an official-looking letter.

Crystal scanned it. "It's from the governor's office, explaining the 'Click It or Ticket' seat belt enforcement program that started," she ran her finger down the page, "yesterday."

Matt added the letter to the pile of things he didn't have time to deal with. He thought of Helen Tyler and the want ads she had circled on her Sunday paper. They were for clerical positions, so he presumed she could type. And since she was new to the area, she didn't have friends to share departmental secrets with . . .

Matt picked up the governor's letter and wrote Helen's cell phone number on the back. "Call Helen Tyler at this number and ask her if she wants to be my research assistant."

"Who's Helen Tyler?"

"My new tenant. She needs a job, and I want to make sure that she can pay her rent."

Crystal's eyes narrowed. "Since when do you care about money?"

"That was a joke, Crystal. But I know Helen's looking for a job. She used to be a schoolteacher, so she's got to be smart, and she doesn't have any friends, so she won't gossip."

Crystal's expression became speculative. "Is she pretty?"

Matt shrugged. "She's not ugly."

"And you're sure you don't want to just call a temp service?" Crystal asked.

"Let's give Helen a try," Matt responded, then turned back to his computer screen.

Out of the corner of his eye, Matt saw Crystal frown as she moved toward the door. "I'll let you know what she says."

A few minutes later the phone rang. It was Ed Ramsey again, and Matt could tell by the tone of his voice that he didn't have good news.

"There was a small article in the *Gazette* this morning about Mrs. Freeburg's exhumation, and my wife said both deaths were mentioned in her Bible study class last night," Ed reported. "If the press gets hold of this—"

"They will," Matt interrupted. "We've just got to figure it out before they do."

* * *

Helen went to her job interview on Tuesday morning, and the personnel director said she'd be in touch. Based on the woman's bored attitude, Helen doubted if this were true. Having no references was proving to be a big roadblock in securing employment. A little discouraged, she headed back to her rental house. As she unlocked the door, her cell phone started ringing.

"Hello?" she answered.

"This is Crystal Vines from the Coosetta County sheriff's department," a female voice announced. "May I speak to Helen Tyler?"

"This is she," Helen replied.

"Ms. Tyler, the sheriff needs a research assistant, and he's offering you the job."

Helen was momentarily dumbfounded. Matt Clevenger wanted to hire her, and he was willing to do so without references, a typing test, or even an interview. "O-okay," she stammered.

"The position pays $10.50 an hour and is only temporary," Crystal continued.

"That sounds fine." Helen was getting used to the idea. Working for Matt Clevenger was certainly preferable to continuing her futile job search. "When does he want me to start?"

"He needs an assistant pretty badly," Crystal replied. "Could you come now?"

Helen looked at her reflection in the black television screen. Her cotton blouse was limp with perspiration, and her makeup had melted off. "How about noon?" she proposed.

"Fine."

Crystal disconnected abruptly, and Helen stared at her phone. She couldn't remember the last time she'd had even a tiny speck of good luck, and this new job falling into her lap left her feeling slightly unnerved. Helen changed clothes, brushed her teeth, and reapplied her makeup. Then she climbed into the old Escort and was halfway to the sheriff's department before she realized that Matt Clevenger had somehow managed to obtain her cell number. *Chalk one up for the sheriff,* she thought with a wry smile.

Helen followed her map to the address listed for the sheriff's department in the phone book. When she reached the appropriate spot she pulled to the curb and studied the building. The sign said *Coosetta County Jail.* She double-checked the address and verified that she had the right place. Then she looked at her watch. She had left early to give herself plenty of time, but it was still only eleven-thirty. She didn't want to seem overly eager, so she circled the block. When she passed the library, she remembered that she wanted a book on Vietnamese customs and decided she might as well make good use of her extra thirty minutes.

Once inside the library, she walked to the circulation desk and found Judith Pope. "Hello," the librarian greeted when she saw Helen. "Have you learned a lot about home repair?"

"Oh!" Helen said. "I meant to return the books you brought me, but I left the house in a hurry and . . ." Since Judith didn't like the sheriff, Helen decided not to mention the reason for her trip into town. "I just forgot. But they brought me good luck. Nothing at the house has broken since I got them."

"Don't worry about returning them. I'll stop by on my way home from work sometime and pick them up."

"Well, I may take advantage of your helpful mood. I have another favor to ask. There is a Vietnamese family living next to Nelda Lovell, and on Sunday I found the children in my backyard. They wouldn't speak to me, so I gave them a bag of Oreos."

"Why?" Judith asked in confusion.

"So they'll come back."

Judith frowned. "You shouldn't encourage children to play in your yard. If one of them gets hurt, you could be sued," she warned ominously.

"I'll remember that." Helen was careful not to show her amusement. "Anyway, when they accepted the cookies, their mother felt obligated to give me their dinner."

Judith nodded. "Oriental people are very polite. But if you gave them cookies and she gave you their dinner, you should be even."

"Yes, but I don't want to make another social faux pas. I was hoping a book on Vietnamese customs might help me."

Judith smiled. "I'll see what we have." She typed on her keyboard. "There's nothing specifically on Vietnamese culture. There's one on Asian marriage traditions."

Helen shook her head. "Tan's way too young for me, so I don't think that book will do me any good."

Judith looked up with a blank expression, and Helen regretted the joke.

"Never mind."

"I'll keep looking and let you know if I find something," Judith promised as Helen headed for the stairs. "You might try the Internet."

Helen thanked Judith, then left the library and drove back to the Coosetta County jail. She entered the building through a set of tinted glass doors and walked into a lobby. The air in the small space was stale, as if the door wasn't opened often. Two wilted plants were the room's only decorations, and a couple of the overhead lights were out.

Helen's footsteps echoed faintly as she crossed the tile floor to a building directory mounted on the wall beside the elevator. The sheriff's department, fire chief, and Coosetta County Board of Education all had offices on the second floor. The upper stories of the building were devoted to the jail facilities. Telling herself that she wasn't nervous, Helen got into the elevator.

The elevator was so slow that Helen actually reached for the emergency button twice on the trip up one floor. She sighed with relief when the doors opened and she stepped out into a smaller version of the lobby downstairs. After taking a deep breath, Helen opened the door marked *Sheriff's Department.*

The suite was larger than she expected. It had several cubicles along the right wall and a couple of small offices to the left. The floors were covered with gray indoor-outdoor carpet, and the walls were painted a utilitarian off-white. Wiping her sweating palms on her skirt, Helen walked over to a woman sitting at a desk by the door. "My name is Helen Tyler."

The woman nodded. "Crystal Vines," she replied, looking up from a complicated switchboard. Crystal was young, probably in her early twenties. She had a no-nonsense, short haircut and a sprinkle of freckles across her nose. She was solid rather than heavy, but her choice of khaki pants belted at the waist was not flattering. She extended a hand and Helen took it. "Matt said you weren't ugly, but I'd say that's an understatement."

Helen blinked. She was astounded that the sheriff would have an opinion about her appearance, much less share it with his secretary. "Thanks—I think."

Crystal laughed as Matt Clevenger walked out of his office.

"Good, you're here. Come on in," Matt said to Helen. He led the way to the office directly behind Crystal.

After a quick survey of the chaos, she turned to him in wonder. "I don't know how you can find anything in here."

"I can't," he admitted. "That's why I hired you."

Helen was daunted. "What can I possibly do?"

"You can sort through these files." He waved at one of several piles on his desk. "Once you're through with them, they can be refiled, and that will reduce the clutter a little."

Helen looked around again. "Not much."

Matt shrugged. "Once you get through with that, I'll give you another pile to work on."

"I see. You're planning on being able to see your desk in about," she paused to think, "a year?"

Matt looked surprised. "Are you saying you're not equal to the task?"

"A magician wouldn't be equal to this task."

"The journey of a thousand miles begins with a single step," Matt reminded her.

"Keep telling yourself that," she recommended.

Matt offered a half grin. "So, what did Crystal tell you about the job?"

"Just that you needed help desperately and that the position was temporary."

"That about sums it up. I need you to work as many hours as you can for the next couple of weeks. Keep track of your time and give it to Crystal by noon on Fridays." Matt paused and looked at her. "So, is it a deal?"

Helen nodded. "It's a deal."

Matt walked over and typed a few instructions into the keyboard. "I've got a checklist I want you to fill out on each of these files. When you're finished you'll enter the results into the computer, then look for matches." He pulled a sheet from the printer and handed it to Helen. She scanned it quickly.

It was a very strange list, and she frowned as she asked her next question. "So I look in each file, and if any of the dead people lived alone, I write the name in this space."

"Correct."

"If anyone had a white Bible on the end of their bed at the time they died, I write the name here," she continued.

"That is also correct," he confirmed.

"If they died in their sleep or had chicken soup listed as stomach contents, I make a note of that as well?"

"Exactly."

She looked around his office, then back at his list. "It's hard to believe that this is the most important project you have for me."

"Unfortunately, it is," Matt replied. "And if you see anything else that just seems, I don't know, *odd,* write that down too."

Helen felt a little chill. "Can you explain why I'm doing this?"

"Yes," Matt said. "But not right now because I want you to get busy. Once you've got the checklist complete, we'll talk." He turned his head toward the door. "Crystal! Where are we going to put Helen?"

Crystal appeared in the doorway. "She can choose between the ladies' room or the other side of my desk."

Helen didn't have to give this any thought. "I'll share your desk if you don't mind."

"I'll be glad for the company," Crystal told her.

"Both of you grab a stack of files and follow me," Matt instructed on his way out the door.

Helen worked on files for the rest of the afternoon. Matt came out occasionally and read over her shoulder, then returned to his office. Finally, at six o'clock, Crystal sent her home. "You can take a few files to work on tonight if you want to, but I'm the only person allowed to stay later than this," the secretary informed her.

"I guess I can finish these at home," Helen said, referring to the remaining files. She stacked them, then looked toward Matt's office.

"He's on the phone," Crystal said, pointing at the switchboard. "He's talking to the chief of police, so I don't think we should disturb him. But I'll tell him good-bye for you."

"Thanks," Helen replied as she hefted the files. "See you tomorrow."

"Bright and early!" Crystal called out. "And take the stairs." She indicated toward a door at the far left corner of the room. "That elevator ought to be condemned."

"Thanks again," Helen said over her shoulder as she stepped into the stairwell. She walked quickly down the stairs and out to her car.

During the short drive home, Helen felt optimistic. Crystal was odd but nice, and working with Matt Clevenger was proving to be interesting. She was getting so involved with her new life in Eureka that she rarely worried about Harrison Campbell and his crazy obsessions anymore. When she turned onto Ivy Lane, she saw Nelda Lovell standing on Glida Mae's porch.

"Are you having trouble getting Glida Mae to come out again?" Helen asked as she climbed out of the Escort.

"I'm afraid I'm having more than trouble," Nelda said. "Today getting Glida Mae outside looks impossible."

Helen offered her assistance, but Nelda shook her head. "Thank you, dear, but you're busy." She waved at the files in Helen's arms. "And I've already called Dr. Baker. He'll be here in a few minutes, and I think she'll open the door for him."

Helen was surprised by this information. "I didn't know doctors made house calls anymore."

"Most don't, but Dr. Baker does. He's served this community for many years, and he has a wonderful bedside manner. Call him if you ever need a doctor."

"I will," Helen promised with a smile. "And let me know if there's anything I can do for Glida Mae."

Nelda nodded and Helen went into the rental house. She changed into a pair of jeans, then spread the files out on the coffee table. She worked steadily, making notations on Matt's checklist until her phone rang at seven. She stood up, and her muscles protested at the quick movement after an hour in the same position. Massaging her lower back, Helen dug in her purse and pulled out the phone.

"Hello?"

"Helen?" It was Matt.

"I meant to ask earlier how you got my cell number," she responded.

"Caller ID," he admitted shamelessly. "How's it going with the files?"

Helen didn't really mind that he had her number, but she disliked being tricked. "I'm almost through," she said. "And I haven't found much."

"I didn't really expect you to," he told her. "I'm about to leave here and thought I'd stop and get us some barbecue sandwiches for dinner."

She was surprised by the offer. "You don't have to do that."

"I figure it's my turn," he replied simply. "I know that Mormons have dietary restrictions, so I just wanted to be sure that you can eat pork."

Helen controlled a laugh. "I *can* eat pork, but only on Tuesdays," she told him.

There was a brief pause, then he asked, "Are you teasing me?"

"Yes."

"So barbecue is okay?"

"Sounds good."

"I'll see you soon then."

Helen put her phone in her purse and was headed to the bathroom to brush her teeth when there was a knock on the door. She looked through the peephole and saw Hugh and Thelma Warren standing on her porch. "What a pleasant surprise," she said as she opened the door. It *was* a surprise anyway. "Won't you come in?"

"We can't stay," Thelma said as she stepped into the small living room. "But I am curious to see what you've done with the place." She looked around, then back at Helen. "You haven't done a thing."

Helen resisted the urge to laugh. "I haven't had much time, and I told you this move was just temporary."

"Looks fine to me," Hugh said, leaning in from the porch.

"What do you know?" Thelma demanded as she extended a jelly jar. "I heard Nelda say she was going to give you some Mayhaw jelly. Now you know I love Nelda better than anything in the world, but when it comes to making jelly, well, she just doesn't have the knack. So I brought you some of mine."

"Nobody makes jelly like my Thelma," Hugh said from the doorway.

Helen accepted the jar with a smile. "Thank you very much."

"And I wanted to check and see if you still needed my help writing a thank-you note for those foreign folks," Thelma offered.

Helen covertly checked her watch. Matt would be here soon with barbecue sandwiches, and she didn't want to explain his presence to her neighbors. "I appreciate the offer, but I managed by myself."

"You got ESPN?" Hugh asked, pointing at the nice television. "The Braves are playing."

"Don't even think about it." Thelma put an end to this idea. "We've got to get home. It's almost bedtime."

"Oh Thelma, you are so romantic!" Hugh gave her a friendly pat.

Thelma took Hugh's hand and pulled him to the door. "Come on, you crazy old man!" Then she looked over her shoulder at Helen. "Good night!"

* * *

Matt was still staring at the phone after his conversation with Helen when it rang, and he reached for it automatically.

"Hello?"

"I'm looking for the sorriest sheriff in Coosetta County." Alex Jordan's voice came through the phone lines.

"Speaking," Matt replied.

"Good, because I just got a fax of the toxicology report on Mrs. Freeburg and Robyn Howell."

Matt sat up straight in his chair. "That was quick."

"I called in a few favors. You owe me big-time."

"I'll send you a pecan log at Christmas."

Alex laughed, then cleared his throat and began reading. "Mary Jane Freeburg had high levels of Digoxin in her system, even after embalming and several days underground. But that didn't really surprise me since she was old and her heart was in bad shape. It makes sense that she would be on heart medication." Alex paused dramatically. "Then I checked Robyn Howell's report."

"She had Digoxin in her system too?"

"Tons of it, and there was nothing wrong with Robyn Howell's heart."

"That's what killed them then?" Matt whispered. "A heart medicine?"

"I think so," Alex confirmed. "It's a fairly common drug used to regulate the heart rate. But given in large doses, it would slow the heart too much and eventually prove fatal. It was a pretty smart choice on your killer's part. We wouldn't ordinarily even check for it, so if I hadn't ordered every test known to man, you still wouldn't have your answer."

"You're my hero, Alex," Matt said.

"There are a few more results still outstanding. It's weird stuff that takes awhile. I don't expect to find anything significant, but if I come up with something else, I'll call you."

"Thanks for your help," Matt said as he disconnected. Then he dialed Ed Ramsey's number. "I just talked to Alex Jordan in the ME's office," he said when the chief answered. "He believes that both our victims were killed with an overdose of a heart medication called Digoxin."

"You wouldn't kid an old man, would you?" the police chief cursed.

"Not about something like this. How are you coming with your lists of people a woman might trust even if she didn't know them—like delivery people, utility workers, doctors?"

"Almost done. I'll fax you a copy when we're through."

"Based on Alex's findings, I'd say we need to concentrate on people who provided health care for Mrs. Freeburg. We need to find out if she had a current prescription for Digoxin, and if so, what her usual dosage was and who administered the medication. Since you have more resources than I do, I was hoping you could handle that."

"Okay, but how will this help us with Robyn Howell?" the chief wanted to know.

"It will give us a place to start. We also need to find people who have access to large amounts of Digoxin."

"Doctors, pharmacists, drug company reps," the chief itemized.

"And every person who has had Digoxin prescriptions filled during the past six months or so."

"You'll never get pharmacy records without a court order," the chief stated flatly. "Since you're more handsome than I am, maybe you could charm one out of our lady judge. I'll work on the others."

"Fair enough. I'll talk to the judge first thing in the morning," Matt promised.

"We're getting closer," Ed said.

"I wish I felt like we were," Matt said softly. "We might have identified the crime, but we're a long way from finding the killer. And I'm afraid that we're running out of time."

"Call me tomorrow when you get that court order, and I'll have some of my boys distribute it to our local pharmacies," Ed offered.

"Thanks," Matt said, then hung up. He sat in his office for a few minutes and reflected on the changes that had taken place in the course of a few days. He'd contacted a friend he'd avoided for years, he'd become almost buddies with the police chief, and he'd hired Helen Tyler. Of course, she was just a temporary part of his life. He didn't have room for more than that.

Matt said good night to the dispatcher, then headed out to his Bronco and drove to the Pork Belly Restaurant, where he ordered two barbecue sandwiches with fixings. When he knocked on the door at 126 Ivy Lane, Helen answered the door with a smile.

"Oh, that smells so good," she said as she stepped back to let him in.

He looked at the files scattered on the coffee table. "How many more files to go?"

"Just a few."

Matt was impressed. "You *are* a magician."

Helen seemed pleased by this remark. "No, just a hard worker. You can put the food here." She moved the files to the floor.

Matt put the bags of food on the coffee table while Helen got some plates and two glasses of milk from the kitchen. He gave her a sandwich and some angel hair coleslaw covered with the Pork Belly's famous sauce.

"What is that?" Helen asked, pointing at the orange-coated cabbage.

"Special, award-winning coleslaw," he told her. "Try some."

She looked apprehensive, but she tried the coleslaw and finally nodded. "It's good." They ate in companionable silence until all the food was gone, then Helen leaned back on her side of the couch. "I'm so full I can barely move," she moaned.

"No point in getting food from the Pork Belly unless you're going to eat until you're sick," Matt said, licking his fingers.

Helen laughed, then asked for the explanation he had promised her about the case they were working on. "It's not that I'm nosy, really," she clarified. "I *am* curious, but I also think I can be more of a help to you if I know what I'm looking for."

Matt polished off the last of his milk and leaned forward. "We're looking for people who may have been murdered, even though officially their deaths were classified otherwise."

Helen sat up straight. "So there *is* a murderer in Eureka?"

Matt nodded. "I'm afraid so. We think the killer uses a heart drug called Digoxin, which, by the way, needs to be added to your checklist."

"Digoxin?" Helen clarified.

"Yes," Matt said. "He mixes it with chicken soup."

"Maybe Glida Mae really did see someone over here," Helen said, looking around the room anxiously.

Matt smiled. "I doubt that Glida Mae actually saw the murderer."

"And why am I looking for Bibles?" Helen asked.

"Because the murderer left one on the foot of each woman's bed," Matt told her. "Everything about this case is strictly confidential, but almost no one knows about the Bibles."

"I told you I can keep a secret," Helen assured him, then frowned. "But leaving a Bible at a murder scene seems particularly . . . sick."

"All murder is sick—especially if there are multiple victims," Matt pointed out.

"Right now the only thing that connects the two women is the way they died."

Matt shrugged. "And there could be more. Most people who die are not autopsied, and the medical examiner told me they don't ordinarily even check for Digoxin. So we might have missed a couple."

"And this case could be bigger than it seems?" Matt saw Helen repress a shudder.

"I'm afraid so. I've got about a hundred printouts cross-referencing the victims with more information coming in all the time. Once you're through with the files, I'm going to get you to help me put everything into my computer so we can merge files and look for matches."

"I'll finish these files up tonight, and we can start on that in the morning," Helen promised as she stacked up their dinner dishes.

"Let me help you wash those," he offered, but she shook her head.

"Two plates? They'll only take me a minute."

Matt stood and stretched. "I guess I'll go over and check on Miss Glida Mae before I head home."

Helen turned back to face him. "Oh, I forgot to tell you that Nelda had to call a doctor to come over this afternoon. She couldn't get Glida Mae to let her in."

"I'll walk down and talk to Nelda first and see what the doctor had to say." Matt stepped outside and crossed Miss Glida Mae's yard into Nelda Lovell's. There was a light on in the living room, and Miss Nelda opened the door almost immediately.

"Good evening, Matt. What a nice surprise."

"Hey, Miss Nelda. Helen told me that Miss Glida Mae had a bad day."

Nelda Lovell's eyes clouded. "Glida Mae is not doing well, Matt. Dr. Baker said she was dehydrated and her delusions are interfering with her ability to sleep or eat. He's going to arrange for a home health care nurse to come daily, but if this current trend continues, she'll have to be put in a nursing home."

"Helen suggested that Miss Glida Mae might feel safer with new locks. And I was wondering about putting bars on her windows."

"That might help some, but it would be very expensive, and Glida Mae lives from month to month on her social security check."

Matt thought about all the insurance money that was sitting in his bank account and nodded. "Well, I'd better get home." He turned to leave, then hesitated. "Miss Nelda?"

"Yes, Matt?"

"Keep your doors locked."

Nelda smiled. "I will." She glanced down the street at his rental house. "And tell Helen I said hello."

It was late, so Matt headed toward his Bronco. Then he remembered a question he wanted to ask Helen.

"It's going to take me just a little longer to make it through the rest of these files," she said when she opened the door.

Matt smiled. "I know you haven't had time to finish that project, but I have a question for you. One of a religious nature."

"Uh-oh."

Matt looked up in surprise. "Will that make you uncomfortable?"

Helen shrugged. "Only if I can't answer it."

"I'm kind of desperate on this case and really need a break," he began. "So I was just wondering . . ."

"What?" Helen prompted.

"Do all Mormons have visions?"

"Visions?" Helen confirmed.

"I've been reading the Book of Mormon, and it's full of visions. Lehi said he had one, then Nephi, and, of course, Joseph Smith."

"I can't speak for all Mormons," Helen replied slowly. "But I know *I've* never had a vision. Regular members are entitled to personal revelation, but I think actual visions are reserved for prophets."

Matt sighed. "I sure could use a vision right now." He turned toward his car. "Well, this time I really am going home."

"Thanks for dinner," she said, stepping out onto the porch.

"It was the least I could do since you're working around the clock for me."

"I'll finish the files tonight."

"And I promise not to make a habit of coming over and talking about the case at night, but you're new to the town, so you're an objective sounding board. And you don't seem interested in romance, so I don't have to worry about you getting the wrong idea." He paused, searching for the right words. "I guess what I'm trying to say is that I feel safe here."

Helen stared back for a few seconds, then cleared her throat. "I'm comfortable, Sheriff Clevenger? Kind of like a worn-out pair of sneakers?"

Matt shrugged. "Something like that."

"That may be true, but it's not very flattering. I wouldn't recommend that you use that line on a girl you actually want to impress," Helen advised.

He gave her a tired smile. "There are no girls I want to impress."

CHAPTER 7

After Helen finished her search of the files, she went back through, checking for any mention of Digoxin. It was early on Wednesday morning when she finally fell into bed and set her alarm for seven-thirty. But she was awakened at six o'clock by the sound of hammering. Mourning the loss of much-needed sleep, she staggered to the kitchen window and looked outside. Several workmen with a security company logo on their shirts were installing bars on Glida Mae's windows. The actress was standing in her front yard, watching the process. Surprised to see Glida Mae outside the confines of her pink house, Helen pulled on some clothes and went out her front door.

"Good morning, Glida Mae," she greeted the older woman.

"Hello, Helen," Glida Mae responded. Helen noted that her neighbor had apparently not taken the time to put on makeup or comb her hair. However, she was dressed, although her gown was buttoned incorrectly and was wet along the hemline where it had dragged across the dew-dampened ground.

"It's good to see you up and about," Helen added, then pointed to the house. "You've got visitors."

Glida Mae giggled. "The sheriff hired these nice men to put new locks on my doors and bars on my windows so the murderer can't get in."

"Well, that was very nice of him."

Glida Mae leaned forward and lowered her voice. "I told you he was sweet on me."

Helen went back inside and took a shower, then dressed in a pair of jeans and a blue oxford shirt. Not exactly the kind of clothes she normally wore to work, but they were practical. She collected the files and put them in her car. Then, with a final wave to Glida Mae, she headed to the sheriff's department.

Crystal greeted her with a nod as Helen took a seat at the secretary's desk. She glanced at Matt's office, but the light was still off. "He had to go to the courthouse this morning," Crystal provided, and Helen felt her cheeks get hot.

"Is there a computer I can use?" Helen asked. "I'd like to type my summary of Matt's checklist."

Crystal leaned forward. "Did you find anything?"

Helen shook her head. "There was not a single file that had all the items on Matt's list."

Crystal sighed. "Well, I guess you might as well use Matt's computer since he's gone."

Helen followed the secretary into the sheriff's office. Crystal flipped on the light and looked around. "Try not to make a mess," she said sarcastically. "The computer's pretty basic, but if you have trouble, call me."

After Crystal returned to her own desk, Helen sat down in the old chair.

"Don't get too comfortable in there," Crystal called. "Matt will be back soon."

Helen felt another blush stain her cheeks as she turned on the computer and started typing.

* * *

Matt ate a bowl of cereal with his mother before leaving for the courthouse. She was thrilled to have his company and offered to make a more substantial breakfast, but he assured her that bran flakes were fine.

"Mama, do you remember some Bibles the church sold a few years ago?" he asked, and she nodded. "I think you bought a case."

Rita Clevenger thought for a minute. "I believe I did buy some to give as Christmas gifts. You have a very good memory."

"Do you still have one?"

"I think so, but I can't remember what I did with that box." Rita gave him a brilliant smile. "If I can't find it, I'll be glad to buy you another one. You've worn Julie's old Bible to shreds."

"I'd really like one of those white ones," Matt told her.

"Okay," his mother replied. "I'll look."

"Thanks, Mama." Matt finished his bowl of cereal, then pushed back from the table. "What do you know about Mormons?"

His mother considered his question. "Those traveling evangelists from Chattahoochee County were here a few months ago, and Minerva Westfall said they showed a movie that made the Mormons sound worse than the devil himself." Lines formed between her eyes as she concentrated. "But Nelda Lovell says they read the Bible and believe in Jesus—just like regular Christians."

"And Sydney seems nice."

"Sydney was always an odd child," Rita said with a frown. "Playing baseball with the boys and acting like a hoodlum. Then she got divorced and worked in a bar . . ."

"Miss Nelda says Sydney has settled down now, and plenty of Baptists get divorced and have to take rotten jobs."

Rita nodded. "I guess the correct answer to your question is that I don't really know much of anything about the Mormons." Rita's eyes narrowed. "Why do you ask? Have some of those Mormon bicycle boys been bothering you?"

Matt shook his head. "No, I was just curious." He kissed his mother's cheek and hurried down to the courthouse. He wanted to talk to Judge Sandra Weldon before she had a chance to get in a worse mood than the one she woke up in.

Matt bought a couple of stale Danish rolls and two cups of weak-looking coffee from a street vendor near the courthouse steps. The styrofoam containers were flimsy, and he managed to burn himself twice before he located the judge in her office behind a mountain of paperwork that rivaled the one on his own desk.

"Good morning, Matt," the judge greeted as she glanced up. "Don't tell me that's some of the incredibly bad breakfast food sold by the vendor on the courthouse steps."

His shoulders sagged. "Okay, I won't tell you."

The judge shook her head. "You are the most helpless case I've ever seen. Throw that mess in the garbage and have a seat. Then talk quick while I'm still feeling sorry for you."

Matt dropped the food into her garbage can as instructed, then wiped his hands on a napkin before sitting in one of the uncomfortable chairs in front of her desk. "I'll bet you had to look far and wide to find chairs this unappealing," he ventured.

She gave him a grim smile. "They discourage people from sitting in my office and bothering me."

"I had heard you were brilliant."

The judged waved this aside. "Sympathy works better than insincere flattery. What do you want?"

Matt regretted the need to tell the judge all the details of the case, but he knew there was no way she would give him a court order for prescription records otherwise. So he divulged everything—the Bibles, the odd murder scenes, the chicken soup, and the Digoxin.

"So, you haven't found a connection between the two women?"

"Not while they were alive," Matt admitted. "But both had Aunt Clara's Chicken Noodle Soup laced with Digoxin as their final meal."

The judge nodded slowly. "I'll give you the court order for pharmacy records in Coosetta County for the past six months, but you'll have to serve them."

Matt kept the satisfaction from showing on his face. "Ed Ramsey has agreed to help me with that."

"I'm glad you're sharing the responsibility on this one, Matt. And I'd look for a reason to consult with the FBI soon." When she saw that Matt was about to object, Judge Weldon held up a hand. "I didn't say give them the case. You just need to mention it, so if it blows up in your face, you can say you called them."

Matt nodded and stood. "I will."

The judge gave him a sour look. "I doubt it. But remember— people who ignore my advice usually live to regret it. The court order will be ready this afternoon. And Matt," she added as he stepped toward the door. "Next time you want to bribe me, stop by the Starbucks on Fifth Avenue. They have the most incredible apple-oatmeal muffins."

He smiled and hurried out the door before she could change her mind. Back in the Bronco, he called Crystal. "Is Helen there?" he asked.

"Here and making herself at home in your office."

"As long as she's working on my case, she's welcome to it. Now I need you to do something for me."

"What?" Crystal's tone was wary.

"I talked Judge Weldon into giving us a court order for the pharmacy records we need. I want you to go by the Starbucks on Fifth Avenue and pick up a dozen apple-oatmeal muffins for the judge, then come camp on her doorstep until the court order is ready."

"Who's going to answer the phone while I'm gone?"

"Tell the dispatcher to do it."

"She won't like it," Crystal warned.

"But she'll do it. Once you have the court order, take it to Chief Ramsey at the police department. I'm going to stop and check on Miss Glida Mae, then I'll head to the office."

"I'll tell Helen. She's been asking about you."

Matt smiled as he disconnected. He was anxious to tell Helen about his morning. He could only imagine the way her turquoise eyes would light up when he described his encounter with the ornery Judge Weldon. He hadn't felt this comfortable with a woman since . . . Julie. He blinked hard and concentrated on the traffic.

He reached Ivy Lane and parked in front of Miss Glida Mae's house. The new security bars looked impressive and took some of the sting out of the price. He decided to check in with Nelda Lovell before trying to get Miss Glida Mae to let him in. He walked around to Miss Nelda's back door and knocked. She opened the door promptly, wearing an apron over her dress and waving a wooden spoon.

"You got here just in time, Matt," she told him as she pulled him into her cozy kitchen. "Sydney is on her way over, and I'm making banana pudding to celebrate."

"I really just came to ask about Miss Glida Mae."

"She's been a little better since you had the bars and locks installed. She's still reluctant to come out of her house, but she doesn't seem so confused. Here, have a seat."

Matt took a chair at the table. "I can only stay a minute," he warned.

Miss Nelda smiled at him. "Sydney will be pleased to see you, and banana pudding is her favorite food. She's been miserable during these last few weeks of pregnancy, so I thought this might be just the thing."

The back door slammed, and the subject of their conversation waddled in. "Are you talking about me again, Grandma?" Sydney asked. "Hey, Matt," she added, then collapsed into a chair across from him.

"I was just telling Matt that I made you some banana pudding to cheer you up."

Sydney grimaced. "Better give me some quick," she muttered. "I'm very low on cheer right now." She turned to Matt. "So, how's law enforcement?"

"Better since your husband quit having witch parties on his farm."

Sydney sat up straight. "Cole never had a witch party on our farm, and you know it. Lauren explained the whole misunderstanding."

Matt leaned forward, enjoying himself. "Well, it would have helped if the person clearing his name wasn't also his sister. The police bought their story, but I thought it looked a little . . . fishy."

"Fishy?" Sydney cried, half rising from her seat. "Are you calling my husband a liar? And his sister too?"

Miss Nelda turned toward the table in alarm. "Sit down, Sydney. You'll hurt the baby."

Matt held up both hands in surrender. "I'm just kidding," he assured his old friend. "Gosh, you never could take a joke."

"Some things just aren't funny," Sydney said as she settled back in her chair.

"So, do you like being a farm girl?"

Sydney nodded. "I love it."

Miss Nelda placed a big bowl of banana pudding before each of them, and Matt sighed. "This reminds me of old times." He took a big bite, then addressed Miss Nelda. "Except usually the only time I got invited inside for banana pudding was when Sydney had punched me in the eye or hit me with a baseball bat."

"All well deserved," Sydney remarked absently as she ate.

"I won't deny that." Matt stirred his pudding. "I would give anything if I could go back to being a kid again when the worst thing we had to worry about was a bad curveball."

Sydney looked up in horror. "Not me! I wouldn't want to go through my awkward teenage years and my divorce again. And as much as I love my kids, if I thought I had to be pregnant three more times . . ." Her voice trailed off.

"I'd go through anything again, even the tornado, just to hold my boys and Julie one more time," Matt whispered, and Sydney reached across the table to touch his hand.

"I'm so sorry, Matt. That was thoughtless of me."

He took a deep breath and changed the subject. "Do you ever hear from Craig?" he asked, referring to Sydney's ex-husband.

"All the time," she answered with a nod. "He calls regularly and comes down a couple of times a month to see the kids."

"He lives in Nashville now, doesn't he?"

"Yeah. His wife is a wheeler-dealer up there, and Craig runs the emergency room at a big, private hospital. They have more money than they can count, but no children." Sydney glanced up at Matt. "Craig comes here so often I told him he really ought to consider buying a condo on the lake."

"Sounds like things may not be very happy at home."

Sydney shrugged. "I think you might be right."

"I remember that you were real torn up about the divorce. It must give you some satisfaction to know that he's unhappy in his new marriage."

Sydney considered this. "I would have thought so. For a long time all I could think about was getting revenge against him. But now I have Cole, and honestly, I just feel sorry for Craig."

Matt smiled at her. "That sounds like a good, healthy sign."

"Cole says it shows that I've truly forgiven Craig," she admitted. "Of course, Cole is an optimist. I do think I've learned to do my best and leave the rest in the Lord's hands. That's something you might want to try."

Matt scraped the last of the pudding from his bowl. "I guess I don't have much choice."

"I thought that I didn't have a choice either, but I did. I couldn't change the situation, but I could control my reaction to it."

"Sydney the philosopher," Matt teased, anxious to get away from the painful subject.

Sydney's eyes narrowed. "You can make fun of me if you want to, but you know what I'm saying is true." Matt didn't comment, and after a few seconds, Sydney continued. "I met your renter on Sunday." Sydney paused again, but Matt remained silent. "She's gorgeous."

"I guess," he replied casually.

"All that booze you drank after the tornado might have pickled your liver, but I know it didn't ruin your eyesight. She's gorgeous, and now I heard she's working for you too."

"For someone who lives out on a farm, you hear a lot."

Sydney acknowledged this with a wave of her spoon. "Cole's sister Lauren is my source for local gossip. She keeps her eyes and ears open when she's at Shear Delight for her weekly manicure."

Matt held his breath, waiting for Sydney to say that Lauren had told her about murders in Eureka, but Sydney turned and asked her grandmother for more pudding instead. With a sigh of relief, he pushed his chair back from the table. "Well, what you heard is true. Helen's very pretty, and she is working for the sheriff's department on a temporary basis. And I'd better get back to work." Matt stood up.

"Yeah, three or four people probably ran a stop sign while you were in here eating banana pudding."

"Probably," he said, wishing that crime in Eureka was limited to traffic violations. "Thanks for the dessert!" he called to Nelda, and she told him to come again soon. Then Matt turned back to Sydney. "Good luck with that baby. Is it a boy or girl?"

Sydney made a face. "Cole won't let me find out. He wants it to be a *surprise*."

Matt laughed and stepped outside.

* * *

The morning went by quickly for Helen, but she caught herself watching the clock as noon approached. She had finished her reports, and since Matt hadn't given her another assignment, she had volunteered to sit at Crystal's desk while the secretary went to the courthouse on an errand for Matt. Helen was handling about one call in three, and the dispatcher was picking up the rest.

When Matt walked in, she tried to hide her pleasure, but she was afraid she failed. "Well, did you have a good morning?" she asked him.

"Very good. The judge agreed to give us the court order we need to get pharmacy records." He held up a McDonald's sack. "And I brought you a Big Mac to celebrate."

Before Helen could answer, three lines rang at once. She cut off one, ignored another, and actually managed to answer the third. Matt waited patiently while she took a message for one of the deputies.

"You're making me nervous," she told him. "And I can't celebrate anything until Crystal gets back." The phone rang again and she groaned.

"Well, I'll just leave your lunch here." He put her hamburger on the desk and walked into his office.

"Thanks," she said as the switchboard lit up. "The completed checklist for those files is on your desk!" she called after him.

Matt stuck his head out the office door. "I see it."

By the time Crystal returned an hour later, Helen was on the verge of a nervous breakdown. "I don't see how you do that every day," she said as Crystal reclaimed her chair and eased effortlessly into answering multiple phone calls.

"I enjoy a challenge," Crystal replied as Matt walked over.

"You get the court orders delivered to Chief Ramsey?" he asked the secretary.

"Dropped them off about ten minutes ago."

"Good. Helen, you come with me."

Crystal arched her eyebrows as Helen followed Matt into his office. He led her to the desk and picked up her report. "You did a good job on this," he said, then leaned over to point out particular names. "There are a couple of partial matches, like Judith Pope's grandmother. She did die unexpectedly, and she was taking Digoxin. But she didn't live alone, and there was no Bible on her bed."

Helen smiled. "So I guess you can cross Judith off your suspect list."

Matt ignored her joke and pointed to a different name. "And this woman didn't live alone, and she had been on the verge of death for years, but there was a Bible on her bed . . ."

"But it wasn't new," Helen finished for him. "It was a family heirloom."

"Probably just coincidence," Matt said as he put the list back on his desk. "We still don't have anything that connects the two victims. Mrs. Freeburg was bedridden with poor health, and Robyn Howell was a marathon runner. Mrs. Freeburg lived on a fixed income, Ms. Howell had lots of money. Ms. Howell had tons of insurance, Mrs. Freeburg had a three-thousand-dollar burial policy that was paid up in 1958. It looks like the only thing they had in common was warm blood."

"And the fact that they were female."

"Which is probably significant," Matt conceded. "But it's still not much, and the murderer killed them both for *some* reason."

Crystal walked in with two phone messages and added them to the pile already on Matt's desk. "Myron called and said that the prisoners are calling a hunger strike to protest the inhumane conditions in our county jail," she told Matt.

"Good," he replied. "If they don't eat, they'll save the county a few dollars."

Helen frowned. "You're not worried about an uprising?"

"Not the least little bit," he assured her. "We never have more than two or three prisoners at a time. And Myron, the chief deputy in charge of the jail, has twenty years of experience. The hunger strike is his problem and he'll handle it just fine."

"Probably by making the conditions *more* inhumane," Crystal predicted.

"Are you this Myron guy's boss?" Helen asked.

Matt shrugged. "Yes and no. As sheriff, I'm responsible for the jail, but I don't have anything to do with the day-to-day operations."

"Who else are you 'sort of the boss of,' besides me and Crystal?" Helen asked.

"There are two chief deputies, Myron, who runs the jail, and Riley Hunkapillar, who handles the uniform squad."

"We have twelve uniformed deputies, and they work rotating shifts," Crystal reported proudly.

"Mostly patrolling the back roads of Coosetta County and ticketing speeders," Matt said, downplaying Crystal's announcement.

"So you just sit in this nice office while your chief deputies do all the work?" Helen asked with a smile.

Matt nodded, but Crystal jumped in to defend him. "He has to attend meetings and political fund-raisers and file reports and handle all kinds of paperwork."

"And catch serial killers," Helen added.

He sighed. "If I can."

Helen looked for a reason to be optimistic. "And you have twelve deputies to help you."

"For now we're trying to keep a lid on the case, and the fewer people who know the details, the better. Eventually we'll have to involve them, but for now it's just us."

Helen picked up her report off his desk. "You said earlier that there had to be a connection between the women for the killer to choose them both."

"I remember saying something to that effect."

"Did you ever read Agatha Christie books when you were a kid?" she asked.

"No, I was more of the Marvel Comics kind of guy," he replied, and turned to Crystal. "How about you?"

Crystal held up a hand. "Don't look at me."

"Well, for your illiterate information, she wrote this book called *The ABC Murders*," Helen informed them. "The first victim's name started with *A*, the second with *B*—"

"Let me guess," Matt interrupted. "The third one's name started with a *C*."

"You're not such a bad detective after all," Helen said with a smile. "Anyway, all through the book they kept looking for a connection between the victims, but there wasn't one."

"The killer was just a kook who randomly chose his victims in alphabetical order?" Matt guessed.

Helen shook her head. "The killer wanted Mr. C dead—for some reason which escapes me now—but he didn't want to be an obvious suspect. So he killed two innocent people first, and by the time Mr. C died, no one was looking at relatives or business partners anymore. They thought they had a serial killer on their hands."

"Are you saying that maybe someone wanted to kill Robyn Howell and just killed Mrs. Freeburg to throw us off?"

"I don't know about that, but you shouldn't ignore the obvious people—ones who had something to gain."

"Thank you, Miss Tyler," Matt said. "That is very good advice."

She gave him a small bow. "It's the least I could do since I didn't find any big clues for you today."

"Eliminating possibilities is as important as finding facts," he assured her.

"Really?" She was surprised.

"Well, almost," he admitted.

Crystal looked between them. "I'm getting out of here before I throw up."

"Crystal is moody," Matt remarked after the secretary left.

"I've noticed," Helen said with a smile. "What now?"

"Chief Ramsey is compiling a list of pharmacists, doctors, and drug company reps who have access to Digoxin. It would be a long shot, but we might find a match with your checklist summary. We'll add the names of everyone in Coosetta County who had a prescription for Digoxin filled during the last six months. Then we can compare all of that with the victims' phone records, coworkers, known associates, etc."

Helen was daunted. "It's so much information."

Matt nodded. "That's the hard part. You want to compile enough data that you don't leave out something important, but if you get *too* much, you just cloud the issue."

"So, when will I have this new information to stare at until I'm blind?"

"Hopefully tomorrow," Matt replied with a smile. "And in the meantime, could you enter these phone numbers into my computer? I started, but I'm a slow typist."

"What are you going to do while I'm sitting at your desk?" she asked.

"I might try to make a dent in those phones messages," he said, but he didn't look enthusiastic.

"Chief Ramsey's on line two!" Crystal hollered from the outer office.

Matt frowned. "Then again, maybe I won't," he said, and picked up the phone.

Having Matt in such close proximity was distracting, but Helen did her best to concentrate on entering numbers for the rest of the afternoon. When she finally finished at five-thirty, her neck was stiff and her back ached. She walked out and found Crystal alone in the outer office.

"Where's Matt?" she asked, hoping she just sounded curious.

"Myron asked him to come up," Crystal responded. "He thinks he's negotiated an end to the one-day hunger strike."

"Oh, that's good."

"A matter of opinion, I guess. Eat jail food or go hungry? Which is worse?"

Helen shrugged. "I hope we never find out. I'm going home for the day. Tell Matt he can call me if there's something else he wanted me to do."

"So, what am I now? Your social secretary?"

"No," Helen told Crystal with a smile. "You're his secretary, and this is strictly business."

"Yeah, famous last words," Crystal muttered.

Helen went to the stairwell and hurried to the ground floor. It felt so good to be out in the open air. She took a deep breath, then climbed into her Escort and drove home. When she pulled into the driveway at 126 Ivy Lane, she found the Nguyen children in her backyard. They were looking over the fence at the new bars on Glida Mae's back windows.

Helen slipped quietly into the house, grabbed a bag of Oreos, and stepped out the back door. "Hello!" she called to the children. Both turned, poised for flight. "I've got you some more cookies." Lin's eyes lit up, but Tan seemed reluctant. "You can eat them here instead of taking them home," Helen suggested. "And I'll keep the leftovers for tomorrow."

Lin stepped forward and accepted the bag of cookies.

"Before you leave to go home, knock on my back door. I need to return your mother's dish."

Tan nodded solemnly, then Helen went back inside and watched them through the window. Lin grabbed another handful of cookies. Tan resisted for a minute or two, then got several for himself. When Tan knocked on the door, Helen gave him the casserole dish with her thank-you note inside, and he handed her the half empty bag of Oreos.

"I'll save these for the next time you come," Helen told him, and he nodded. "And maybe you don't have to mention the cookies to your mother," Helen suggested.

Tan didn't actually smile, but his eyes sparkled a little. Then he rejoined Lin by the fence and they hurried from the yard. Helen was sorry to see them go, but pleased with the progress she had made toward a friendship.

Helen ate one of the leftover cookies herself and turned on the news. When it was over, she decided to make a quick trip to the store, anxious to maintain an ample Oreo supply.

* * *

After the meeting at the jail, Matt went back to his office. Crystal was gone, but had left him a note. Crystal's handwriting was terrible, but it said something about Helen wanting to talk to him about more work. He had planned to stay at the office for several hours, but since Helen was eager to get busy on something else, he decided to take her some homework.

It was almost seven-thirty when he parked in front of his rental house on Ivy Lane. Helen's car was not in her driveway, which both surprised and disappointed him. He walked up to Miss Glida Mae's house. In answer to his knock, the actress cracked open the door and peeked out.

"Oh, Sheriff. I'm so glad you came by. I wanted to thank you for having these bars put on my windows."

"You're very welcome," Matt told her. "I hope it will make you feel safer."

"Oh it does!" she assured him. "I won't ever come out again where that murderer can get me!"

This was not exactly the result he had hoped for, and Matt was trying to think of a response when Helen's car pulled into her driveway. Finally, he gave up and said good night to Miss Glida Mae. He walked over to Helen, and she handed him a bag of groceries and led the way into the kitchen.

"Just put the bags there." She indicated toward the small counter next to the sink.

Matt did as he was told, then watched as she unloaded several packages of Oreos. "You must have quite a sweet tooth," he said.

"The Oreo is the world's most perfect food."

He studied her thin frame for a few seconds. "You must have the world's most perfect metabolism if you eat this many Oreos and stay slim."

Helen laughed. "I don't eat them. I use them to bribe Tan and Lin."

Matt nodded, remembering. "The Vietnamese kids."

"They still don't say much, but they will come into my yard as long as I have Oreos."

Matt eyed the cookies. "Do you think the kids would mind if I ate a couple?"

Helen found the open package. "Help yourself." She poured him a glass of milk, then put the carton in the refrigerator. "That was nice of you to pay for security bars to be put on Glida Mae's windows."

"I have my good moments," he said with a mouthful of cookie. "But it may have backfired. When I was over there a few minutes ago, she said she never plans to leave her safe house again."

Helen sighed. "Oh well. You tried anyway."

Matt finished his cookies and milk, then they walked into the living room. "Crystal left me a note that you wanted more work to do," he told her.

"Well, actually what I said was that if you needed me to do anything else tonight, you could call."

Matt felt a little foolish. "Crystal's handwriting is hard to read. And here I thought you were just a tireless worker."

Helen raised an eyebrow. "So, what have you got for me?"

Matt handed her the printouts. "More lists."

"Oh boy."

Matt smiled. "Don't feel obligated to finish this tonight, but do keep track of your hours so we can pay you."

Helen nodded. "I'll do as much as I can."

"Well, I'd better leave you alone so you can work." He started for the door, then turned around. "I'm expecting a big breakthrough."

"You mean like the murderer's name and address?" Helen asked.

Matt smiled. "I'd settle for one or the other."

* * *

On Thursday morning, Helen packed up the home repair books and turned them in at the library on her way to work. Then she went by the circulation desk to let Judith know that her card was clear. "And I got my own little key chain library card in the mail yesterday, so I won't need you to check out books for me anymore."

The librarian frowned. "I didn't mean for you to return all those books. I was planning to stop by your house on my way home from work tonight."

"It was the least I could do after you went to so much trouble to help me," Helen replied. "See you later," she whispered over her shoulder as she headed for the front door.

When she arrived at the sheriff's department, Helen took her seat across from Crystal and resisted the urge to look in Matt's office. "Good morning," she told the secretary.

"You just think so because you haven't seen all the faxes waiting for you."

Helen couldn't control a groan when Crystal stacked the pile of new information in front of her. "And this isn't all of it. The fax machine is still humming away."

Helen started sorting the pages into some kind of reasonable order. Matt stepped into his doorway to wave hello, but before Helen could respond, a man walked up and said he needed to talk—immediately. Matt frowned, then led the guest into his office and closed the door.

"That's Murray Monk from the mayor's office. He wants Matt's job," Crystal explained.

Helen stared at the closed door to Matt's office. "How could he take Matt's job?"

"By winning the election in November. He's campaigning like crazy, and Matt won't even let me have signs printed for his own campaign."

"It sounds like he doesn't want to be sheriff anymore."

"He doesn't know what he wants," Crystal muttered.

The switchboard phones rang unceasingly, foot traffic was continual, and by lunchtime Helen had accomplished next to nothing. Finally she stacked up her lists and stood. "I'm going home to work where it's quiet." She glanced at Matt's office, where he was still trapped with his competitor. "Tell Matt to call me or come over after work—whatever is most convenient."

"Matt didn't hire you to work at home," Crystal said crossly as Helen moved toward the door.

"He hired me to work period, and I'm not getting anything done in all this confusion," she said, waving to encompass the entire room. "But if he doesn't like it, he can fire me." With that parting shot, Helen walked outside.

On the way home Helen stopped by the Wal-Mart Super Center. She bought the ingredients for lasagna and told herself that she was not planning to share her meal with Matt Clevenger, nor was she trying to impress him with her culinary skills. She was just in the mood for Italian food.

Matt called on her cell phone while she was driving back to Ivy Lane. "Did you quit already?"

"I won't desert your hopeless cause," she promised him. "But I couldn't work at Crystal's desk. I'll be better off at home without all the interruptions."

"I'm sure you're right," he agreed. "I'll come by tonight, and we can go over your lists."

When Helen pulled up to her rental house, she saw Nelda Lovell and a woman dressed in hospital scrubs on Glida Mae's front porch. "Hey!" she called.

"Hello, Helen," Nelda returned.

Helen took a step forward. "Are you checking on Glida Mae?"

Nelda frowned as she crossed over to speak to Helen. "The nurse is here to give her a bath, but I can't get her to let us in. I thought Glida Mae was better, but if she won't open the door, the doctor will have to commit her."

Helen frowned. "Maybe I can help. Let me get these groceries into the refrigerator and I'll be right back." Helen unloaded the car quickly, then walked up her neighbor's porch and called through the door. "Glida Mae? This is Helen and I've come to visit. It would be impolite not to let me in."

Glida Mae spoke from the other side. "I'm sorry, Helen, but I can't open the door."

"Why not, Glida Mae?" Nelda asked.

"Because he'll kill me."

"Who?" Nelda asked in exasperation.

"The murderer. He already killed my cat, and I know I'm going to be next."

"Oh, Glida Mae," Nelda began, but Helen interrupted.

"Glida Mae, you know that Nelda and I are not murderers, don't you?"

There was a pause, then Glida Mae whispered, "Yes."

"And you know that the nurse won't hurt you, so it's safe to open the door for just a second."

"No," Glida Mae whimpered. "If I open the door, he might come in."

"But the nurse has to give you your medicine and a bath," Nelda tried to explain to the confused woman. "And I've brought you lunch."

"If you open the door for just a second, no one will get inside except Nelda and the nurse," Helen promised. "I'll stand right here by the door to be sure." There was no response. "And I have a gun," she added. Nelda raised her eyebrows, but Helen concentrated on the door.

There was another long pause, and Helen had almost given up hope when the door opened slowly. Glida Mae's appearance was startling, and Helen and Nelda exchanged worried looks.

"You'll stay right here?" Glida Mae asked, and Helen nodded. "You have your gun?" Helen removed the revolver from her purse so Glida Mae could see it. The older woman relaxed. "Thank you," she whispered, then stepped back and admitted Nelda and the nurse.

Helen paced the front porch until the door finally reopened. The nurse came out first, followed closely by Nelda. Then the door closed, and they heard the lock slide into place.

"I'm going to have to report her condition to Dr. Baker," the nurse warned.

Nelda nodded. "But she *did* let you in."

The nurse shrugged and walked toward her car, which was parked at the curb.

Nelda watched the woman leave, then turned to Helen. "I've always been able to get through to Glida Mae, and it concerns me that lately I can't influence her."

"You're doing all you can."

Nelda nodded. "I hope so. Maybe I'll call Dr. Baker myself before the nurse gets a chance. That way I can tell him our side of the story." She glanced up at Helen. "Would you come with me while I call? For moral support?"

Helen had work to do and a dinner to make, but she couldn't refuse Nelda's request, so she nodded. "Okay."

They walked across Glida Mae's lawn, and Nelda opened the back door of her home. "As a bonus, I'll feed you lunch. I have leftovers from last night."

"I haven't eaten today," Helen replied gratefully.

She offered to help prepare the meal, so Nelda gave her a bowl of tomatoes and a knife. "Slice them thin." Nelda demonstrated a few times until Helen nodded.

Nelda heated up the cornbread, then stirred the turnip greens on the stove.

"What will the doctor decide about Glida Mae?" Helen asked reluctantly.

"That she needs to go into a nursing home."

Before Helen could answer, the back door slammed. "Grandma!" a voice called.

"Sydney?" Nelda wiped her hands on her apron and stepped forward to greet her granddaughter with a hug. "She's been to the doctor," Nelda said for Helen's benefit. "What did he say?"

"That I am glowing with good health, which confirms my suspicions that he's a total quack," Sydney muttered as she settled herself in a kitchen chair. "Hey, Helen," she added, looking around. "Where's Miss Glida Mae?" Sydney asked as Nelda put the food on the table and passed out plates. "Doesn't she usually eat with you?"

Nelda poured each young woman a glass of milk. "Lately I've been taking her meals to her place."

"Why?" Sydney asked in surprise.

"Because Glida Mae is afraid to come out of her house," Nelda explained.

Concern clouded Sydney's eyes. "She's always made up things— like her marriage to Humphrey Bogart and all those imaginary cats— but she loved to visit people." Sydney turned to Helen. "Especially Grandma."

Nelda sighed. "She thinks that someone is trying to kill her."

Sydney put her fork down. "Then she's finally gone completely crazy?"

Nelda reached over and patted Sydney's hand. "Just eat your dinner, dear. I'm going to call Dr. Baker after we're through and let him decide what to do about Glida Mae."

They ate in silence for a few minutes, and then Nelda asked Sydney if her obstetrician thought the baby would come soon. "He said he wouldn't let me go past my due date, so that means I only have another two weeks in agony."

"It can't be that bad," Nelda said firmly.

"Pregnancy was never intended for women as old as I am," Sydney commented around a mouthful of cornbread.

"Sarah in the Bible was over a hundred when she had Isaac," Nelda pointed out.

"She didn't have the Georgia heat or humidity to deal with."

Nelda looked like she would like to say more, but stood instead. "How about some banana pudding?" She turned to Helen. "I made it yesterday, and it's always better after a night in the refrigerator."

"You know *I* won't be able to resist," Sydney said as she pushed away from the table. "But just give me a little bit. I've gained too much weight already."

Helen accepted a bowl as well.

"Well, you girls help yourselves," Nelda encouraged. "I'm going to call Dr. Baker."

Helen took a bite of the pudding, but concern for Glida Mae had ruined her appetite. Nelda returned a few minutes later with the doctor's verdict. "I talked Dr. Baker into leaving Glida Mae at home for the time being, but he says that he'll do a reevaluation in a week or so."

"You bought her some time, anyway," Helen said.

"Maybe she'll get over this nonsense about murderers before they evaluate her."

Helen felt certain that Glida Mae's condition would worsen with time rather than improve, but she didn't have the heart to tell Nelda, so she just nodded. "Well, thanks for lunch, but I've got to get to work." With a wave to Sydney, Helen hurried outside.

Back in her quiet house, Helen went into the kitchen and preheated the oven for her frozen apple pie. While the pie baked, she browned sausage and ground beef, then chopped onions and garlic. She sautéed, stirred, and simmered the tomato sauce until it was ready. Then she assembled the lasagna and put it in the oven after the pie was done. She laid out breadsticks to thaw, tossed a salad, and went into the living room, where she worked on the printouts until six-fifteen, when there was a knock on her door.

Helen hadn't expected Matt so early, and felt a little thrill of anticipation as she pulled open the door. But it was Judith Pope, not Matt, who was standing on her front porch. "Judith!" Helen said in surprise.

"Sorry to drop in again," the librarian apologized. "But I found you a book on Vietnamese people."

Helen accepted the book. "That was so thoughtful of you!" She opened the front cover. There was no thick protective covering or pocket for date-due cards. "Did you get this from another library branch?"

Judith blushed. "No, I bought it at Books Galore," she admitted. "The library will reimburse me, though, since we don't have another one on the subject. But it takes forever to get a new book cataloged, and I didn't want you to have to wait."

"You are incredible," Helen said. "And you're going to have to come in and eat dinner with me so I won't be hopelessly indebted to you *and* the Nguyens."

Judith shook her head. "I ate a hamburger on the way over here."

"Well, you can at least eat a piece of apple pie," Helen insisted. "It's just one of those frozen kinds, but they're pretty good."

Judith didn't look happy, but finally stepped inside.

"Have a seat on the couch." Helen had to move some files to the coffee table so that Judith could sit down. She briefly explained that she was working part-time for the sheriff, and Judith's expression became more grim.

"Now I'll get your pie," Helen promised, then hurried into the small kitchen. When she returned, Judith was perched on the very edge of the couch. Every muscle looked tense as she accepted the dessert. "You don't really have to eat it if you don't want it," Helen said.

Judith shook her head and took a tentative bite. "I just hate to be a bother." Judith glanced up. "Aren't you having a piece?"

Helen certainly wasn't going to admit that she hoped to eat later with the sheriff, so she just smiled. "I haven't eaten dinner yet, so I'll wait until later."

Judith took another bite. "This *is* good."

"I'm glad you like it," Helen said. "My homemade ones are even better, but I didn't have time to make one this afternoon."

"My grandmother didn't believe in eating sweets except on special occasions," Judith told her. Helen remembered Thelma's comment that Judith's grandmother didn't allow her to have tea cakes as a child. "And I haven't cooked much of anything since she died."

"Were the two of you very close?" Helen asked with sympathy.

Judith considered this for a few seconds. "She was all I had," she said finally.

"It must have been lonely growing up in a neighborhood of elderly people," Helen remarked.

"I didn't need friends," Judith replied. "Not when I had books."

"Have you always been this serious?" Helen teased.

"I guess," Judith responded without so much as a smile.

"Then I'll bet you were a straight-A student in school. And probably president of the debate team, and editor of the school paper."

Judith's expression tensed. "I did make straight As, but my high school didn't have a debate team, and Grandmother didn't believe in extracurricular activities either."

Helen was developing a healthy dislike for "Grandmother," but she controlled her reaction carefully. "Did you go away to college?"

"Grandmother wanted me to live at home, so I accepted a scholarship to City College."

"You had to make a lot of sacrifices," Helen said slowly.

"Grandmother made sacrifices for me too," Judith said. "It wasn't easy for a woman her age to raise a young child."

Helen thought Judith's attitude was very generous. They were quiet for a minute, then Helen introduced a new but related subject. "So, does this place still look the same as it did when you came to watch bridge games?" she asked her guest.

Judith glanced around. "Pretty much."

"Matt seems drawn here," she commented. "I think he misses his grandmother."

Judith shrugged, obviously uninterested in Matt's emotional state, so Helen redirected the conversation.

"Did you and Matt go to high school together?"

Judith looked up. "We were in the same graduating class, but moved in very different circles. He participated in *every* extracurricular activity, and he had no interest in good grades."

Helen was disappointed by this news, but curiosity forced her to ask for more. "Nelda said his wife was a cheerleader."

Judith acknowledged this with a small shrug. "Julie was okay. I never understood what she saw in Matt Clevenger."

As Judith said these words, there was another knock on the door. The sound seemed to startle Judith, and she almost dropped her plate. Helen looked through the peephole. "Well, speak of the devil," she said with a smile over her shoulder, then opened the door. "Hey, Matt."

"Sorry to drop by at dinnertime again, but . . ." His voice trailed off when he saw Judith. "Oh, I didn't know you had company."

Judith put her plate on the cluttered coffee table and stepped toward the door. "I was just leaving."

"Please stay," Helen said automatically.

"Don't rush off on my account," Matt added.

Judith looked at the ground as she walked past Matt and out onto the porch. "I have to go."

They watched as Judith rushed off, then Helen turned to Matt. "Well, you had quite an effect on her."

Matt sighed and collapsed onto the couch. "I told you I wasn't nice to Judith when we were kids. She holds a grudge."

Helen frowned, remembering Judith's defense of her grandmother. "She doesn't seem like a vindictive person."

"Everyone has their limits," Matt said. "I was a mean kid."

"I think there's more to this than you've told me."

"What do you want me to do? Bare my soul?"

Helen considered this. "It might help if you talk about it and kind of sort things out. What did you do to her besides not letting her play baseball?"

"I used to tease her because she stuttered," he admitted.

"Oh, Matt," Helen whispered, a little knot of pain forming in her chest.

"I was ten years old, for goodness sake," he responded with feeling, then looked up at Helen.

"You didn't tease her when you were older?"

Matt ran his fingers through his hair in a weary gesture. "I don't even remember seeing Judith after the sixth grade until the night we graduated from high school."

"Not even one time?"

Matt shook his head. "No, if I'd have stopped to think about it, I would have wondered if she moved. But I never stopped to think about it."

"Being invisible might have been worse to Judith than being teased," Helen mused.

"I'd like to apologize," Matt told her. "But after all these years, I really don't know how. I already have enough problems in my past. I can't let Judith become another one."

Helen ached for poor Judith, but couldn't really hold youthful mistakes against Matt. "Maybe someday you'll get the opportunity to make it up to her."

Matt shrugged. "Maybe."

The timer on the oven went off, indicating that the lasagna was done. Helen offered to share her dinner, and Matt accepted. Helen fixed them both plates and brought them to the living room so they could work while they ate.

"Well, your lists are getting longer anyway," he commented. "And this food is delicious. More handouts from the Vietnamese people?"

Helen laughed. "No, I made this myself."

"So, are you coming into the office tomorrow?" he asked.

"Unless you fire me."

Matt took another bite of lasagna. "Naw, I can't go through that grueling interview process again, so I guess I'll keep you. I know it's hard to concentrate at Crystal's desk, so I figure we'll just share my office."

Helen's cheeks turned pink. "I won't inconvenience you to that extent. I'll make do at Crystal's desk."

"No, really, it's the perfect solution," he insisted. "I don't know why I didn't think of it sooner." He drank his milk, then held up his empty plate. "You got any more of this?"

Helen smiled and pointed him toward the kitchen.

CHAPTER 8

Matt berated himself as he left Helen's house. He'd eaten her food again and wasted her time confessing his childhood sins. He knew she didn't care about the food, but she had seemed disturbed by his treatment of Judith Pope. As he drove toward his parents' house, he tried to think of something he could do to apologize to Judith. Flowers sounded too easy. Maybe a good book.

When he got home, his parents were still up watching television in the small den and invited him to join them, but he shook his head. "I'm going to try to get a good night's sleep for a change," he said as he walked by. He went upstairs, took a quick shower, and settled onto the bed he'd slept in as a child. He read several chapters in Julie's old Bible, but his eyes kept straying to the paperback copy of the Book of Mormon on his nightstand. Finally he gave in and turned to 1 Nephi.

* * *

Matt was back in his office at the sheriff's department by six o'clock on Friday morning. He found more Digoxin sales records from a local pharmacy in the tray of the fax machine. He put them in an envelope and wrote Helen's name on the front, then called Ed Ramsey at home and woke him up.

"I've got most of the Digoxin reports," he said when the sleepy police chief answered the phone.

"I presume that since you woke me up, you must have found something earthshaking," the chief growled.

"Haven't even looked at them yet. I'll let my researcher see what she can find. But I wanted to let you know that I've got them."

"Next time, wait until you have some actual information before you call and wake me up," Ed Ramsey requested. "I've got my list of all the people who treated Mary Jean Freeburg, doctors who make house calls, and other people who had access to large amounts of Digoxin. I'll fax you a copy when I get to the office."

"I don't want to wait that long. I'll send somebody over to pick up a copy. Did you find anything?"

"Just a possible lawsuit. I sent a couple of uniforms out to talk to the people who administered medication to Mrs. Freeburg. One of the nurses didn't appreciate being questioned—thought we were calling her incompetent and blaming her for the old lady's death. She's gotten a lawyer, and he's making all kinds of noise."

"Hmmm." Matt considered this. "It could be a case of protesting too much."

"If we had a simple medical connection between the two victims, I'd say you might be right and we'd have a possible suspect. But since Robyn Howell was healthy . . ."

"We'll have to keep looking."

"We may be running out of time. It was a week ago today that Robyn Howell was killed."

Matt sighed. "I'm aware of that." As he hung up the phone, Matt saw Crystal arrive at her desk, so he punched the intercom button. "Crystal, come into my office and make it quick. I have an important assignment for you."

"What?" she asked irritably when she reached his doorway.

Matt waved the envelope full of pharmacy records. "Is Helen here yet? I need to give her these."

Crystal frowned. "I don't think answering questions about your girlfriend falls into the 'important assignment' category."

The girlfriend remark didn't deserve a reply, so Matt ignored it. "There's a list over at police headquarters that might contain the name of our murderer. I need you to go and pick it up."

Crystal looked slightly impressed. "In that case, I'll do it. As long as you don't mind if I stop and get breakfast on the way," she said over her shoulder as she left.

Matt worked on payroll until Crystal got back. She offered him a bacon, egg, and cheese biscuit, and he accepted gratefully. He looked through Ed's list as he ate. "Helen's still not here?"

"It's not even eight o'clock yet," Crystal reminded him with her mouth full of biscuit. "And that Miss America look doesn't come easy. It probably takes her hours to get ready in the morning."

"We need to get all this information into the computer," he said with a speculative look in her direction.

"Don't even think about it. I've got a switchboard to handle." Crystal stood up and brushed the crumbs from her lap. "I'm sure Helen will be in soon, but before she gets here . . ."

Matt raised an eyebrow.

"You might want to wipe the egg yolk off your chin."

Matt used a napkin to clean his face, then finished his breakfast while returning week-old phone calls. Helen arrived thirty minutes later, and Matt met her in the outer office by Crystal's desk.

"Good morning," he said to Helen. She was wearing a dark business suit and her honey-blonde hair was brushed up into a neat bun at the back of her head. She looked pretty and smart, which made it hard for Matt to drag his eyes away. Finally he told both women to follow him.

Matt walked into his office and cleared a small section of his desk. "I need another chair brought in here for Helen," he told the secretary. "She doesn't want to work with you anymore, so I'm going to share my office."

"Matt!" Helen protested.

"It's okay," Matt said with a smile. "Crystal knows I'm kidding."

The secretary gave them a speculative glance.

"There's so much confusion at your desk," Helen tried to explain. "I can't concentrate."

"Tell me about it," Crystal replied as she went into the outer office. She returned a minute later with a chair for Helen, which Matt put in front of his computer. Then he gave Helen the pharmacy records and Ed Ramsey's list. "Get everything entered, and we'll see what we've got," he told her. Crystal went back to the switchboard, and he started working on an overdue mileage report.

Helen worked steadily for two hours. Finally, she sat back and looked over at Matt. "I'm done."

Before he could respond, his phone started ringing. He ignored it. "Print it out."

"Phone's for you!" Crystal hollered from her desk.

Matt nodded but didn't reach for the phone.

Finally Crystal appeared in the doorway. "Sorry to bother you two, but it's your creepy medical examiner friend from Atlanta."

Matt grabbed the receiver. "Alex?"

"Hey, Matt old man. I've gotten all the test results back on those two cadavers you brought me, and I found something odd, although I doubt it has any bearing on your case."

"I'm desperate. I'll take anything—even something odd," Matt assured him.

"Well, the marathon runner who was in perfect physical condition was also HIV positive."

Matt was profoundly shocked. "You're kidding."

"It's no fun kidding a serious guy like you," Alex promised him. "It hadn't progressed into full-fledged AIDS yet, but it was in a stage advanced enough that I'm sure she was under a doctor's care."

"We checked every doctor in Eureka, and none of them had her listed as a patient."

"She would have been seeing a specialist—probably infectious disease. I'd try Columbus or Atlanta."

"Robyn Howell made monthly trips to Atlanta."

"Sounds like doctor's appointments to me," Alex predicted.

"Thanks, Alex. You're the best."

"Don't go overboard. It's just an odd little detail that no one else in the world would have ever found."

Matt didn't laugh. "And it may be the key to a murder investigation."

"An immune deficiency disease?"

"No, a medical connection between the two victims."

"Well, I'm glad I could help."

"I'll let you know how it turns out," Matt said, then disconnected. As soon as he had a dial tone, Matt called Ed Ramsey's office. The secretary said the police chief was in a meeting, so Matt left a message. Then he yelled for Crystal. When the secretary poked her head in, he explained the situation. "We need a list of infectious disease specialists in Atlanta—quick."

Helen spun around in her chair and pulled up the Internet. "I'll handle that for you." She began typing.

"Just how do you plan to get doctors in Atlanta to give you information about Robyn Howell?" Crystal asked. "Putting the squeeze on doctors and pharmacists in Coosetta County is one thing, but people in Atlanta won't be impressed by your badge."

Matt gave Crystal an impatient look. "Nobody here is impressed by my badge either, and I've never 'put the squeeze' on anyone. You've got to stop watching reruns of *Miami Vice*."

Crystal blushed as Helen put a piece of paper in front of them. "Here's the list. There are twenty-three infectious disease doctors in Atlanta, but only eleven of them treat AIDS patients."

They studied the list in silence for a minute, then Crystal made a proposal. "Would you be against an outright lie?"

Matt sat up a little straighter. "When it comes to catching a murderer, I don't have any limits as to how far I'll go. What do you have in mind?"

"I was thinking that I could call these doctors and pretend to be Robyn Howell."

"What if they know she's dead?" Helen asked.

Matt looked at Crystal. "She's got a point."

"Instead of impersonating Ms. Howell, why don't you say you are calling to check on the date of her next appointment?" Helen suggested. "That way you won't actually be lying."

A smile spread across Crystal's face. "I can say I'm calling to *cancel* Robyn Howell's next appointment. She certainly won't be needing it!"

"Brilliant," Matt told her appreciatively. "You make the calls from my desk. Helen and I will go over here and look at this list." He pointed to a corner piled with boxes. "And when you find the right doctor, hand the receiver to me."

Matt dragged in another chair, and they used the biggest box as a table. "So, what do we have?"

"There are a few names on the pharmacy records that you might find interesting. Glida Mae Magnanney has been taking Digoxin since the first of the year."

Matt nodded. "That doesn't surprise me."

Helen's finger moved down the page. "Mary Jean Freeburg took the drug too."

"I knew that."

"And last but not least, your friend Elvis takes two tablets a day."

"Elvis Hatcher?" Matt confirmed. "I didn't know he had heart problems."

"Maybe he doesn't. Maybe he faked symptoms so that the doctor would put him on Digoxin. Then he stockpiled the pills until he had enough to kill his victims."

Matt frowned. "I know you don't like Elvis, but that plan would take more sense than he's got."

"Think about it," Helen insisted with enthusiasm. "Everyone knows him, and I'll bet most of the women around here would let him in their homes without giving it a second thought."

"You think they'd let him make them a bowl of chicken noodle soup?" Matt asked with skepticism.

Helen shuddered. "His fingernails are filthy."

"And Elvis Hatcher won't even kill a *rattlesnake*," Matt told her. "He catches them and keeps them in cages at his house."

"Like I said, he's as weird as the day is long."

"But he doesn't *kill* things," Matt reiterated.

Helen put an asterisk by the handyman's name. "You'd be crazy not to check him out."

"Okay," Matt agreed. "But he's not the killer."

Helen narrowed her eyes at him. "You just don't want to admit that I might have been right about something you scoffed at."

Matt laughed. "I don't even know how to 'scoff,' and I'll be the happiest man in the world if you solve this case."

Matt caught a movement out of the corner of his eye and turned to see Crystal gesturing frantically. Matt hurried to the desk, and Crystal handed him the phone. He identified himself and asked to speak to Robyn Howell's physician. The receptionist tried to stall, but after Matt made a few mild threats, she put him on hold and went to find the doctor. Matt waited impatiently until a male voice with a distinct edge of annoyance spoke into the phone.

"Hello?"

"My name is Matt Clevenger, and I'm the sheriff for Coosetta

County," Matt said, giving his credentials again.

"My receptionist told me who you are. That's why I've left my patients cooling their heels in my waiting room to talk to you."

A wise guy, Matt thought to himself. "I'm sorry to take you from your busy and no doubt lucrative practice, Doctor. . . . ," Matt glanced down at the list, "Sizemore, but I have a couple of murders on my hands, and I'm trying to avoid another one. So I need you to answer a few questions."

"What does any of this have to do with Robyn?"

"She was the second victim," Matt said bluntly, and he heard the doctor's quick intake of breath. "The autopsy report showed that she was HIV positive, and we found you by process of elimination."

"How did she die?" the doctor asked quietly.

"In her sleep," Matt replied. "Poisoned."

"I'm terribly sorry about Robyn, but I can't give out confidential information on a patient—even a dead one." There was a pause, then the doctor continued. "I mean, I'm sure you can imagine what would happen if people got the idea that I can't keep a secret."

Matt sighed. "Yeah, it could cost you millions. I'm not asking for embarrassing specifics about Ms. Howell or any of your other patients. I just need to know the types of medication you had prescribed for her."

"I can't tell you that. It would be a breach of confidence."

Matt gritted his teeth. "People's lives are at risk here. Didn't I mention that earlier?"

"I have a reputation to maintain," the doctor insisted.

"Can you at least tell me if you prescribed the drug Digoxin—a particularly large dose?"

"There was nothing wrong with Robyn's heart. Why would I prescribe Digoxin?"

Matt smiled grimly. "You're sure."

"Absolutely."

"Thank you, Doctor. You might have inadvertently helped to save a life."

"If you need anything else, get a court order," Dr. Sizemore responded, then disconnected.

"A real prince," Matt said, staring at the receiver.

"Hopefully you'll never need his services," Crystal murmured as she took the phone from his hand.

"So he didn't prescribe the Digoxin?" Helen asked.

"No," Matt confirmed. "It was obviously administered by our murderer."

"Someone who had access to large amounts of the drug," Crystal thought out loud.

Matt nodded. "Okay, we have a medical connection. Both women were sick. Helen, cross-reference all your other lists with the people who provided medical care to Mary Jean Freeburg. Doctors, nurses, pharmacists, dentists, even family members. Once you have that done, let me look at it. Crystal, fax this report for me while I call Ed Ramsey."

Crystal glanced at the report. "This was due in April."

Matt reached for the phone. "I know I'm making all the other sheriffs look bad with my efficiency, but that's their problem." He gave her a quick smile, then started dialing.

* * *

It took Helen an hour to compile her list. There were six people who had provided some type of health care service for Mary Jean Freeburg who also appeared on at least one other list. Matt and Ed Ramsey divided the possible suspects, then went out to question them. After Matt left, Helen stacked up a bunch of lists and told Crystal she was headed home.

Once she arrived at 126 Ivy Lane, she changed into jeans and reheated some lasagna for dinner. She was watching the news when the doorbell rang. Helen opened the door to find Matt on her porch holding two strawberry slushies from Jiffy Mart. Helen stepped back to let him in and took the large plastic cup he extended toward her.

"I hated to come empty-handed," he explained as he took a big sip that left a bright red mustache above his lips.

Helen looked down at her own slightly melted drink. "Well you should have. Really."

Matt gave her a smile, then walked over and sat on the couch. "Our investigation of health care providers was a big success or a terrible disaster, depending on how you look at it."

She sat on the other end of the couch. "What do you mean?"

"Our most likely suspect is probably the most respected citizen in Eureka, Dr. Ira Baker. He has served the community for almost fifty years, has more nonpaying patients than Mother Teresa, and was recently voted Physician of the Year by the Georgia chapter of the American Medical Association."

"But you think he's guilty of murder?" she asked.

He took another sip of his slushie and returned his eyes to Helen. "He's on several lists. He had access to large doses of Digoxin and would know of its capabilities. He's the kind of person women would trust and probably let into their homes at night. He was Mary Jean Freeburg's primary care physician, and his wife says he was home watching television on the night Mrs. Freeburg was killed. But even though Robyn Howell was not a patient of his, he stopped by her house on the evening of the murder."

Helen felt her heart beat faster. "He admits that?"

"Yep. Said the neighbor, Mrs. McBride, told him at choir practice that Ms. Howell was suffering from a stubborn cold. He said he wanted to help."

Helen shook her head in wonder. "Wow. The guy's either a saint or a demon."

"Pretty big room for error there," Matt replied. "He says that she did let him inside, that he gave her a limited examination in her living room, and that when he left her, she was very much alive."

"Do you believe him?"

Matt shrugged. "He's offered to take a lie detector test."

"But you're worried that he might be able to trick it?"

"I'm a little worried about that, but what really scares me is that if Dr. Baker is our murderer, he might have killed hundreds of people over the course of his career."

Helen frowned. "But we've checked cases for the past six months, and there were no other white Bibles."

"The Bibles and the Digoxin may be a new thing. He knows all about drugs and how they affect the human system. He could probably kill people in different ways and never cause any suspicion."

"Sounds like I need to make a new list of patients under Dr. Baker's care who have died during the past . . ."

"Let's make it two years," Matt suggested.

Helen made a note. "I'll start on it first thing in the morning."

"He said his office would cooperate, so call his nurse. If she'll send you the information, it will save a lot of time."

"Well, at least we have a suspect."

Matt acknowledged this with a nod. "I'm not sure I'd feel much worse if I were investigating my own mother." Matt polished off his slushie. "So, how do you like working in law enforcement?"

"It's exciting," Helen admitted. "And Crystal is . . . interesting."

"She's gotten the idea that you're my girlfriend."

"It's been hard to resist you, I'll admit," Helen teased back. "You come over all the time, bringing me romantic gifts like sloshies and lists of dead people."

"It's a slushie," Matt corrected.

Helen waved her hand. "Whatever. So, I guess like all the other women in Eureka, Crystal is in love with you."

Matt looked surprised and slightly alarmed by this comment. "Women in Eureka love me?"

"Well, a high percentage of the ones I've met so far seem to. There's Glida Mae, the judge who gave you the court order, Crystal, and Judith Pope."

"Miss Glida Mae is crazy, so she doesn't count. The judge doesn't love me; she just felt sorry for me. And Judith Pope absolutely hates me."

"That's why I suspect that deep down she really cares for you. What else would generate that much animosity?"

Matt shrugged. "Who knows? And as for Crystal, she's just one of the boys."

Helen raised an eyebrow. "Crystal is not a 'boy,' and she's crazy about you."

Matt put his cup on the coffee table. "I know Crystal cares about me. All the guys do. We're like a family." He paused, then pressed on. "I guess by now you've heard about the tornado that killed my wife and kids?"

Helen nodded and he continued.

"I fell apart after that. It didn't seem like I had anything to live for—any future at all. So I stayed in a drunken stupor for several months after the funeral." He cut his eyes toward her. "I'm not proud of that, but honestly, if I had to do it again, I don't know if I could handle it any better."

"It must have been awful."

"Those months are a blur. When I finally stopped drinking, I expected to find out that I'd been fired, my car had been repossessed, and that my credit had been ruined. But the other deputies had been working my shifts, clocking in and out for me just like I'd been at work every day. Crystal deposited my checks, paid my bills, filed for insurance."

Helen saw his hands tremble. "They took care of you," she said.

"They are some of the best guys in the world, and they all still worry about me, especially Crystal. But there's never been anything romantic between us."

Before Helen could point out that this didn't necessarily mean that Crystal hadn't hoped for something to develop, there was a knock on the door. Helen opened it to find Nelda Lovell standing on the porch.

"I'm so sorry to disturb you while you're trying to work," the older woman began as Matt joined them at the door. "But Glida Mae called me in hysterics. She says that the murderer came to her house and tried to get in. I was walking down to check on her when I saw Matt's car and thought maybe he should come with me."

Matt stepped out onto the porch. "Lock the door behind us," he instructed Helen as he led the way to the house next door.

Helen locked the door, then watched out the front window. She saw Matt and Nelda disappear into Glida Mae's house. After thirty minutes she got tired of standing at the window, so she went back to work. Over an hour later, Matt knocked on her door.

"Where's Nelda?" she asked, stretching her tired muscles.

"I walked her back home."

"And Glida Mae?"

"I couldn't see any evidence of an attempted break-in. She probably just let her imagination get the best of her. Miss Nelda gave her some medicine, and we waited until she fell asleep. I think she'll be okay."

"Poor Glida Mae."

"Yes." Matt reached over and picked up the list of common denominators and the pharmacy records. "I'll take these back to the office. I guess you can have the weekend off."

"Thanks," Helen said with a smile.

After Matt left, Helen stacked all the information pertaining to the case in a corner of the living room, then took a shower. She put on a pair of pajamas and made herself a glass of lemonade. Then she curled up on the couch and used the remote control to search the television channels until she found an old movie. It was a Cary Grant picture, and she was thoroughly enjoying it until there was a knock on her door. She looked at the clock and saw that it was after ten o'clock.

Thinking of Harrison Campbell and the reasons she had taken refuge in Eureka, Helen approached the door and looked through the peephole. Matt Clevenger was standing on her porch. With a sigh of relief, she unhooked the chain and pulled the door open a few inches. She intended to tell him that she couldn't invite him inside since she was dressed for bed, but the look on his face silenced her.

"What's the matter?" she demanded.

He stepped into the house and pushed the door closed. "We have another victim."

The dread in his eyes terrified her. "Not Glida Mae," she whispered, clutching his hands in hers.

"No," he shook his head. "It's Judith Pope."

Helen felt the air desert her lungs. She didn't know Judith well, but she wasn't a complete stranger. This time the murderer had hit a little too close to home. "Poor Judith."

"She's alive, Helen," Matt told her, and she looked up in surprise. "But barely. The doctors aren't making any promises, but they're hopeful. I didn't want you to just hear it on the news."

"It's going to be on the news?"

"Oh yeah. Ed said the local stations were represented at the hospital, so they'll all have a piece about it on the eleven o'clock news."

"At least that might make the community aware of the danger."

Matt sighed. "Yeah, we would have had to make an announcement of some kind anyway."

"Who found Judith?"

Matt looked uneasy. "Elvis Hatcher."

Helen raised an eyebrow. "Well, that's interesting."

"He said he came by to check a roof leak and found her unconscious."

"I know you don't believe that."

"Ed and the police department are investigating his story, but if he killed her, why would he call 911?"

"Maybe he thought she was already dead and just wanted to give himself an excuse for being in the area."

"Maybe." Matt didn't look convinced. "Anyway, I'm headed to the hospital. Hopefully Judith will regain consciousness and can tell us who brought her the poisonous soup."

"Then your case will be solved." Helen knew she should be glad, but once the murderer was arrested, her job at the sheriff's department would likely end. And that was a sad thought.

"Yes, the case will be solved," Matt put his arm around her shoulders, and she didn't know if he was trying to comfort her or himself. "Well, I'd better get to the hospital."

"I'm coming too," Helen told him. "It will just take a minute for me to get on my clothes."

"It will probably be a long, boring night."

"I won't be able to sleep anyway, and at least we can keep each other company," Helen replied.

He considered this for a few seconds, then smiled. "Yeah, I guess you're right."

Helen dressed in five minutes, and the two of them got into Matt's Bronco. As they drove through the dark streets of Eureka, Helen pulled out her cell phone. "I need to tell Nelda about Judith." Matt provided the number, and she placed the call. She gave Nelda the details, then turned back to Matt. "She wants to come to the hospital."

"Tell her to wait until tomorrow morning. And remind her to keep her doors locked. Eureka has become a dangerous place to live."

* * *

Matt parked in front of Lakeside Hospital and then led Helen through the reporters and cameramen by the entrance. Ed Ramsey was standing in the lobby and approached them when they walked through the door. The men exchanged brief nods. "Ed, this is my new assistant, Helen Tyler."

The police chief removed his hat and addressed Helen. "Ms. Tyler."

"How's Judith?" Matt asked.

"She's still unconscious," the chief said. "They say it's too soon to tell if she'll make it."

"What are we going to do about these reporters?"

"Nothing. They're the hospital's problem."

Matt sighed. "For now, but soon we're going to have to make a statement. Something that doesn't give away too much, but sufficiently warns the public."

"Yeah, I'll get the lawyers on it first thing tomorrow."

"So, what happened?"

Chief Ramsey took a deep breath, then began. "Elvis Hatcher called 911 at 9:18. He said he was coming to check out a roof leak that Ms. Pope had reported. He knocked and got no response, so he tried the front door. It was unlocked. He opened it and called from the porch but never got an answer. Finally, he went inside and found Ms. Pope unconscious on her bedroom floor."

"That seems kind of late to be making a service call," Helen remarked.

"That's probably not so unusual for him," Matt said, then looked at the police chief. "Do you think he's the killer?"

"The repairman?" Ed clarified, then shook his head. "He barely has walking-around sense. I can't picture him being the mastermind behind a series of murders."

Matt was relieved. "They're sure it was Digoxin?"

The chief nodded. "Oh, yeah. She's loaded with it."

"Did she eat chicken noodle soup?" Matt wanted to know.

"The folks in the emergency room pumped her stomach and said it looked like chicken noodle soup," Ed told him. "They packaged a sample for us, and I've got an officer on the way to Atlanta with it now."

Matt looked around the lobby. "Well, I guess we might as well make ourselves at home."

"Since you're here, I think I'll go to Ms. Pope's house. I've got a team there taking pictures and dusting for fingerprints."

"Was there a Bible on the bed?"

"No," the chief said. "It was still on the counter by the sink. I think our murderer was surprised by the arrival of Mr. Hatcher and didn't have time to put the victim or the Bible on the bed."

"I suppose you have a guard in her hospital room."

"Yeah, we won't give our murderer another shot at Ms. Pope tonight."

"Well, let me know if you find anything interesting at Judith's house, and I'll call you if she wakes up."

The chief settled his cap on his head and walked out through the automatic doors. Matt and Helen chose seats on the least unappealing couch. "I wonder where Dr. Baker was tonight."

"I sent a deputy to question him. He said his wife went to bed early and he fell asleep watching television."

"No alibi," Helen concluded.

"That pretty much sums it up."

A doctor came into the waiting room and approached them. "How's Ms. Pope doing?" Matt asked.

"I think she'll live, but I can't rule out the possibility of residual effects."

Matt hated to ask, but felt like he had to. "Like what?"

"Brain damage, hearing loss, visual impairment."

Matt stood and took a step closer to the doctor. "I don't mean to seem insensitive, but as soon as she shows any signs of consciousness, I need to talk to her."

The doctor nodded. "I understand. I'll ask the nurse to keep you informed of any changes in her condition throughout the night."

After the doctor left, Matt got two Sprites from the drink machine in the hallway and returned to the couch. Helen drank a few sips of her drink, then dozed. He watched her sleep, her lips slightly parted, and he felt a tenderness that was not completely welcome.

A nurse came by every hour or so to report on Judith. At seven o'clock she said that Judith's pulse rate was up, but she was showing no other signs of wakening.

"Do you think she'll regain consciousness soon?"

"It will probably be awhile."

Helen woke up as he was talking to the nurse. "Judith still isn't awake?"

"No, not yet."

Helen stood and stretched. "I'm stiff, but at least I got some sleep. Aren't you exhausted?"

"I'm used to sleepless nights," he told her with a tired smile.

Ed Ramsey walked in at eight-thirty. His wrinkled uniform and the whiskers on his face were indications that he had not been home since the last time they saw him.

"Find any prints at Judith's house?" Matt asked.

The chief shook his head. "No, and that didn't surprise me. Whoever we're dealing with is smart enough to wear gloves. I do have some news, though."

Matt stood, and Helen sat up straighter. "What?"

"I think we've got another surviving victim."

Matt didn't even try to hide his astonishment. "Who?"

"A woman named Iris Whited. She's in her early fifties, recently widowed, and lives over in the Merrywood community."

"That's a neighborhood across town," Matt said for Helen's benefit. "It looks like our killer is expanding his area a little. You're not too excited, so apparently this 'surviving' victim can't identify the murderer."

"No, she called this morning and said she heard about Ms. Pope on the news and it made her start thinking. A little basket was delivered a few days ago with a can of chicken noodle soup and a white Bible in it. She's a member of the Eureka Baptist Church, and she thought it was from them because of the Bible. On Wednesday evening she heated up the soup for dinner. She said she only ate a few bites and started feeling dizzy. Luckily her daughter was there and took her to the emergency room. They pumped her stomach and assumed it was food poisoning. She didn't want to cause trouble for the church, so she didn't say anything."

"Who delivered the basket?"

"A man from a local delivery company. She couldn't remember the name."

Matt turned to Helen. "We need to find all the companies who provide delivery services and see if any of them have delivered little baskets with Bibles and chicken soup."

"Or if any of them are missing uniforms."

"That too, although it might be harder to determine," Matt said with a frown. "I don't guess she saved the basket?"

"No, she threw away the can and the basket, but she still has the Bible," Ed told him. "I sent some boys over to pick it up. We did find a can of Aunt Clara's Chicken Noodle Soup in the garbage at Ms. Pope's house. There was a tiny hole drilled along the top edge that had been covered with wax."

"He probably puts the Digoxin in with a hypodermic needle," Matt guessed.

"That's my theory," Ed agreed.

"But if Judith got her soup in a basket too," Matt said slowly, "that means she probably won't be able to identify the murderer either."

The police chief nodded.

"Was there a basket at Judith's house?" Matt wanted to know.

"On the counter in the kitchen. We didn't think anything about it at first, but after Ms. Whited called, we gave it a closer look. It's just a little wicker basket with what looks like paper Easter grass in the bottom."

"We need to check the houses of the other victims for a basket," Matt thought out loud. "And I'd like to interview Ms. Whited."

"I'll ask her to come by the station about two o'clock, and you can talk to her there."

Matt nodded. "Was Ms. Whited by any chance sick or a patient of Dr. Baker's?"

"Ms. Whited says she has no medical problems, and while she has met Dr. Baker, she is not a patient of his."

"What about Judith?"

"According to the emergency room doctor, she seems healthy too. We'll have to wait for her to regain consciousness and ask permission before we can get her medical records."

"Can we at least snoop around and see who might have her medical records?"

"I already have, and no doctor in Eureka admits to having her as a patient. Dr. Baker did handle childhood illnesses for her, but his secretary says she hasn't been for an office visit in almost twenty years."

"Well, that seriously weakens our medical theory and our case against the good doctor," Matt said with a sigh.

"Don't give up yet. We still need to talk to Ms. Pope, and we might find out something interesting from Ms. Whited this afternoon. In the meantime you'd better go home and get some sleep. Ms. Pope will be safe with a policeman at her door, and the hospital will call us when she wakes up."

Matt ran a hand through his hair. "I guess you're right. I'll meet you at the police station a little before two o'clock."

"Are we ready to announce that we have a suspect?"

Matt shook his head. "No, but I think it would be wise to put a twenty-four-hour tail on Dr. Baker. Tell your boys to be discreet."

The chief nodded and Matt led Helen outside.

* * *

Once they were in the Bronco, Helen reached for her cell phone and told Matt she wanted to give Nelda a report on Judith.

"We'll just stop by there and tell her in person," Matt said, and Helen let the phone drop back into her purse.

When they got to Nelda's house, she insisted that they come in for breakfast. Since they were both starving, they didn't argue much. She had eggs, bacon, homemade biscuits, and fresh-squeezed orange juice. They had barely settled around the table before Thelma and Hugh walked in.

"Have a seat," Nelda said. "I made plenty."

"Thelma won't let me eat real food for breakfast," Hugh replied with a longing look at the bacon. "She gives me bowls of oats and barley and bran flakes just like a darn horse."

"You know you have to watch your cholesterol," Thelma said, helping herself to some of everything.

"Can Hugh at least have a cup of coffee?" Nelda asked.

Thelma shook her head. "No, the caffeine is bad for his prostate."

"Don't worry about me, Nelda," Hugh said with a wave of his hand. "Thelma will probably give me some hay and a cube of sugar when we get home."

"Not if you keep misbehaving," Thelma threatened mildly as she buttered a biscuit.

Nelda stood and hurried to the refrigerator. "Here, Thelma, let me get you some Mayhaw jelly for that biscuit."

Thelma looked over at Helen and pulled a face. "That would be real nice," she said to Nelda.

"And here's a jar for you to take home, Helen." Nelda placed a jar identical to the one Thelma had given her on the table beside her plate.

"Thank you," Helen replied with a smile at Thelma.

"So, tell us about Judith," Thelma requested.

"Not much to tell," Matt answered. "She's unconscious, and the doctors don't know if she'll recover. Even if she does, they can't tell whether or not she'll have brain damage."

Nelda returned to the table. "Chief Ramsey said on the morning news that someone has been giving people baskets that contain tainted cans of Aunt Clara's Chicken Noodle Soup. He said not to accept gifts or deliveries unless you know the person who sent it."

"Personally, I wouldn't eat chicken soup no matter where it came from," Helen murmured.

"It's just awful that someone would want to poison people," Nelda added.

"It *is* awful," Matt agreed. "And you all need to be very careful for the next few days until we catch this guy. Keep your doors locked and don't even talk to strangers, much less accept deliveries from them."

Thelma reached over and patted her husband's gnarled hand. "Hugh here will protect me."

Helen was not comforted by the thought that sweet little Hugh Warren was all that stood between Thelma and danger. In an effort to change to a more pleasant subject, she turned to Nelda. "How's Glida Mae?"

Nelda sighed. "She's convinced that the murderer turned to Judith only when he was unable to get past the new locks and security bars on her house. So now she feels guilty as well as confused and terrified."

"She's going to give herself a heart attack," Helen predicted.

Thelma nodded. "It won't take a murderer to kill her."

"She's not eating or sleeping, and goodness knows if her medicine is being administered properly," Nelda told them. "I talked to Dr. Baker this morning, and he's checking to see if Medicare will pay for round-the-clock nursing care."

"Do you think they will?" Matt asked.

Nelda shook her head. "No. Glida Mae will be in a nursing home before the end of next week."

After this depressing announcement, they finished breakfast in silence. Then Matt and Helen left the others sitting around the kitchen table and went outside. "Try to get some rest," Matt told Helen as they walked up to her house.

"I will, and you need to do the same."

He nodded and climbed the steps ahead of her. She was digging in her purse for her keys when he put a hand on her arm. "You don't need your keys. Your door isn't even closed all the way."

Helen stepped up beside him and stared at the slightly open door. "I'm very careful about things like that," she said, trying to keep her voice steady. "I wouldn't have left the door unlocked."

"You were upset when I told you about Judith," Matt reminded her. "And the old wood sticks sometimes. Maybe in the confusion of trying to get to the hospital the door just didn't get closed all the way."

Helen was almost positive that she had both closed and locked her door, but arguing with Matt served no purpose, so she nodded. "That's possible, I guess."

"I'll go in with you and look around to make sure there's no one inside," he offered, and she nodded again.

The house looked just as she left it. Her half-empty glass of lemonade was on the coffee table and her pajamas were piled on the bed. But Helen couldn't shake the feeling that someone had been in her house. Matt checked each room, under beds, inside closets. He even pushed back the shower curtain and looked inside the medicine cabinet.

Helen laughed at that. "If our murderer is small enough to fit in there," she said, pointing at the medicine cabinet, "I think I can take him on."

Matt smiled back. His uniform shirt was untucked and his hair was sticking up around his head. Oddly, Helen thought he had never looked better. "Just being thorough," he said.

"I was thinking that in a few hours I might go up to your office and work on our new lists. Do you think that would be okay?"

Matt nodded. "There's always a dispatcher there, and the weekend shift will wander through from time to time, so it should be safe. I'll ask Ed to fax over what they already have on Iris Whited, and that will give you a starting point. But Dr. Baker's office will be closed because it's Saturday."

"I was hoping that his secretary might be convinced to come in and compile a list of dead patients, given the seriousness of the situation." Matt considered this for a few seconds. "You're right. I'll tell Crystal to call her. Crystal knows everybody, and the woman might be a friend or even a relative. But if that doesn't work, Crystal can strong-arm her."

"I hate for Crystal to have to work on Saturday."

"Like you said, the situation is serious enough for extreme measures, and she won't mind." Matt paused for a few seconds, thinking. "In fact, I'll tell her to come by and get you. That way neither one of you will be driving around Eureka alone." He took a step toward the front porch. "And this time when you leave, try to remember to lock your door." With a quick smile, he let himself out, and Helen watched through the open door as he hurried down the street to his Bronco. Then she closed the door and locked it.

CHAPTER 9

After dropping Helen off, Matt called Ed Ramsey. "One of us is going to have to notify the FBI that we have a possible serial killer in Eureka," the chief said.

Matt sighed. "Judge Weldon suggested that we just call and discuss the case with an agent. We can ask them if they have any perps on record with similar MOs. That kind of thing."

"But not invite them to come in on the case?"

"Not yet. They'd attract attention from the press and terrify Judith Pope, thereby making her useless to us. But as long as we contact the Feds and they are aware that we have a possible repeater . . ."

"We'll be covered," Ed Ramsey finished for him. "Okay. I'll go with that. You gonna make the call?"

"I worked with an agent from Columbus last spring. I could call him."

"Let me know how it goes," Ed commanded before he disconnected.

Matt had to call Crystal at home to get the number for the FBI office in Columbus.

"Haven't you ever heard of 411?" she grumbled.

"Why would I bother with that when I can call you?" Matt teased.

She recited the number, and he wrote it on the back of his left hand. "And would you be interested in working a little overtime this afternoon?"

"Is *interested* anything like *happy?*"

"No, it's something like wanting to catch a murderer. We've got two new victims, but both survived the Digoxin poisoning." Matt thought about Judith still unconscious at the hospital. "So far, anyway."

"I know," Crystal replied. "I watch the news."

"We need to compile lists of delivery companies," he paused, hating to say it. "We also need to get a list of Dr. Baker's patients that have died during the past two years."

"Why?"

"We have to check out all possibilities, Crystal."

"He took out my tonsils when I was six, then brought me ice cream afterward."

"I'm sorry, Crystal, but it has to be done. Do you know his secretary?"

"Mary Charles Henderson. We graduated from high school together."

"Dr. Baker said he would cooperate, so try to get your friend to go to the office and fax us a list. I'm going home to sleep for a couple of hours, then I have a meeting with one of our survivors at two o'clock. I'll come see how much progress you've made as soon as I can."

He disconnected the call, then dialed the FBI's number while driving down the road. He got an answering machine and left a message. At his parents' home, he took a quick shower and collapsed onto the bed. He slept for three blissful hours before his mother woke him up.

"It's an FBI agent from Columbus," she whispered, her eyes full of concern. "He said he had to talk to you right away."

"Thanks, Mama." Matt pushed himself into a sitting position and took the phone.

"Sorry to disturb your beauty rest, Clevenger," the voice on the other end of the line quipped.

"I'd rather talk to you than sleep any day, Barry," Matt assured him.

There was a guttural laugh. "So, what's up?"

"I'm not really sure that anything is, but I've got two dead women and two attempted murders. It looks like they all overdosed on Digoxin."

"Which is . . ." Barry Stanger prompted.

"A heart medication. All the women had high dosages in their systems."

"Were the survivors able to identify the guy?"

"One's still unconscious, and the other said a basket containing poisoned chicken noodle soup and a Bible was delivered to her house. She didn't know the delivery person. Said he was from a delivery company. I'm meeting with her this afternoon, and I should know more after that."

"So, are you calling us in?"

"Not yet," Matt replied carefully.

"What do you want from us, then?"

"Support, suggestions, that kind of thing. I was hoping you could run this MO through your computer and see if you have any others."

"I can do that," Barry agreed. "All the cases have taken place in Coosetta County?"

"Yes."

"Hmmm," Barry said thoughtfully. "Any new folks move into that particular area recently?"

"A few," Matt responded. "We've checked them out." He thought of Helen. She had moved right into the neighborhood on the night of the second murder, but she couldn't possibly be considered a suspect. She wasn't a resident at the time of the first murder, and the fact that she had a gun and was very secretive about her past shouldn't be held against her.

"You still there, Clevenger?" the FBI agent asked.

"I'm still here," Matt replied.

"I might drive down there on Monday. Nothing official, just kind of look around."

Matt was disappointed but not surprised. Barry had to cover himself too. "Meet me at the sheriff's office, and I'll go over what we've got."

"And I'll bring whatever I can come up with. Give me the names of your victims."

Matt recited the names and ended his call. Rubbing his eyes, he tried to think clearly, then pushed the number three on his speed dial. He got Brian's answering machine and left a brief message. The phone rang almost immediately.

"Put me to work!" the PI said in salutation.

"There was another murder attempt last night," Matt informed him. "And one on Wednesday that we just found out about."

"Since you used the word *attempt*, I'm assuming the most recent wave of victims are still alive."

"Yes, but the murderer sent the tainted soup in an anonymous little gift basket, so the victims can't identify him."

"Man, if you don't have *all* the bad luck," Brian expressed his sympathy. "You need me to check something out?"

"I want you to get me everything you can find on Judith Pope and Iris Whited. Fax your reports to the office."

"I'll get right on it. What kind of a timeline am I looking at?"

"I need it in two hours."

"Man, you're not easy to please."

"Thanks, Brian. And in your spare time, go ahead and dig a little deeper on Helen Tyler," Matt added reluctantly. "I'd like to know what day she left West Virginia and if she came directly here. And maybe a few more details about the romance with her student."

There was a brief pause. "Okay."

"Call me as soon as you have something."

Feeling like a traitor, Matt fell back against his pillow.

* * *

Crystal knocked on Helen's door at 1:45 and woke her up. Helen took time to brush her teeth and pull her hair into a ponytail, then joined Crystal outside. She saw Nelda and Sydney standing on Glida Mae's front porch and told Crystal she needed to check on them.

"We've got work to do," Crystal replied irritably.

"This will only take a few minutes, and you're early anyway," Helen said, then walked down the steps and over to the house next door. Crystal muttered something under her breath as she walked to her car.

"Well, good afternoon," Nelda greeted Helen.

"Hey, Nelda. And Sydney, you're still glowing with healthy pregnancy," she teased. The other woman gave her a smirk, then Helen realized that Glida Mae was standing in the open doorway. "Well, Glida Mae! What a wonderful surprise!"

"The nurse just left after giving Glida Mae her bath," Nelda said. "Doesn't she look nice?"

"Just like Joan Fontaine," Helen agreed, and Glida Mae laughed.

"Oh, Helen, today I applied my makeup using Tallulah Bankhead's signature style."

"Get your ancient actresses straight, will you?" Sydney said to Helen from behind her hand.

Helen smiled. "Well, you look very pretty anyway."

Glida Mae took a step forward, actually out of her house and onto the porch. "I've had some good news," she confided. "Dr. Baker came over and talked to Nelda and me. He *believes* me about the murderer," she said with a disapproving look at Nelda.

"It's not that the rest of us don't believe you," Nelda began, but Glida Mae waved her hand.

"You all think I'm crazy, but Dr. Baker recognizes the danger and wants to put me in a nice assisted-living complex for my own safety until the murderer is caught."

Helen was uneasy about their best suspect providing "safety" for Glida Mae, but she nodded. "I think that is very wise."

Glida Mae pulled a pamphlet from her pocket and handed it to Helen. "It's called Gentle Haven. Doesn't that sound peaceful to you?"

"And secure," Helen agreed. "So, when do you move?"

"First thing on Monday morning. Sydney's going to drive me," Glida Mae announced.

"Unless I die of a heatstroke first," Sydney muttered. "Or have this baby."

"Is there any chance that the baby will come early?" Nelda asked in surprise.

Sydney rubbed her distended abdomen. "With my luck? None whatsoever."

"Who will take me to Gentle Haven if you have your baby before Monday?" Glida Mae wanted to know.

"I will," Helen promised.

"Oh thank you, Helen." Glida Mae seemed pleased.

"Well, I'd better go. I just wanted to say hello." Helen stepped down to the lawn and Sydney joined her.

"I heard about those women who ate poisoned soup. It's hard to believe anything that exciting could happen in Eureka," Sydney whispered.

Helen wanted to explain just how unexciting the recent events were, but knew she couldn't. "Did you bring your family to visit your grandmother?" she asked instead.

"No, the kids have gone to Dollywood with their father, and Cole is at a veterinary convention in Panama City. Ordinarily I would have gone with him, but the doctor said it was too late in my pregnancy for me to travel." This comment elicited another smirk. "Grandma didn't want me to stay out on the farm by myself, so I'm going to spend the weekend with her."

"That's a good idea with all this poisoned soup around," Helen told her. Then before Sydney could ask any more questions, Helen turned and called to Glida Mae. "And let me know if you need a ride on Monday."

The butterscotch curls bobbed. "I will."

* * *

When Matt reached the sheriff's department that afternoon, it was almost four o'clock. He was pleased to see Crystal's Accord in the lot across the street and parked his Bronco right beside it. Crystal and Helen were in his office when he walked in. "So, what did y'all find out?"

"Dr. Baker's patient death rate is twice the AMA average for general practitioners in the state of Georgia," Helen announced.

Matt raised an eyebrow. "Impressive research."

Crystal waved this aside. "She's a show-off. It only took her two minutes to come up with that statistic thanks to the Internet. And you have to keep in mind that Dr. Baker treats a lot of elderly people so of course some of them are going to die. And even if he was a murderer, he'd have to be more than crazy to kill his own patients," Crystal defended the doctor.

Helen looked back at Matt. "That would eventually cause suspicion."

"Not if he chooses his victims carefully and changes the death methods," Matt replied.

Crystal crossed her arms over her chest. "I will never believe that Dr. Baker killed anyone. We're wasting our time investigating him."

Matt winked at Helen, then asked about delivery companies.

"There are three official delivery companies in Eureka, one industrious housewife who runs a casual one from her home, and several florists who will deliver items upon request and for an outrageous fee. We contacted all of them, and no one has any record of delivering baskets of chicken soup and Bibles. But one of the owners said they all do a lot of cash business that doesn't get written down."

"To avoid paying taxes," Matt guessed.

"That would be a reasonable assumption. Anyway, she said that if someone walked in with four or five little baskets, gave them the addresses and paid cash, they probably wouldn't keep a record."

"The employee who handled the job might remember, though."

Helen nodded. "We asked them all to check with their delivery people and let us know. How did things go with Ms. Whited?"

"Oh fine. She's a very nice lady who doesn't know a thing about the murders." Matt was frowning. "What we need is a way to look at all this information at one time and figure what direction to go."

"You mean a victim board like on *CSI?*" Crystal asked.

"Exactly." Matt looked around. "But since here at the Coosetta County sheriff's department we're a little below the cutting edge of technology, I think we'll have to use the wall. Crystal, I need a bunch of index cards."

"What? Now you want me to run to the Piggly Wiggly?"

Matt pulled out his wallet and handed the secretary a five-dollar bill. "If necessary, but check upstairs first. I think Myron uses them to keep up with prisoners' personal effects. He might sell us some."

"And what's Helen going to do while I'm searching for index cards?"

"She's going to help me set up the wall, but I think the note cards are the key to solving this case."

Crystal looked mildly appeased as she walked toward the stairs.

Matt used some electrical tape to divide the wall into four columns. "First we'll do a victim wall, then a suspect wall. We'll start with Mary Jean Freeburg since she was the first to die." Matt wrote the name across the top of the first column in permanent marker.

"She's the first one that we know of," Helen said.

Matt glanced over his shoulder. "Don't cheer me up." He moved to the next column and wrote *Robyn Howell.*

"That won't wash off," Helen pointed out. "That's the reason they call it *permanent.*"

Matt didn't even turn around. "Murray Monk can paint over it when he gets here in November."

There was a picture of each victim in their file, and Matt had Helen tape them beside their name. "They seem more real when you can see their faces," Helen said softly.

"It makes this personal," Matt agreed. "Here's a map of Eureka." He spread the map out and held it against the wall while Helen taped. "We'll pinpoint each victim's address and see if that tells us anything."

"Like if the murderer is killing people in locations that make the shape of a star?" Crystal asked, walking back through the door with a stack of index cards.

"You've really got to stop watching so much television," Matt said. "Helen, if you'll tape up pictures from the crime scene, I'll start writing pertinent information on the cards. Then we'll move on to Robyn Howell."

"What am I supposed to do?" Crystal wanted to know.

"How about ordering pizza? Get one with everything on it," Matt suggested.

The secretary put her hands on her hips. "Are you going to tell me that pizza is also crucial to the case?"

"We'll never find the killer if we starve to death," Matt countered.

"You'd better get your wallet back out because I'm not paying for the pizza," Crystal muttered as she walked back to her desk.

* * *

It took them two hours and a large pizza to get all the victims onto Matt's wall. Then they stood back and studied it.

Crystal stepped closer so she could read the index cards. She pointed at one, then turned back to Matt. "What's this?"

He joined her by the wall. "Ed called and said that there were traces of a yet-unidentified substance on the wicker baskets delivered to Judith Pope and Mrs. Whited."

Crystal processed this information. "When will we know what it is?"

Matt shrugged. "The lab in Atlanta is trying to identify it."

"There's something that's been bothering me," Helen said, pointing at two additional cards. "If Robyn Howell and Mary Jean Freeburg received baskets, why didn't the police find them? And why did both of those women put the white Bible on their beds? Was it just coincidence?"

Matt shook his head. "My guess is that our killer changed delivery methods. I think he took the soup and Bible personally to the first two victims. Then he must have decided that was too risky. So he hired a delivery company."

"Which was safer but less effective, since the two cans of soup he sent by messenger weren't fatal," Helen pointed out.

Crystal frowned. "Maybe he mixed up a weak batch of poisoned chicken soup."

"Or the victims just didn't eat enough since he wasn't there to encourage them," Helen suggested.

Matt moved to the wall on his left. "We'll worry about that later. For now, let's list possible suspects." He wrote Dr. Baker's name in permanent marker, and Crystal groaned. "Who else?"

"Robyn Howell's ex-husband," Helen suggested. "He's a wealthy man now, thanks to our murderer." Matt wrote *Scott Howell* on the wall. "And your friend Elvis Hatcher."

Matt looked back over his shoulder. "I thought we'd established that Elvis doesn't have the mental capabilities to commit multiple murders."

"He has enough sense to fix houses. You might be underestimating him," Helen insisted.

"Go ahead and write my name up there," Crystal said.

Matt turned and looked at her. "Why would I do that?"

Crystal shrugged. "Because I'm more likely to kill someone than Dr. Baker is. And what about the nurses who took care of Mrs. Freeburg? I thought we were investigating them."

"The police did, and none of them had anything to gain by her death or any connection to the other victims," Matt replied.

Helen stared at their small list. "I hate to bring up another literary reference that doesn't involve comic books," she began slowly, "but I read a Sherlock Holmes book one time where the murderer was one of the victims. He faked his own attack to divert suspicion."

Matt nodded. "So you think we should include Judith and Mrs. Whited on our suspect list?"

"Well, we at least need to look them over."

Matt smiled. "You might have a career in law enforcement," he teased. "Ed and the police department are already investigating Mrs. Whited. We'll handle Judith if she ever wakes up," he added grimly, then printed the names of the two surviving victims at the bottom of his list in parenthesis. "If we follow the money, which we must, we'll also have to add Martin Freeburg."

"Mrs. Freeburg's son?" Crystal demanded. "That's as bad as Dr. Baker."

Matt ignored her. "Judith has no family, and Mrs. Whited's estate is still tied up in probate since her husband just died a few weeks ago. I don't see that anyone would have profited from their deaths, so now we'll look for connections between the victims."

"Mrs. Freeburg and Robyn Howell were both sick, but not the other two."

"Mrs. Freeburg and Mrs. Whited were members of the Eureka Baptist Church, but Robyn Howell was an atheist and Judith didn't attend church anywhere."

"Iris Whited and Mary Jean Freeburg were both widowed, Robyn Howell was divorced, and Judith is single."

"All the women lived alone," Matt agreed with a nod. "That would make killing them easier."

"But why did someone *want* to kill them?" Helen asked, and they all stared at the writing on the wall.

"I don't know," Matt said with a sigh.

"Judith worked at the library, and Mrs. Whited was on the library board."

"But Mrs. Freeburg was homebound, and Robyn Howell didn't even have a library card."

Matt raised an eyebrow. "You're sure?"

Helen nodded. "We checked."

"Judith and Robyn Howell both have college degrees. Mrs. Whited and Mary Jean Freeburg just graduated from high school."

Crystal shook her head. "It doesn't make sense," she said, her frustration obvious. "They have nothing in common."

"Except that somehow they attracted a murderer," Matt replied. "We just have to keep looking. Either we'll find a new connection or evidence to support one of these. But it's getting late, so I think we should call it a night. I'll be back up here in the morning, and we can work on a list of alibis for our suspects."

Helen looked down at her hands. "I'm sorry, Matt, but I don't work on Sunday. It's against my religion," she added so he wouldn't think she was just lazy.

He smiled. "That's okay. Crystal and I can handle the investigation until Monday."

Crystal frowned. "What about me? I think working on Sunday is against my religion too."

"Yeah, well murder is against mine," Matt told her. "Be here at ten o'clock. Helen, I'm going to check with the hospital and see how Judith Pope is doing, then I'll take you home."

Crystal raised an eyebrow. "You don't want me to drop her off?"

Matt shook his head. "No, I have to check on Miss Glida Mae anyway."

Crystal left and Helen stared at the wall while Matt made his phone call. He joined her a few minutes later. "They said that Judith is waking up. Would you like to ride to the hospital with me?"

Helen nodded and they moved toward the door.

* * *

Matt called Ed Ramsey on his cell phone as they drove to the hospital. Ed was taking his wife out to dinner, but promised to meet them at the hospital as soon as he could. Matt parked the Bronco, then led the way inside. A woman at the information desk directed them up to the third floor. Matt showed his identification to the policeman guarding Judith's door, and they were admitted.

Judith was lying very still on the hospital bed. Her plain face was pale, and her hair was matted and tangled. They approached the bed as a nurse came in. She took Judith by the shoulders and shook her gently. "Come on, now. It's time to wake up. You've got company," she added, and Judith's eyes flew open.

"I'm going to go let the doctor know she's awake," the nurse said. "I'll be at the nurses' station if you need me." She slipped out into the hall, and Matt returned his attention to Judith.

The patient held a hand up to shield her eyes from the light, then looked around the room. "Where am I?" she asked.

Helen stepped closer and gave her a reassuring smile. "You're in the hospital. You've been sick."

Judith processed this information, then nodded. "I remember getting so dizzy. Then I fell down and couldn't get up."

Matt moved forward. "You ate poisoned soup, Judith, and I need to ask you some questions."

Judith's mouth tightened at the sound of his voice, but she nodded.

"During the last few days, did someone deliver a basket with the soup and a Bible in it?"

Judith nodded again. "On Monday, I think."

"Do you remember which company delivered it?"

She shook her head. "No. It came at night. I was surprised to be getting something, anything." She paused as color stained her cheeks, and Matt realized that she regretted this admission. "No, I don't know what company delivered it," she concluded firmly.

"Did you have to sign for it?"

Judith thought for a minute. "No, he just verified my name and address, then gave me the basket."

"So the delivery person was male. Old, young, tall, short?" Matt asked.

Judith looked irritated by all the questions. "Young, I think, and sort of medium height." She put a hand to her head. "I have a terrible headache."

"I'll go tell the nurse," Helen offered.

Matt waited until the door closed behind her, then turned back to Judith. "I'm sorry you're not feeling well, but this is very important.

Two women have been killed, and we have to find out who is doing this before more people die."

Judith nodded warily, so he continued.

"Has Dr. Baker been to see you lately?"

Judith thought for a few seconds. "You think Dr. Baker tried to kill me?"

"We aren't accusing anyone yet. We're just collecting information."

"Dr. Baker comes by sometimes. I can't remember if he did this week."

"He was your grandmother's doctor, and you went to see him as a child, but not recently."

"I'm never sick," Judith said. "Dr. Baker used to give me immunizations and things when I was young, but I don't need a doctor now."

Matt tried not to let his disappointment show. "What about Elvis Hatcher? He's the one who found you. He said you had a roof leak and he was coming to check it out."

Judith frowned. "I did tell him a couple of weeks ago that I had a leak, but I didn't know he was coming last night."

"Has he ever said anything threatening or tried to hurt you in any way?"

Judith looked at him as though he was crazy. "Elvis?"

Matt glanced down, embarrassed. "What about Scott Howell—do you know him?"

"I've never even heard of a Scott Howell."

"How about Martin Freeburg?"

Judith's expression became guarded. "He comes to all the library board meetings. He's not an official member and he can't vote, but they let him sit in."

The fact that Martin Freeburg regularly went to meetings he didn't have to attend surprised Matt. "Why would he want to do that?"

Judith shrugged. "His mother was bedridden and got deliveries from our bookmobile. Mr. Freeburg wanted the library to buy a new one and he came to the meetings so he could put pressure on the board members."

"Were there any plans to buy a new bookmobile?"

Judith nodded. "The Eureka Literary Guild had donated the proceeds of the annual cookbook sale to add a Braille section to the library. Mr. Freeburg wanted the board to take the money and buy a new bookmobile instead. The board was actually considering it," Judith's tone became indignant, "so I called the Literary Guild and told them. They threatened to withdraw their donation if the funds weren't used as they had specified."

"So you and Martin Freeburg are not best friends," Matt concluded.

Judith shrugged. "He wasn't pleased by my interference."

"Are you a member of the library board?"

Judith blushed again. "Oh no. I just take minutes."

Helen walked back in, followed by a nurse. "The doctor says you can take these for your headache." The nurse poured two capsules from a little paper cup into Judith's hand. Judith swallowed them dry, then leaned her head against her pillow. "I think you've talked long enough for tonight," she said to Matt. "You can come back in the morning if you like."

Matt accepted their dismissal reluctantly. "We'll see you tomorrow," he told Judith, and she acknowledged this with a weak nod.

On the way home, Matt asked Helen if she was hungry.

"No, that pizza is still with me. And I've got Oreos at home if you want something sweet."

He glanced over at her wide, innocent look. She was sweet all right, and spending so much time with her was giving him all kinds of contradictory feelings. He had to concentrate on the murder case right now and didn't need distractions. "Thanks anyway, but I think I'll just check on Miss Glida Mae and head home."

"Oh, that reminds me," Helen said, twisting toward him slightly. "Glida Mae is going to a nursing home called Gentle Haven on Monday. Sydney Brackner's going to take her."

Matt felt a wave of sadness. "I knew it would happen eventually, but . . ."

Helen nodded. "Don't feel bad about it. Glida Mae is excited. She'll probably show you the brochure."

Matt smiled. "I'm glad she's not unhappy about the move."

Matt parked behind Helen's old Escort. "Well, if you and Crystal need me tomorrow, I guess I could consider the ox to be in the mire."

Matt raised an eyebrow. "What ox?"

Helen laughed. "It's an old Mormon phrase meaning an emergency that causes a person to do something that wouldn't ordinarily be considered appropriate for the Sabbath day."

"Thanks for the offer. I think we can get through tomorrow without you."

Helen put her hand on the handle, but didn't open the door. Instead, she looked up at him. "I worry about you, Matt. You work so hard, and you never sleep . . ." She stopped, a blush rising into her cheeks. "I'm sorry. It's none of my business."

Matt clutched the steering wheel and stared through the windshield as a tense silence filled the Bronco. Helen made no further attempt to get out of the car, and finally Matt sighed, then turned to her. "I have to work hard," he admitted. "Otherwise I'll have to think, or even worse, remember."

Helen reached over and put a hand on his arm. "About your family?"

He nodded.

"I don't know how you survived it—losing them all at once like that."

Matt wanted to answer but didn't know if he could. He opened his mouth and closed it again. Then somehow he found the courage to respond. "Honestly, I don't know either."

"Do you have a picture of them?" Helen asked softly.

Matt rarely looked at their pictures himself and couldn't imagine showing them to anyone else, even Helen, so he sidestepped the question. "Most of them were destroyed in the tornado."

She accepted this with a little nod, then opened the door and climbed out. "Sure you don't want an Oreo for the road?" she asked with a smile.

"I'll take a rain check on that," he told her. "I'm going to check on Miss Glida Mae, then head home."

Helen waved as she walked into the house. He waited until she had disappeared inside, then got out of the Bronco and walked to Miss Glida Mae's front porch.

* * *

Helen woke up on Sunday morning with a migraine. She was nearly blind with pain and had to search through all her things before she found her prescription medication. Gratefully she took the pills, then got back into bed and waited for the agony to recede.

By one-thirty she was feeling better, so she climbed out of bed and started toward the kitchen, but a knock on the door stopped her. She looked through the peephole to see the very pregnant Sydney Brackner standing on her front porch holding a pie. Helen pulled the door open, and Sydney gave her a smirk.

"If you ask me why I haven't had this baby yet, you'll get this pie in your face."

Helen smiled. "I don't have to ask. I know you're just prolonging this pregnancy to get attention."

Sydney blinked, then laughed. "You've gotten to know me pretty well in a short period of time. Grandma sent you this." She extended the pie.

"Thanks." Helen accepted the gift. "Won't you come in?"

"Naw, I just came up to see why you weren't at church." Sydney held up a hand. "Don't get the wrong idea. I'm not a very caring person, and I never spend my Sunday afternoons looking for lost sheep. So don't expect a pie every time you skip church."

It was Helen's turn to laugh. "I don't plan to make a habit of missing my meetings, but I get migraines and I had a terrible one this morning."

Sydney was instantly contrite. "Are you feeling better?"

"Much better, thank goodness. How about a piece of your grandmother's pie?"

"I ate two pieces at Grandma's house already," Sydney said with regret. "I'm going to weigh three hundred pounds by the time this baby is born."

"You're the most attractive pregnant woman I've ever seen."

Sydney narrowed her eyes. "Did Grandma tell you to say that?"

"No," Helen denied.

Sydney looked pleased as she turned away from the door and started down the porch steps. Then she stopped abruptly. "Oh, and

Glida Mae has decided that she wants you to take her to Gentle Haven tomorrow. She's afraid I'll go into labor and mess up her trip." Sydney rolled her eyes. "Only someone as crazy as Miss Glida Mae would think *that* was possible before my due date."

"I'll take care of Glida Mae," Helen promised. "You concentrate on having that baby."

Sydney nodded and started across Glida Mae's lawn.

CHAPTER 10

On Sunday morning, Matt decided cutting the grass could wait a week and drove to the cemetery instead. Then he went into the office. Crystal arrived at ten-thirty and they tracked down alibis, then added them to his wall. Matt gave Ed Ramsey time to finish Sunday dinner before he called the chief at home.

"You haven't heard anything back from the delivery companies?" Ed wanted to know.

"No," Matt replied. "And I was wondering if your boys could question them. An official visit might jar some memories."

"I'll send out a couple of guys tomorrow. When's your FBI friend coming?"

"First thing in the morning," Matt said morosely.

After his conversation with Ed Ramsey, Matt and Crystal worked for a couple of hours, then he sent the secretary home. Alone in the quiet office, Matt stared at the wall until his vision started to blur. Finally, he said good-bye to the dispatcher and headed for Ivy Lane. He spoke briefly with Miss Glida Mae, who was all packed and ready for her trip to Gentle Haven the next day.

"Helen's going to take me," she informed him with a smile.

Matt was surprised. "I thought Sydney was taking you."

Miss Glida Mae shook her curl-covered head. "Sydney's right ready to have her baby, and it's been years since I did any work as a midwife. So I decided it was more sensible to let Helen drive me."

Matt raised both eyebrows. "You were a midwife?"

"Back in the thirties before I went to Hollywood. I trained under Dr. Baker's father, and he said I had a real gift for medicine. He begged me to continue my training, but my artistic talent would not be denied."

Matt nodded. "No, of course not." They talked for a few more minutes, then Matt found an excuse to leave. After saying good-bye to Miss Glida Mae, he turned toward the street. He knew he should go home and spend some time with his parents, but his grandmother's old house drew him like a magnet. Helen answered the door, looking pale and tired. He was immediately concerned. "Is something wrong?"

Helen shook her head. "I had a bad headache this morning."

"Probably eyestrain from staring at all those lists," Matt muttered, feeling guilty. "I've been working you too hard."

"No, I just get them sometimes. I was about to make a grilled cheese sandwich for dinner. Would you like one?"

Matt was going to decline, but his stomach growled at that moment and Helen laughed as he put a hand to his midsection. "Actually, I haven't eaten anything since this morning."

"Come on in," Helen invited, then turned back toward the kitchen.

The dreary old kitchen seemed warm and cozy as Matt sat at the tiny formica table and watched Helen cook.

"So, did you and Crystal make any progress on the case today?" she asked as she put two sandwiches on his plate.

"We found out that Judith was at work when Mary Jean Freeburg and Robyn Howell were killed. Mrs. Whited was out of town with her daughter on the night of the first murder and at a Literary Guild meeting the night of the second. So I think we can forget the Sherlock Holmes theory."

Helen nodded. "What about our other, more reasonable suspects?"

"We already knew that Dr. Baker has only the weakest of alibis. Martin Freeburg has none at all, and neither does Elvis. Scott Howell was home alone the night of Mrs. Freeburg's murder, but he was with a bunch of friends hunting when his ex-wife died."

"That sounds kind of convenient."

"Yeah, Mr. Howell is not off the hook."

Helen stood. "Would you like some of Nelda Lovell's coconut cream pie?"

"I'd love some," he said, and Helen sliced him a large piece.

"I'm going to be a little late coming into the office tomorrow. I promised to take Glida Mae to the nursing home."

"She told me," Matt said as he finished his second sandwich. Then he forked a piece of pie into his mouth. "But don't leave me alone with Crystal for too long."

"I'll hurry," Helen promised.

Matt ate the rest of his pie, then pushed back from the table and stretched his arms above his head. "Well, I'd better get home. I try to spend a little time with my parents on Sunday."

"A good, loyal son," Helen replied with a smile.

"I don't know about that," he said as they walked into the living room. Then he pointed to the stack of computer printouts she had brought home with her. "I'll pack this stuff up and take it with me tonight so you won't have to lug it in tomorrow."

"I don't know why we're even bothering to take this stuff back," Helen said. "I've got it all memorized."

Matt smiled. "We'll have the information from my private investigator, Brian West, on Iris Whited and Judith tomorrow."

"We can make more index cards, and then maybe we'll find a connection."

"We have to find a connection," Matt replied.

He drove home and just had time to take a shower before Ed Ramsey called. "What?" Matt, still dripping wet, demanded into the receiver.

"Meet me at the hospital," Ed said without preamble. "Judith Pope had a dream about the murders."

Matt clutched the phone. "You mean the attempt on her life?"

"No, she saw the murderer's lab."

"How is that possible?" Matt asked.

"That's what we've got to find out."

* * *

After Matt left, Helen took some more of her migraine medication as a precaution, then washed their dishes. She heard a noise in the backyard and peeked out to see the Nguyen children slip in through the gate. She picked up a bag of cookies and opened the back door.

"Hello," she greeted them, and they turned to look at her. "I'm so glad you came to see me. I'm in the mood for cookies, but I hate to eat alone." She removed a cookie from the bag and took a bite, then crossed the lawn to the spot where the children were standing. She extended the bag, and after a brief hesitation, Tan accepted it. "It's such a beautiful evening," she continued, hoping she would eventually say something that would prompt them to respond. "I love summer nights when it stays light so long." Still no response. "Why don't we eat over here under this big oak tree?"

They followed her to the huge oak tree, then waited for her to sit on the soft grass before following suit. She noticed that they would not eat while she was watching, but if she looked over at the house or into Glida Mae's yard they would quickly take a bite. "I wish I had some toys or books for you," she said, thinking that she needed to make another trip to Wal-Mart soon.

"If you have some paper, we could draw pictures," Tan suggested, and Helen smiled at him.

"I'll be right back," she promised.

She found a tablet of stationery and two felt pens and returned to the big tree. She distributed the writing equipment, then settled back against the tree trunk. She always felt a little drained after a migraine, so she was content to sit quietly and enjoy the gentle breeze. She looked around the yard and could almost see a small boy with curly, dark hair playing baseball with a miniature Sydney near a somewhat smaller tree.

Tan interrupted her reverie by handing her his piece of stationary. On it he had written *Thank you for the cookies* in a neat, precise script. Lin stepped up beside him and extended her sheet of paper. She had drawn a stick woman with yellow hair and blue-green eyes. "That's you," Tan explained unnecessarily.

Helen nodded, unaccountably touched by the childish drawing. "Thank you both. I will put these on my refrigerator." And she did as soon as the children left. As she stared at the pictures in the quiet house, she wondered if her parents had been so wrong to encourage her to marry and raise a family. The life she had chosen would have been solitary, but the life she'd been stuck with was downright lonely.

Before she had a chance to get too depressed, there was a knock on the door. It was Nelda accompanied by the Warrens. "We won't come in," Thelma said before Helen had a chance to offer. "But Sydney said you were sick, and we just wanted to stop by and check on you."

"That was very kind," Helen said with a smile. "I'm much better now, and I'd be glad if you'd visit for a while."

"We're taking our evening walk," Thelma said. "I'd be satisfied to walk around the block a few times, but Hugh likes to go down to the park. Says it's because of the track, but I think he just likes to ogle the jogging girls."

"Not ogling anything they aren't displaying for all the world to see," Hugh defended himself. "Come on, Thelma."

The Warrens left, and Helen turned to Nelda. "You'll come in, won't you? I've got some delicious coconut pie."

Nelda smiled. "I can visit for a few minutes. Sydney's gone back home, and it always seems a little lonely at my house when she leaves. And I'm glad you liked the pie." Nelda followed Helen inside and to the kitchen.

Helen opened the refrigerator and removed the pie. "I really am going to have a piece, and I'd be happy to share some back with you."

"Thank you, dear, but I wouldn't care for any." Nelda looked at what was left of the pie. "My goodness, you *do* like coconut pie!"

Helen laughed. "It is wonderful, but I didn't eat all this. Matt had a big piece when he was here earlier."

Nelda's expression became thoughtful. "Matt is over here quite a bit."

Helen put her pie onto a plate and got a fork from the drawer. "Just work stuff," Helen said quickly, then felt heat rise in her cheeks.

"Oh, I'm sure," Nelda replied. "It's just that . . . well, I don't know exactly how to say this, and the last thing in the world I want to do is offend you."

Helen smiled. "You couldn't possibly offend me. What do you want to say?"

"It's just that Matt is such a handsome, charming man, but he's damaged—emotionally, I mean. The death of his family was devastating, and I'd hate to see you fall in love with him if he can't return the feelings."

Helen's smile dimmed a little, but she nodded bravely. "Don't worry. I know better than to fall in love with any man, especially one with as much emotional baggage as Matt Clevenger."

Before Nelda could reply, there was a knock on the door. Helen opened it to find Matt standing on the porch. Hoping that the walls were thick enough that he hadn't heard her recent conversation, she invited him inside. "You're just in time to eat the last of Nelda's pie."

"I won't say no," he said, then nodded at the older woman. "Hey, Miss Nelda."

"Good evening, Matt. Tell your parents I said hello. Now that I work in children's church, I rarely see them."

"I sure will."

Helen saw the tension around his mouth and frowned. "Where have you been?"

"The hospital," Matt said as he took a seat at the little table. "Ed Ramsey called and told me that Judith had a dream about the murderer's lab. Not her attempted poisoning, but preparations made by our killer in a workroom of some kind."

Helen frowned. "How?"

Matt shrugged. "We're not sure. She says she's had several dreams during the time she's been in the hospital, and they are fairly detailed."

"Was she able to identify the murderer?" Nelda wanted to know.

"No, but the dreams incriminate one of our major suspects," Matt said, casting a look at Helen. She nodded, realizing that Matt didn't want to mention any names in front of Nelda. "They wouldn't be admissible in court, of course, but if they are for real, they could help us."

"What could they be besides real?" Helen asked.

"They could be hallucinations induced by some of the medication she's been given. It may be she really does know something about the murders and she's suppressed it for some reason. Or . . ." He hesitated.

"Or what?" Helen asked, leaning toward him.

"Ed thinks she might be psychic."

"And you think *Crystal* watches too much television," Helen said, dismissing this theory automatically.

Matt shrugged. "I'm too desperate to ignore anything, even help from another realm. I've arranged for a psychiatrist to come and see Judith tomorrow morning. I'm hoping the doctor will be able to determine if the dreams are authentic, and if so, enhance them."

Nelda was frowning, and Helen finally asked if something was wrong. "Oh, I hate to sound unkind."

"What?" Helen insisted.

"Well, it's just that Judith is rather starved for attention, and it makes me wonder . . ."

"You think Judith poisoned herself just to get attention?" Matt asked incredulously. "That's impossible. The police found a basket and a Bible at her house."

"Oh, no, I didn't mean that. But I think she might be enjoying the role of celebrity-victim," Nelda clarified. "And these dreams could be a way to keep attention focused on her."

Matt nodded. "I guess that is also a possibility. Unfortunately, it isn't one that will help us."

"I could be wrong, Matt," Nelda was quick to say. "You go on with the psychiatrist just as you planned." She stood. "Well, I'd better get back home. Good luck with your case."

Helen walked Nelda to the door, and when she returned, Matt was staring dejectedly at his half-eaten pie. "Nelda was just giving her opinion," Helen pointed out.

"But she has good instincts, and she knows Judith as well as anyone. I'll still have the psychiatrist work with her, but I don't think we'll find the killer through psychic means." He scraped what was left of his pie into the garbage, then rinsed his plate in the sink. "Well, I've eaten enough of your food for one day. I'll see you in the morning."

Helen followed him to the door.

Matt paused as he reached for the doorknob. "When you get Miss Glida Mae to the nursing home, will you do me a favor?" he asked.

"Of course," Helen replied promptly.

"Tell them to make a big note on her chart saying that all visitors are to be cleared with me personally, including Dr. Baker."

Helen blinked, then nodded. "You think Glida Mae really has seen the murderer?"

"I just want to play it safe. Lock your door," he instructed, then stepped out into the fading light.

* * *

On Monday morning when Helen arrived at Glida Mae's, Nelda was already there trying to get the actress to eat her breakfast. Helen picked up the suitcases waiting by the door. "You'd better hurry and eat or we're going to be late!" she called to Glida Mae.

Glida Mae hesitated for a second, then spooned some cereal into her mouth.

Helen took the suitcases to her car, and by the time she had returned, Glida Mae had eaten enough of her cereal to satisfy Nelda. After a round of hugs, Glida Mae climbed into the passenger seat of Helen's car. Then Helen saw tears in Nelda's eyes.

"I thought Glida Mae was going to be the one to cry," Helen teased gently.

"Glida Mae doesn't have a firm enough grip on reality to recognize the significance of this moment," Nelda explained. "This neighborhood was built at the end of the depression, and up until recently, most of the original owners still lived here. Now the Warrens and I are the only ones left."

"I'm sorry."

Nelda gave her a sad smile. "Me too, but I guess there's no stopping time." She looked around. "Some people would call a metal fabrication plant progress, but I keep remembering this street the way it used to look when I was a young mother. People called it Diaper Row because we all dried our laundry on clotheslines. It didn't seem like such a special sight back then—diapers flapping in the wind as far as your eye could see. But now, I'd give a lot to see some diapers drying on the line."

"Like you said, there's no stopping time," Helen said softly.

Nelda wiped her eyes. "Thank you for taking Glida Mae to Gentle Haven, dear. I'd offer to go with you, but I think it will be easier to say good-bye here." Helen nodded that she understood, and Nelda turned to wave at Glida Mae. "Drive carefully."

For the first few minutes Helen had to concentrate on the traffic and her directions to the nursing home. Glida Mae was so quiet that Helen thought she'd fallen asleep. Then the older woman spoke. "You'll have to take care of Nelda while I'm gone. She'll be lost without me."

Helen was amused by Glida Mae's skewed concept of her relationship with Nelda. "I will."

"And I don't know what poor Dr. Baker will do with himself now that he won't have to check on me during the night."

"Dr. Baker checks on you at night?" Helen asked in surprise.

"Not every night, of course," Glida Mae said with a trace of impatience. "But often. Sometimes he rings the doorbell, but I tell him it's not proper for a single girl to receive male visitors after dark."

Helen gripped the steering wheel. She would have been truly alarmed by the thought of Dr. Baker walking around near her house during the night if she didn't know Glida Mae was delusional. "I thought it was the murderer that you saw at night."

"Oh, I see them both," Glida Mae claimed.

"How can you tell them apart?" Helen asked with flagging patience.

"I can recognize Dr. Baker by his bow tie," Glida Mae exclaimed as if Helen's question were ridiculous.

Helen frowned. "How do you recognize the murderer?"

Glida Mae shuddered. "He wears a hat and coat even though it's summertime. But I don't have to see him to know when he's near. I can *feel* him."

"You feel him?"

"I think I must have some undeveloped psychic powers," Glida Mae replied in complete seriousness.

Helen considered this, then came to a decision. "I'm going to write down my cell phone number for you, and I want you to do me a big favor. If Dr. Baker comes to see you at Gentle Haven, I want you to call me."

"Why?"

"There's something I need to ask him, but he's so busy. If he comes to see you, I could just ask him then."

Glida Mae looked perplexed for a few seconds, then nodded. "I'll call you if he comes."

Helen sighed with relief as Gentle Haven came into view. "Well, here we are." The facility appeared to be a beautiful combination of comfort and safety. The brick security walls were covered with ivy, which softened their appearance. After checking in with the security guard, Helen drove to the administrative building.

Glida Mae twisted in her seat to look out the window as they passed a small park. "I already love it here," she whispered, then glanced back at Helen. "For weeks I've been afraid to close my eyes at night." She sighed. "It will be so nice to sleep again."

Helen parked the car and turned off the ignition. "I'm going to get your suitcases out, and then we'll go inside."

Glida Mae reached over and grabbed her hand. "But please don't tell them who I really am," she begged. "I'd hate to cause a scene on my first day."

It took Helen a few seconds to realize that Glida Mae was referring to her imaginary movie career. Then she agreed with a solemn nod. "I won't say a word."

Throughout the check-in process, Helen kept expecting Glida Mae to break down, but her former neighbor followed every instruction and waved good-bye with a smile when it was time for Helen to go. Helen reminded the admission clerk about the instruction to call if Glida Mae received any visitors. Then she climbed into her car and fought tears all the way back to Eureka.

* * *

Barry Stanger from the FBI arrived at the sheriff's department at nine o'clock on Monday morning. Matt gave him a brief summary of the case, then showed him the victim wall and the suspect wall. "As you can see, we have narrowed our investigation down to these suspects. Our most promising is Dr. Ira Baker, who has connections to all our victims. Also under consideration are Robyn Howell's ex-husband, a local handyman named Elvis Hatcher, and the first victim's son, Martin Freeburg. Mr. Howell benefited in a major way from his ex-wife's death. Martin Freeburg will inherit a very small estate from his mother. As far as we can determine, Dr. Baker and Elvis have no motive for the murders."

Barry studied the walls for a few minutes, then asked, "Is there a physical characteristic that the victims all share, like blue eyes or left-handedness?"

Matt stared at the files on his desk. "I don't know."

"You're looking at the murders logically, but when you're dealing with someone who kills repeatedly, you have to look for triggers that go beyond the obvious. I've seen cases where the only thing the victims had in common was the fact that they wore glasses."

Matt frowned. "I guess we'll have to make more index cards."

"And you can't rule out the possibility that an established kook has moved in from somewhere else and set up shop in Eureka."

"We had your buddies at the FBI check for a similar MO, and they didn't find anybody."

Barry nodded. "No, so your murderer is probably homegrown, with a reason, however twisted, for the murders he's committed. But it's too early in the game to rule out anything. So keep your eyes and mind open, follow the leads you've got, and dig up more."

Matt chewed his bottom lip. "If we dig up much more, I'm going to have to expand into another office."

Barry ignored this attempted joke and continued staring at the wall. "For instance, the second victim wasn't religious, but maybe she had another association with the Eureka Baptist Church."

Matt spread his hands in frustration. "Like what?"

"Maybe that's where she was assigned to vote, or maybe she attended Weight Watchers meetings there. I suggest you contact the church and ask for a list of members, janitorial staff, the company who cleans their carpets, caterers used for wedding receptions, everything. Then look for a connection again."

"And I presume you want me to do the same with the library."

Barry nodded. "And don't overlook the geographic angle. All of your victims live in a very limited area. That could mean something."

"Eureka only has a population of about thirty thousand. Everybody lives close to everybody else."

"Yeah, but this is what?" Barry approached the map on the wall and pointed. "A mile radius."

"Maybe the murderer doesn't have a car and has to kill close to where he works or lives."

"Killing people close to home is risky. It could be that he used to live here and holds a grudge against some of the residents. Ms. Howell was a teacher. Maybe the killer is one of her students and a member of the Baptist Church."

"But Ms. Howell has only been teaching here for a couple of years."

Barry shrugged. "That's just the kind of thing I think you should look at."

Matt walked over to his desk and picked up the phone. He called Brian West, and when the PI returned his call, Matt told him to continue digging on all the suspects. Then, after checking his Rolodex, he dialed the number for the Eureka Baptist Church. Once he had Maybeth Hadder on the line, he requested all the information Barry had suggested.

"Why, Sheriff, this is going to take me just forever to collect."

"I'm sure the church would want you to provide this service to the community. We are investigating a serious crime," he reminded her.

"Oh," she breathed, "I'll be helping to catch a criminal, almost like a deputy."

"Almost," Matt agreed, trying to maintain his patience. "If you'll call Crystal Vines here at the department when you have it ready, she can come pick it up."

"Oh, I'll drop it off myself," Maybeth promised. "Since I'm helping you and all."

After murmuring an insincere thank-you, Matt disconnected and called the Eureka city library. He made an appointment to meet with the director at eleven-thirty, then called Helen. "Where are you?" he asked.

"Just turning onto Ivy Lane," she responded.

"I thought you were coming here."

"I am, but I wanted to let Nelda know how things went at the nursing home."

"How *did* things go?"

"Fine."

"I've got an appointment with the director of the Eureka library system at eleven-thirty, and I thought you might want to come along. Kind of take notes for me."

"Okay," Helen agreed.

"I'll pick you up at your house. That will give you time to fill Miss Nelda in on the happenings at Gentle Haven, then we can talk on the way to the library."

"I'll be ready."

After his phone conversation with Helen, Matt told Barry Stanger that he was going out for a while. "Make yourself at home," he offered.

"Thanks," Barry replied. "I would like to go back through all your files. Sometimes a fresh pair of eyes can spot something interesting."

"Feel free to make new index cards as you deem necessary," Matt suggested. "Are you headed back to Columbus tonight?"

Barry shook his head. "No, I'm going to get a hotel room for a couple of days and hang around here."

Matt had expected as much, but was still disappointed. "Well, I guess I'll see you later, then."

* * *

When Helen parked her car in the driveway of 126 Ivy Lane, Tan and Lin were in her backyard. They were on their hands and knees, looking through the grills that covered the air vents in her foundation.

"Are you looking for Oreos down there?" Helen asked pleasantly, and both children jumped.

Tan stepped forward. "We are looking for the cat."

Helen walked over to the children. "What cat?"

"The black one that belongs to the lady in this pink house."

"Glida Mae?" Helen asked more sharply than she intended, and both children retreated a step. She softened her tone and tried again. "You have seen her cat?" Helen pointed toward the now-vacant house next door.

Tan nodded. "We came to play with it every day until it got lost." Tan leaned forward and lowered his voice. "We still look for it because I don't want to tell Lin it is probably dead."

"That's why you've been coming in my yard," Helen realized aloud. "Not because you like cookies." *Or me,* she added in her mind.

"We do like cookies," Tan corrected earnestly. "But Lin really loves the cat."

"Well, I'll keep an eye out for it too. You said it was black?" Helen confirmed.

"With white front feet," Tan repeated.

Helen sighed. "Come on around to the back and I'll give you some cookies. That might cheer Lin up a little." Helen opened her back door, then passed a package of Oreos to Tan. He thanked her, then herded Lin toward the gate and out of the yard.

* * *

While Matt drove toward his rental house, he called Dr. Sylvia Appling. The secretary put him on hold for several minutes until the psychiatrist finally picked up. "I presume you're calling to ask about my new patient, Judith Pope."

"Yes, ma'am. I'm hoping you can tell me if there's anything to her dreams or not."

"It's impossible for me to say at this stage. I've only met with Judith once, and psychic phenomena is not my field of expertise."

"Could you meet with her more often—maybe try hypnosis or something?" Matt tried to keep from actually pleading. "If Judith's dreams are real, she might be able to give me the key to arresting a murderer."

"I understand your position, Sheriff," Dr. Appling replied patiently. "But I am responsible for Judith, and I can't do anything until I'm certain that she won't be adversely affected. Judith will probably be released from the hospital today, and I can try to arrange to see her twice a week, but that's all I can promise."

Matt sighed. "Call me if you come up with anything. Day or night. You have my cell number."

Dr. Appling laughed. "I hope when I make a big breakthrough it's late at night and that you're in the middle of a wonderful dream."

"You're out of luck there, Doctor," Matt told her. "I don't have wonderful dreams."

Matt closed his cell phone as he pulled in front of his rental house and honked, then watched Helen appear on the front porch. She hurried across the small yard, her blonde hair blowing in the wind. "So, how was your morning?"

"Fine. Glida Mae is looking forward to her first good night's sleep in weeks." Helen glanced over at him. "She said she's been afraid to close her eyes."

Matt nodded. "I know how she feels."

Helen paused in the process of buckling her seat belt. "You're afraid the murderer will come after you too?"

"No." Matt shook his head. "I'm afraid that when I wake up, someone else will be dead, and it will be my fault since I haven't been able to catch this guy."

"What did you do this morning?" Helen asked.

"Listened to a cocky FBI agent tell me how to solve this case."

"Did the agent have any new ideas?"

"No, just a variation of our old ones. He wants a list of anyone who has access to the Eureka Baptist Church or the city library. That includes employees, patrons, custodians, voters, overweight people, etc."

Helen gave him a look, but she didn't comment.

"I had to call and ask Maybeth Hadder to compile all that information for the church, and now she thinks she's a deputy."

Helen had to smile. "The first thing you should do is make her take an oath of silence."

"I thought it was only monks who took those."

"She probably doesn't know that."

He considered this for a second, then nodded. "You're right. It's worth a try."

Helen looked out the window. "Glida Mae is quite a piece of work."

Matt couldn't disagree. "She's always been crazy."

"But sometimes she's almost shrewd. Like today she told me that Dr. Baker has come to check on her in the middle of the night on more than one occasion, but she didn't let him in because it wouldn't have been proper."

Matt raised an eyebrow. "I'd say that strengthens my case, but I'm trying to picture Miss Glida Mae on the witness stand . . ."

Helen smiled again. "And she says she can *feel* the murderer's presence."

Matt laughed out loud. "Maybe I should go get her and drive her around Eureka. Whenever she feels a presence I'll stop and look for the murderer."

"She was quite serious about it," Helen replied. "But you remember the cat Glida Mae has been looking for ever since I moved in? The one we all assumed was a figment of her imagination?" Matt nodded and Helen continued. "Well, the little Vietnamese kids saw it too. Tan said the cat was black and belonged to the lady in the pink house."

"Finally a clue I recognize! Miss Glida Mae's house is pink!" Matt responded with exaggerated enthusiasm, and Helen gave him an impatient look. "I just wanted to prove that I was following you," he said with a smile. "So the kids saw a cat and this means . . ."

"That Glida Mae didn't make the cat up. It really exists and has been missing since about the time I came to Eureka."

"So are you suggesting we start a list of people who have seen black cats?"

"Are you making fun of me?" she demanded, and Matt's heart pounded. She looked so cute with her lips pursed in disapproval.

"Of course not," he said, pulling his eyes away from her mouth. Then he opened his door.

Helen hesitated for a few seconds, then did the same. "What I was trying to say, in case you were too busy cracking jokes to notice, is that we can't discount everything Glida Mae has said."

Matt smiled down at her. "You're right. Go back to Gentle Haven and get her immediately so I can deputize her along with Maybeth Hadder."

Helen narrowed her eyes. "You *are* making fun of me."

"On the contrary, I'm agreeing with you," Matt countered. "Miss Glida Mae is only completely crazy part of the time."

"Thank you for proving my point."

"Which was . . ."

"Glida Mae could have seen or felt someone lurking around her house and maybe it was the murderer."

"Let's forget about Miss Glida Mae for the moment." Matt waited as Helen circled around to join him on the sidewalk. Together they walked into the cool confines of the Eureka Public Library. Matt told the clerk at the front desk that they had an appointment with the director, and the young woman led them to the back, where several offices lined a wall.

The girl stopped in front of the corner office and pointed inside. "This is Ms. Fagan's office."

Matt thanked her, then waited for Helen to go inside. The woman behind the desk stood. She was tall and heavyset, with short, gray hair and a faintly masculine air. "Come in, Sheriff," Ms. Fagan invited, then turned inquisitive eyes to Helen.

"This is Helen Tyler," he introduced. "She's my research assistant."

"Nice to meet you," the director said with a wave at two chairs in front of her desk. "What can I do for you?" she asked as she resumed her seat.

Helen sat in the first chair, and Matt took the one beside her. "We need your help in a murder investigation," Matt began, hoping to shock Ms. Fagan into a cooperative attitude. The director didn't even blink; she continued to watch him calmly. "I need a list of all your employees, service personnel, patrons, and anyone else who comes to the library on a regular basis."

Ms. Fagan considered this for a few seconds. "The list of employees and service people will be easy." There was a pause, then she continued. "The list of patrons might be a problem. I'll have to get permission from the library board. And as far as 'anyone else who comes to the library on a regular basis,' we have no record of that. People don't have to sign in, and there are no security cameras. We have hundreds of people who come in every week just to cool off."

Matt nodded. "I realize that, but any names you can give us will be helpful."

Ms. Fagan picked up the phone and pressed a button. When the call was answered, she directed someone to prepare a list of current employees and service people, then bring it to her office. "I'll check with the library board, and if they give permission for me to release the names of our patrons, I'll call you."

"We also need to know about your program that takes books to people who are confined to their home."

"We have an entire Outreach department. Books and audiovisual materials are mailed to some of these patrons, and we have a bookmobile that runs on Fridays."

"I understand that Mary Jean Freeburg was receiving Outreach services."

Ms. Fagan nodded. "She had been on one of our bookmobile routes for several years."

Matt leaned forward. "Who drives the bookmobile?"

"We try to staff it with volunteers, but that's under the direction of the Outreach director, Sonny Webster."

"I need copies of the routes, a list of library patrons serviced by your bookmobile, and the names of volunteers who drive the book-mobile," Matt told the director.

"Sonny can show you the routes," Ms. Fagan replied. "And we have a log for volunteers to sign, but I'm afraid it's fairly haphazard."

Matt saw Helen's shoulders sag in disappointment, then said, "We'd like to see that log."

Ms. Fagan nodded. "Follow me and I'll introduce you to Sonny."

Matt and Helen accompanied the director through the bowels of the library to a garage. The bookmobile was parked on a platform in the middle, and an old, metal desk was pushed into one corner. The man behind the desk had a fringe of stringy, gray-streaked hair that hung to his shoulders. The library director made introductions, and he gave them a collective peace sign. Ms. Fagan explained the information they needed, then turned back to Matt. "I'll have the list of employees and service people waiting at the front desk for you to pick up as you leave. I'll call about the patron list as soon as I hear from the board." Matt nodded, and Ms. Fagan left them with the aging hippie.

Mr. Webster opened a drawer of his desk and extracted a spiral notebook. "Everybody who drives for us is supposed to sign in here." He handed Matt the notebook. "But nobody ever does."

Matt took the notebook and handed it to Helen. "We'll make a copy and return it."

Sonny Webster smiled, exposing two rows of coffee-stained teeth. Matt watched Helen recoil, and he had to control a smile. "Just be sure we have it by Friday in case somebody gets the urge to record their hours of service to the community," Sonny continued.

"Ms. Fagan said you would know the bookmobile routes," Matt

said.

"There are four that run on Fridays." Sonny pointed to the maps taped on the wall behind him.

Matt studied the maps. "And the bookmobile is driven by volunteers?"

Sonny shrugged. "When I can get one."

"Who drives when no one volunteers?"

Sonny raised an eyebrow. "I do."

"Did you ever make deliveries to Mary Jean Freeburg?"

Sonny gave them another discolored smile. "All the time. She was on the third Friday route."

Matt looked up from the maps. "How does the bookmobile process work?"

Sonny rocked back in his chair and put his arms behind his head. "People call and ask to be put on a route. Once they are assigned, they request books through the Internet or over the phone. Mrs. Freeburg was a big reader, and she wanted the most recent releases, so she did her choosing on the Internet."

"Since she was bedridden, how did you deliver her books?"

"She had a little remote control unlocking thing, kind of like a garage door opener. Whoever delivered just spoke into a little intercom, then she'd open the door and we'd take the books inside."

Matt clutched the arms of his chair and resisted the urge to look at Helen. "Do you know a Judith Pope who works here?"

Sonny's expression became sour. "Yeah, I know her."

"But you don't like her?"

"She stopped the library board from buying a new bookmobile a few months ago, and I didn't appreciate that. I mean, what's it to her whether the library has a Braille book section or a new bookmobile? She ain't blind, and she should have minded her own business."

This time Matt did give Helen a quick glance before continuing his questions. "Have you ever met Iris Whited?"

"She's on the library board," Sonny volunteered. "Kind of snooty."

"And what about Robyn Howell? Do you know her?"

Matt saw Sonny's eyes narrow. "No, don't know her."

Matt was certain that Sonny was lying, but couldn't imagine why.

"You're sure."

"Sure as shootin'," Sonny claimed as he stood. "I'd be glad to give you a quick tour of the bookmobile," he offered.

"We appreciate that, but I think we have all we need for now." Matt took Helen's arm, then led her to the door.

Matt left the garage without waiting for a response from Sonny Webster. They passed through the library, stopping at the front desk to retrieve the lists Ms. Fagan had waiting, then walked outside. Helen waited until they were settled in the Bronco before making a comment about the Outreach supervisor.

"That man was so creepy," she said.

"Yeah, I see why they keep him in the garage."

Helen laughed, then put on her seat belt. "And he had a connection to three of the victims. I say he should be added to your list of suspects."

Matt started the car, then reached for his cell phone. "He's as good as there. And I think he explained how the murderer got into Mrs. Freeburg's house."

"The automatic door opener?" Helen guessed, and Matt nodded.

"Which means she recognized the killer's voice and let him in."

"Probably not an anonymous delivery person," Helen deduced.

"Probably not," Matt agreed. "Although a lonely old woman might let in the mailman or the UPS driver or a florist."

"You're right. She might have let in a stranger delivering a basket."

Matt flashed her a quick smile, then dialed his office number.

"We'll be there in a few minutes," he said. "Call Brian West for me and tell him to do a complete check on Sonny Webster pronto."

"Yes sir!" Crystal hollered so loud that Matt held the phone away from his ear.

Matt hung up, then turned to Helen. "If she wasn't such a good secretary, I'd fire her."

Helen laughed. "Crystal has the most job security of anyone I've ever known. So, what will you do now?"

"We'll get all these new names, cross-reference them with what we have, make hundreds of additional index cards, and plaster them all over another wall in my office."

"But having another suspect is good, isn't it?"

Matt shrugged. "It's good if Sonny is the killer. If he's not, he just confuses the issue and distracts us from the real murderer."

"But there's no way to know for sure until we investigate him."

Matt smiled. "Right. You're getting pretty good at all this."

"Remember that when you solve this big case and get famous."

Matt parked the Bronco in its usual spot, then turned to face Helen. "I'll do better than that. When the big story finally breaks, I'll let you handle all the press interviews."

"A simple 'I owe all that I am to Helen' will do," she said as they climbed out of the car.

They reached the entrance, and Matt held the door open for Helen, then led the way inside. "Crystal!" he yelled as they passed the secretary's empty desk. "Crystal!" he tried again.

The secretary stepped out of the break room with a startled look on her face. "Where's the fire?"

"Did we get that report from Brian yet?"

Crystal stared back incredulously. "I just ordered it five minutes ago."

"Well, bring it in as soon as it comes. And I'm expecting a call from Ms. Fagan at the library. Put it through." Matt looked around his empty office. "Where's Barry Stanger?"

"Lunch," Crystal replied. "Some employers actually allow people to *eat*."

Matt shook his head. "Big waste of time. He's going to be here for a couple of days, and I need you to find him a work area so he won't be in my office," Matt continued.

"The ladies' room and break room are both still available," Crystal proposed.

"As appealing as the ladies' room sounds, it would probably be better to put him in the break room. Give him a table and a chair. If he needs more equipment than that, he can get it himself."

"Will do."

Once Crystal was gone, Matt took the lists Ms. Fagan had given them and asked Helen to enter them into the computer. "Then cross-reference them with what we've already got while I make note cards on Sonny Webster."

Helen nodded as she began typing. "He acted funny when you asked him about Robyn Howell."

"Yeah, I'd be willing to bet that he knew her."

"I wonder why he lied," Helen mused without looking up from the computer screen.

"Because the truth hurts," Matt told her with a quick smile.

Ms. Fagan called an hour later. She had polled the library board by phone and they had agreed to provide him with a list of patrons. "But only the names—no addresses and phone numbers, since that would be giving out information that was provided to us confidentially."

"That's fine. Thank you," Matt told her. "How long will it take to print a list?"

"We have close to twenty thousand names on file, so give me an hour."

Matt checked the clock. "My secretary will be there at two o'clock." He hung up, then called for Crystal. When the secretary appeared in the doorway, he gave her the assignment. "She said they have almost twenty thousand names, so as soon as you get back, start scanning."

Crystal shook her head. "That will take . . ."

"All day," Matt finished for her. "But it has to be done."

"Why are we looking at library patrons?" Crystal asked. "I thought you were convinced that Dr. Baker is the murderer."

Matt and Helen took turns describing their visit to the library. "So now we have an additional suspect," Matt concluded, waving the new stack of index cards.

"Sonny Webster admitted to knowing all the victims except Robyn Howell," Helen said, staring at the card-covered wall.

"But we think he was lying about her," Matt added.

Helen stood and walked over to the wall. After a few seconds of careful study, she turned to them with a look of wonder on her face. "Come here," she commanded, and both Matt and Crystal hurried to her side. "What is that?" She pointed to a picture taken inside Robyn Howell's house on the night she died.

Crystal squinted at the black-and-white photograph. "It looks like a book on the coffee table."

"On the otherwise bare coffee table, and not just any book, but a *library* book," Helen clarified. "See the way the light's reflecting off the plastic cover? And there's a little tag on the bottom of the spine."

"Robyn Howell didn't have a current library card," Crystal reminded them. "If it is a library book, someone else checked it out."

Matt picked up her train of thought. "Maybe Sonny Webster."

"We've got to get that book," Helen said. "And if this turns out to be the key that solves the case, don't forget who thought of it first."

Matt glanced at Crystal. "Helen has self-esteem problems and needs praise when she finds a clue."

Crystal turned to stare at the other woman. "I can see why she'd lack confidence, being so ugly and all."

Crystal's gaze moved back to Matt, and he cleared his throat. "Stay by the phone, Crystal. When Ms. Fagan has that list of library employees and patrons ready, go pick it up and start scanning. Helen and I are headed to Robyn Howell's house to look for a library book."

Crystal put a hand to her heart. "It doesn't seem fair for me to have all the fun."

Matt ignored this and pulled his keys from his pocket. "When Barry gets back from lunch, show him his workstation in the break room and try to keep him out of here." He motioned for Helen to join him and headed toward the door. "We'll be back soon."

They met Barry Stanger coming in as they were going out. "We're checking out a lead," Matt told the FBI agent. "Crystal is setting up an office for you. Anything you need, just ask her."

Barry looked from Matt to Helen, then back at the sheriff. "Okay."

"If you need me while I'm gone, Crystal has my cell number."

CHAPTER 11

When Matt parked the Bronco in front of Robyn Howell's house, Helen looked around. The grass was long and the flower beds overgrown, but she could tell that the yard had once been well tended. "This house looks a lot like your grandmother's," she said to Matt as they walked up the sidewalk. "Except cuter."

"Wait until you see the inside," Matt said as he inserted a key. "You'll probably want to call Ms. Howell's ex-husband and make an offer."

They stepped into the dark interior, and Helen couldn't suppress a shudder. "No, I don't think so."

Matt flipped the light switch, but nothing happened. "I guess Mr. Howell has already had the electricity turned off. So much for him not caring about money."

"And it's terribly dusty," Helen said, peering through the dim light seeping in around the closed blinds.

"Fingerprint filament," Matt explained. "Robyn Howell kept this place immaculate."

"Nice furniture," Helen commented.

"Yeah, she had good taste," Matt agreed. Then Helen gasped, and Matt turned around quickly. "What?"

Helen pointed at the coffee table. "The library book is gone."

* * *

They went back out to the Bronco, and Matt called Ed Ramsey. He put his phone on speaker so Helen could hear. The police chief said that the house had been turned over to Scott Howell earlier that morning. "He's been bugging us about it for a week. Wants to put it up for sale. Since we have pictures, I didn't see any reason to hold on to it."

"I'm not complaining, Ed, just surprised," Matt told him. "There was a library book on the coffee table. You know what happened to it?"

There was a brief pause. "No, I told my boys not to touch anything."

"Maybe Scott Howell turned it in."

"That would be awfully *responsible* of him," Ed commented.

Matt frowned. "Yeah, that does seem unlikely. Could you call and ask him if he knows anything about the book? Because if he doesn't, the killer might have returned to the scene of the crime."

"You know, on television they do that, but in my experience it doesn't happen all that much. I'll call him, though. And by the way, Judith Pope was discharged from the hospital this morning. I've got a policewoman with her."

"That's a good idea," Matt agreed. "I talked to Dr. Appling, and she hasn't formed an opinion yet about Judith's dreams. She said she would increase their sessions to two a week and see what happens."

"I guess that's the best we can do."

Matt thought about this for a second. "Maybe it's not. I'm near her house right now. I think I'll stop by and ask her some questions myself."

"It's worth a try," Ed agreed. "Oh, we did get one little piece of information, for whatever it's worth. The lab boys said that the unexplained substance found on the wicker baskets is coal dust."

Matt considered this. "We only have one mine still operating in Coosetta County."

"Yeah, and guess who provides occupational therapy for miners wounded on the job."

Matt smiled at Helen. "Let me guess. Dr. Ira Baker."

"You've got it."

As soon as Matt disconnected, his phone rang. It was Crystal. "You've got to get back to the office. Maybeth Hadder is here, and she's driving me crazy," Crystal whispered into the phone.

"We're going to stop by Judith Pope's house, then we'll be on in. Did you get the list of library patrons?"

"Yeah, I finally caught a break on that one. Ms. Fagan had them on disks, so I don't have to spend hours scanning."

Matt was pleased. "That is good news. Is Barry in the break room?"

"No, he's digging through that mess on your desk."

Matt sighed. "I guess I can't have everything."

A grouchy policewoman answered Judith's door when Matt knocked. He showed the officer his identification, then explained the purpose for their visit. "All visitors are supposed to be cleared through the chief," she told him.

"I told Chief Ramsey I was coming over. You can call him if you'd like."

The woman nodded, then stepped back. "She's in here."

This house had a similar floor plan to his grandmother's, but it was even less appealing. The walls were covered with dark wood paneling, the carpet was a deep shag, and most of the room was occupied by a large hospital bed and various equipment that had obviously been used to care for Lavenia Pope until her death.

He looked down and saw that Helen's eyes were even wider than usual. "I'll bet this place hasn't been updated since the fifties," he whispered. "It makes my grandmother's old house look downright modern. Maybe I should raise your rent."

Helen smiled. "You can't. I have a lease." Then she looked around the living room. "The carpet and paneling I could live with, but the dead grandmother's stuff would have to go."

"I guess you never know when you might need a hospital bed and a respirator," Matt teased and watched Helen shudder as they reached the bedroom. Judith was propped up on several pillows in the middle of a large bed.

"How are you feeling?" Helen asked.

"Tired," Judith responded, keeping her eyes away from Matt.

"How are your sessions going with Dr. Appling?" Matt asked.

Judith shrugged. "My dreams probably don't mean anything except that I'm crazy."

"What can you tell us about Sonny Webster?"

Judith looked up at Matt briefly. "The Outreach supervisor? Not much. I rarely see him."

"He wasn't happy that you blocked the purchase of a new bookmobile."

Judith waved a hand. "Are you suggesting that he tried to kill me because of that?" Her tone was disdainful.

"We're just covering all our bases," Matt answered, trying not to sound defensive. "Mr. Webster has a connection to most of the victims, and we wanted to see if he'd ever threatened you, anything like that."

"He called me a few names after the board meeting that canceled his bookmobile, but he didn't frighten me."

"We're getting a list of all employees and patrons from Ms. Fagan, but I know the library uses a lot of volunteers, and there are other people who come to the library regularly who won't be on any list. I was hoping you could help us identify some of them."

"You think the poisoned soup has something to do with the library?" Judith asked with skepticism.

Matt shifted his weight from one foot to the other. "It's a possibility."

Judith considered this for a few seconds. "Wynette Sowell at the Rescue Mission could tell you homeless people who visit the library often. As far as volunteers, your best bet would be to contact Dr. Baker."

Matt and Helen exchanged a quick look, then he turned back to Judith.

"Why?"

"Because he's the president of our volunteer committee."

Matt smiled, then wrapped the conversation up quickly and hurried Helen through the door. "Every time I start looking in another direction, something leads me back to Dr. Baker," he whispered to Helen once they were outside.

"It does seem that way," she agreed.

They started down the sidewalk and met Nelda Lovell by the Bronco. "Hey, Miss Nelda," Matt greeted. "Have you come to visit Judith?"

"Good afternoon, Helen, Matt," she replied. "And yes, I've brought Judith a pie."

"That should cheer her up," Helen predicted, and Miss Nelda smiled. "Has Sydney had her baby yet?"

"No, but she can't get much crabbier, so it has to be soon."

"Well, let me know when something happens."

"I will, dear," Nelda promised.

"And speaking of crabby," Matt entered the conversation. "Good luck getting past the policewoman at Judith's front door."

* * *

When they got back to the sheriff's department, Maybeth Hadder had a chair pulled up to Crystal's desk. The secretary gave them a pleading look as they approached.

"Well, Miss Maybeth, I presume your presence here means that you have collected all the names I asked you for," Matt said pleasantly.

"Oh, yes indeed," Mrs. Hadder gushed. "It took me just forever, but I knew it was like you said—doing a service to the community."

Crystal covertly rolled her eyes. "My luck ran out and her lists are not on disks, so I've been scanning."

Matt smiled. "Good girl. Helen will help you finish up, then she can do her regular cross-referencing," he said. "I guess I'll go see what Barry has come up with."

Matt took a step toward his office, and Mrs. Hadder stood to follow. "Is there anything else you need me to do, Sheriff?"

He turned and shook his head. "Oh no, you've done quite enough already."

The church secretary looked a little hurt, but she nodded and headed for the elevator.

* * *

When Matt walked into his office, Barry stood and offered to relinquish his chair, but Matt waved him back down. "Keep your seat. I'll sit here." He sat down in the chair they had moved in for Helen. "So, what have you come up with?"

"Not much," Barry admitted. "You got a report on Sonny Webster from your private investigator. The library guy has a criminal record. Mostly juvenile stuff, but he has a recent conviction in Muscogee County for possession of marijuana. The judge let him do his jail time on the weekends, presumably so he wouldn't get fired from his cushy job at the library."

"If somebody found out and threatened to tell . . ."

"It could be a motive for murder," Barry agreed. "I had my partner run through our mainframe the names of people who had recently moved into the area," Barry said, then pointed to Helen's name. "Isn't that your girlfriend?" he asked.

"Helen is not my girlfriend," Matt denied. "She's a temporary employee."

Barry looked embarrassed. "Oh, sorry. Did you know there's an outstanding warrant for her arrest in West Virginia?"

Matt nodded. "It's just a civil dispute and has no bearing on this case, so I've decided to ignore it for the time being."

Barry watched him for a few seconds, then nodded. "I guess that's your call."

The phone started ringing, and Crystal yelled from the outer office. "Chief Ramsey for you, Matt!"

Matt picked up the receiver. "What you got, Ed?"

"That Howell fellow says he doesn't know anything about a library book. Says he doesn't remember seeing it on the coffee table."

Matt looked at the victim wall. "Well, it was there. We have a picture."

"Maybe you can check with the library."

Matt walked closer to the picture and squinted. "Since I can't read the title, I doubt the library can help me, but I'll try. Thanks, Ed."

"What?" Barry asked when Matt hung up the phone.

"See this book on Robyn Howell's coffee table?" He pointed to the picture and Barry nodded. "We've already established that Robyn didn't have a library card, and we need a connection between Ms. Howell and Sonny Webster. So we went over there to get the book, intending to take it to the library and see who had checked it out. But when we got there, it was gone."

Barry raised an eyebrow. "You think the murderer got it?"

Matt nodded. "That *is* what I think. The husband didn't turn it in, and no one else had access to the house. Besides, why would anyone—except the killer—*want* to take the book?"

"But if the book is gone, how can it help you?"

"I'm hoping the library can help me identify it." Matt checked a number on his desk, then dialed. "Ms. Fagan, please," he told the woman who answered. After a short wait, the library director answered.

"This is Ms. Fagan. How can I help you?"

Matt explained about the book and the need to locate it.

"If you'll give me the title, I'll be glad to check for you," she offered.

"I don't have a title," Matt admitted.

"Sheriff, there are over a hundred thousand books in the adult fiction section alone. Without a title, I can't possibly help you." Matt sighed. "Can you at least give me a list of books that are overdue and who they are checked out to?"

There was a brief pause, and Matt realized that he was reaching the limit of Ms. Fagan's cooperation. "Very well. I will have that printed and faxed to you as soon as possible."

"Thank you," Matt said. Ms. Fagan hung up without replying. "Well, so much for that."

Barry was still staring at the picture. "We have a guy who does computer enhancements back at my office. I wonder if he could blow this up enough to see the title of the book?"

Matt smiled. Maybe having the FBI on board wasn't such a bad thing after all. "It's worth a try. I'll have Crystal scan it, and then you can e-mail it to him."

Matt called Crystal and gave her the picture. Helen came in with the lists from Maybeth Hadder and the resulting cross-references. After Matt added these to the growing stack on his desk, he explained about the picture to Barry.

The FBI agent nodded, then looked around the room. "You've collected a lot of data—almost too much. You may be missing the forest for the trees."

"What do you mean?"

"Just don't overlook the obvious," Barry recommended.

Helen gave Matt a satisfied look, and he nodded in acknowledgement. Then he turned back to Barry. "Thanks for the advice."

Barry looked at the clock. "Well, I'll see if your secretary has that picture scanned, then I'll send it to my office. After that, I think I'll call it a night and check into my hotel."

Helen walked out to Crystal's desk as Matt escorted Barry to the door. He was on his way back to his office, just about to heave a sigh of relief, when Crystal told him that Maybeth Hadder was on line one. Matt trudged into his office and picked up the phone. "Hello?"

"Oh, Sheriff, I know you are so busy, and I hate to bother you," Mrs. Hadder told him, "but I found something when I was looking through my file, and I thought I should bring it to your attention."

"What did you find?" Matt tried to sound interested.

"Well, I'm responsible for printing the weekly church bulletin, and today I started on the one for next Sunday. Most people think the bulletin is an easy job, but it's really quite difficult. You have to make sure you have everyone's name spelled right, and you can't leave out anyone's birthday. And if you type in the wrong scripture for the week, people will be unprepared when they come to Sunday School class."

Matt tried to get Helen's or Crystal's attention, hoping one of them could save him, but neither of them would look up.

"One of my most important responsibilities is the prayer list," Miss Maybeth droned on. "Accuracy is so important. I mean, imagine how I'd feel if everyone was supposed to be praying for one of our members and I left their name off the list! Why, they could die and it would be my fault!"

Matt closed his eyes. To keep the conversation from being a total waste, he considered taking a quick nap.

"I always check the prayer lists for the past several weeks because we have some people who are rollovers."

This odd statement dragged Matt from semiconsciousness. "They're what?"

"Rollovers. We keep them on the prayer lists week after week for one reason or another. For instance, Miss Mary Jean Freeburg was a rollover because she had been sick for so long."

"Oh, I see," Matt replied.

"And I have to check the old programs to make sure I roll over everyone who still needs our prayers."

"Yes ma'am, I can see how that could be time-consuming." Matt checked his watch.

"Well, today I started working on the bulletin for Sunday."

"Yes, I believe you already mentioned that," Matt reminded her.

"And I checked the past few programs for rollovers."

Finally, Matt accepted his doom. "Yes, ma'am. You checked the rollovers."

"And I found something odd. On Sunday, June 27, the prayer list included Miss Mary Jean. But then it always did."

"Because she was a rollover," Matt provided helpfully.

"Exactly." Miss Maybeth sounded pleased that he understood the process. "But that other woman who died in her sleep, Robyn Howell? Her name is on the list too."

Matt sat up straight, all vestiges of boredom evaporating. "Why would her name be on the list? She wasn't even a member of the Eureka Baptist Church."

Mrs. Hadder giggled. "You don't have to be a member of the church to be on our prayer list. A few months ago when the Pope was sick, someone put *him* on the list and he's not even Baptist!"

Matt's mind was racing. "So, Robyn Howell was on the prayer list for June 27, but she didn't roll over?"

"Oh, no. She was just a one-time request."

And by the next Sunday she was dead, Matt thought to himself.

"But the really surprising thing is that Judith and Iris are on the list too."

Matt felt his heart skip a beat. "All four of the poisoning victims were on the prayer list for June 27?" he repeated.

"Every single one of them," Maybeth Hadder replied in her singsong voice.

Matt cleared his throat and mentally repented for every bad thing he'd ever thought about the secretary of Eureka's largest church. "I'd like to see a copy of that program as soon as possible, and I need to know how names are put on the list."

"Well, the rollovers . . ."

"Not the rollovers," Matt interrupted. "I think I understand about people like Mrs. Freeburg who had chronic illnesses. But what about the other three?"

"Well, mostly people call them in, but there are slips outside the sanctuary that can be filled out too."

"Do you save the slips?"

"No, I'm sorry."

"Do you keep a list of people who call in?"

"Not the requester's name," Mrs. Hadder said regretfully. "But I have a pretty good memory, and I can tell you who called in the specific requests you're interested in."

Matt held his breath. "Who?"

"Well, Edith McBride called in Robyn Howell. She said the girl had a bad cold."

"What about Iris Whited and Judith Pope?"

"That's easy. Dr. Baker made both of those requests."

If Maybeth Hadder had been in his office at that moment, Matt would have kissed her right on the lips. "When do you think you'll be able to bring me a copy of that program?" he asked, struggling to keep the excitement from his voice.

"Why, I'll bring it over right now."

"That would be mighty convenient," Matt told her, then hung up and called Ed Ramsey.

* * *

Helen glanced through the open door into Matt's office. He was still on the phone. "Poor Matt," she said. "I wish his luck could improve a little."

The secretary raised an eyebrow. "Oh, I don't know. His luck seems pretty good to me."

"What do you mean?" Helen asked.

Crystal laughed. "I mean that since you moved here, he's almost acting like a regular person."

Helen was determined to keep the conversation light. "Are you saying he was irregular before I got here?"

Crystal didn't smile. "I'm saying that for three years, he's been like the walking dead." Helen inhaled sharply, and Crystal continued. "Those first weeks when he was drinking were terrible. Since then, he's functioned, but during the last few days he's really seemed alive. He's started smiling, and yesterday I actually heard him *whistle*."

Helen didn't know whether Crystal was fishing for information or issuing a challenge, so she chose her words carefully. "He told me how much you did for him after his family died. I know he must mean a lot to you."

Crystal shrugged. "I'd have done it for any of the guys." She glanced up and saw the knowing look in Helen's eyes. "All right. I'll admit that I used to have kind of a crush on him, but he never felt that way about me, and now I'm over it. But there's been a little spark of hope in his eyes lately, and I think it must be because of you."

The possibility of a continued relationship with Matt Clevenger was something Helen only allowed herself to think of at night when she was almost asleep and could pretend she was dreaming. So in front of Crystal, she laughed it off. "Matt just likes me because I'm willing to work almost as hard as you do for less money."

"Matt likes you, all right, but it doesn't have anything to do with hard work." There was an awkward pause while Helen tried to think of something to say, then Crystal cleared her throat and continued. "We haven't known each other very long, and I don't want to overstep the bounds of our friendship, but I think it's only fair that I warn you."

Helen raised an eyebrow. "Warn me? About what?"

"That Matt loved Julie very much. He was crazy about his boys, and when they died, it broke his heart. I just don't know if he'll ever really get over them. So if it's not already too late, you might want to try to keep from falling in love with him."

Helen was saved from an answer by Matt's appearance in his office door.

"Helen, Crystal, come in here quick." He turned and walked back to his desk.

Crystal gave Helen an exaggerated shrug, then stood to obey. Inside the office, they found Matt staring at the victim wall. Helen sat in her chair, and Crystal picked the most sturdy-looking box. "What?" Crystal demanded. "Do you want me to get a list of all the registered voters in Eureka and scan them into my computer?"

Matt turned to face them, a look of wonder in his eyes. "We've just gotten our first big break." He explained about the program and told them that Maybeth Hadder was on her way over with a copy. "Once we get that, we'll need to call all the people listed and warn them specifically. Then tomorrow, I want them all questioned." He turned to Crystal. "It's time to call in the guys. Full staff meeting tomorrow morning at seven o'clock."

Crystal nodded.

"We'll divide up the prayer list. Each deputy can take a few names, and hopefully everyone will have been questioned by the end of the day."

"That will upset the rotating schedule," Crystal reminded him.

Matt nodded. "I know that, but this is urgent."

"Maybe I could question a few folks myself," Crystal suggested without meeting his gaze.

"You're interested in fieldwork?" Matt asked in surprise.

"I wouldn't mind trying my hand at it," Crystal admitted.

Matt shrugged. "Okay, I'll count you in."

Crystal notified the deputies of the meeting the next day, and when Maybeth Hadder arrived with her program, Matt greeted her like visiting royalty. She was pleased by all the attention and promised to keep her "find" to herself, although Matt expressed doubt about this after she left. "Telling her friends that she's been instrumental in solving a murder case will probably prove irresistible," he predicted. "But I can't be mad at her."

Helen stared at the church bulletin in his hand. "So, you think the murderer used this bulletin to choose his victims?"

Matt nodded. "Dr. Baker put two of the victims on the list himself, and Mary Jean Freeburg was on there perpetually. He might have even suggested that Mrs. McBride put Robyn Howell's name on the list."

Crystal nodded. "But what if by some crazy chance, Dr. Baker is not the insane killer? Then what?"

"Then the church bulletin is still the key," Matt insisted. "Just for a different reason."

"Maybe he hates the preacher or the church or Baptists in general," Crystal proposed.

Matt considered this. "Some people check the obituaries and rob houses when they know families are gone to the funeral. Maybe it's something like that."

"He picked people from the prayer list to ensure that his victims were in a weakened condition?" Helen asked.

"But Judith Pope and Iris Whited weren't sick," Crystal pointed out.

Matt chewed his bottom lip, thinking. "Did we ever find out why our surviving victims were on that prayer list?"

"You should have asked your new girlfriend, Miss Maybeth Hadder," Crystal suggested.

"You ask her for me," Matt said, then turned to Helen. Crystal made a face at his back, then went to follow his orders.

"Either the killer made sure all the names of people he wanted to kill were on that prayer list, or he used the prayer list for a victim pool," Helen clarified.

"There's no other explanation for all the victims being on this list. It cannot be coincidence," Matt said. "And other women may have received baskets and not opened them, which is why you need to start making phone calls."

Helen started toward his door, then stopped and turned around. "Matt, if he plans to kill again, do you think he'll use this same list?"

"It makes sense to me."

Before Matt could respond, Crystal returned. "Lavenia Pope's birthday was that week, and Maybeth said Dr. Baker was afraid Judith might be sad," she announced. "He added Iris Whited's name because she'd been struggling with depression since her husband died."

At this moment, Ed Ramsey walked in. "Show me what you got," he commanded.

Matt gave Helen the program and asked her to make a copy and start her phone calls. Then he led the police chief into his office.

* * *

Matt showed Ed Ramsey the church program, and the police chief shook his head. "Well, I'll be. We could have looked from now till doomsday and never found this. God works in mysterious ways."

Matt nodded. "Maybeth Hadder is mysterious all right."

"So you think Dr. Baker is our man?"

"I'm about ninety-nine percent sure. You're still having him followed?"

"Oh yeah, and he's been the picture of Christian charity."

"He knows we're watching, and he's on his best behavior," Matt predicted.

"At least maybe that will keep him from killing again."

"Unless he gives your boys the slip."

* * *

Crystal helped with the phone calls until they finished at eight o'clock. Then she said she was calling it a night and offered Helen a ride home, but Helen declined. "I'll wait on Matt."

Crystal looked like she wanted to say something, but she apparently thought better of it and left. When Matt and Ed Ramsey came out of his office, Helen was sitting at Crystal's desk, trying hard to stay awake. Matt gave her a sweet smile, then said he was walking Ed downstairs.

Helen nodded, then went into his office. She absently started stacking files and printouts and her endless cross-referencing lists. Then she saw her own name and pulled out a thin sheaf of papers. She was still reading when Matt walked back in.

"What's that?" he asked, obviously tired but encouraged.

"Just a report from your private investigator," she replied, then looked up. "On me."

The regretful expression on his face was instant and sincere. "I'm sorry, Helen. But you were new to the area, and you live right in the middle of Eureka's version of Death Valley. If I hadn't requested the background search, Ed Ramsey at the police department would have."

She put the report down, blinking back tears. "I guess I shouldn't be surprised, but I am. I thought you trusted me." She couldn't believe how much that report hurt.

Matt crossed the room and put his hands on her shoulders. "I do trust you. It was just a formality."

Helen sighed. "I guess it's time I told you the whole sad tale."

Matt smiled. "I'd like to hear your side of the story."

"We'd better get comfortable." Helen sat cross-legged on the floor and leaned against one of the boxes. "This could take awhile."

Matt sat beside her, close but not quite touching. She appreciated his sensitivity as she stared straight ahead and began her narrative.

"I've wanted to be a teacher for as long as I can remember. For Christmas I always asked for stuff like a chalkboard or a real desk or some other school supply. My room was so full of classroom equipment there was barely room for my bed."

Helen sensed Matt's smile more than saw it.

"My parents were supportive. Neither one of them had finished college, although they were very successful. They were proud of my grades and my scholarship to William and Mary. But once I finished my undergraduate work, they couldn't understand why I went on and got my master's. And they really didn't understand my desire to get my doctorate. But I wanted to teach on a collegiate level, and that's pretty much the standard now."

"Your parents objected to your continued education?"

"It was more disapproval than actual objection. They wanted me to marry and have a family. In fact, they thought going to school had become an obsession for me. I was a grown woman and they couldn't have stopped me if they had tried, but it made things a little awkward during my visits home. Anyway, I got my doctorate and applied for professorships. I was offered one at Brownley College."

"Brian said it's an expensive private school."

Helen nodded. "It was a very prestigious appointment, and the learning environment is incredible. I was extremely happy there until last year, when a graduate student named Harrison Campbell took one of my English literature classes."

"And you fell in love with him," Matt said.

Helen laughed, but there was no humor in her voice. "I never loved Harrison. At first I liked him. He was handsome and charming in a pushy, you-can't-say-no-to-me kind of way. He would hang around after class, wanting to help with papers, things like that. Then he started asking me out to dinner, buying me gifts and flowers. At that point I explained firmly that I did not date students. So Harrison offered to drop my class—even change universities so we could pursue a relationship." Helen shook her head at the memory. "Finally I had to tell him that I would not date him under any circumstances."

"But this guy was hard to discourage?"

"Harrison was impossible to discourage, and it didn't take long for me to start hating the sight of him. He made a point to be wherever I was. If I ate in the cafeteria, he'd be sitting at the next table. If I took a walk around the park, he'd be right behind me. Then he started following me home at night. I would look out my front window well after midnight and see his car parked at the curb in front of my house."

"You should have called the police."

"I did!" Helen turned to face him. "They told me to get a restraining order, but Harrison took that as a challenge—like I was playing hard to get or something crazy like that. He changed to my dentist, he got his hair cut the same day I did, and if I went into the library, he'd be there. The police soon became weary of my calls since Harrison never threatened me in any way. Then he started the rumor that we were," she paused, trying to find the right word, "involved. He told people we had been living together and planned to get married as soon as he got his master's."

"But it wasn't true?"

Helen shuddered. "Nothing could be further from the truth. But he did little sneaky things to make it appear that a relationship existed, like hiring a man to build a gazebo in my backyard without my permission and buying stocks in both our names."

"But why? Did he actually think he could pressure you into marrying him?"

"I'm not sure what motivated Harrison," Helen said with a sigh. "I guess it was partly obsession, partly a refusal to admit defeat. But whatever his reasons, he made my life a living nightmare. The dean called me in several times asking about the rumors and my alleged relationship with Harrison. I told the truth, but . . ."

"He didn't believe you?" Matt guessed.

"I don't know if he believed me or not. The truth didn't really matter. It was the fact that I had brought negative publicity to the school. Brownley has a reputation to maintain, and I was becoming an embarrassment. So they fired me."

"That stinks."

"Yes, it does. But it was my reality. Harrison had destroyed my professional life, but he wasn't satisfied with that. He went to see my parents and told them he was worried about me. He thought I was unstable since I had promised to marry him, made elaborate wedding plans, and then changed my mind. He led them to believe we were involved in an immoral relationship, which horrified them even more than my possible instability."

"And *they* believed him too?"

"Maybe not completely, but enough to destroy what was left of our already-tenuous relationship."

"So, you packed up and came to Eureka?"

Helen nodded. "My dad used to bring us here for fishing trips during the summer when I was a kid, so I had good memories associated with the town and a general knowledge of the area. I moved here intending to hide out for a while in hopes that Harrison would forget about me," she told Matt, "or turn his attention to some other poor woman."

"Maybe he has."

Helen shrugged. "Or maybe he just hasn't found me yet."

They were quiet for a few minutes, then Matt reached out and took her hand in his. He had the long, strong fingers of an athlete, and Helen clung to them pitifully. "I'm sorry I had you investigated," he said gently.

"I guess you didn't have a choice," Helen replied.

He smiled. "I really didn't, but I'm still sorry."

"So." Helen scooted a little closer to him until their shoulders were touching. The warmth was intoxicating, and she lost her train of thought.

"So . . . ," Matt prompted, and she continued.

"You think Dr. Baker is our killer."

"I think we have a good circumstantial case against him, but we need something to tie him to the Digoxin. Somewhere in that pile of information is a list of drug company representatives that Ed Ramsey collected. Tomorrow could you call them and see if Dr. Baker requested Digoxin samples? And maybe could you talk to the local pharmacists and ask them if Dr. Baker ever picked up prescriptions of Digoxin for his patients or anything strange like that."

Helen nodded and tried to suppress a yawn.

"After my meeting with the deputies in the morning, I've got to drive to Columbus and testify in federal court. I may be gone most of the day."

"Is the judge who's presiding over the trial tomorrow the same one you sweet-talked into the court orders for the Digoxin prescriptions?"

"No, it's a different one—a man who doesn't like me nearly as well."

Helen smiled. "Then you really do need to get some beauty rest."

Matt squeezed her hand. "You've been working late a lot. I hope you're keeping track of your hours."

Helen didn't really care about the money, but she nodded. There was a companionable silence, then he spoke. "I usually read the Bible every night before I go to sleep, but lately I've been reading the Book of Mormon instead."

Helen was surprised by this announcement, but didn't comment.

"Last night I read the verse in Mosiah that says children who die will have eternal life." He paused for a second, then turned to face her. "What does that mean?"

Helen took a deep breath before attempting to answer. "It means that when children die, they go straight to heaven."

Matt considered this, then stared at their intertwined hands. "At the funeral, the preacher said my family was safe in the arms of Jesus, but I can't picture them that way. Julie loved being outside. She would hate sitting around in an angel dress playing a harp all day long. Chase couldn't be still for a minute, so why would he want to sit on Jesus' lap forever? And Chad was just learning to crawl . . ." His voice trailed off. "That picture of them in Jesus' arms doesn't give me much comfort or peace."

"We Mormons believe in eternal families, so even though they are in heaven with the Savior, I think they're just like they were before. The boys probably run and play, and Julie . . . ," Helen paused, praying for the right words to come, "well, she still takes care of them." Matt was watching her closely, and she searched for an analogy. "It's like you were all going on vacation, but you couldn't get off work and had to let them go on ahead. You know where they are, you know they are happy, and you know that eventually you will join them. You're just apart for a while."

Matt looked away, and Helen was afraid she had said the wrong thing.

"I didn't mean to oversimplify. I'm not very good at explaining. If you'd really like to know more about our beliefs on life after death, I could set up an appointment with our missionaries or our bishop."

Matt considered this. "Is a bishop like a minister? he asked, and she nodded. "Then I think I'd be more comfortable with him."

Helen hadn't expected him to accept, and it took a few seconds for her to formulate a response. "I'll try to set up an appointment for tomorrow night."

Matt smiled, then stood and pulled her to her feet. "Tomorrow's going to be a long day, so I'd better get you home."

* * *

Helen set her alarm clock for six o'clock on Tuesday morning, but there was a brief power outage during the night, so when she woke up, her clock was flashing twelve o'clock but it was actually seven-thirty. She called the sheriff's department and talked to one of the dispatchers, who told her that both Crystal and Matt were in a meeting. She left a message that she'd be late, then rushed to get ready.

By the time she arrived at the sheriff's department, the meeting was over and Matt had left for Columbus.

"If you can't get here on time, just get here when you can," Crystal muttered when she saw Helen. "And you didn't even bring us breakfast."

Helen waved her empty hands. "Sorry. I didn't think about it."

"That's one of the many things I can't stand about skinny people. They don't think about food nearly enough."

Helen glanced at Matt's office. "I see the FBI agent is back."

"Oh yeah, and he said his partner is coming this afternoon as they prepare to make the mistake of their careers by arresting Dr. Baker." Crystal turned to Helen for support. "You've got to convince Matt he's wrong before it's too late."

"I'm not sure he is wrong," Helen began slowly. "There's a lot of evidence against Dr. Baker."

"I'm telling you—he's a good man and certainly not a killer."

Helen decided not to argue. Then she looked back at Matt's

office. "I thought Mr. Stanger was supposed to use the break room for his office."

"He was, but he likes Matt's office better."

Helen frowned. "Well, I need to make a phone call, and I guess I'll have to go to the break room." Crystal didn't comment, so Helen went into the small space between the bathrooms and called Nelda Lovell. "I hope I didn't wake you, but I need Sydney's phone number," she explained.

"You didn't wake me, but I'm afraid Sydney might be sleeping in. Let me have her call you."

Helen recited her cell number, then thanked Nelda for her help. After hanging up the phone, she walked back out to the switchboard and sat in the chair in front of Crystal's desk.

"I thought you'd be out questioning the people on your list," Helen said to the secretary.

Crystal scowled. "Somebody's got to answer this telephone, so I'll have to wait."

Helen was faced with a difficult decision. She hated that complicated switchboard, but Crystal had been kind to her, and she really wanted to help further the secretary's law enforcement career. Finally, she sighed. "Okay, I'll try to answer at least every other call while you're gone."

Crystal's face brightened. "You mean it?"

"Yes, I mean it. But ask your questions quickly and get back here as soon as possible."

Crystal nodded and hurried out of the office as if she were afraid Helen would change her mind. Then four lines started ringing at once, and Helen groaned.

Barry Stanger came out of Matt's office a little while later and asked if Helen knew when the sheriff would be back. "He said it might be late this afternoon," she told the agent without taking her eyes off the blinking lights.

"Well, the computer guy in my office in Columbus was able to get the title of that book in the picture, and I just wanted to let him know."

Helen picked up a pencil. "If you'll give it to me, I'll check with the library and maybe we can save some time."

Agent Stanger looked at the piece of paper in his hand. "The title is *Dream of Death*. Kind of ironic, don't you think?"

Helen suppressed a shudder and nodded politely. Once the agent was back in Matt's office, she took off Crystal's headset and ignored all the blinking lights. The minute she saw an open line she dialed the library's number. "Could I speak to Ms. Fagan, please?" she asked the woman who answered. Ms. Fagan came to the phone promptly. "This is Helen Tyler. I work for Sheriff Clevenger."

"Yes, I remember you," Ms. Fagan replied.

"I was going to ask one of your employees to look something up for me, but I wanted to get your permission first," Helen said in her most diplomatic tone.

"We'll do our best to assist you." Ms. Fagan sounded marginally cooperative, and Helen was thankful for the years she'd spent playing politics in the academic world. "What do you need?"

"To know who checked out a particular book."

"I can handle that for you. What is the name of the book?"

"*Dream of Death,*" Helen read off her note.

There was a brief pause, then Ms. Fagan spoke again. "We have three copies of that book, two in adult fiction and one in our large-print section. According to the computer, only one is currently checked out, and it is listed under the name of . . . staff."

"What?" Helen asked.

"Staff. That means that the person who checked the book out is someone who has special status and doesn't actually have to use a card."

"Who would have this special status?"

"All of our employees, board members, the mayor and city council, and even some of our longtime volunteers."

"So there's no way to tell who checked out the book?"

"I'm sorry, no."

"Would it be possible to get a list of everyone who has staff status?"

After the briefest hesitation, Ms. Fagan replied, "I will fax it over in a few minutes. And then surely, Ms. Tyler, once you receive this last list, the sheriff's department will know us as well as we know ourselves."

Helen had to smile. "Thank you, Ms. Fagan. You have been extremely helpful. When this case is solved, you will have the satisfaction of knowing you saved lives."

There was another short pause, then Ms. Fagan spoke again. "And I have to say that hiring you was one of the sheriff's better decisions. Your fax should come through shortly."

Helen thanked the director of the Eureka library system again, then hung up as the dispatcher came in from her office. "Why isn't anyone answering the phone?" she asked.

Helen glanced down at the switchboard. She'd been so involved in collecting information that she forgot she was doing Crystal's job. "I'm supposed to be, but I'm trying to track down some information for the sheriff, and this switchboard requires more than even my total attention."

The dispatcher stared at her for another second, then nodded. "I'll handle the phones. You get the information Matt needs."

Helen didn't know whether the offer came out of loyalty for Matt or prejudice against blondes, but she accepted quickly. The fax from Ms. Fagan came through a few minutes later, and Helen scanned it quickly. Dr. Baker, Martin Freeburg, and Sonny Webster all had staff status at the library. Scott Howell and Elvis Hatcher did not. With a frown, Helen realized that she was probably going to have to abandon her attempts to tie Elvis to the murders.

While she was pondering this, her cell phone rang. She answered it absently. "Hello?"

"Helen? This is Sydney. Did you want to talk to me?"

"Oh, thanks for calling back. I need to set up an appointment with the bishop tonight, and was hoping you could give me his number."

There was a pause on the other end of the line. Then Sydney asked, "Are you at work?"

"Yes."

"Then tell me what time you want the appointment, and I'll set it up. Bishop Middleton runs a little tourist fishing business on the lake, and it might take awhile to track him down."

"I didn't mean to inconvenience you."

"I can make a few phone calls. I'm certainly not doing anything else," Sydney added.

"About seven-thirty would be good."

"If I don't call you back, that means you're set. If the bishop can't meet with you then, I'll let you know."

As Helen was returning her cell phone to her purse, Barry Stanger's partner arrived and she showed him into Matt's office. Barry introduced the new man as Agent Tucker. "He brought a technician with him," Agent Stanger told Helen, and she looked at the other man, wondering if he were mute. "We're going to install an extra phone line and set up another computer," Barry glanced around the room and finally settled on a corner, "there. Is that okay?"

Helen shrugged. "You'd need to ask Matt. He's the sheriff, and this is *his* office."

Barry smiled. "I know this looks intrusive, but we really are all on the same team, trying to solve the murder case before someone else dies."

Helen acknowledged this with a small nod. "Then go ahead and do whatever. I'm sure Matt won't object."

Before Barry could reply, another man walked in carrying a big box. For the next hour, Helen called the drug company representatives from Chief Ramsey's list and watched the FBI take over the Coosetta County sheriff's department. At first it was almost exciting, as if the cavalry had arrived. Then she started to feel as if Matt and the other local folks were being pushed into the corners like dunces, and her excitement changed to resentment.

In between giving the FBI disapproving looks, Helen managed to reach all but one of the drug reps. A Mr. Dewey Piper was unavailable, according to his office, so she left him a voice mail message. None of the people she talked to remembered Dr. Baker or anyone else asking for large samples of Digoxin.

At noon the dispatcher returned. "Matt's on line three," the woman said. "It's the little flashing red button with a big 'three' on it."

So it was the blonde prejudice, Helen thought to herself as she replaced the headset and reached for the blinking light.

* * *

Matt settled comfortably into the contours of the Bronco's seat, then pressed his cell phone to his ear as Helen answered. "Where's Crystal?"

"Interviewing the people on her section of the prayer list," Helen replied. "I'm supposed to be answering the phone for her, but the dispatcher finally took pity on me and the rest of Eureka."

"Other than phone problems, is everything going okay there?"

"Barry Stanger's computer friend was able to come up with a title for the library book at Robyn Howell's house. Get this—it was a mystery novel called *Dream of Death.*"

Matt frowned at the road through the Bronco's windshield. "That's appropriate. We need to know who checked out that book."

"According to Ms. Fagan, there's no way to tell. It was checked out to 'staff.' I asked for a list of everyone who has staff status, and it turns out that most of our suspects do, except Scott Howell and Elvis."

Now Matt had to smile. "Does this mean Elvis is finally off the hook?"

"I still don't like him, but I don't think he's the murderer. How did the trial go?"

"It was a big waste of time. One of the witnesses didn't show up, so the defense attorney got the judge to reschedule for next week. But while I was pacing the halls of the courthouse waiting to be released, I got a call from Brian West. He gave me some new information on Sonny Webster and Martin Freeburg. He found the connection between Robyn Howell and Sonny Webster."

"What was it?" Helen asked.

"Sonny was required to take a computer applications class as part of his drug rehabilitation program, and Robyn was the teacher. It was held at the Muscogee County Courthouse, and that's why Sonny didn't show up on her lists of students."

"I guess he lied because he didn't want to admit that he'd been arrested," Helen predicted.

"I can't really say I blame him."

"So, you don't think this new information makes him a suspect?"

"He already was a suspect. I don't think it makes him a *better* one. Now Martin Freeburg is another story. Brian says that he found an application for an insurance policy that was filled out just a few days before Mrs. Freeburg died. It's still in the processing stage, and that's why he didn't find it in his initial search."

"Who filled out the application?"

"Martin himself. He has a little estate planning company and sells insurance as part of that. The policy was only for $100,000, which isn't much as policies go. But the interesting part is that it doesn't have a sixty-day waiting period, which is standard on most life insurance policies. So even though he hasn't paid the first premium, he'll still get the money."

"That does look bad."

"Oh, and that's not all. His company does job-related injury claims for Bob Walters' Mines, and he makes a trip out there every Friday."

"And probably gets some coal dust on his clothes."

"And Martin's had some financial difficulties lately. He had to file for protection under federal bankruptcy laws, and he laid off his secretary. Brian made a date to take the woman out to lunch and hopes to know more about Martin's financial woes afterwards."

"Is that legal?" Helen wanted to know.

"There's nothing illegal about taking someone out to lunch. Asking questions about Martin Freeburg may not be completely ethical, but if it helps us solve this murder, I don't care."

"I guess we need to make some more index cards for Mr. Freeburg."

Matt sighed. "Yes, I guess we do. I was all settled on Dr. Baker, but this new information can't be ignored."

"I'll make them up and put them on the suspect wall, assuming I can fit in your office with all those FBI agents."

Matt was mildly alarmed. "How many of them are there?"

"Just two agents and a technician at the moment, but if they keep multiplying at this rate, you'll have hundreds by the end of the week."

Matt laughed. "I'm going to call Ed Ramsey and have him meet me at the office to go over this new information. If he gets there before I do, try to find him a chair that the FBI isn't using."

"It will probably have to be in the ladies' room."

"Could be worse."

* * *

After Matt hung up, Helen started making phone calls to local pharmacies, asking about prescription fraud. All the pharmacists had stories to tell, but most were about narcotics, muscle relaxants, or diet pills. When she talked to the pharmacist who filled Mary Jean Freeburg's prescriptions, he asked her to hold for a minute while he went into his office. When he came back on the line, he said that he didn't want to talk where his employees could overhear.

"Mrs. Freeburg's son always picked up her prescriptions, and in the month of April he had the same prescription filled twice. He said his mother accidentally threw the first bottle away, so we replaced it."

Helen's heart started beating faster. "How many pills would that be?"

"Two a day, sixty pills."

"And how many would be a lethal dose?"

"I'm not sure about that, but I'd say half that many," the pharmacist estimated. "But the craziest thing of all is that he filled his mother's prescription one last time a couple of days *after* she died. He had several of his own prescriptions refilled, and I didn't notice that one of Mrs. Freeburg's was mixed in with them until later. I called and offered to take them back and give him a refund, but he said it was his mistake and he'd just discard them."

"Thank you so much for this information," Helen told the man. "It will be a big help to us."

Helen hung up the phone and started writing more index cards. Ed Ramsey did arrive before Matt, but Helen put him in the chair beside Crystal's desk instead of in the ladies' room.

"This place is crawling with Feds," he whispered to Helen, and she nodded.

"By the time this is over, they may decide to open an office in Eureka."

Helen was kidding, but the chief looked concerned by this remark. "What's that you're doing?" He pointed at the cards.

Helen passed them across the desk and explained their latest discoveries.

"Darn. When we get closer on one suspect, something comes up on another."

Helen had to smile. "I know. Why can't one guy just look guilty, and stay that way?"

Matt came through the door from the stairwell, then stepped carefully over the roll of cable that the FBI technician was installing. "Welcome to crime central, Ed," he told the police chief, then turned to Helen. "I hate that Crystal's missing this. It's bound to be just like something she's seen on a television show." He looked down at the cards in Ed's hands. "What's that?"

"New information," Helen spoke for the chief. "It looks like Martin Freeburg was stocking up on Digoxin."

Matt's face registered shock as he took the cards and read them quickly. "Well, I'll be."

Crystal burst through the doors, her eyes wide with excitement. "There's a big van outside blocking the whole parking lot. I had to park in the deck two blocks away, and they charge five bucks a day!" she told them.

"It's the FBI," Matt informed her with relish. "They're taking over the sheriff's department."

"They are just here temporarily to help Matt with his murder case," Helen corrected with a stern look at the sheriff. "Now you'd better sit back at this switchboard before the dispatcher kills me. Because of my ineptitude, she's been having to answer calls ever since you left."

Crystal resumed her position at the switchboard, and the chief spoke to Matt. "Oh, I did get a little piece of news myself today. A college kid who makes deliveries for Fiona's Florist said a guy approached him after work a couple of weeks ago and asked him to deliver two baskets. The baskets had a white Bible and some chicken soup, and he recognized the addresses of Judith Pope and Iris Whited."

"Did he describe the man?" Matt wanted to know.

"Said it was an older guy with gray hair. He wore a hat and kept it down low so it shadowed his face. Could have been either Baker or Freeburg."

"And he probably paid the kid in cash?"

"Oh yeah," the chief said as he stood. "One of us had better get in there and keep an eye on those FBI boys, and I guess it's going to have to be me." He stepped toward the office door.

Matt nodded. "I'll be there in a minute."

The phone rang and Crystal answered it with casual competence. "It's for you," she told Helen. "Some guy named Dewey Piper."

"He's one of the drug company reps I contacted this morning. I'll get it in the break room." She walked to the other room and picked up the phone, then explained what information she needed. There was a long pause, and she was beginning to wonder if he had been cut off. Finally, Mr. Piper said he had something that might help her, but didn't want to discuss it on the phone. "I'm at the Starbright Café. Meet me here." Then the phone went dead.

Helen walked back to Crystal's desk and was surprised to see Matt still standing there. "What did the drug guy say?" Matt asked.

"He wants me to meet him at the Starbright Café," Helen told him. "He says he has information he can't give me over the phone."

"That sounds a little strange," Matt said with a frown.

"Sounds delicious to me," Crystal disagreed. "Will you bring me a take-out vegetable plate with cornbread and a piece of peanut brittle pie?"

Helen nodded, but Matt was shaking his head. "I don't like it. For all we know, this Piper character could be the murderer."

"The restaurant is a very public place," Helen pointed out. "If Mr. Piper wanted to hurt me, he'd ask to meet in a dark alley or a deserted warehouse."

"Matt!" Chief Ramsey called from the crowded office. "Are you coming in here or not?"

Matt looked over his shoulder. "I'll be there in a minute." Then he turned back to Helen. "I guess you can go, but keep your cell phone on and call Crystal if the guy starts acting funny."

"She's not going anywhere in her car unless you get the FBI to move their van," Crystal reminded them. "I'd loan you my car, but you'd have to walk two blocks and pay five dollars to get out of the deck."

"Just take the Bronco," Matt interrupted. "I parked on the street right in front of our building."

Crystal looked up in astonishment. "Either I'm in the twilight zone or I've just witnessed a miracle."

Helen narrowed her eyes at the secretary. "What? You don't think I'm a good enough driver to handle his car?"

"It's not what I think that matters. It's what *he* thinks." Crystal pointed at Matt. "In all the years I've known him, I've never seen him invite *anybody* to drive his precious car—not even his . . ." Crystal trailed off, a horrified look on her face.

"What?" Helen asked in confusion.

Matt finished the sentence for Crystal. "Not even my wife."

"I'm so sorry, Matt." Crystal seemed next to tears.

"It's okay," Matt told her. "If the past few years haven't taught me anything else, I've learned that *things* don't mean much. Even classic Ford Broncos."

Crystal still looked devastated, and Helen stepped in to help lighten the mood. "I guess that means you wouldn't let me drive your car if you still valued it, right?" she teased, and Matt gave her a grateful smile.

"That's it." Matt pulled his keys from his pocket and handed them to Helen. They were still warm from his body heat, and Helen wrapped her fingers around them. "All you have to do is turn the key and put it in drive."

Helen batted her eyelashes. "Gee, I think even a dumb blonde like me can handle that."

"You may be blonde, but you're sure not dumb," Crystal replied, then looked at Matt. "You'd better get in your office before the FBI adds *you* to the suspect wall."

Matt smiled. "And I've got to tell them about our new clue," he said and Helen raised an eyebrow. "Don't worry. I'll give you full credit."

She nodded, then turned to Crystal. "How do I get to the Starbright Café?"

Matt walked into his office while Crystal drew a small map. Then Helen walked down the stairs and out of the building. Matt's Bronco was parked right in front, just as he'd said. It took a few minutes to get the seat and mirrors adjusted, then Helen started the car and followed Crystal's directions to the restaurant.

When Helen arrived at the Starbright Café, she placed Crystal's to-go order, then gave the hostess Mr. Piper's name and was taken to a booth in a far corner. Dewey Piper was a heavyset man with gray hair and a red nose. Based on the empty beer bottles that littered the table,

Helen assumed the facial discoloration came from excessive drinking rather than playing golf. He didn't rise when Helen approached, but waved at the other side of the booth and offered to buy her a drink.

"No, thank you," Helen declined as she slid into the seat across from him. "I only have a few minutes," she added, hoping to hurry Mr. Piper.

He took a long sip of beer. "I must be crazy, agreeing to talk to you at all," he told her, his speech a little slurred. "I'm already on probation with the company, and if they find out that I've broken another rule, they'll can me." He looked up at Helen with a smile that closely resembled a leer. "But you sounded pretty on the phone, and in person, you're even better than I expected."

Helen wanted Mr. Piper to talk to her, but didn't want to give him a wrong impression, so she chose her words carefully. "What rule did you break?"

"Well, Merrill Pharmaceuticals is in the business of selling drugs, not giving them away. But in January Doc Baker told me he had a patient that was having trouble paying for her prescriptions. There are charities that help old folks with stuff like that, but he said this woman was too proud for that. He wanted me to give him samples of Digoxin for her every month."

Helen leaned forward. "And you agreed?"

Mr. Piper shrugged. "Yeah. Doc was real good to my wife when she was diagnosed with diabetes, and so I thought—what the heck? As long as I gave the pills directly to the doctor, who would ever know?"

Helen's cell phone started ringing and she reached for it impatiently. "Hello?"

It was Matt. "Are you okay?"

"I'm fine, but I'm busy. I'll be back in a few minutes."

"You'd better be, or I'm coming to get you."

Helen hung up without replying. "Who was the patient that Dr. Baker wanted the Digoxin for?" she asked Mr. Piper.

"I don't know. He never told me."

Helen frowned. "So, for all you know, there may not have even been a patient who needed the medication?"

Mr. Piper blinked, then shook his head a couple of times. "Doc isn't in any kind of trouble, is he? I mean, I can't testify against him in court or anything. Besides, if my supervisor finds out, I'll get fired!" Mr. Piper's words attracted attention from neighboring tables.

Helen spoke in a harsh whisper. "We're investigating a series of murders, Mr. Piper. If the doctor is involved, you will have to testify against him, even if it costs you your job." She took a deep breath. "But you did the right thing by telling me. You might have helped to save someone's life." Mr. Piper made no comment. "Give me a number where you can be reached in case the sheriff has more questions."

Dewey Piper pulled a business card from his pocket. "He can leave a message on voice mail just like you did."

Helen put the card into her purse and stood. "Thank you, Mr. Piper."

He didn't answer, just raised his hand to alert the waitress that he needed another drink.

Helen paid for Crystal's lunch, then drove quickly back to the sheriff's department.

* * *

Matt was pacing around Crystal's desk when Helen walked back in. "Why didn't you call me from the car so I'd know you were on your way?" he asked.

"I thought I'd better keep both hands on the wheel so I wouldn't wreck your Bronco, even though you don't care that much about it anymore," she said as she handed the styrofoam container to Crystal.

Matt narrowed his eyes. "What did Piper have to say?"

"That he's been delivering a monthly supply of Digoxin to Dr. Baker at his office since the first of the year for an unknown patient with a limited income."

"Dr. Baker probably really is giving the medicine to a poor patient," Crystal called from her desk. "Why don't you just ask him?"

Matt nodded. "I think it's time we have a talk with Dr. Baker and Martin Freeburg." He looked back at Helen. "While you were gone, Brian West called and reported on his lunch with Mr. Freeburg's secretary. She said Martin and Robyn Howell almost became business partners a couple of months ago."

"How would they have even met?"

"I told you Martin was having financial problems. Apparently a nasty divorce and the expense of taking care of his mother had taken its toll, and he was looking for an investor. He placed some ads in financial magazines, and Robyn answered one. She was interested—even had partnership papers drawn up, according to the secretary. Then she changed her mind at the last minute, and Martin had to file for bankruptcy."

"I don't know if that's a motive for murder, but I can see how he would be mad at her."

Matt pointed toward Crystal's desk. "Brian is faxing Martin's financial records now."

"And for someone who doesn't have any money, he has a *lot* of records," Crystal muttered.

Matt smiled at Helen. "You come with me and tell the FBI agents and Ed what the drug guy said."

After listening to Helen's report, all the law enforcement officials agreed that their two major suspects should be questioned. "Since this is your case, Matt, you should be the one to bring them in," Barry Stanger suggested.

Matt raised an eyebrow. "*Is* this still my case, Barry?"

The FBI agent shrugged and gave Matt a sheepish smile. "For the moment."

Matt nodded, then stared at the suspect wall for a few seconds. "While we're questioning people, we might as well question all our major suspects. Ed, maybe you could talk to Sonny Webster at the library and tell him I don't appreciate him lying to me about knowing Robyn Howell."

Ed nodded in assent. "And since we don't want you FBI boys to be bored while we're questioning people, why don't y'all talk to Elvis Hatcher?" Matt suggested with a quick look at Ed. The police chief winked back. "He might be a little hard to track down, but Crystal will help you."

"Fine by me," Barry agreed.

Matt turned his head and called for Crystal. When the secretary arrived in his doorway, Matt told her to help the FBI agents locate Elvis. Then he asked Ed which policeman was watching Dr. Baker at the moment.

"Billy Weller," the chief replied.

Matt turned to Crystal. "Who do we have on Martin Freeburg?"

"Steve Pahos."

"Crystal, find out where both suspects are and tell Weller and Pahos to be prepared to bring them in."

Crystal nodded and left the office. Matt handed Helen some index cards, and they started adding the new information while the FBI agents and Chief Ramsey discussed the wisdom of another press conference.

"The local stations are breathing down my neck," Ed told them. "And yesterday I even got a couple of calls from out-of-town reporters."

"I guess it wouldn't hurt to keep the public informed," Barry finally said.

"Will we tell them that we have a suspect?" Ed wanted to know. "The voters always feel better when they hear that."

Matt shook his head. "It's too soon."

"I think it will be okay as long as you don't give any names," Barry countered.

Matt shrugged, then went back to writing on index cards as Crystal yelled from her desk. "Dr. Baker's making rounds at Lakeside Hosptial, and Freeburg's at the dentist."

"Call Dr. Baker's office and find out what time he's expected back there, and make me an appointment to talk to him. Then tell Pahos to bring Freeburg in for questioning," Matt returned.

"Can he wait until Mr. Freeburg's teeth are clean, or do you want him to yank the poor guy out of the dentist's chair?"

Matt walked to the door and gave Crystal a look of annoyance. "Tell Pahos to wait in the parking lot and approach Mr. Freeburg when he leaves the dentist office. He doesn't need to arrest him, just ask him to come in and answer a few questions. Mr. Freeburg won't give him any trouble."

Crystal gave him a curt nod, then waved at a stack of paper. "You want this financial stuff or what?"

Matt sighed. "I guess I'll add it to the rest of the confusion in my office."

Ed used Matt's phone to set up the press conference for five o'clock that afternoon, in time for the evening news. While they were discussing what they would say, Crystal walked in and said that Martin Freeburg was on his way to the sheriff's department. Then she turned to Matt. "And you have an appointment with Dr. Baker at two-thirty."

Matt checked his watch. That gave him over an hour to grill Martin Freeburg before he had to leave for Dr. Baker's office.

"We'll do the questioning upstairs in the jail conference room," Matt told the FBI agents and Ed Ramsey.

"Sounds fitting to me," Barry agreed.

Matt stepped to the doorway and spoke to Crystal. "When they get here, send them up to Myron's conference room. We'll be waiting for them." He turned to Helen. "Come with us and take notes."

Agents Stanger and Tucker, Chief Ramsey, Matt, and Helen were all seated around the conference room table when Officer Pahos ushered Martin Freeburg in. Matt asked the policeman to guard the door, hoping to rattle their suspect a little. It must have worked, because Martin Freeburg's hands were shaking and he looked next to tears.

"I can't imagine why you want to talk to me, Sheriff," Martin said after a quick glance around the room.

"We want to question you about the murders of your mother and Robyn Howell," Matt said bluntly, and the color drained from Martin's face as he collapsed into a chair.

"You're sure, then, that they were killed?"

"Positive," Matt affirmed. "I have representatives from the FBI and the city police here," he waved in the general direction of the room's other occupants, "and I recommend that you call your attorney before the questioning procedes." Matt paused, hoping Martin would waive his right to have a lawyer present.

"I'm innocent!" Martin said fervently. "I don't need a lawyer!"

"If you can't afford an attorney, the court will appoint one for you," Matt added.

Martin Freeburg blushed at this reference to his financial condition, but shook his head. "Go ahead and ask me whatever you want to know."

Matt cleared his throat and continued. "The first thing I'd like you to explain is why you didn't tell me that you knew Robyn Howell when we talked before."

Martin looked at the table. "I didn't think it was important."

Matt nodded as though he accepted this weak excuse, then changed directions. "You've had some financial problems lately."

Martin acknowledged this with a nod. "It's been a bad year."

"Your wife filed for divorce in January and asked for a large percentage of your assets, but you didn't contest it."

Martin shrugged. "Our marriage had been over for a long time, and I was relieved to finally end it. She made sacrifices in the early years when I was building the company, and I figured she deserved something. Besides, business was good, and I thought I could build my cash reserves back up. So I let her have the house and most of our savings and some company stock."

"Which she promptly sold."

Martin nodded. "Yes. Then the economy took a nosedive, and I couldn't get my company going again."

"And at this point, Robyn Howell answered an ad you had placed in *Fortune* magazine and agreed to become your business partner?"

Martin looked surprised, but didn't ask how this information had been obtained. "Yes. Robyn had some money to invest, and I showed her how successful my company had been in the past. She saw the earning potential, and we had partnership papers drawn up."

"But Ms. Howell backed out at the last minute."

"Making money was the driving force in Robyn's life," Martin said slowly. "She found a better, more secure deal and pulled her offer."

"That must have made you hopping mad."

"It didn't make me happy," Martin admitted. "But I don't think Robyn realized that by canceling the partnership she was essentially destroying my company."

"So you were understanding about the whole thing?" Matt asked incredulously.

"I know you find that hard to believe, Sheriff, but I did understand. Robyn had to make money—and lots of it—since her insurance wouldn't cover the cost of some experimental treatments she was receiving . . ."

"For the HIV, you mean?"

Martin's eyes widened. "You knew about that too?"

"You find out a lot about a person during an autopsy," Matt said, purposely being callous.

Martin flinched, then blushed again, and Matt got an idea. "Your relationship with Ms. Howell wasn't completely a business one, was it Mr. Freeburg?"

Martin looked away. "We were both lonely. We loved classical music and the Braves, so we became friends."

"Just friends?" Matt asked.

Martin bristled. "I'm an old man. Why would a girl like Robyn be interested in me? Besides, her creep of an ex-husband had turned her against men for life."

Matt raised an eyebrow. "How so?"

"By divorcing her, then blackmailing her."

Matt felt as though he'd been sucker punched. "Why don't you tell me a little more about that?" he suggested through a clenched jaw.

Martin sighed and clasped his fingers together. "Robyn developed a bleeding ulcer a few years ago and had to have a transfusion. One of the blood donors had AIDS, but it was too early to detect it and Robyn ended up with HIV. She said Scott acted all loving and supportive in front of the doctors when they gave them the bad news, but when they got home he said there was no way he was living with her anymore."

"He wanted a divorce?"

Martin nodded. "But the bum had a lot of expensive hobbies that were supported by Robyn's hard-earned income. He told her he was going to file for a quiet divorce, then instructed her to give him a huge amount of money every month and anything else he asked for. Otherwise he threatened to tell everyone about her disease and ruin her career—which was her life."

Matt's original negative feelings for Scott Howell returned. "So she agreed?"

Martin nodded. "She had no choice, even though she was a danger to no one."

"Mr. Howell told us that she visited him in Atlanta one weekend a month. He claimed that they were still good friends."

"She hated Scott. If *he'd* turned up dead, I'd say she would be your prime suspect. She had to go to Atlanta once a month to see her specialist and to give Scott his check. I guess she figured she ought to stay at his place since she was paying for it."

Matt shuffled the pages in front of him, then looked back up. "Can you explain why you had your mother's prescription of Digoxin filled twice in the month of April?"

"She threw away the new bottle by mistake, and I had to get a replacement."

"And why did you refill her prescription for Digoxin after her death?"

Martin squirmed a little. "Things were very confusing right after Mother died. I have some medication that I take daily. I called the refills in and must have given them a wrong number. Or maybe they made a mistake. I don't know."

"The druggist said he offered to give you a refund if you'd bring the pills back. Since money is tight for you right now, it seems like you would have taken him up on that."

"The cost was negligible, and besides, I had already thrown the pills away."

"Why did you apply for a life insurance policy on your mother just a few days before her death?" Matt pressed.

"My business was to provide overall estate planning for people, and as a part of that, I sold life insurance policies. In order to keep my agent status with Beneficial Life Insurance, I have to submit a certain number of policy applications each month. I was short for the month of June, so I wrote one on Mother. I also did one on myself and a couple of friends. I didn't expect them to ever actually be in force since no premiums would be paid, but it was a way to keep from losing what I have left of my business."

"And the $100,000 will come in handy since your mother conveniently died and there was no waiting period in the policy on her life."

Martin frowned. "That's a rather cruel remark, but it's true that I can use the money. I had to refinance my car to pay Mother's funeral expenses."

Matt could feel Helen's disapproving look, but steadfastly kept his gaze from hers. "Can you tell us about the fight you had with Judith Pope over the new bookmobile at the library?"

Martin looked startled again. "There was no fight. The library had some money to spend, and I had seen how much happiness the bookmobile brought into my mother's life, so I suggested they buy another one. Ms. Pope took exception since the money was earmarked for a Braille book section. She won, I lost. That's all there was to it."

"Mrs. Iris Whited is a member of the Literary Guild, and she argued against you as well."

Martin spread his hands in supplication. "Do you seriously think I would try to kill two women over a new bookmobile?"

Matt was a little uncomfortable with the question, but shrugged. "You tell me."

"I *am* telling you, Sheriff. I had nothing to do with Robyn's death, and I spent years caring for my mother. It's obscene for you to even consider that I might harm her. And I barely knew Ms. Pope and Mrs. Whited. I probably wouldn't recognize them if I met them on the street."

"You're sure that you can't verify your whereabouts on these dates?" Matt slid a piece of paper across the table to the man.

Martin shook his head. "I live alone, and I don't have employees anymore. I was probably at home on each of these dates, but I can't prove it."

Ed Ramsey leaned forward and spoke for the first time. "This doesn't look good, Mr. Freeburg."

Martin wrung his hands. "I know. But everything I've said is true."

"We may not have any choice but to arrest you soon," Matt told him quietly.

Martin looked around in exasperation. "Well, I didn't kill anyone, and while you're sitting here asking me all these meaningless questions, the real murderer is out there getting ready for his next victim."

Matt blinked, trying to keep his reaction from showing. "We're going to let you go for now, but please don't leave the city limits without notifying my office first. And if you think of anything that would clear your name, let me know."

Martin Freeburg sighed as he stood. "You'd better listen to me . . ." he waved his hand to include the others sitting silently around the table, "all of you, or it will be your fault when someone else dies."

Matt waited until Officer Pahos had escorted Martin Freeburg out into the hallway, then turned to face his companions.

"Well, what did you think?" Ed asked.

Matt shook his head. "I'm afraid he's telling the truth."

* * *

When they got back downstairs, Helen sat by Crystal's desk and filled the secretary in on the interview with Mr. Freeburg while Matt went into his office to confer with the other men. They all came out together at two-fifteen. "Did you find Elvis?" Matt asked Crystal.

"Yeah, he's at his house waiting for the FBI agents."

"Helen and I are headed to Dr. Baker's office," Matt continued. This was news to Helen, and she stood quickly. "Chief Ramsey will be at the library if anyone is looking for him."

Crystal nodded as Helen followed Matt outside. Matt was quiet during the drive to Dr. Baker's office, frequently chewing his bottom lip and scowling at the road in front of him. "Do you take shorthand?" he asked when they parked in front of an unimposing building.

"No, but I write fast," Helen replied.

He nodded without a trace of humor. "Good. I want a record of every word Dr. Baker says, but I'm afraid a tape recorder might spook him."

The waiting room was filled to capacity with people of all ages, races, and economic conditions, united in the misery of illness. Some looked up when Helen and Matt entered; most did not. Matt stepped up to the receptionist and told her he was there for a two-thirty appointment with Dr. Baker. The woman stood and motioned them to a door on the right.

"Come right this way." She ushered them into a small, cluttered office that reminded Helen vaguely of Matt's. "The doctor will be with you soon."

A few minutes after the receptionist left, Dr. Baker rushed in. He was a little under six feet tall, thin with gray hair and tired, brown eyes. His white lab coat hung open, exposing a dress shirt and bow tie. Matt stood, and the doctor extended his hand. "Nice to see you, Matt. Who's your friend?"

Matt accepted the doctor's hand. "This is Helen Tyler. She's my research assistant."

The doctor's expression dimmed. "I guess this is an official visit, then."

Matt nodded. "Yes, sir. I need to ask you some questions."

"Have a seat." Dr. Baker waved toward the chair Matt had been sitting in, then moved around behind the desk and sat heavily in his swivel chair. "What do you need to know?"

"Glida Mae Magnanney said that before she moved to the nursing home, you knocked on her door during the middle of the night and tried to get her to let you inside her house. Is that true?"

Helen watched the doctor's eyes widen. "Glida Mae also says she was a movie star," Dr. Baker pointed out, and Matt looked away. "I did check on her regularly, but never in the middle of the night. Of course, since Glida Mae's grasp on reality is slim, she may have thought it was later than it really was when I came by."

"Did you visit Robyn Howell on the night she died?"

Dr. Baker nodded as if he had been expecting this. "Yes. Her neighbor, Edith McBride, is a longtime friend of mine. She was worried about Ms. Howell because of a cold she'd had for a couple of weeks. I stopped by and offered to do a strep test, but Ms. Howell declined. She said she had an appointment with her own doctor in Atlanta the next week and would wait until she could see him."

"So when you left, Ms. Howell was alive."

The doctor gave him an amused look. "Very much so."

"You were listed as Mary Jean Freeburg's primary physician. Did you make regular house calls to see her?"

"At least once a week."

Matt seemed surprised by this. "Mrs. Freeburg needed treatment that frequently?"

"No, she was just lonely and enjoyed the visits, so I made a point to go by."

"Did you ever administer medication to her?"

"Quite often," the doctor admitted. "If I was there and it was time for her to take her medication, I'd count them out for her."

"Do you know a representative for Merrill Pharmaceuticals named Dewey Piper?"

Dr. Baker considered this for a few seconds. "I see so many drug company representatives, but yes, I think I remember Mr. Piper. Kind of a big, gray-haired man?"

"With a red nose," Helen contributed, and the doctor nodded.

"Oh, yes. I do remember him. Well on the road to alcoholism."

Matt ignored this comment and leaned forward. "Did you ever ask Mr. Piper to give you free Digoxin samples for one of your patients?"

For the first time since they arrived, Dr. Baker looked a little uncomfortable. "Yes," he admitted softly.

"What was the patient's name?" Matt demanded.

"I don't see why that is important."

"It's important because four women in this area have been poisoned with that drug during the last couple of weeks, and anyone who has access to large amounts of it is suspect."

The doctor nodded. "Well, it doesn't seem like it would matter anymore, but I asked Mr. Piper to give me the samples for your grandmother."

Helen had to control a gasp as she watched Matt's face go pale. "My grandmother?"

"She lived on such a limited income—less than most people pay for a car each month. But she believed in taking care of herself and wouldn't hear of asking for help. Even when I told her I had arranged for samples, she refused to accept them. To convince her, I finally had to say that they would just go to waste if she didn't use them."

Matt finally found his voice. "But my grandmother has been dead since February, and Mr. Piper told Helen that he was still delivering the samples to your office every month."

The doctor rubbed his forehead in a weary gesture. "I guess I forgot to tell Mr. Piper that we didn't need them anymore."

"Do you have a medicine cabinet where you keep drug samples?" Matt asked.

Dr. Baker stood. "Come and I'll show you."

The "medicine cabinet" turned out to be a huge plastic tub full of various drug samples. There was no organization that Helen could see.

"So, when a drug rep gives you samples, they are just dumped in here?" Matt asked incredulously. "Some of these medicines are dangerous and probably even controlled substances."

Dr. Baker shrugged. "An overdose of vitamins can be fatal. We can't keep everything under lock and key."

"You don't keep track of the samples you are given or who gets them?" Matt sounded desperate.

"No. We put them here, and whenever a patient requests samples, one of the nurses looks through and gives them what we have."

Helen ran her hand through the hundreds of sample packets. "There are quite a few Digoxin packages here," she told Matt, and Dr. Baker gave her a smile.

"But there's no way to be sure all of the ones Mr. Piper delivered for my grandmother are there without counting."

"That would be a waste of time," Dr. Baker said. "I have many patients who take Digoxin, and I'm sure we've given away some of the samples intended for your grandmother."

"But you don't have an alibi for the nights of the murders?" Matt asked.

"No. All I can give you is my word that I had nothing to do with the deaths of those women."

Helen saw the look of frustration on Matt's face.

"I want to believe you, Dr. Baker," Matt said finally. "But the time might come when your word isn't enough."

Dr. Baker nodded. "If that time comes, I'll deal with it then. But right now I have a waiting room full of sick patients, so I'm going to have to ask you to excuse me." The doctor turned to Helen and gave her a small bow. "It was nice to meet you, Ms. Tyler. Maybe we'll have a chance to talk again under better circumstances."

"I hope so," Helen said, and she meant it.

Once they were back in the Bronco, Helen looked at Matt. "I'm sorry, but I have to agree with Crystal on this. Dr. Baker is not a killer."

"I don't want to think so," Matt said softly. "But I can't ignore the evidence. And he might not be killing for recreation. He might be trying to save people from pain."

"But Judith Pope and Iris Whited aren't sick."

"No, but they are lonely and grieving. Having lived through that, I can tell you it's worse than being sick."

Helen thought for a minute. "So you're saying that just because Dr. Baker is a nice, compassionate man doesn't mean he isn't the killer?"

"Unfortunately, that's exactly what I'm saying," Matt told her.

* * *

"Well, you look like something the cat dragged in *yesterday*," Crystal announced when they walked back into the office. She stared pointedly at Matt. "Have you cut back to fifteen minutes of sleep a day and quit shaving altogether?"

Matt rubbed the stubble on his chin. "Are the FBI guys back?"

Crystal shook her head. "Naw, but Chief Ramsey called. He said his conversation with Sonny Webster was uneventful, and he'll give you the boring details when you come to his office for the press conference."

As Crystal completed this sentence, Agents Stanger and Tucker walked in. "That Elvis Hatcher is a *nut!*" Barry exclaimed without preamble, and Helen had to cover her mouth to keep from laughing out loud.

"He's a little unusual," Matt admitted, the corners of his mouth turning up.

"Unusual?" Barry demanded. "His house is full of animals, and I don't mean just cats and dogs. He has squirrels and birds and even a possum."

Agent Tucker stepped forward and made a rare comment. "Mr. Hatcher said he used to have a *snake,* but hasn't been able to find it lately."

This time Matt did smile. "So, do you think Elvis is our man?"

Barry shook his head. "He won't kill a cockroach and uses herbal concoctions to repel fleas." This was said with a small shiver. "So I doubt murdering women with prescription heart medication is his hobby," Barry concluded. "He is weird enough to keep an eye on, though."

Matt sighed. "Well, let's go into my office and make new index cards," he told the FBI agents. "Then we'll finish our statement for the press conference in," he looked at his watch, "one hour."

Helen stood and put her hand on Matt's arm, delaying his departure. "I think I'll go home if you don't mind."

He gave her a weary smile. "You've put in a long day. You deserve a break."

"I want to be able to watch you on the news," she teased, and he groaned. "And I want to take a shower before our appointment at church tonight. Unless you think we should reschedule for another night."

Matt shook his head. "The press conference won't last long. What time are we supposed to be there?"

"Seven-thirty."

"I'll pick you up about seven."

Matt went into his office, and Helen looked around to see Crystal staring at her. "What?"

"Matt's going to *church* with you?"

"Well, it's not an actual worship service. He just wants to talk to my bishop about some questions he has."

"Religious questions?" Crystal clarified, and Helen nodded. "Wow, I don't think Matt has been inside a church since the funeral." Crystal gave Helen a worried look. "This might be more serious than I thought."

CHAPTER 12

As Matt drove toward Ivy Lane, he wondered if he'd finally lost his mind. He'd blamed recent decisions on fatigue, but he hadn't had a decent night's sleep in three years and this was the first time he'd agreed to talk to a Mormon bishop. The main question that nagged him was whether he was really interested in the Mormon point of view on life after death or just wanted to impress his lovely renter.

The subject of his confusion was standing on her porch when he pulled up. She was wearing a simple dress, and Matt was fascinated by the way the material floated around her calves as she walked. She climbed inside the Bronco and gave him a breathtaking smile. He felt his throat constrict and pulled against the collar of his uniform shirt. "I'm underdressed."

"You're fine," Helen assured him as they passed Nelda's house. The Nguyen children were standing on the sidewalk, and Helen waved. "So," she twisted slightly to face him, "you looked almost as grim as the FBI agents during the press conference."

Matt frowned. "That wasn't exactly my intention."

"No, your intention was to stand in the background and let Ed Ramsey and the FBI guys do all the talking."

Matt acknowledged this with a little nod. "My strategy in a nutshell."

"So, after the interviews this afternoon, who is our major suspect?"

"We can't choose between the two, and I keep thinking that I'm missing something. Something obvious that I'll hate myself for when I realize what it is." Matt paused, then shook his head in frustration.

"Not that it really matters. The FBI is about to take over the whole case anyway."

"I'd be glad to let them have it if I were you."

Matt looked over in surprise. "What? A glory seeker like you? I thought you'd want to solve the case single-handedly so you could be interviewed on the *Today Show*."

Helen shuddered. "That's the *last* thing I want," she assured him.

When they arrived at the church, Matt parked his Bronco and they walked inside. Bishop Middleton met them at the front door, and Helen introduced the men. "I appreciate you meeting with Matt on such short notice," Helen said. "He's been reading the Book of Mormon and has some questions. I didn't feel qualified to answer them, so we called you."

"I'm pleased that you want my opinion on theological questions," Bishop Middleton told Matt. "Surprised, but pleased."

"It was a last resort," Matt admitted, and the bishop laughed.

"The pressure is really on, then." The bishop led the way to his office.

When they reached the lobby, Helen sat on the couch right outside the bishop's door and Matt raised an eyebrow. "You're deserting me?"

She shook her head. "No, but this is something you need to do alone."

Feeling slightly abandoned, Matt followed the bishop into his office. Bishop Middleton walked around his desk and invited Matt to sit. "So, you've been reading the Book of Mormon?"

"Yes."

"What do you think?"

"It's very interesting and I wish I had more time to read, but things have been really busy at work and . . ."

"Yes, I watch the news." The bishop spared him from an explanation. "How far have you gotten?"

"I'm about halfway through Mosiah."

"Well, I'll be glad to try and answer any questions you might have, but the Spirit will be your best resource there."

"The Spirit?"

"The Holy Ghost," the bishop clarified. "Moroni was the last prophet to write on the gold plates, and he issued a challenge to his readers. He said, 'And when ye shall receive these things, I would exhort you that ye would ask God, the Eternal Father, in the name of Christ, if these things are not true; and if ye shall ask with a sincere heart, with real intent, having faith in Christ, he will manifest the truth of it unto you, by the power of the Holy Ghost.'"

"So after I get finished reading, I'm supposed to pray and ask God if the book is true?" The bishop nodded, and Matt continued. "I guess you know that my family died in a tornado a few years ago?"

"Yes, Sydney told me." The bishop was silent for a few seconds, then posed a question. "Do you blame God for the deaths of your wife and children?"

Matt shook his head. "No, I blame myself."

"What do you think you could have done against the strength of a tornado?"

Matt raised his eyes. "Maybe I could have saved them. At least I could have been there to comfort them at the end. And I could have gone with them instead of being left behind."

Bishop Middleton leaned forward onto his desk. "Sheriff, I believe that God has a plan for our lives. There are things we all need to accomplish, and apparently your wife and sons were able to complete their life's mission in a short time. You still have more to do."

Matt remembered Helen's analogy. "Yeah, like they're on vacation and I had to stay at work."

Bishop Middleton frowned. "I'm sorry?"

Matt shook his head. "Never mind." He took a deep breath and pressed on. "One of the few things that survived the tornado was my wife's Bible, and I've gotten in the habit of reading from the New Testament every night. Sometimes all night," he added. "And the thing that intrigued me about the Book of Mormon from the very beginning is that I can't tell the difference."

"The difference?" the bishop asked.

"Between the Book of Mormon and the Bible. I have to look to see which one I'm reading. They feel the same to me."

Bishop Middleton smiled. "They might have been written by different men, but they were inspired by the same source."

Matt acknowledged the possibility with a shrug. "But actually that's not why I wanted to talk to you tonight. I'm concerned about something else, and I thought that since you didn't know my family, you might be able to give me an unprejudiced opinion."

"I'll be glad to help you if I can."

"Since my wife died, I've had no interest in women," Matt began carefully. "Until Helen arrived in town."

"She's very beautiful," Bishop Middleton stated in an objective tone.

"There are hundreds of beautiful women in Eureka, and none of them attracted my attention. But Helen stirred up feelings in me that I thought had died with my wife." Matt glanced at the bishop, and he nodded in encouragement. "My attraction to her is growing stronger, but I feel so guilty and," Matt stopped, searching for the right word, "conflicted."

"You feel disloyal to your wife because you have feelings for Helen?" the bishop asked. Matt nodded miserably.

"If I really cared for my wife, then why am I falling in love with Helen?"

"You had two sons, isn't that right?"

Matt ignored the little stab of pain in his chest. "Yes. Chase and Chad."

"Did you love the older one more than the younger, or vice versa?"

Matt's head jerked up. "Of course not."

"So even though they were separate individuals, you were able to love them both at the same time. You shared memories with your first son that were particular only to him, and the same with the second son. But one relationship did not diminish the other?"

Matt felt a sense of peace envelop his heart. "No. I love them both equally."

"Mormons believe in eternal families. If you live worthy, your first wife and your sons can be sealed to you. If you marry again in this life, that wife can be sealed to you as well. In heaven, happiness is possible for everyone."

The bishop reached into his desk and pulled out two books. One was a well-worn paperback book. "This is a favorite book of mine," he said.

Matt read the title: *Our Search for Happiness.*

"And this has a lot of good information about the eternities." The bishop held up a hardback entitled *The Teachings of Joseph F. Smith*.

"Thank you." Matt stood. "I'll return them soon."

The bishop stood too. "There's no hurry. But you'd better be careful."

"About what?" Matt asked.

"If you're not careful, you'll turn yourself into a Mormon."

Matt was smiling when they stepped out of the office, and he found Helen asleep on the couch. He walked over to stand beside her and had to press his hands to his sides to keep from reaching out and stroking her cheek.

"I've been working her too hard lately," Matt said.

The bishop nodded. "I'm praying that you'll solve this murder case quickly."

"I need all the help I can get," Matt acknowledged, then shook Helen gently. "Time to go home."

She uncurled her legs and stood with a stretch. "Sorry. I didn't mean to fall asleep."

The bishop led the way toward the front doors. "I hope to see you back here on Sunday, Sister Tyler."

She smiled. "I plan to be here."

"And bring the sheriff with you," Bishop Middleton suggested, then pushed the door open for them.

"I might just do that," Helen said with a quick look at Matt. As Bishop Middleton waved good-bye, Matt took Helen's hand and pulled her outside.

* * *

Helen was still groggy and didn't notice Matt was still holding her hand until they got to the Bronco. Self-consciously she pulled her hand away, then cleared her throat. "Well, was the bishop able to answer your questions?" she asked. He was very close, which set her nerves on edge, so she leaned against the car to put some distance between them.

"Actually, yes. He even gave me homework." He raised the books, and she smiled. "I tried to tell him your analogy about Julie and the boys going on vacation without me, but he hadn't heard that one before."

"Well, it's about time he did," Helen said. He leaned forward, and for a terrifyingly wonderful moment, she thought he was going to kiss her. But instead, he opened the car door. She climbed inside, then clasped her hands together to keep them from trembling.

Matt walked around to the driver's side and slipped behind the wheel. Then he started the car and Helen stared out her window, mentally chastising herself for her lack of emotional discipline. She didn't have room in her life for romance, and she couldn't drag anyone else into her problems. Not even Matt. Especially not Matt. The car stopped, and she looked out the window with a sigh, expecting to see her little house on Ivy Lane. Instead, she saw countless headstones.

"Where are we?" Helen asked.

"I think it's time for you to meet the rest of my family," he said softly, then climbed out of the car.

Helen opened her door and followed him up a stone pathway to the top of a small rise. She saw the three markers and read the names in the moonlight. The letters blurred as tears filled her eyes.

"Don't cry," he whispered.

A light breeze lifted the hair around her face as Helen studied the peaceful spot. "It's a beautiful place. Do you come here often?"

"I try to limit myself to once a week. More than that seems obsessive."

Helen reached down and righted a vase of daisies that had fallen over in front of Julie Clevenger's grave marker. "You bring them flowers."

"No," Matt corrected. "The flowers are from Crystal and my parents and Julie's parents. I rarely bought her flowers when she was alive. It seems hypocritical to do it now."

Helen frowned as Matt continued.

"I don't mean that I was a bad husband or anything. I loved Julie and she knew that, but money was always tight, and Julie was a practical kind of person. I always assumed she'd consider flowers a waste of money."

"And you were probably right," Helen said, trying to comfort him.

He looked up at the cloudless sky. "You know those few minutes just before you fall asleep when you can indulge in a short daydream?"

Helen nodded, glad he couldn't see the heat that rose in her cheeks. Those few minutes of her day were usually dedicated to thoughts of him.

"My favorite one is coming home to our house—which is now a pile of rubble—and finding everything just like it was the last time I saw them. The kids are playing in the den, and Julie is making dinner in the kitchen. I have a big bouquet of flowers." His voice cracked, and he paused for a second. "I pull out the flowers, and her eyes light up. Then I tell her how beautiful she is and thank her for all the sacrifices she makes for me and the boys . . ."

He fell silent, and Helen took both his hands in hers. "She knows, Matt."

"I wish I could believe that," he whispered, then looked down at her. "You're *sure?*"

Helen nodded. "Trust me."

Instead of answering, Matt pulled his hands free and reached into his back pocket. He removed his wallet and took out a picture, then extended it to Helen. The boys were just as she had pictured them—small replicas of Matt. But Julie was a surprise. The cheerleader classification had led Helen to expect Matt's wife to be the glamorous type, but Julie Clevenger looked like a woman who spent more time at the park than in a beauty parlor and more money on her children's clothes than her own. Helen felt the tears flood her eyes again.

"They're beautiful," she told him.

"Yeah," he agreed as Helen handed the picture back.

Matt stared at the graves for a few more seconds, then took Helen's hand and started down the slope. Helen allowed him to lead her a few steps, then turned and looked back at the thick green grass that covered the final resting place of Matt's family. "I think you're wrong about the flowers," she said, and he gave her a questioning look. "It's not too late."

Matt tried to smile, then turned away, and she pretended that she didn't see the tears on his cheeks.

* * *

After taking Helen home, Matt spent most of Tuesday night reading the books Bishop Middleton had given him. They were so interesting that he stayed up later than he intended and was on his third cup of coffee when he pulled into the parking lot next to the sheriff's department the next morning. Helen was just getting out of her car, and Matt walked over to meet her.

"That's something you'll have to give up if you decide to actually become a Mormon," she told him, pointing at the styrofoam cup.

"Coffee?" he asked in surprise as they walked toward the building.

"Coffee, tea, tobacco, alcohol, and if you're an extremist, even caffeinated soft drinks are a thing of the past."

"How come?"

"It's a dietary law called the Word of Wisdom. It advises us not to eat much meat, mostly grains, fruits, and vegetables, and none of the things I mentioned earlier."

"But Mormons *can* eat pork on Tuesdays?" Matt clarified with a smile.

"And coconut pie any day of the week," she added as they reached Crystal's desk.

The secretary looked at them. "Morning, Matt, Helen."

"Good morning," Helen responded. Matt just nodded, still staring at his coffee cup.

"So, what's on our agenda for today? Scanning? Faxing? Browbeating old men?" Crystal itemized, and Matt looked up to give her a scowl.

"I've got a meeting with Ed Ramsey and the FBI agents at police headquarters in an hour."

"What are you fellows going to do? Discuss your favorite fishing holes?" Crystal asked.

"We're going to decide if we have enough evidence to arrest Martin Freeburg for murder."

Crystal was pleased by this. "So, you're not investigating Dr. Baker anymore?"

Matt frowned. "I didn't say that. I just think we have the best case against Martin. So while I'm gone, you and Helen go back through all

Mr. Freeburg's financial records, the PI reports, and anything else we have on him. Since most of our evidence is circumstantial, I'm going to need a lot of it, and I'm sure the DA will want everything organized."

"Oh boy!" Crystal said.

Matt ignored his sarcastic secretary and pulled Helen into his office.

"So, your case is almost solved."

"Well, I think we have enough evidence against Martin Freeburg to get a warrant, but I'll have to check with the DA first. And I'm still hoping that Judith will remember something that will incriminate Freeburg."

"Will you charge him with his mother's death or just Robyn Howell's?"

Matt shrugged. "I'll let the DA decide."

Helen seemed depressed. "I guess my job here will be ending soon."

Matt looked around the room. "Are you kidding me? Even without a murder investigation to distract you, it will take at least six months for you to organize this office."

Helen smiled. "You don't have to worry about me. I'm sure I can get a job substitute teaching."

"I'm worried about me, not you. One day I'm going to get so lost in here I won't be able to find my way out."

* * *

After Matt left, Crystal helped Helen arrange the information they had on Martin Freeburg in a semilogical order. While they worked, they discussed the press conference. "I thought it went pretty well," Helen ventured.

"Yeah, considering that we've got a serial killer running loose and a weak case against a leading citizen, it could have been worse," Crystal acknowledged.

Helen rested her elbows on a stack of computer printouts. "Do you think Mr. Freeburg really killed his mother and Robyn Howell?"

"Honestly? No. But I'd rather him get arrested than Dr. Baker, so I'm not complaining."

"Who do you think the killer is?"

Crystal shrugged. "Somebody we haven't considered yet. Probably a homeless person or drifter."

"You should tell Matt."

"He's not convinced he's got the right man. That's why he's dragging his feet."

"What do you mean?"

"Having meetings with the FBI and Chief Ramsey," Crystal said. "Telling us to organize this information. If he was sure about Martin Freeburg, he'd have been in the DA's office yesterday and would have taken this stuff with him in a wheelbarrow. Matt's waiting for something to click."

It was almost four o'clock when Matt came back from police headquarters. Helen was in his office, trying to sort through the mess on his desk. "Well?" she asked, and he sat down.

"The FBI has recommended that the DA indict Martin Freeburg. I have a meeting with him tomorrow," Matt told her, but he didn't look enthusiastic, and Helen knew Crystal was right. Matt didn't feel good about his case.

"You don't look very happy about it," she said.

"I just want this whole nightmare to be over," Matt said.

Before Helen could respond, Matt's phone rang and he picked it up.

"It's Dr. Appling," he mouthed to Helen, then pushed the speaker feature on his telephone. "So, how are things going with Judith Pope?"

A woman's voice responded. "I don't have much to report. She's still having dreams, and on the surface it seems that she is somehow able to see into the murderer's mind," the doctor began tentatively. "But only while she's asleep, and only for a few seconds. I need to do some research before we proceed."

"You mean try to enhance her dreams?"

"Or suppress them. These dreams are terrifying for Judith. I know you think they'll help you solve your case, but I want to be sure they won't damage her."

"I need her cooperation," Matt said, his voice tense. "And it's more about saving lives than solving a case."

"Sorry, Matt," the doctor replied. "But Judith's life is important too. She will not be questioned further until I'm convinced it will be safe."

Matt stared at the phone for a minute or two after his conversation with Dr. Appling ended, then shook his head and stood. "Well, so much for that."

Helen nodded in sympathy. "You've done the best you can. The FBI and the DA's office can take it from here."

Matt looked up, then blinked as if he'd been far away. "If you're not busy tonight, I was thinking that I could take you out to dinner at the finest eating establishment in Eureka."

Crystal walked in during his invitation. "You two celebrating already?"

"The murders aren't solved yet," Helen pointed out.

"Try to think positive," Crystal recommended, then turned to Matt. "You taking her to one of those places on the lake?"

Matt shook his head. "No, I'm taking her to my parents' house," he said, and Helen's stomach flipped. "My mama's the best cook in town."

Crystal raised an eyebrow in Helen's direction. "Meeting the folks. Now *that* sounds like loads of fun."

Matt ignored her remark and spoke to Helen. "I'll pick you up at seven o'clock."

Helen's hands were trembling as she drove home. What if Matt's parents hated her? What if they liked her? Could her life possibly get any more complicated? She had just pulled into her driveway when Thelma and Hugh strolled up. "We're going for our walk," Hugh explained.

"We'd be glad for you to join us," Thelma invited.

"Thanks," Helen said. "But I'm eating dinner with Matt and his parents tonight."

The Warrens exchanged a startled look. "Nelda told us you and Matt were dating, but we didn't think it was so serious."

Helen laughed. "It's not serious. He just wants to show off his mother's home cooking."

Hugh pulled on Thelma's hand. "Let's get going."

"Wait a minute, Hugh. Goodness gracious." She turned back to Helen. "I just feel that I should warn you about Matt. He's a wonderful person, and I like him very much—"

"Even if he did go to the University of Georgia instead of Auburn," Hugh interjected.

"But he was so devoted to Julie and the boys, and well, I just don't want to see you get hurt," Thelma finished.

Helen smiled as she started toward the front door of her rental house. "I understand, and I appreciate your concern. Have a nice walk."

The Nguyen children were in her backyard, so Helen walked through the kitchen, pausing only long enough to pick up a bag of Oreos, and went out the back door. After a few minutes of one-sided conversation, she finally handed them the cookies and went inside to take a shower.

Matt picked her up at seven o'clock, and they drove a few miles to a modest, ranch-style home. Both Matt's parents met them at the door, and he made introductions. Then Mrs. Clevenger returned to the kitchen while the men settled in the den. Helen offered to help Matt's mother, but she insisted that Helen relax, so she sat on the couch by Matt.

"Watch this, Helen," Mr. Clevenger said as he rewound a video with the remote control, then played it back in slow motion.

It was a football game, and the picture quality was poor. Helen squinted at the screen, trying to determine which teams were playing. The quarterback threw a long pass, and the receiver caught it for a touchdown. Helen looked up and saw that Mr. Clevenger was watching her expectantly. "That was very nice," she said.

"Yeah, Matt was the best."

Helen jerked her head around to Matt. "That was *you?*"

He nodded. "About a million years ago."

"State championship game during his senior year of high school. That touchdown won the game and got him a scholarship to the university."

"Nelda said that you hurt your knee," Helen said, looking down at his khaki-covered legs.

"Yeah, ACL injury. I had surgery, but the doctors told me I couldn't play football anymore."

"You like football?" Mr. Clevenger asked Helen.

"My father is a big Dolphins fan, so I've watched my share of games," Helen told Matt's father.

Mr. Clevenger's face lit up. "I've got a football signed by Dan Marino. Would you like to see it?" Helen said that she would, and Mr. Clevenger left in search of the autographed football.

"Don't tell your father, but I never really cared for the game," she told Matt under her breath.

Matt leaned closer. "Why not?"

"Because it's senseless and unnecessarily violent," she whispered. "Football is a perfect example of all that is wrong with our society today."

"Here it is," Matt's father announced as he reentered the room. He handed Helen the football, and she examined it thoroughly.

"This is great."

"It's a collector's item and worth a lot of money, but I wouldn't ever sell it. Has a lot of sentimental value," Mr. Clevenger explained as he stepped up to the television. "You want me to rewind this video so you can watch it from the first, Helen?"

"Oh, please do," she replied, then smiled up at Matt. Once the video was playing again, Mr. Clevenger went into the kitchen to check on his wife. Helen watched the youthful Matt lead his team to victory, and in spite of her feelings about football, she was impressed. "You were pretty good," she finally told Matt.

"For years, football was my life."

"Do you miss it?"

He considered this for a few seconds. "It's not the thing I miss most, but I do love the game. I planned to make a career of it."

This was a surprise. "You wanted to play football professionally?"

"No, I wanted to coach on a high school level, where it's still fun. Once you get higher than that, all the emotion's gone and it's just business."

"So, why didn't you pursue your dream?"

Matt shrugged. "The high schools here didn't need a coach. Julie already had a job at Lakeside Hospital, and her parents had given us land to build a house on, so moving wasn't much of an option. Then Sheriff Bridger offered me a deputy job with the department, and it just seemed like everything was falling into place."

"It's not too late," Helen told him.

"For what?"

"Being a coach."

Matt frowned. "I'd probably have to go back to school and get my master's to make myself competitive in the job market."

"So?"

Before he could answer, Mrs. Clevenger called them to dinner. While they ate the veritable feast, Matt's mother explained that she always cooked a big meal at night. "Just in case Matt makes it home," she said. "But he's so busy, we rarely see him. I'm glad you're working for him. Now that he's got some help, maybe he can get home at a decent hour."

Matt smiled. "Helen's been a wonderful addition to the department. She's a natural sleuth, but kind of a glory hog."

Both Clevengers turned their eyes to her, and Helen resisted the urge to kick Matt under the table. "In my brief experience with the Coosetta County sheriff's department, it seems that few cases actually get solved. Most of them just become files that clutter up your son's desk."

Matt laughed, and Mrs. Clevenger gave him a perplexed look, then addressed Helen. "Were the two of you investigating a case last night? Matt was out even later than usual."

Helen deferred this question to Matt with a glance. He put down his fork and faced his mother. "No, ma'am. Last night I had an appointment to talk to Helen's minister."

Mrs. Clevenger paled as she leaned forward and lowered her voice. "But didn't you say she is a *Mormon?*"

"Yes," Matt replied.

"Are you going to start being a Mormon too?" Mrs. Clevenger asked, her voice barely above a whisper.

Matt shrugged. "Maybe. I haven't decided for sure."

The room was deathly silent. Helen was at least as surprised as Matt's parents. Finally, Mr. Clevenger pushed away from the table. "Well, that was a delicious meal as usual, Rita. How about some of your famous carrot cake for dessert?'

Mrs. Clevenger pasted a smile on her face. "Everyone go sit in the den and let your food digest. I'll bring you some in just a few minutes."

The men stood and walked back to the den, but Helen had no desire to watch more football, and she felt that she owed Matt's mother some kind of explanation. So she stacked up dirty dishes and followed the other woman to the kitchen. She found Mrs. Clevenger leaning over the sink, weeping.

"I'm sorry," Helen apologized quickly. "I know you probably think that Mormons are bad, or that I've been pressuring him about religion, but really I haven't . . ."

Matt's mother held up a hand to stop her. "I'm the one who should apologize, and I'm not crying because Matt has shown an interest in your church. I'm crying because I've prayed so hard for Matt to find some peace. He's had such a hard time since Julie and the boys . . . well, you know. He's not comfortable in our church because of all the painful memories. So I asked the Lord to help him find another church." She glanced up at Helen. "Of course I was hoping the Lord would lead him to the Methodists or Presbyterians, something more . . . mainstream." Matt's mother shrugged.

Helen studied this woman who had lost her daughter-in-law, her grandchildren, and for a time, even her son. She wanted to offer some sort of comfort. "Matt is a good man," was all she could think to say.

Rita Clevenger nodded, then picked up one of the several jars of pale pink jelly that lined the counter. "I'd be pleased if you'd take some of my Mayhaw jelly."

Helen accepted the gift. "Thanks."

Rita put the dinner dishes into the sink full of soapy water. "Like we were saying, Matt *is* a good man, and in time I think he'll come to accept things and move on with his life. But I saw the way you looked at him tonight, and I feel I should warn you. He loved Julie dearly and may not be able to give his heart to another woman."

Helen smiled, thinking that the list of people warning her about Matt was growing almost as fast as her collection of Mayhaw jelly. "Matt and I are just friends."

Mrs. Clevenger studied her for a second. "Well, you brought him home to dinner and I thank you for that," she said. "And if it's the Lord's will that he be a Mormon, I can deal with that too." She dried her hands, then sliced the cake. After deftly distributing pieces onto saucers, she put them on a tray. "I've got to get this into the den before Henry starts that football video again."

"Can I help you, Mrs. Clevenger?" Helen offered.

"I've got it," Matt's mother responded. "And call me Rita."

* * *

When Matt got back from taking Helen home, he walked through the quiet house to his bedroom. He paused in front of what his mother called his trophy wall. It was covered with awards and souvenirs from his various sports careers. He thought of it as sort of a shrine to happy days gone by.

He picked up the football signed by all the members of his high school championship team. His fingers rubbed the dimpled surface and stroked the laces. For some time he had believed that football, like love and happiness, was a part of his past. Remembering Bishop Middleton's words from the night before, he wondered if he had a future after all.

CHAPTER 13

Helen slept fitfully on Wednesday night. At one point she thought she felt a presence in her bedroom and opened her eyes. She saw Glida Mae Magnanney sitting in a chair by her bed. "Hey, Glida Mae," she said. "Why aren't you at Gentle Haven?"

Glida Mae smiled. "I had to come back to keep watch over you while you sleep. Go ahead and close your eyes. I won't let any harm come to you."

Helen curled into her pillow and drifted off to sleep, grateful for Glida Mae's attendance.

At 3:00 A.M. Helen woke up and looked around. There was not a chair by her bed, and Glida Mae was nowhere to be seen. Realizing that her neighbor's appearance had been a dream, Helen climbed out of bed and walked to the kitchen for a glass of water. As she drank, she looked across to the pink house next door and saw a light on. She blinked, then rubbed her eyes, but the light was still there.

She thought about calling Matt, but she hated to wake him and his parents in the middle of the night. She convinced herself that Nelda had probably left the light on to discourage vandals, and went back to bed. But she didn't sleep any more that night, and called Nelda at seven o'clock the next morning.

"Why no, dear, I didn't leave any lights on in Glida Mae's house, although that is a good idea," Nelda told her.

Helen thanked the older lady and ended the conversation as quickly as possible. Then she called Matt's cell phone number. He answered on the second ring and said he was on his way to the courthouse for his appointment with the district attorney. "He told me to be there at eight o'clock sharp," Matt told her.

Helen explained the reason for her call, half expecting him to laugh it off, but he didn't.

"Wait until I get through at the DA's office," he said. "Then I'll come, and we'll check out Miss Glida Mae's house before going to the sheriff's department."

Helen agreed, then hung up the phone. She walked to the kitchen and looked across at Glida Mae's house. There was no light inside anymore. Her heart started to pound. Either she was seeing things or someone had been inside the house next door.

* * *

Matt arrived at the district attorney's office fifteen minutes early, then had to wait thirty minutes past his scheduled meeting time before Richard Rolland walked in. The DA had a gym bag in one hand and a cup of steaming coffee in the other. "Want some?" he asked, raising the styrofoam cup, and Matt shook his head.

"I'm trying to give it up. It's full of caffeine."

The DA frowned. "Of course it is. Why do you think I drink it?" Richard put his gym bag down and pointed to a small conference table. "Show me what you've got."

Matt unpacked his briefcase and spent the next forty-five minutes outlining the evidence they had against Martin Freeburg. When he finished, the DA leaned back in his chair and stared at the ceiling. "It's weaker than I had hoped. Trying anyone for murder is always tough, but I try to be especially cautious when accusing a respected member of the community."

"Once the community finds out some of these things about Martin Freeburg, he'll no longer be respected."

Richard Rolland nodded. "That's the other thing that worries me. What if we destroy his reputation and then find out we were wrong?"

Matt considered this for a few seconds, then shrugged. "So, what do you want to do?"

"Let's hold off for a few days," the DA suggested. "The FBI can dig around a little more, and by the first of the week, we ought to have a strong enough case to haul Mr. Freeburg in."

Matt was disappointed. "And what if he kills someone else before then?"

"That's always a risk in our business. You know that, Matt."

Since there didn't seem to be any room for negotiation, Matt collected his files and stood to go.

"But Matt," Richard said.

"Yeah?"

"Keep Freeburg under surveillance under we're ready to make a move."

Matt closed his briefcase and took a step toward the door. "Thanks, Rich. I never would have thought of that."

* * *

As she waited for Matt to return, Helen watched *Good Morning America* and *Regis and Kelly*. Then she started to feel stir-crazy, so she went outside. The Nguyen children were playing in their front yard, and when they saw Helen, they walked down the street toward her.

"Good morning," she greeted. Tan gave her a polite nod, but Lin smiled. "What are you up to today?"

"Today we are pulling weeds from our flower bed," Tan informed her with dignity.

"Well, it sounds to me like you need some cookies for energy with a project like that ahead of you."

Lin nodded, so Helen went inside for the cookies. Just as she handed them to Tan, Matt's Bronco pulled up, and the children disappeared into their own backyard.

Matt told Helen he was going to walk down and get a key to Glida Mae's house from Nelda Lovell. "I don't want to alarm her, so I'm just going to say I'd like to have a look around since the house has been vacant and we've got a crazed killer in the area."

Helen raised an eyebrow. "That certainly shouldn't alarm her."

Matt smirked, then started down the sidewalk. He returned a few minutes later with a key, and they approached Glida Mae's house cautiously.

"You don't think there's anyone in there, do you?" Helen asked as he inserted the key in the lock.

"If so, they'll probably run out the back door."

With this encouraging comment, Matt led the way inside. The house looked like a poorly organized thrift store. Stuff was heaped everywhere. It wasn't so much dirty as it was just cluttered. "How can she live in this mess?" Matt asked in wonder.

"She doesn't," Helen reminded him. "She's at Gentle Haven."

Matt gave her a quick look over his shoulder, then proceeded through the house. There were no intruders or any sign that someone had been inside recently. "Well, so much for that," Matt said as he turned back toward the front door.

Helen stayed close behind him, but as they stepped back into the living room, her eyes were drawn to a table in the far corner. It was piled high with dusty magazines, and perched right on top was a small wicker basket wrapped with pink netting. Helen took a step closer, then gasped.

"What?" Matt asked, and Helen pointed to the basket. "Well, I'll be," Matt said as he walked over for a closer look. "Miss Glida Mae was the only recipient of the poisoned soup smart enough not to eat it."

Helen stared at the basket, feeling a terrible sense of uneasiness. "I told you she's shrewd sometimes."

Matt called Ed Ramsey and asked him to send a lab team over to pick up the basket, then they went back to Helen's house and called Gentle Haven. Glida Mae was brought to the phone, but she couldn't remember when she had received the basket. Matt wanted to know why she didn't open the gift, and her response was immediate.

"I didn't want to ruin it! It was so pretty just the way it was."

Matt said good-bye and disconnected the call. "Well, so much for Miss Glida Mae being shrewd."

On the drive to the sheriff's department, Helen asked Matt about his meeting with the DA.

"Is he going to indict?"

"Not yet, and I'm afraid the killer will strike again before the DA gets up the courage."

"Maybe the police lab will find something conclusive on Glida Mae's basket, and the DA won't be able to refuse you."

Matt considered this, then smiled. "It doesn't hurt to think positive."

* * *

It was late that afternoon before they heard from Ed Ramsey about the basket. "No fingerprints, fibers, or hints of any kind, except the trace of coal dust," Ed reported.

After his phone call with the police chief, Matt sent Crystal home. "Everybody get a good night's sleep, and maybe we'll be able to think this thing out tomorrow."

"What about Helen?" Crystal wanted to know as she closed down her computer.

"She's riding with me," Matt explained. "And I think tonight I will take her out to one of those restaurants on the lake. Which one do you recommend?"

Crystal thought for a minute. "The Lure is the most fun, but The Reserve has the best food."

Matt looked at Helen. "Food or fun?"

"Definitely food," she replied.

They went to The Reserve. Matt ordered a fried catfish plate, and Helen had a seafood salad. The meal was good, but Helen couldn't keep from yawning throughout the evening. Finally, Matt commented on it. "I guess I must be boring," he teased.

Helen felt her cheeks get hot. "I'm so sorry."

"I'm the one who should apologize," Matt said quickly. "I've been working you too hard."

"I am tired," she admitted. "But it's something else that's causing me to be so distracted. Today while we were in Glida Mae's house, I almost remembered something, and I think it was important. But then it escaped me, and I can't get it back."

He smiled and her heart pounded. "Maybe a good night's sleep will restore your memory," he said, then motioned for the waitress to bring their check. Matt signed the charge slip, then stood. He walked around the table and caught her hands in his. "Ready to go?" He pulled her to her feet.

"Thanks," she said, holding his hands tightly. They were close, and his warmth was almost magnetic. As she leaned toward him, a busboy rushed up and started clearing their table, effectively breaking the mood.

Matt smiled, then led her outside. He drove to Ivy Lane and insisted on walking her to the door, unlocking the house, and doing a thorough walk through it before he would leave. Finally, they were back on the front porch.

"Thanks for dinner," Helen said softly. "And good night."

After Matt was gone, Helen checked the doors to be sure they were locked, then took a shower and climbed into bed. She expected to sleep soundly, but she tossed and turned.

Finally, at six o'clock on Friday morning, Helen remembered what had eluded her since the previous evening. When she was walking through Glida Mae's house, she noticed the clutter and the thin film of dust that covered everything—everything except the hardwood floor in the hall. The only reasonable explanation was that whoever had turned on the light during the night had also dusted the floor to keep from leaving footprints.

As she stared at the ceiling, her thoughts returned to the first time she had seen her rental house. It was uniformly old, worn, tattered, and covered with dust. But the day she looked around the basement, something had seemed odd, and now she knew what it was. The basement was much cleaner than the rest of the house.

Helen waited until eight o'clock, then with her cell phone in one hand and her gun in the other, she went outside. Approaching the basement door with caution, Helen turned the key, then raised her gun before stepping inside.

She flipped on the light and glanced around to be sure the room was empty. Then she closed the door behind her. The room was much as she remembered it—dark and cluttered with junk. Helen walked over to a metal table in one corner that was covered by a canvas tarp. She pulled back the cloth and exposed several blister packages of pills, a small propane stove, and a hypodermic needle.

With trembling hands, Helen examined the boxes stacked against the wall behind the table. Two were filled with old clothes. In the third she found white Bibles. The next box contained cans of Aunt Clara's Chicken Noodle Soup, and on a hook behind the water heater was a white lab coat.

Helen rushed outside to keep from suffocating with fear. She hurried around to the front yard, putting as much distance as possible between herself and the murderer's laboratory. Then she pulled out her cell phone and called Matt. His answering machine picked up, so she left a message, then dialed 911.

Helen couldn't bring herself to go into the house, so she stood on the sidewalk, waiting for the police to arrive. She saw a movement from the corner of her eye and clutched the little gun tightly. Then she saw two dark heads pass through Glida Mae's backyard into her own.

Terror caused her to react strongly. "Tan!" she called as she charged toward them. The boy approached her cautiously, Lin trailing a few steps behind. "You and Lin must stay out of my backyard from now on. Do not come here for any reason!" she said with a wave at the back of her house.

Hurt sprang into Tan's eyes, but their safety was more important than their feelings. Helen pointed her finger at Lin. "The cat is dead. Do you hear?" Tears glistened in the big, brown eyes, but Helen steeled herself to do what had to be done. "If I catch you in my backyard again, I'll tell your mother. Is that understood?"

Lin nodded, then Tan took her hand and led her home.

Helen was standing on the sidewalk, feeling like the lowest life form when Nelda Lovell waved from her front porch. "Hey, Helen! I thought I heard you out here. I was just heading up to see you." Nelda walked down her front steps and joined Helen on the sidewalk, carrying a big cake saver. "Were you calling me?"

Helen shook her head. "No. I found something disturbing in my basement, and I don't want the Nguyen children to play in my backyard when I'm not home anymore. So I had to ruin my hard-earned friendship with Tan and Lin to ensure their safety."

"I'm sorry, dear," Nelda said as she extended the Tupperware container. "I've made you a Mountain Dew cake. Maybe that will cheer you up. Have you ever tried one?"

"No, but that was very nice of you," Helen responded, gazing at the Nguyens' door.

"These cakes are delicious, and they freeze beautifully!" Nelda praised just as sirens rent the humid air. The older woman looked up at Helen, her eyes wide. "You *did* find something disturbing in your basement," she remarked as the first police car pulled to a stop in front of 126 Ivy Lane.

* * *

Matt was driving to work when he thought to check the messages on his cell phone. He heard the one from Helen and did an illegal U-turn, then headed toward his rental at top speed. He had to park a block away from his grandmother's old house because numerous emergency vehicles already crowded the quiet street. He jumped out of the car and ran without even pausing to close his door. A set of policemen met him in the sidewalk.

"We were just going to find you," one said. "The chief is around back."

Matt turned the corner of the house at a trot and came to an abrupt halt when he saw the group of people around the basement door. Ed Ramsey emerged from the crowd and approached him. "Is my grandmother's basement really the murderer's lab?" he asked, and Ed nodded. "Any fingerprints?"

"The guys are checking now, but we don't expect to find any. Our man is too smart for that," Ed predicted.

"What else did you find?"

"Particles of Digoxin, empty medicine packets, cans of chicken noodle soup, Bibles, everything." Ed paused, then looked up at Matt. "Even a lab coat with Dr. Baker's name embroidered over the pocket."

Matt frowned. "If our guy is too smart to leave fingerprints, why would he leave his own lab coat?"

Ed nodded. "Exactly. I figure the lab coat was planted by Martin Freeburg to throw us off."

Matt considered this. "Miss Glida Mae claims she saw Dr. Baker and the murderer on several occasions. Maybe Mr. Freeburg used the lab coat as a disguise to get into the women's homes."

The chief shrugged. "Maybe so."

Matt saw Helen standing on the edge of the crowd by the basement door. She looked like she'd been crying, and his heart started to ache. He moved toward her, almost involuntarily. She glanced up and reached out as he approached. He pulled her to his chest and stroked her hair.

"Are you okay?"

"Just scared. It's so unnerving to think that the murderer has been using this basement to make poison soup while I was upstairs asleep." He felt her shiver.

"You can't stay here anymore. I'm sure Miss Nelda will let you sleep at her house for a few nights until you can make other arrangements."

Ed Ramsey walked up as Matt was making this statement. "That won't be necessary. The DA has just given us the go-ahead to arrest Martin Freeburg."

* * *

Helen took a hot shower, allowing a few rebellious tears to fall, then got dressed. She arrived at the sheriff's department a little before noon and Matt was at the police department, participating in yet another press conference. Helen refiled case folders and opened mail until Matt returned. At that point Helen vacated the office so Matt could confer with the FBI agents. Feeling a little extraneous, Helen sat by Crystal's desk and watched the secretary work until five o'clock, at which point Crystal suggested that they call it a night. Helen's eyes strayed toward Matt's office of their own accord. An attorney for the city of Eureka had now joined the group to discuss the legal ramifications of the case.

Crystal followed the direction of her gaze. "It could be hours before they finish. We'll leave Matt a message to call you when he's through," Crystal promised. The secretary scribbled a little note, stuck it on her computer screen, then ushered Helen outside.

When Helen got home, she put on pajamas and curled up on the couch. She dozed off and was startled awake several hours later by a knock on the door. Helen's heart was pounding as she looked through the peephole to see Nelda Lovell standing on the front porch.

"You shouldn't be out so late," Helen scolded as she drew the old woman inside.

"I just wanted to check on you after all the excitement this morning," Nelda explained.

"I appreciate you coming by, but I'm very tired."

"Of course you are, dear. You go on to sleep and call if you need me."

Helen nodded. "I will."

Matt called at ten-thirty and said he was at the jail with Martin Freeburg and would see her in the morning. After their conversation Helen turned off the television and climbed into bed.

Helen slept fitfully and woke up on Saturday morning feeling dull and listless. She couldn't remember the last time she had eaten, so she forced herself to make sausage and pancakes. Then she mixed up orange juice concentrate, but once she sat down at the table, she couldn't eat more than a few bites. Matt showed up on her doorstep at nine o'clock and consumed her breakfast leftovers.

"Did you get *any* sleep?" he asked around a big bite of pancake.

"Not much," she admitted.

"Judith had another dream last night, a bad one from what Dr. Appling says. She's meeting with her later this morning and promised to call me as soon as they are finished."

"Dr. Appling sees patients on weekends?"

Matt waved his fork. "Only emergencies."

"Where are you headed?"

"To question Martin Freeburg again. Then bad weather is predicted this afternoon, and that always means trouble."

Helen stood and started clearing the table. "Well, let me know what Dr. Appling says about Judith when she calls."

"I will, and you might want to take a little nap. You look kind of peaked." He turned toward the back door. "I'll just let myself out." Matt opened the door, then paused. "Looks like someone has left you a little gift," he said, and she turned around from the sink. Matt was pointing at a bag of Oreos on the top step.

Helen wiped her soapy hands on her jeans, then reached down and picked up the cookies. "They must be from Tan and Lin," she said as her vision blurred with tears.

"I thought you gave them cookies instead of vice versa," Matt said, studying her closely.

Helen spoke around the lump in her throat. "Yesterday I told them to stay out of my backyard." She forced her eyes to meet his. "I couldn't explain about the murder lab in my basement, so I just told them not to play here when I'm not home or I'd tell their mother." She looked back at the package of cookies. "They must be trying to make up."

Matt reached down and touched her chin. "Oreos are a pretty serious gift. I think they really like you." He gave her a quick hug of encouragement, then walked down the steps.

After Matt left, Helen took a shower, hoping to improve her mood. She did feel refreshed initially, but as rain started pelting the roof, her anxiety returned. So she called Nelda and asked about the weather situation.

"The best thing to do is turn on your television so you'll know if you need to go to the basement," Nelda recommended as thunder rattled the walls.

"Why would I need to go to the basement?" Helen asked.

"In the case of a tornado, dear," Nelda explained. "It's the safest place to be."

Helen thought of Matt's family and shuddered. Then she remembered the police tape and padlock that blocked entry to her own basement. "If the weather gets that bad, I may have to sit in your basement, since mine is a crime lab."

"Dear me," Nelda said. "You'll be more than welcome here."

CHAPTER 14

Matt called Dr. Appling's office from the Bronco on his way back to the sheriff's department. "I was expecting your secretary," Matt said when Dr. Appling answered.

"My secretary doesn't work on weekends," the doctor replied.

"You meet with crazy people alone?" Matt asked in alarm.

"The world is full of crazy people, Sheriff. At least I have a little warning about the ones I deal with."

"You've got a point there," he conceded. "Has Judith Pope arrived yet?"

"Her appointment isn't until eleven o'clock, and I have a new patient scheduled right afterwards, so it may be early afternoon before I can call you and report on our session."

"I'll be at the sheriff's department," Matt told her. "You can reach me there or on my cell phone."

After disconnecting the call, Matt went by the cemetery for his weekly visit. Then he went to see Martin Freeburg in the county jail. The man still insisted that he was innocent and earnestly advised Matt to keep looking for the murderer. Thoroughly depressed, Matt descended the stairs into the sheriff's department. When he walked into his office, he found Crystal sitting at his desk, eating a taco.

"What are you doing here on a Saturday?" Matt asked, startling the unsuspecting secretary. "Trying to get the feel of my office so you can take over as sheriff when I get fired?"

"You scared me to death," she scolded, brushing lettuce and cheese off her shirt. "And sheriffs don't get fired; they just aren't reelected."

"I can only hope," he said as he sat in Helen's chair. "You got any more of those?"

Crystal passed him the bag, and he removed the remaining taco.

"I heard about the stuff they found in your grandmother's basement," she said. "What a bummer."

Matt agreed that it was not one of his happier moments.

"I heard Helen was real brave about it, though."

"Yeah, she's a trooper."

"And she's crazy about you."

Matt looked up from his donated lunch. "You think so?"

"I know so."

"That gives me a little hope," Matt said.

Crystal frowned. "What's her story? She's so sad and mysterious. I know she's got some kind of deep, dark secret."

Matt crumpled up his taco wrapper. "I can't tell you."

"I could call Brian West and ask him to fax another copy of the background check he did on Helen."

Matt smiled. "You could, but you won't because you, Crystal Vines, are a good person."

"Yeah, living proof that nice guys finish last." Her remark was punctuated by lightning and they both looked at the window. "Are there any watches or warnings out?"

Matt shrugged. "Not that I know of." He stood and waited for her to relinquish his chair. Crystal collected the remains of their lunch and started for the door. Then she paused and turned back toward him. "This murder case might turn out to be kind of a good thing."

Matt looked up. "I don't see how that could be possible."

"Well, since you've solved the case, that creep from the mayor's office may not be able to defeat you in November."

"Crystal, I'm not even going to run for sheriff in November."

The secretary walked back to the front of his desk. "Oh, come on Matt. You're a good sheriff," Crystal said earnestly. "If you'd just try a little harder . . ."

Matt laughed. "I'm an awful sheriff! I was a good deputy, but I'm way over my head with all this paperwork!" He waved at the mess that surrounded him.

"I'll help you," Crystal offered.

"You do help me. I'd never have made it this long without you. But I'm ready to find something else, and so are you."

Crystal's shoulders slumped forward. "You think Murray Monk will bring his secretary from the mayor's office with him when he takes over and I'll be out of a job?"

"No, you'll still have a job because I'm going to promote you to deputy before I leave," Matt told her. Crystal was stricken speechless, and he laughed again. "Sheriff Bridger made me finish out his term because he wanted me to care about *something*. And even though I don't want to be sheriff, his plan still sort of worked."

"How?" Crystal asked.

"Because I do care about stopping this murderer. I care a lot about that."

"And maybe you care a lot about your research assistant and renter too," Crystal teased.

"Maybe," Matt conceded. "And I definitely care about the phone call I'm expecting from Sylvia Appling. When she calls, put her through immediately."

"Like I'd keep her on hold for hours," Crystal muttered as she walked to her desk.

Matt returned long overdue phone calls for a while, then filled out an equipment inventory and tried to sort through the piles of mail. Finally, he gave up and checked the weather on the Internet. "Crystal!" he called when he saw the profusion of multicolored radar.

The secretary poked her head through the door. "What?"

"Look at this!"

The secretary walked in and looked over his shoulder at the computer screen. "The whole state is under some kind of watch or warning, and the National Weather Service radio hasn't made a sound."

Matt frowned. "You'd better make sure it's plugged in."

Crystal hurried out and came back a few seconds later carrying the radio. "I've told Wiley a hundred times not to use that socket to charge his cell phone."

"It's okay, Crystal. If anything was really wrong here, I'm sure we'd have had calls." He took the radio and plugged it into his surge protector. Immediately a list of various watches and warnings poured from the machine.

"Any tornadoes?" Crystal asked as the phone began to ring.

"For now, all we have is a severe thunderstorm watch."

Crystal turned back toward her own desk. "Maybe it won't get any worse than that."

Matt nodded and continued to stare at the computer screen, pressing redial on his phone every few minutes. After a half hour, he went into the outer office and paced around Crystal's desk. "That's it," the secretary said finally. "I'm going home."

"What?"

"You're making me dizzy, that's what! And I've got more comp time than I can ever use as it is."

"Don't you think Dr. Appling has had time to finish her sessions by now?" Matt asked as he watched Crystal pull an umbrella out of her desk drawer.

"I'm not a psychiatrist. I have no idea how long sessions take."

The weather service radio siren went off at this moment. "The National Weather Service has just issued a tornado watch for Coosetta County," the voice droned until Crystal pushed the alert button and silence filled the room.

After a few tense seconds, Matt reached for the phone on Crystal's desk and dialed Dr. Appling's private line again. "No answer," he reported after two more tries.

"Maybe she decided to come over and talk to you in person."

"She would have called me first."

"With this weather, the phone lines might be jammed."

"Well, whatever the problem is, I can't just sit here twiddling my thumbs," Matt said, taking the umbrella from Crystal's hand. "I'm going to Dr. Appling's office. If you hear from her, call me on my cell."

"I just said I was going home," Crystal reminded him as he walked to the door.

"If you'll stay for another hour, I'll pay you double your usual overtime wage."

"You don't pay me overtime!" she cried as he disappeared.

* * *

Helen paced nervously with the telephone in her hand. "I've never been in a tornado before," she told Nelda Lovell.

"And you're not in one now," Nelda assured her. "We just have a watch, which means atmospheric conditions are favorable for a tornado. But if you feel nervous, come to my house. We'll watch the weather radar together."

Helen felt a little silly, but relieved. "I'll be down in a little while."

After Helen ended the call, she looked out her front window as lightning streaked across the prematurely darkened sky. She couldn't resist a squeal of terror, then she picked her phone back up and called the sheriff's department. "Hey, Crystal," she said when the secretary answered. "Is Matt there?"

"No, he's on a wild goose chase," Crystal replied. "Why?"

"This weather is nerve-racking, and I want to hear a strong male voice."

"Turn on Channel 5 and listen to Max Cochran. He's got a great voice and he gets his forecasts 'right the first time,'" Crystal quoted the television slogan.

"I'm watching Mr. Cochran as we speak," Helen replied. "But I'd rather talk to Matt. Where is he?"

"Gone to Dr. Appling's office. She was supposed to call him and never did, so he decided to go see her. But from the traffic reports I'm hearing on the police radio, it might be Valentine's Day before he gets there."

Helen laughed. "Well, when you hear from him tell him I'm going down to Nelda Lovell's house until this storm blows over."

"Will do," Crystal said, then hung up.

Helen got her raincoat and umbrella out of the closet and walked to the front door. She put on the coat, then adjusted the umbrella before pulling the door open. When she looked out, a scream burst from her lips, but the sound was swallowed up in a loud clap of thunder.

Harrison Campbell pushed his way inside and closed the door behind him. "Now is that any way to greet me after all these weeks?" he asked as his eyes raked her up and down. "I have to say, Helen, you've really let yourself go. You look like you haven't slept in days, and this house is way below your normal standards."

"What are you doing here?" She hoped she sounded more menacing than afraid. "You know you can't be within fifty feet of me."

"There's no restraining order against me in Georgia, Helen. I am free to visit you whenever I want."

"That is an oversight that will be corrected immediately," she assured him.

"Why can't you just accept my presence in your life, Helen?" he asked, tilting his head to one side. "I know that your feelings for me are not as strong as mine are for you, and I'm willing to give you some time. I'm going to rent the house next door . . ."

"Glida Mae's house?" she demanded, instantly furious. "How could you possibly manage that?"

He shrugged. "A nice lady at the city clerk's office is helping me to arrange it. But in the meantime, since it's empty, I've moved in."

"You were there the other night," Helen realized suddenly. "That's why I saw the lights. But you hid from Matt when we came to look around."

Harrision scowled. "I thought it might be better to save my little surprise until we could be alone."

Helen reached for her phone. "I'm going to call Matt."

"I think that's a very good idea," Harrison agreed with a smile. "Then when he gets here, I can tell him about that outstanding warrant for your arrest in West Virginia. If he's honest, he'll have no choice but to take you into custody."

Harrison was right. Matt would follow the letter of the law. Her chest heaved with futile fury as she dropped her cell phone back into her purse. "How did you find me?"

"I tracked you as far as Columbus, but then your trail evaporated. I figured you had to be close by, and I'm a very patient man." He gave her another grin. "So I got a hotel room and was systematically checking the area. I would have found you eventually, but I have to admit that seeing you on the evening news with the sheriff was a real stroke of luck. I've been with you ever since, biding my time."

"With me . . . ," Helen began, then she remembered the open door a few days before. "You've been in my house?"

Harrison nodded. "Several times. While you were at work, I slept in your bed, ate your food, even used your toothbrush."

Helen slumped against the wall, defeated by the depth of his obsession. "If you'll go away, I'll give you everything I have," she promised. "The equity in my house, my stock in my parents' business, and my retirement account . . ."

"I don't want your *money*," Harrison whispered. "I want your *love*."

She spread her hands in supplication. "That is something you will never have! And if you really loved me, you'd want me to be happy."

"I do want you to be happy, Helen," Harrison insisted. "And I can make that happen. I'm sure of it. Someday you'll realize that we are meant to be together."

Harrison took a step toward her, and she shuddered. "Don't touch me." Then the doorbell rang, and both of them turned to stare.

"Aren't you going to answer it?" Harrison asked finally.

Helen didn't want to open the door. It might be Matt, and explaining Harrison's presence in her house without telling him about the warrant would be difficult. The bell rang again, and she realized that she was going to have to respond. Reluctantly she moved to the door and pulled it open. Judith Pope stood on her porch, soaked to the skin and holding a grocery sack.

"I hope I haven't come at an inconvenient time," Judith said. "But I hate bad weather and hoped if I brought lunch, you'd let me wait out the storm here with you."

Helen was trying to decide what to say when Harrison pulled the door wide. "Come on in," he invited. Helen turned to him, and he shrugged. "We can't very well turn her away under the circumstances." He waited until Judith was inside, then introduced himself. "I'm Harrison Campbell, Helen's fiancé."

Judith looked uncertain, but Helen didn't dare contradict him, so finally the librarian nodded. Harrison closed the door behind her and locked it. "I'm glad you've brought lunch. I'm starving."

Judith glanced at Harrison, then moved her eyes to Helen. "I didn't know you had a guest, so I really only have enough for two people."

"Harrison understands," Helen assured her. "He was just leaving anyway."

Harrison raised an eyebrow, but didn't dispute this as Judith walked toward the kitchen. "It will just take me a minute to heat the food up," she told them.

Helen followed Judith to the kitchen and showed her where the limited supply of pans and utensils were kept. Then she returned to the living room and found Harrison Campbell still standing just where she had left him.

"Judith is nervous around men, and you're making her uncomfortable," she said softly. "If you'll go next door and wait, I'll get rid of Judith as quickly as I can. Then I'll come over and we can discuss things further."

Harrison considered this for a few seconds. "So, if I leave, you'll come see me in just a little while?" he confirmed.

Helen nodded, encouraged by his semicooperative tone. "Yes, as soon as possible."

"Okay," he agreed, and she felt limp with relief. Then Harrison reached over and picked up her purse off the coffee table. "But I'll take this with me so you won't be tempted to leave without saying good-bye."

Helen did her best to hide her disappointment since that was exactly what she had planned. Before she could respond, Judith walked through the kitchen door carrying a tray.

"Lunch is ready," she announced. She put the tray on the coffee table, and Helen saw two steaming bowls of soup.

"Smells good," Harrison said with a charming smile.

"I hope you like soup." Judith looked at Helen anxiously.

Helen glanced down at the bowls on the table. "It's chicken noodle." She'd never particularly cared for chicken noodle soup, but after the recent poisonings, she had a complete aversion to it.

"Aunt Clara's," Judith affirmed with a nod. "It was my grandmother's favorite meal, especially during thunderstorms."

Helen stared at the soup, speechless. There was no way she could eat it.

"Would you like some crackers and milk?" Judith asked, and Helen nodded.

"Yes, please." Helen waited until Judith had left the room, then looked around for a way to dispose of the soup. Her eyes settled on a drooping silk plant, nestled in a tarnished, brass planter in the corner of the room. She stood and dumped the contents of her bowl into the dusty moss that mostly covered the fake roots, then returned to her seat on the couch.

Harrison watched her throughout this process, and when she looked at him, he raised an eyebrow.

"Your unexpected arrival has caused me to lose my appetite," she told him. "But I don't want to hurt Judith's feelings."

He smiled. "Don't worry, Helen. Your secrets are safe with me."

She ground her teeth in frustration as Judith came in and put a glass of milk on the table. "My goodness, you *were* hungry," she said when she saw Helen's empty bowl.

"Mmmm," Helen murmured without meeting her gaze.

"I have just a little left in the kitchen if you'd like some more," Judith offered. Helen shook her head, and Judith turned to Harrison. "Then I guess you can have it."

"Thanks anyway, but I'm headed home," he said. "I'll see you *soon,*" he told Helen, patting her purse.

She mentally reviewed the contents of her purse, trying to decide if she could live without them. Inside the purse was her cell phone, her gun, her identification, her money, her credit cards, the keys to her house and car—everything. Unless she wanted to try life in a cardboard box, she would have to negotiate with Harrison, so she nodded. He moved toward the back door and Judith followed.

"I forgot the crackers," she explained.

Alone in the living room, Helen took a few sips of her milk and watched the weather report on television. As if she needed anything else to depress her, the tornado watch for Coosetta County had been extended another thirty minutes.

When Judith returned with the crackers, she offered the package and Helen took a few. She nibbled a cracker, then pointed at the television screen. "Maybe we should go down to Nelda's since my basement is locked up."

Judith studied the radar for a few seconds, then shook her head. "There's no point in getting wet until you have to. We can wait until an actual warning is issued."

"Is Harrison gone?" Helen asked, and Judith nodded.

"Yes, and it's a good thing you have plenty of Oreos. He took two bags with him."

Helen sighed. "He's not my fiancé. That was kind of a sick joke."

Judith considered this for a second. "I'm glad. He seemed like an unpleasant sort of person."

If you only knew, Helen thought to herself as Judith sat beside her on the couch. "Aren't you going to eat your soup?" Helen asked.

Judith shook her head. "I'll let it cool for a while first."

"How was your appointment with Dr. Appling?"

"Same as always," Judith said with a sigh. "We're not making any progress, so I've decided to stop seeing her."

Helen knew that Matt would be disappointed, but Judith had a right to make her own decisions and the case was pretty much settled anyway. The wind howled, and Helen shivered.

"I'm scared of storms too," Judith commiserated. "Grandmother considered my fear a sign of weakness and wanted me to overcome it, so she never let me go to the basement with her when we had bad weather."

Helen looked at the other woman in horror. "Your grandmother left you upstairs alone during storms?"

Judith nodded. "Even tornadoes. Sometimes I wondered if she actually wanted me to die, but then she wouldn't have had anyone to take care of her, so that doesn't make sense, does it?"

Helen was unsure how to respond. She couldn't imagine purposely leaving anyone alone during a storm, but deserting a terrified child was unspeakably cruel. Then she remembered Nelda's concern that Judith may have fabricated the dreams about the murderer to get attention and wondered if the current conversation fell into that same category. "No, that doesn't make any sense," she said finally. "I can't believe that your grandmother would do such a thing."

"Oh, she did much worse," Judith replied matter-of-factly. "I wet the bed until I was a teenager, and Grandmother absolutely hated that. She'd threaten to beat me with her cane every night before I went to sleep, and the only way I could be sure that it wouldn't happen was to stay awake. I tried so hard not to close my eyes, but eventually I would give in to exhaustion."

"Surely your grandmother understood that you couldn't control the bed-wetting."

"My grandmother didn't understand a lack of control on any level. She thought she could beat the bad habit out of me, and maybe she did. Or maybe I just outgrew it."

Judith was calm but seemed completely serious, and Helen was tempted to believe her. "Your grandmother was very harsh."

"I was born out of wedlock," Judith explained abruptly, and Helen had to work to control a gasp. "They never knew who my father was, and my mother deserted me at the hospital. Grandmother hated scandal above all else, and I think that whether she realized it or not, she spent the rest of her life punishing me for my mother's sins."

Helen felt tears fill her eyes. "Oh, Judith. Why didn't you tell someone?"

"No one would have believed me. My grandmother was a good Christian woman who had taken in her little orphan granddaughter. If I had complained, people would have considered me ungrateful."

"Someone might have listened."

Judith shook her head. "When I was seven, I said something Grandmother considered disrespectful, so she pushed me down the basement stairs. I broke my arm, and she called Dr. Baker. She told him that I had fallen, and I didn't contradict her, but he took me to his office to put on a cast and when we were alone, I told him what really happened."

"What did he say?" Helen asked, although she was afraid she didn't want to know the answer.

Judith sighed. "He said I was mistaken, that my grandmother loved me very much and would never deliberately hurt me."

"Did you tell him that she punished you for wetting the bed?"

"I was too embarrassed."

"I wonder why he didn't report the incident to the police and let them check it out?"

"That is a question that I've been asking myself for almost thirty years," Judith replied, then turned to Helen. "Are you feeling okay? You look a little pale."

"I'm fine," Helen said as her fingers and toes started to tingle. She wiggled them, trying to improve her circulation and took a few more sips of milk. "I haven't been sleeping well lately, and I think it's starting to catch up with me."

Judith curled up into the corner of the couch, facing Helen. "It's nice and cozy in here."

Helen was going to agree, but her fingers went numb and she almost dropped her glass. "It feels a little warm to me," she said, then leaned forward and put the glass on the coffee table.

"It's good that you ate your soup so fast," Judith commented as she picked up her own bowl and took a bite. "It's really much better that way."

Helen's chest felt tight, and she rubbed it absently. "The soup is better if you eat it fast?"

Judith nodded. "And the Digoxin takes effect more quickly."

"Digoxin?" Helen asked, more confused than alarmed.

"I put some in the soup. The milk too, just to be sure." Judith waved toward Helen's half-empty glass on the table.

Helen frowned. She was a little dizzy and found it hard to concentrate. "Sure of what?"

"Sure that we die."

"Die?" Helen put a shaking hand to her forehead.

"I didn't keep track of how many pills I put in each can of soup, so I'm still not sure of the lethal dosage. The milk is my insurance against error."

Helen blinked as the sinister meaning of these words registered. "*You* poisoned Mrs. Freeburg, Robyn Howell, and Iris Whited?" Helen asked incredulously. It was impossible to tell whether Judith had lost her mind or was truly confessing, but in either case, the situation was decidedly dangerous.

"Of course," Judith admitted with a weary sigh.

Helen wanted to get up and run, but her legs felt strange and she wasn't sure that they would support her. She hadn't eaten any soup, but she did drink some milk, and there was no way for her to know if she had enough Digoxin in her system to kill her. Matt would come eventually and Harrison could return at any minute, so Helen decided her best course of action was to stall and pray for help. "Why would you want to poison people?"

Judith picked up her bowl of soup and took a few more bites. "It's a long, sad story. Are you sure you want to hear it?"

After a surreptitious glance at the front door, Helen nodded. "I want to hear it all."

"I dreamed about killing Grandmother for years, but I never seriously intended to *do* it," Judith said as she finished her soup and took a big sip of milk. "That last night I was so tired after work. Grandmother wanted chicken noodle soup for dinner, but when I brought it to her, she said it was cold and slapped me across the face."

Helen shuddered as Judith continued calmly.

"I reached for a tissue to stop my lip from bleeding and saw her medication on the bedside table. I thought that if I gave Grandmother a few extra pills mixed in with her soup maybe she would sleep through the night and leave me alone. I crushed one and then another and another." Judith shrugged. "She ate every bite and never woke up."

"And it was assumed that she died of natural causes."

Judith inclined her head in agreement. "I thought freedom from Grandmother would bring me happiness, but instead I was racked with guilt and was, strangely, lonesome. So I decided to punish myself by joining her."

"You tried to kill yourself?"

Judith nodded. "I took a handful of Grandmother's Digoxin, but before I lost consciousness Nelda Lovell came by to check on me. She figured out what I had done and called Dr. Baker. He pumped my stomach and unfortunately for him and the rest of Eureka, saved my life. He attributed my suicide attempt to depression, gave me a prescription, and recommended that I see a therapist."

"You didn't take his advice?"

Judith shook her head. "I knew I didn't deserve to live, but Grandmother spent her life protecting our family name, and it was wrong for me to create a scandal as my last act on earth. So I had to think of a way to die without casting suspicion on myself. The Eureka Baptist Church sends me their bulletins every week. In June I saw the announcement that Dr. Baker had been named Physician of the Year and I was livid! How could he be rewarded after the way he had failed me?" Judith demanded. "There was also an article about Matt Clevenger being appointed to finish Sheriff Bridger's term, but no mention of his alcoholism."

Helen's lethargy was getting worse, and she tried to move her legs but couldn't. Forcing herself to concentrate, she addressed Judith. "I understand your feelings for Dr. Baker, but why do you hate Matt so much?"

Judith clasped her hands to her heart in anguish. "Because I loved him with the pure affection of a child who had never experienced a single act of kindness, and he rejected me. Not once, but hundreds of times. He teased me and played cruel tricks on me," Judith itemized Matt's childhood crimes. "He managed to make my time outside of Grandmother's house almost as miserable as the hours spent inside."

Helen closed her eyes against the pain. "He was wrong, Judith, but he was a child, and he didn't understand how awful your circumstances were."

Judith waved this aside. "I was a child too. A lonely, pitiful child. Matt wasn't nice to people, but he had friends. He didn't try to make good grades, but he got a scholarship to the University of Georgia. He never saved a dime, so his in-laws gave him the land to build a house on. And he didn't even have to apply for the job of deputy sheriff—they called up and offered it to him! He consistently made wrong choices, but everything he touched turned to gold."

"He lost his entire family," Helen said and Judith nodded.

"Then turned into a worthless drunk—an object of scorn, and I felt a measure of satisfaction. But when he was appointed sheriff, and the community rallied around him . . ." Judith shook her head. "It was his turn to *suffer!*"

Helen was still searching for a response when Judith moved on. "Then I saw the prayer list in the church bulletin, and it gave me an idea. One that would give this whole neighborhood a taste of what it's like to be afraid to close your eyes at night."

"You made baskets of poisoned soup," Helen said, and Judith nodded.

"My grandmother dragged me to church every Sunday when I was a child. The members of the Eureka Baptist Church saw my bruises and turned a blind eye. By delivering my baskets to people on their prayer list, I hoped to generate some bad publicity for the church. When several victims died in the same way, I hoped Matt would assume he was dealing with a serial killer. And then I planted a trail of evidence that led directly to Dr. Baker."

"It was a clever plan," Helen had to admit.

"All I needed was a place to prepare the baskets. Matt's grandmother's house was empty so I decided to use his basement and the box of Bibles stored there seemed like a sign from heaven that I was doing the right thing."

"You think the Lord approved of your plan to kill people?" Helen clarified.

Judith nodded. "Sometimes innocent lives must be sacrificed for the greater good."

Helen recognized the futility of trying to argue. "So it was you Glida Mae saw going into Matt's basement?"

Judith shrugged. "That didn't concern me at first, since nobody believes anything Miss Glida Mae says. She has a short attention span, and I thought she would drop it after a few days, but she kept on."

"So you made her a basket."

"But she wouldn't let me in!" Judith said in exasperation. "I tried all different times of the day and night. I even put on Dr. Baker's lab coat and pretended to be him. But she would not open her door. I finally left the basket on the porch."

Helen felt tears spring into her eyes as she realized that Glida Mae had truly been in grave danger. "Where did you get all the Digoxin?" she asked.

"I never cancelled Grandmother's prescriptions from her mail-order pharmacy, so I had plenty of medicine."

"But you were working at the library on the nights Mrs. Freeburg and Robyn Howell died."

Judith shrugged. "On both occasions I told my supervisor that I was going to sort through the donated periodicals. That's a job everybody hates, and I knew that no one would come looking for me. I brought some of my grandfather's clothes to work in a small bag and changed in the staff rest room. With a hat on, I looked just like an old man. I slipped out and back in without anyone noticing."

"So you had an ironclad alibi."

Judith acknowledged this with a little smile. "The plan should have worked perfectly, but Matt kept finding other suspects, and I'd have to return his attention to Dr. Baker."

Helen remembered Matt's comment that every time he looked at another suspect, something led him back to Dr. Baker. That *something* was Judith. "So you made up the dreams?"

Judith nodded. "And put Dr. Baker's lab coat in Matt's basement."

Time, Helen thought to herself. *Just a little more time.* "How did you get Mary Jean Freeburg to let you into her house?"

Judith rubbed her cheek against the back of the couch and closed her eyes as if she were getting ready for a nice long nap. "I told her I was making a delivery for the church. She was so pleased to get the basket, I almost felt guilty. She died with a smile on her face."

Helen fought against the Digoxin-induced fatigue and tried to hide her revulsion. "What about Robyn Howell?"

Judith opened her eyes and frowned. "Robyn Howell seemed amused rather than honored by the gift, and I wasn't sure she'd actually open it. So after work, I stopped back by in my regular clothes. I told her that in an attempt to increase circulation the library was delivering books to selected area residents. Then I showed her a book I had checked out for myself."

"And she believed that?" Even in her drowsy state, Helen was surprised.

"I don't know if she did or not. Before she could answer, she had an awful coughing fit. I helped her get into bed, then fixed the soup, and she ate it without protest. My only mistake was leaving the book on her coffee table."

"So you came back to get it later?"

"Yes. I was afraid that it would be traced back to me."

"And then you ate some of the poisoned soup yourself."

Judith sighed. "It would have all been over then if that dim-witted Elvis Hatcher hadn't remembered about my leaking roof." Judith yawned. "I'm getting sleepy, how about you?"

Helen forced her eyes to focus. "Why do you want to kill *me*?"

"I'm sorry," Judith said, and she really did seem to be. "But I was afraid you might remember the books I brought to you and make the connection with the one I left at Robyn Howell's house." Judith looked at her earnestly. "I have to die, but it's my responsibility to protect the family name. Grandmother would insist."

Helen realized that it was time to throw caution to the wind. "Help!" she called out, but her voice was barely above a whisper.

Judith smiled sweetly. "Oh, Helen, it's too late for that."

* * *

Matt parked his Bronco in the small lot that faced Dr. Appling's office. A cream-colored Volvo was the only other vehicle in sight. Matt stepped out into the driving rain and approached the office door at a trot. He tried the knob, and it turned easily under his hand. There was a lamp on in the reception area, but the room was quiet. He took a step down the hall.

"Dr. Appling!" he called. There was no response. "Dr. Appling!" he tried again with the same result. He passed a rest room and a storage area. Then he found a door with the doctor's name painted in gold script. He tried the doorknob, but it was locked. "Dr. Appling!"

Silence. With a shrug he turned back toward the front door. Then he heard a faint banging sound. He knocked on the office door again and the sound was repeated. Matt put his shoulder to the door and broke it open. The office was dark and empty. Then the noise came again from a door to his left. He forced the lock and found Dr. Appling lying on the floor of a small bathroom. She was bound and gagged and had a nasty gash on her head.

"What in the . . ." Matt reached down and gently pulled the fabric from her mouth. "Did your new patient do this?"

"No," the doctor whispered. "It was Judith Pope. Today I asked her some questions about her childhood." Dr. Appling paused for a big gulp of air. "She told me that she had been physically and emotionally abused by her grandmother. As she talked she became more and more agitated and finally admitted that she had killed her grandmother with an overdose of heart medication."

Matt's mouth went dry. "Did she say anything about poisoning other people?"

"No, but I think it's safe to assume that Judith is your murderer. I tried to end the session abruptly, and she realized she'd said too much. She pushed me down and I bumped my head on the corner of my desk." Dr. Appling touched the lump on her forehead. "When I regained consciousness, I was here."

Matt leaned the doctor against the bathroom wall, then pulled his cell phone and dialed the number for the sheriff's department. "Crystal," he said when the secretary answered, "call Ed Ramsey and tell him to send a patrol car to Judith Pope's house. I don't want them to arrest her until I can get there, but tell them not to let her out of their sight. And send an ambulance to Dr. Appling's office."

"What's going on there, Matt?" Crystal wanted to know.

"I'll explain later." Matt disconnected and returned his phone to his pocket. Then he knelt beside the doctor and used his pocketknife to cut through the material that bound her hands and feet. "Where did she get this stuff?" He held up a strip of blue cloth.

"I think she shredded my drapes," Dr. Appling told him as she flexed her fingers to restore the circulation to her hands. Then the doctor looked up at Matt. "Judith seemed to have a particular fixation on you. She blames you in part for her unhappy childhood, and I think the poisoning may in some way be a means of revenge against you. It would be wise to warn your loved ones in case she tries to harm them."

Matt shrugged. "I don't have loved ones except my parents, and they're spending the weekend in Atlanta."

Dr. Appling frowned. "That's odd. I thought for sure Judith mentioned your girlfriend."

Matt's heart started to pound as he jerked the phone from his pocket and dialed Helen's cell number. No answer. Then he called Crystal back. "Have you heard from Helen?"

"She's down at Nelda Lovell's house waiting out the storm," Crystal told him.

Matt felt weak with relief. "I'm headed that way as soon as the ambulance gets here." Matt stood as he ended the call.

"I'll be fine, Sheriff," Dr. Appling insisted. "You need to go and locate Judith before she harms herself or someone else."

Matt considered this for a few seconds, then nodded. "I'll check on you later."

* * *

Helen startled awake and looked over to see Judith watching her. "It's time to say good-bye," the other woman said simply.

There was something else Helen needed to know, and she forced her lips to form the words. "Did you kill Glida Mae's cat?"

"The stupid thing followed me every time I came to Matt's basement." Judith's words were slightly slurred. "Finally I realized it wanted some of the soup, so I gave it a bowl."

"Glida Mae never opened her basket."

"I'm glad," Judith replied. "I've always liked her."

Helen was too groggy to contemplate the contradiction. She watched Judith's eyes close as her own consciousness slipped away. After a few seconds, she felt sunshine on the top of her head. Helen opened her eyes and turned her face upward to receive the warmth. She looked around and saw that she was sitting on a lakeshore, a fishing pole in hand. Her father checked her bait, then patted her head and called her his little fisherman. She smiled back, luxuriating in his approval and the beautiful summer day.

Then she heard someone calling her name. She looked at her father, but he was still fishing, oblivious to the noise. Putting down her fishing pole, Helen stood. She couldn't stay there any longer. Someone needed her. Then she recognized the voice. It was Matt.

"Helen!" he screamed and she felt her shoulders shake.

"Matt?" she whispered. Her mouth tasted like cotton, and her throat was on fire.

"Don't go back to sleep!" he commanded. "Don't you dare leave me!"

She nodded, focusing on his soft brown eyes. His hair was wet and stuck out all around his head in little spikes. She would have laughed, but her throat hurt too much. Matt lifted her up, and then she felt cool rain on her face. He kept her cradled in his arms as he climbed into a car. A siren droned on and on, giving Helen a headache. Matt kept talking, but the roar in her ears prevented her from distinguishing the words. Finally the car stopped and strangers wearing masks surrounded her.

"Matt!" she whispered.

"I'm right here," he answered, grasping her hand. "You're going to be okay."

* * *

When Ed Ramsey arrived at the hospital he found Matt in the emergency waiting room and approached cautiously. "You look terrible," he said, and Matt could tell he meant it. "How's your girl-friend?"

"The doctor said she's going to recover—no thanks to me," Matt replied. "The clues were staring me right in the face, but Helen almost got killed because I couldn't figure it out."

"You take yourself too seriously, Clevenger," Ed Ramsey chided. "Who would have thought the librarian was a bona fide nutcase?" Barry Stanger and his silent partner walked in at that moment, and Ed waved in their direction. "Heck, even the FBI boys didn't figure it out."

Barry came to a stop beside Matt. "We'll need to ask Helen some questions."

Matt ran a hand through his damp hair. "I can fill you in on what I know, but it will probably be tomorrow before Helen is alert enough for an interview."

The FBI agents nodded in unison, then led the way to a corner of the waiting room. Everyone sat down, and Matt began. "Judith was abused as a child by her grandmother."

Barry nodded. "We've already talked to the psychiatrist. She says Judith Pope was suicidal and thinks the whole poisoning scheme was a way to get revenge against you and Dr. Baker before she died."

"That's the way I see it too," Matt agreed. "But I don't know whether Judith intended to kill herself or expected us to arrive in time to save her again."

"The lab guys did an on-site test and said Judith Pope had so much Digoxin in her system nothing would have saved her," Ed informed them.

"How did she get all that medicine?" Barry asked.

Matt shrugged, but Ed leaned forward. "The officers I sent to arrest her found a box of pills in her basement. They were from a mail-order pharmacy in Atlanta. They also found a trunk full of her grandfather's old clothes." Ed shook his head. "We should have searched the house more thoroughly after her original 'attack.'"

"You had no reason to suspect Judith," Matt offered as an excuse, but the chief didn't look comforted.

"Who was that guy they found in the pink house next door?" Barry Stanger asked.

Matt answered this question. "His name is Harrison Campbell. He was a former student of Helen's."

"Judith Pope killed him too?" the agent wanted to know.

"He died from an overdose of Digoxin, but I don't know if Judith killed him on purpose. Maybe it was just his bad luck that he liked to drink milk with his Oreos."

* * *

When Helen opened her eyes, she saw Matt's face looming over hers and she smiled. Then she tried to speak, but no sound came from her parched throat. She blinked, and when she opened her eyes again, Nelda Lovell had appeared beside Matt. Crystal was there too, along with Ed Ramsey. The FBI agents were in a far corner, looking grim as usual.

"Good morning, sleepyhead," Matt teased.

Helen frowned. There was something she ought to remember. Something awful. Then the memories came flooding back, and she whimpered. "Judith?" she rasped.

Matt shook his head. "She's gone."

"She was in so much pain."

Matt took her hand in his. "I know."

"She tried to kill herself first, but Nelda and Dr. Baker saved her."

Matt looked at Nelda, and the older woman stepped closer. "I feel so guilty," she said. "I knew that Lavenia was harsh and strict with Judith, but I never dreamed that she was abusive. And when Judith took those pills, I should have realized she had severe emotional problems, but I thought she just missed her grandmother. Judith was always quiet and a little odd, but sweet and gentle. I can scarcely believe that she *killed* people."

Helen turned to Matt. "That's something that bothers me too. Judith didn't seem like a killer. You remember that the doctor told us that Judith might have brain damage after taking all that Digoxin?"

Matt nodded. "I remember."

"Well, I wonder if something happened to her brain when she tried to kill herself the first time. Killing her grandmother was an accident, and then she just wanted to kill herself. It wasn't until after the overdose that she started killing other people."

Matt considered this. "It's a possibility. Or maybe all the years of abuse finally pushed her over the edge into insanity."

Nelda spoke again. "I'll always blame myself for this."

"It was no one's fault," Helen tried to reassure her.

"Or everyone's," Matt amended slightly.

"It wasn't anyone's fault," Helen insisted, then turned back to Nelda and changed the subject. "It was nice of you to come and see me."

"Oh, I would have come to see you under any circumstances, but as it turns out, I was already here when you arrived," Nelda told her, and Helen raised an eyebrow. "Sydney had her baby last night. A beautiful nine-pound boy named Patrick Michael, after both his grandfathers."

Helen smiled. "Congratulations."

"Be sure to go by and see her before you leave," Nelda suggested. "Sydney loves showing the baby off as much as she loved complaining about being pregnant."

Helen promised that she would, and Nelda went back to check on Sydney. Then Crystal stepped up beside Matt. "Some people will go to all kinds of trouble to get attention," she said.

"I wasn't trying to get attention," Helen corrected. "I was trying to solve the case and steal all the glory from Matt before the FBI could."

Crystal gave her a smile. "You're okay, Helen Tyler. Even if you are a Mormon from West Virginia." Then, with a little wave, she left the room.

"Speaking of the FBI," Matt said slowly. "They'd like to ask you some questions if you feel up to it."

Helen nodded, and the agents moved in. For the next thirty minutes she told them everything she knew. Finally Agent Stanger shut his notebook. "Well, that's it for now. We'll contact you if we think of something else."

"So," Helen said to Matt and Ed Ramsey after everyone else was gone. "The case is really successfully closed?"

"With five people dead, Dr. Appling hurt, you in the hospital, and Miss Glida Mae in a nursing home," Matt agreed wearily. "I'm not sure if it can be considered a success or not."

"What happened to Dr. Appling?" Helen asked.

Matt explained, then Helen frowned up at him. "You said five people. There was Judith's grandmother, Mary Jean Freeburg, Robyn Howell, and Judith herself. Who was the other victim?"

Matt and Ed exchanged a quick look. "Do you remember Harrison Campbell coming to your house yesterday?"

Helen twisted her lips into a grimace. "Unfortunately, yes. He plans to rent Glida Mae's house unless I can get another restraining order first. He was tormenting me with his nonsense when Judith arrived. I asked him to wait at Glida Mae's house until I could get rid of Judith." She looked between the two men. "What?"

"He did go over to Glida Mae Magnanney's house. He sat down at the kitchen table and ate half a bag of Oreos," Ed Ramsey began.

Helen nodded. "He stole them from me."

"Apparently he stole some of Judith's milk too. And drank it," Matt added, then waited expectantly.

"A lot of it," Ed Ramsey expanded.

Helen stared back in confusion. "So?" Then she remembered. "The milk had Digoxin in it."

Matt nodded. "He's dead, Helen."

Helen gasped and put a hand to her mouth. Ed Ramsey shifted his weight from one foot to the other. "Was he like an old boyfriend or something?"

Helen shook her head. "No, he was a vile human being determined to make my entire life miserable."

Ed blinked, then glanced up at Matt. "Well, in that case, I say good riddance."

Helen leaned back against her pillow and closed her eyes. "Harrison didn't deserve to die," she whispered.

"You didn't ask him to come here," Matt reminded her gently.

Helen shook her head. "No, but if it weren't for me, he'd be alive and well in West Virginia."

The nurse came in to check her vital signs, and her visitors went into the hall. After the nurse finished, Helen dozed and when she woke up, only Matt was in her room. He put a hand under her chin and kissed her lightly.

"I think I'm going to go home and take a bath. Is there anything you need while I'm out?"

Helen thought for a second, then nodded. "What I really need is a black kitten with two white feet for Tan and Lin."

Matt leaned down and kissed her again. "Consider it done."

* * *

Helen was released from the hospital that afternoon with the understanding that she would get plenty of bed rest for the next several days. Matt offered to take her to a hotel, but Nelda insisted that Helen stay with her. "I'll be spending most of my time at Sydney's house, helping with the baby and the other children. So you'll have plenty of privacy."

Helen couldn't stay in the house where Judith had died, but she needed time to make some important decisions. A few days at Nelda Lovell's house would provide that. "Thank you," she accepted.

"Hugh and Thelma will want to look out for you, but I'll tell them you need lots of sleep," Nelda added.

"I'd appreciate that," Helen said with a smile.

Once Helen was dressed, Matt rolled her wheelchair up to the maternity ward so she could see Sydney. When they got to her door, Matt said he'd wait out in the hall. Helen gave him a questioning look, and he explained, "I'm learning to put the past into perspective, but a newborn baby boy might still be more than I can handle."

Helen gave his hand a squeeze, then rolled herself into the room. The only illumination inside was a small lamp above Sydney's hospital bed. It cast a soft light down onto the mother and child, reminding Helen of paintings she had seen of the Madonna. Sydney waved her forward, and Helen eased up to the bed.

"Grandma told me about Judith, but she says you're okay."

Helen nodded, then leaned closer to see little Patrick.

"Isn't he the most beautiful baby you've ever seen in your life?" Sydney asked, pulling the blanket away to give Helen a better view.

Helen stroked a tiny fist. "He is incredible." Then she looked up at Sydney. "And I'm glad the ordeal is over for you."

Sydney shrugged. "It wasn't really that bad, and I've decided it's not fair to Patrick for him to be off on the end of our family all by himself. So I'll probably have another baby in a couple of years. Somebody for him to play with," Sydney added for clarification.

Helen raised an eyebrow. "What happened to thirty-four being the safe age limit for pregnancy?"

Helen expected a quick, sassy comeback from Sydney, but when the new mother raised her eyes, she saw tears shining. "Motherhood is such a miracle, Helen. There's no way I can adequately describe it, so you'll just have to wait until it happens to you."

Helen turned away, blinking back tears of her own. Motherhood seemed like an impossible dream at that moment.

"Grandma said you're going to stay at her house for a while."

Helen nodded. "Just a few days." Then she glanced at the door. "Well, I've left Matt in the hall so I'd better go."

"Tell him I said hey."

Helen smiled, then waved good-bye and rolled out into the bright hallway.

"Are they okay?" Matt asked.

"Better than okay," Helen assured him. "They're fabulous. And Sydney says hey."

With the help of a nurse, Matt settled Helen in his Bronco, then took her to his rental house to pick up a few personal items. "If you'll tell me what you need, I'll get it so you won't have to go inside," he offered, but she shook her head.

"It's something I'll have to face eventually, and it might as well be now."

Going into the house was not as bad as Helen had expected. She avoided looking at the couch or kitchen, and hurried straight into her bedroom where she packed haphazardly.

When they got to Nelda's house, Helen put her things in the guest room, then sat at the kitchen table with Matt. He reached across the table and took her hand in his. "Now that all this is over, I'd like to take our relationship to the next level."

Helen looked over at him. His dark hair was damp and curling, and his brown eyes were soft and vulnerable. "What is the next level, Matt?"

He shrugged. "Something more than business."

"Friends?" she asked.

"At least."

Helen looked back down at her hands. "I've got some things to clear up in my life before I can even consider other levels," she said.

"Like the warrant for your arrest in West Virginia?"

Helen's shoulders sagged. "You knew about that?"

Matt nodded. "I'm not as bad a sheriff as you thought."

"You're not a bad sheriff at all. And I think a good lawyer can get the charges against me dismissed, but then I need to work out a reconciliation of some sort with my parents."

"So when are you going to leave?"

"Probably tomorrow."

"But you'll come back?"

She nodded. "I promise."

"I talked to Bishop Middleton and arranged to start taking the missionary discussions. I'll go through the motions, but I already know I want to be a member of the Mormon Church."

"How do you know?"

"Because I took Moroni's challenge."

Helen looked over his shoulder and out Nelda's kitchen window. "That's another good reason for me to put some distance between us. You need to concentrate on investigating the Church."

Matt smiled. "Are you calling yourself a big distraction?"

Helen felt her cheeks grow warm. "No, I'm just saying that joining the Church is a serious decision, and you need to be sure you're doing it for the right reasons. And now that the case is solved, your reelection is assured, so you won't have to worry about that."

Matt shook his head. "I'm not even going to run for sheriff in November."

"Why not?"

He looked up into her eyes. "Julie wanted me to get my master's degree so I could coach football and teach. I'd like to honor her wishes now since you don't think it's too late."

"I'm sure she'll be very pleased," Helen whispered as a knock sounded on the back door.

Matt stood and walked through the small laundry room to open the door. He came back into the kitchen a few seconds later. "You have some visitors," he told her. She waited expectantly, thinking it would be Hugh and Thelma with another jar of Mayhaw jelly, but no one appeared. "They'd like you to step outside," Matt added.

Helen walked past him to the back door, then looked out. Tan and Lin stood at the bottom of Nelda's back steps. Tan was holding two pieces of paper, and Lin was cuddling a tiny black kitten with white front feet. Helen felt tears prickle her eyes as Tan extended the homemade cards toward her.

"The sheriff said you are sick, so we made you 'get well' letters," the boy said. "And he says this is your kitten, but you need us to take care of it."

Helen turned to Lin. "And it looks like you're doing a very good job."

"The sheriff bought him a big bag of food and some toys," Tan added with enthusiasm. "He said the kitten can live in the basement of the pink house, and he left the door unlocked so we can go in anytime we want."

Helen smiled first at the children, then at Matt. "Thank you."

"You're welcome," Matt and Tan chorused. Lin just smiled and and hugged the kitten closer.

* * *

Matt waited until Thelma and Hugh came over with dinner, then left Helen in their care and went back to the sheriff's department. The FBI agents were packing up their equipment. "So, you guys heading back to Columbus?" Matt asked.

"Yeah," Barry said with a smile. "Our work here is done."

Matt laughed. "You sure have the easy life. You travel from town to town watching overworked, underpaid local sheriffs do their job, then take credit for their efforts, and leave."

"It's a tough job, but somebody's got to do it." Barry accepted the teasing with a smile.

Matt stared at the suspect wall for a few seconds. "Did you ever figure out where the coal dust came from?"

"Judith Pope's long-dead grandfather worked in the coal mines all his life. Since she wore his clothes to disguise herself as an old man, traces of the dust showed up on the baskets," Barry told him, and Matt nodded.

Barry picked up the last load of FBI equipment and started for the door. "See you next time."

"Good-bye, Barry, Agent Tucker," Matt responded, including the other man as well.

Once they were gone, Matt leaned back in his chair and wondered what he could have done to solve the case sooner. Then he heard a familiar voice from the doorway.

"I hear that congratulations are in order," Dr. Baker said. He was wearing his white lab coat and a bow tie.

"I guess that's a matter of opinion," Matt responded. "Something tells me that Murray Monk in the mayor's office will find my performance during the past few weeks lacking and maybe even irresponsible."

The doctor smiled. "You can't let the opinions of other people discourage you. We all make mistakes, but we have to go on and try to do better in the future."

Matt decided to ask the hard question. "Did you know that Judith Pope was being abused by her grandmother?"

The doctor stepped into the office and sat down in Helen's chair across from Matt. "I could say no and you couldn't prove otherwise."

"You're not on trial," Matt pointed out. "I'm just trying to make sense of it all."

"I suspected that Lavenia was aggressive in her discipline, but thirty years ago, things were different than they are now. Parents spanked their children, and nobody thought it abusive."

"Pushing a child down the stairs and breaking her arm has always been unacceptable."

The doctor acknowledged this with a weary nod. "If I could go back, I would report that incident to the authorities and let them investigate the situation. But Lavenia was the only relative Judith had. If she had been taken from her grandmother and put in foster care, who's to say that she would have been treated any better?"

Matt leaned forward and put his head in his hands. "I'm not in any position to point fingers, Doctor. I was a hateful, mean child, and I contributed to Judith's misery as well."

"So we both have some regrets to carry with us. But that one bad decision does not erase the good I have done in my life," the doctor said with conviction. "I will not let Judith Pope nor her choices destroy me."

Matt nodded. "You're right. Judith had other options." They were silent for a few seconds, then Matt asked another question. "Do you think that the first suicide attempt may have damaged Judith's brain, altering her ability to make rational choices?"

The doctor considered this, then shrugged. "It's certainly possible. Or maybe the death of her grandmother severed her tenuous grip on sanity."

"It would make me feel better if we could know for sure," Matt said in frustration.

"The past is beyond our reach, Matt. All of it. The only thing we can control is today."

Matt stood and extended his hand to the doctor. "I never did thank you for getting those medicine samples for my grandmother."

"You're very welcome, young man. Your grandmother was a fine woman."

"Yes, she was."

"And I think she'd be very proud of you."

Matt coughed to cover a sudden wave of emotion. "Yeah, but she never was very hard to please."

CHAPTER 15

Four weeks later

Helen smiled as she turned onto Ivy Lane. It was good to be back without Harrison Campbell in pursuit or a warrant for her arrest hanging over her head. She had enjoyed her time with her parents, but it was time to see what the future held for her in Eureka, Georgia.

She drove past Matt's rental house and parked in front of Nelda Lovell's small home. The older lady answered the back door and gave her a big hug. "It's so wonderful to see you again! Thelma and Hugh are going to be so sorry they missed you."

"Where are they?" Helen asked as she settled at the kitchen table.

"They bought a motor home and are taking a tour of the United States."

"Really?" Helen was amazed. "I can't believe Hugh was willing to leave his gardens. And who will keep his garbage cans spray painted orange and blue during football season?"

"I guess you didn't hear, then," Nelda said slowly.

"Hear what?"

"The city bought our homes. All of the houses on Ivy Lane, Wisteria Way, and Honeysuckle Drive. The whole area is going to be turned into an athletic complex."

Helen had talked to Matt several times during the past month, but he hadn't told her about this development. "You had to sell your home?" Helen asked, tears springing to her eyes.

Nelda nodded. "The city didn't really give us much choice. It was either sell or have the property condemned. But this neighborhood has been falling into decay for some time now. It encourages me to think of children playing here again, filling the air with laughter."

"What will you do?"

"Sydney and Cole have deeded me an acre of their land. We're meeting with an architect next week to pick out a floor plan for my new house."

Nelda seemed happy, so Helen tried to be. "That sounds exciting."

The older woman smiled. "You know, it really is. I didn't get to choose anything about this house when Miles and I moved in all those years ago. So I'll admit that picking out my own wallpaper has some appeal."

Helen smiled. "What about Glida Mae?"

"The proceeds from the sale of her house will keep her comfortably at Gentle Haven for years."

"And the Nguyens?"

"They were just renting, but I think they found another house closer to their manicure shop. And I hope you don't intend to reclaim your kitten. I believe Lin will fight you for him."

"I'll be glad for them to keep it so they'll have something to remember me by."

Two tears slipped down Helen's cheeks, and Nelda reached out to pat her hand. "Change isn't always easy, dear, but it's often for the best."

Helen nodded. "Well, if Matt's sold his house to the city, I guess I need to get the rest of my things out."

"Oh, there's no hurry," Nelda said. "We have until the end of the year to vacate."

"I wish he would have at least *mentioned* it." Helen couldn't hide the hurt she felt at having been excluded.

"I'm sure he just wanted to tell you in person," Nelda comforted.

Before Helen could reply, Matt walked through the back door. Helen forgot to be mad as her eyes drank in the sight of him. He was wearing blue jeans and a T-shirt instead of the khaki uniform she was accustomed to. There were dark circles under his eyes, and he needed a haircut.

"Still not sleeping, I see," she teased, hoping her longing didn't show in her eyes.

He grinned, and she had to work hard to keep from gawking. "Too busy reading all the books Bishop Middleton keeps giving me."

"How are your parents adjusting to life with a Mormon?" Helen asked.

"They're getting used to it. My mother even signed up to feed the missionaries next week."

Nelda pushed back from the table. "I've got some things to do upstairs if you two can get along without me for a few minutes."

Matt smiled again. "I think we can manage alone."

"There's German upside-down cake in on the counter and milk in the refrigerator," Nelda called over her shoulder as she made a hasty exit.

"I've missed you," Matt whispered, pulling a chair up close beside Helen's.

"Me too," she responded, fighting to keep her composure. "How are Tan and Lin?"

"Ready for school to start," Matt replied. "They're bored with summer."

"I'll bet the kitten is getting big."

"Huge," Matt confirmed.

Helen took a deep breath. "Nelda tells me you've sold your grandmother's house."

Matt frowned. "I was saving that news since it's part of a major announcement."

Helen raised an eyebrow. "What announcement?"

"Well, it's kind of multifaceted," Matt said. "First, I was called as secretary to the Young Men on Sunday."

"That's good," Helen said with a smile.

"Second, I did sell my grandmother's house at the insistence of the City of Eureka. Then I took the money, added it to the insurance proceeds that have been sitting in my checking account since Crystal filed for them, and, by adding just about every other penny I have, was able to set up a perpetual scholarship at the University of Georgia. It's going to be called the Julie, Chase, and Chad Clevenger Memorial Fund."

Two tears slipped down her cheeks. "That is *really* good."

"The university thought so too. In fact, they were so impressed by my generous donation that they accepted me into their master's program."

Helen considered this. "You bought your way into their master's program?"

Matt shrugged. "My undergraduate grades were okay, and I got letters of recommendation from a couple of my old professors. But I figure the money didn't hurt me any."

Helen had to laugh in spite of her tears. "That's even better news, then!"

"An old teammate of mine is an assistant football coach for the Bulldogs, so he talked them into letting me work with their quarterbacks. The pay is next to nothing, but I figure it will look good on my résumé when I start looking for a high school coaching job."

Helen sighed. "And football will be a part of your life again."

He smiled. "Oh yes." Then he scooted his chair even closer. "Now, there's only one little part of my plan that hasn't been implemented yet."

Helen watched him looking happy and hopeful for the first time since they'd met. He had moved on without her, but she wouldn't show him how much that hurt. "And what is that?" she asked bravely.

"Well, I found this dingy little apartment right off campus. The neighborhood's rotten and the furniture is worse than my grandmother's, but the price is right."

"It sounds perfect for a college man," Helen said.

"I also found an opening for an English lit teacher at a junior college nearby. Again, the pay is lousy and there's no prestige attached to the position, but it would be a way to pay for groceries and maybe even affect the lives of a few underprivileged kids."

Helen frowned. "You're going to go to graduate school, coach quarterbacks, and teach English literature all at the same time?"

He laughed. "No, the English lit job is for you. I need somebody to support me while I'm in school, so I thought maybe you'd come along."

Helen looked away so he wouldn't see her anguish. "Don't tease me," she said.

He reached out and turned her face to his. "For years I thought that in order to love another woman I'd have to give her Julie's place in my heart. But Bishop Middleton helped me to realize that there is room for both of you. Julie will always be with me, and so I want you to understand that this is sort of a package deal."

Helen's forehead creased in confusion. "A package deal?"

"Marry me, Helen," Matt said. "Join my family."

Helen opened her mouth, but no sound came out.

"I've talked to Bishop Middleton, and he said that ideally we should wait until a year from my baptism date and get married in the temple. But I'd like to go ahead and get married now, and he said he wouldn't hold it against us. That way you can teach me all the intricacies of Mormon life. Then, once I've been a member of the Church for a year, I'll be ready to take you to the temple and make it forever."

"Oh, Matt." Helen dissolved into tears again.

"Is that a yes or a no?"

"It's a yes."

Matt pulled her onto his lap and cradled her against his chest. "Good, because if it was a no, I was going to start crying too."

EPILOGUE

Helen adjusted the coat of her antique-white suit and moved into the church foyer, where her parents were waiting. She smiled and walked toward them. "You look beautiful, dear," her mother said.

"My little girl," her father added, and Helen's tears began to fall.

"You promised not to cry," Matt said, stepping up beside her. "People will think you don't want to marry me."

Nelda and Glida Mae came over, and Nelda tucked a lacy scrap of material into Helen's hand. "Here, use this handkerchief. It can be your something borrowed. And since it was given to me on the day of my own wedding, it's also something old. Now you just have to come up with something blue and new."

Glida Mae removed a string of blue beads from the several strands around her neck. "Here's your something blue."

Helen gave the actress a hug. "I didn't expect you to be here."

"I got a weekend pass," Glida Mae confided. "But I have to be back on Monday. There are a lot of old people at Gentle Haven and some of them aren't completely right in the head. They depend on me to take care of them."

Helen smiled. "They are lucky to have you."

"Maybe this can serve as your something new," Rita Clevenger said as she handed Helen a silver locket with the initials *H&M* engraved on the front. "It has individual compartments inside for pictures of my future grandchildren," Rita explained, and Helen swallowed a sob.

"Come on," Matt said. "Before this happy occasion disintegrates any further."

They moved on down the hallway toward the bishop's office, passing policemen, sheriff deputies, and several people Helen had never seen before. Maybeth Hadder stepped forward as they walked by the ladies' room. "I'm so happy for you," she said with a toss of her head. "I bought you a silver-plated serving dish at Timmy Spence Jewelers. They said they'd deliver it."

Matt thanked Mrs. Hadder as Ed Ramsey came into view.

"This is my wife, Aurelia," he told Helen.

"We wish you the best," Mrs. Ramsey said.

Hugh and Thelma were next, and Helen embraced them enthusiastically. "I thought you two were off seeing the country!" she exclaimed.

"We made it to Kansas, then turned around and came back," Thelma told her.

"Once you get past the Mason-Dixon Line, you can't understand a word people say," Hugh moaned.

"We're planning another trip, to Florida this time. But I'm glad we were able to attend this auspicious occasion before we leave," Thelma added.

"What kind of an occasion?" Hugh demanded as Helen and Matt moved down the line.

Alex Jordan was next. "I'm still waiting for that golf game," he told Matt.

"Soon," Matt promised.

Right by the bishop's door stood Crystal Vines, Coosetta County's newest deputy sheriff. "We wanted this to be a low-key event." He glanced back down the crowded hallway. "But this wedding is the world's worst-kept secret," Matt told her irritably. "You weren't supposed to tell everyone."

"I didn't tell *everyone*," Crystal defended herself. "I only told people on a 'need-to-know basis'."

Matt sighed, then turned to Helen. "Becoming a deputy has gone to her head already."

Helen laughed as they walked into the bishop's office, where Tan and Lin were standing quietly in one corner. "I know we can't have an official ring bearer and flower girl, but they don't take up much room, so I thought it would be okay if I sneaked them in," Matt whispered. "But I did make them leave the cat at home."

Helen smiled at the children as her parents and Matt's crowded into the small space. The door was closed and the simple service performed. Afterward they went into the cultural hall and accepted congratulations from family and friends at a small reception presided over by Nelda and several of the ladies from the Eureka Baptist Church. They cut the cake and opened a few gifts, then Matt walked to the front of the room and called for everyone's attention.

"Helen and I would like to thank you all for coming and sharing our joy today," he said with simple eloquence. "But Gatlinburg is a long drive from here, so we're going to have to leave now."

They ran through a shower of birdseed to Matt's old Bronco and then left the parking lot, trailing tin cans and bright-colored crepe-paper streamers. Matt concentrated as he maneuvered the car through the downtown traffic. "Sorry about that," he said once they reached the highway. "I know we agreed to save all the fanfare for our temple sealing, but Southern women just don't understand the term *small wedding*."

"You have no reason to apologize," Helen replied as she adjusted the volume on the radio. "There are a lot of people in this town who love you, and they went to a lot of trouble to prove it." She pulled off her shoes and rubbed her aching feet for a few seconds. "My only regret is letting my mother talk me into these shoes."

Matt took his eyes off the road long enough for a quick glance into the backseat. "Miss Nelda said she packed us a snack basket. Do you see it? I'm starving."

Helen leaned over the seat to retrieve the basket, and fed Matt wedding cookies until he'd had his fill. Then she picked up the atlas and asked, "How long will it take us to get to Gatlinburg?"

Matt smiled as he turned off the highway onto a dirt road. "I'm not really all that interested in seeing the sights in Gatlinburg, and I hate to waste any of our honeymoon driving, so I thought we might just spend the weekend here."

Helen looked out the windshield as a small fishing cabin came into view. "Here?"

Matt nodded firmly. "Right here."

"But you told everyone we were going to Gatlinburg."

"I did not. I said it was a *long drive* to Gatlinburg." He parked the Bronco, then walked around and opened the door for her.

"So no one knows we're here?" Helen asked as he led the way up to the cabin door.

"Only Bishop Middleton. This place belongs to him, and he gave me a special weekend rate."

"Which was?"

"Free as long as we're out first thing on Monday morning."

Helen laughed as he lifted her into his arms. "Now what are you doing?"

"I have to carry you over the threshold or we'll have bad luck." He stepped into the dim interior, and Helen huddled close. "This is a little rustic," Matt commented.

"Rustic puts it mildly," she replied.

"Actually, it's luxurious compared to our apartment in Athens."

Helen nuzzled his neck. "Then I'll try not to get too comfortable here."

He put her onto her feet, but kept his arms firmly around her. "We can go on to Gatlinburg if you want. My parents reserved us the honeymoon suite in a fancy hotel there that is bound to be extremely comfortable."

Helen reached up and grabbed the collar of his shirt, then pulled him until their noses were touching. "I don't care where we stay as long as I have you all to myself."

He smiled, but she noticed that his eyes were suspiciously bright. "It's just you and me," he whispered. "Unless there's a mouse or two we haven't discovered yet."

She started to laugh, but he kissed the smile right off her face.

ABOUT THE AUTHOR

Betsy Brannon Green currently lives in a suburb of Birmingham, Alabama with her husband, Butch, and six of their eight children. She is the secretary for the kindergarten campus of Hueytown Elementary School and serves as Primary chorister for the Bessemer Ward.

Although born in Salt Lake City, Betsy was raised in the South. Her life and her writing have both been strongly influenced by the small town of Headland, Alabama, and the people who live there. Many of her characters reflect the gracious gentility unique to that part of the country.

Betsy's other books are: *Hearts in Hiding, Never Look Back,* and *Until Proven Guilty.* Betsy enjoys corresponding with her readers, who can write to her in care of Covenant Communications, P.O. Box 415, American Fork, Utah 84003-0416, or e-mail her via Covenant at info@covenant-lds.com.